ARMED TO THE DENTURES

by Bill Hawkins

Bill Hawkins Publishing, LLC

ISBN: 978-1-7376330-9-9

Library of Congress Control Number: 2021914802

Find recent updates on Bill's novels and novellas,
as well as promotions and free stuff at
www.billhawkinswriter.com

To all the seasoned citizens who fed my
dreams with knowledge and wisdom,
thank you for the inspiration.
To my wife, Ellen, who fed more than
my dreams while I focused on writing,
all my love.

CHAPTER 1

Violet lay her fingers across the rough of a nail file. She scrubbed the edge of each nail across the serrated metal, sorted cards, worked the file, sorted cards. Her eyes scanned the room, tracked the movements, the subtle changes in current. Window light fell across her shoulders. The sun at her back kept her warm, gave her a good view of the room, and sometimes blinded her opponents. Dust danced in the beams reminding her of times long past.

The card game hadn't started. When it did, that would take most of her attention. For now, she let her eyes make another pass, pausing on Irene. Annoying, gossipy Irene had just been let in by Lin, one of the few remaining staff. Lin would be next to go looking for a paying job. Certainly she wouldn't draw another check here. Likely she would land a position in retail where her talents would be wasted. That was too bad. The girl was good with people. Good at caring. Everyone had heard Irene's pounding on the door, but only Lin had responded.

Perhaps not everyone had heard. Mini was deaf as a board and kept her hearing aid turned down to save batteries. There were probably a half dozen others in the room that did the same.

In days past, this room had been bright and full, noisy to the point of irritation. Now it was a ghost, an echo chamber of memories. Almost everyone had left the home, moved in with family, or gone to another home. Violet counted the residents and adjusted her math. Thirteen remained. She felt a familiar loneliness taking hold. Her fingers rubbed the file, then lifted and twirled it slowly as her mind went back to a day when her home, her first home, felt the way this place did today.

It was 1942, and brothers Thomas, Jake, and Wilson boarded a train to Dallas, and from there to fight a war. Violet stood in the ranch house kitchen listening to the awful silence and watching the dust dance in the light from the window. Her brothers gone, the house was the quietest it had ever been in her lifetime. The floor creaked with her slightest movement, and the curtains billowed in the breeze as she passed from one silent room to another closing the windows in anticipation of a spring storm.

The rain didn't fall that day. A few clouds passed, the breeze died, and the house remained silent, nevermore to hear the voices she had grown up with.

Only Thomas returned alive from that war, and he was broken. War had sharpened him in the wrong way. Like a shard from a broken glass, every life he touched bled until his own untimely passing ended the struggle.

Violet scrubbed her fingers on the file as if that would erase the silence of the past. Someone dropped a spoon in the kitchen. The metal rang like a hotel desk bell. Lin leaned on the far wall and scanned the room. Vi could just make out that her lips were moving. She was counting the residents like Violet had. She looked worried and for good reason.

Bernice, her left hand perpetually on her cane, squinted at her cards and blinked. She looked up and restated the obvious, "Lights off."

"Probably not coming back on this time," said Ruby from Violet's left. "That Lin is looking worried."

"She's looking what?" asked Mini.

"Worried," repeated three voices.

Mini shook her head in confusion, "You don't all have to yell at once."

"Look sharp," said Violet, studying her cards while Lin scooted their way.

"Is she coming?" asked Bernice, her back to the approaching girl.

"Ladies," said Lin, passing the table and opening the garden window.

Violet turned, eyeing the young Asian woman thoughtfully. Ruby tried to sneak a look at Violet's cards while her head was turned. Violet covered them without losing focus.

"Do you have another job lined up?" asked Violet.

Lin shook her head.

"Could go home," said Marybeth, an edge to her voice.

"Oh, give the girl a break," said Doris. "Maybe she just thinks a bunch of old busybodies like us don't need to know everything."

Violet tried not to grin behind her cards. She wished that she had the raw charm that Doris seemed to exude like warm breath on a cold day, but wondered if she would have to trade some IQ points for that quality. Doris was clever in her own way. With that simple defense of Lin, she'd put the girl in her debt.

"It's tough not knowing where you're going next," said Doris, setting the hook.

Lin crossed her arms waiting for more.

Doris hid behind her mass of naturally blonde hair and counted her cards.

"Oh, she's young. She'll find something. I saw a Help Wanted sign at a service station last time we were out," said Ruby.

"Service stations are a thing of the past. They call them convenience stores now," said Violet.

"Since when?" said Ruby.

"About thirty or forty years now," said Violet.

Ruby grunted and smiled her little secret smile. Violet always felt a little uncomfortable when Ruby smiled. The woman just seemed too happy. It radiated through her entire lanky, rawboned, hillbilly frame like the afterglow of a nuclear accident. With her long dark hair salted with gray and her thin face, she looked like she belonged in an artist colony or a nuthouse—both the same as far as Violet was concerned.

Doris put her cards down and reached across the table in Lin's direction. "You're not applying to work at convenience stores, are you dear?"

Lin flinched. "I don't know what I'm doing. I need the internship credit if I want to finish my degree, but…"

Doris smiled and sat back, her eyes turning toward Violet who suddenly tilted her chin toward the center of the room. Doris glanced over her shoulder.

"I thought Lester was *your* man," cracked Ruby, turning *man* into a two-syllable statement of territory, her chin following toward the center of the room where a muted drama played out between a thin but sure-footed old man and Irene.

"Lester is what he is, and he is not *my* man," said Doris.

"He sure wants to be," said Marybeth.

"How many times has he asked you to marry him?" said Violet, trying to recall a time when Lester had come by the table without at least hinting that he thought Doris was the best catch left on the planet.

"A few," admitted Doris.

Violet laid her cards facedown, and examined her friend while she ran the file under her nails one at a time. "You really like him, don't you?"

Doris nodded, keeping her eyes on her cards. "I like him. You know that. But he gets on my nerves, always asking me to marry him."

Violet, Ruby, Bernice, and Marybeth all examined Doris over their cards.

Mini, her hearing aid down again, squinted, confused.

Doris broke into red-faced laughter. "Y'all are too much."

Mini scowled and scrolled the volume back up on the hearing aid.

"You should keep that turned up. Now, let's play cards," said Ruby.

The ladies barely got through the first hand before commotion broke out.

***

"Where's my mother?" bellowed Anita Fulsom-Bright, charging through the darkness toward the great room.

Lin attempted to pass, but Anita cast her substantial hips wide, blocking the path. She backed off. A mistimed move would be catastrophic.

"What are these people doing here?" screamed Anita, bursting through the doors. "The lights are off. You people have to leave! What are you doing keeping these people here with the power off?"

"We're not keeping them here. We're taking care of them," said Lin, looking around for help from either of the other two staffers who seemed to have suddenly vanished.

"You're all here now. Are you taking them to a hotel to sleep? Are you taking them on that bus? It doesn't even look like it runs. Where is my mother?"

Irene Fulsom waved her arms from ten feet away, but made no attempt to approach her daughter. Instead, she looked to Lin to push her chair.

Lin ignored her.

Irene put on her *I'm-in-pain* face and pushed the joystick forward the few centimeters it took to engage the chair's motor. Dutifully, her daughter waddled toward her. "Oh, Mother, you look so pale. Have they been feeding you? When did the lights go off? Have you been sleeping in your chair?"

In the kitchen, something crashed.

Lin's head whipped around. Should she stay or go? Her mind conjured up a picture of someone lying on the kitchen floor unconscious. Unfortunately, Irene was accounted for. Breaking from Irene and Anita, she jogged toward the dark back of the room. Irene and her daughter could take care of themselves. It was a short trip to the parking lot.

Lester leaned on a counter with one of the unbreakable plates in hand and a wide sheepish grin on his face. "They make a lot of noise when you drop them," he said.

She nodded her thanks, shaking her head at the same time. *Who really ran this place?*

***

Lin made her way down the hall with the master key, knocking on, then opening each door. Only a few rooms showed signs of still being occupied. The rest she left open to let light into the hall.

There were so many things to do. Laundry was top of the list. The beds in the empty rooms were stripped, and the linens piled in hampers in the laundry room. She needed to get into the files. They were stacked in Mr. Bob's office, in boxes. The police had left them there after the brief investigation. There were things in those files that the residents would need when they left. Medical information, IDs, next of kin—the list went on. She would distribute what she could. The rest would need to be taken somewhere safe to store. She had to do that. No one else would or could.

Bob Robbins had done a number on them all. Comfortably wealthy, the profits from running the home and the prospect of an early retirement for himself hadn't been enough. Bob Robbins took a vacation, a break. In the week that followed, confusion gripped the home as checks began to bounce, and banks notified residents that their payments were being halted due to lack of funds. Residents grumbled and argued. Some wept in confusion. Some demanded that Bob return from vacation. He never did.

Bob had tapped the financial records and accounts of almost every resident. In a matter of hours, their accounts had been emptied. The retirement home deposits also cleared out, the residents weren't the only ones left empty-handed. The paychecks, automatically generated by a payroll firm were nothing more than empty promises.

Each day, fewer of the staff parking spaces were filled. At lunch, Lin counted three cars in the side lot. She hadn't seen the Eastern European woman, Ivanka, since the incident with Irene and Anita. Ivanka had probably taken that as her cue to slip away like the others. Lin pulled a curtain back to check the parking lot. An overgrown shrubbery blocked her view.

She rolled the laundry cart down the hall, letting it carry her weight, her slight frame exhausted from too many hours without pause. She floated through the propped open door, not sure what she would find. It was hard to tell these days. With so few staff, it seemed like they were always chasing problems instead of heading them off.

Other than a few toppled chairs, all seemed in order. But it would be dark in a few hours. What then? Time was slipping away. Her eyes swung uneasily over to the poker ladies' table. Violet, Bernice, Ruby, Ms. Doris, Marybeth and Ms. Barone, who they all called Mini. Those ladies played cards like nothing was wrong. Didn't they know that they would have to leave, today, before dark, while they could still see to pack?

Doris spun cards across the table, dealing another hand.

Lin watched the cards spin, desperation filling her. It was all coming apart. Their world, her world, the whole world. The tiny cracks had become fissures, and those had become crevasses that they tumbled into like so many lemmings walking over a cliff. She launched herself toward the ladies' table, making as much noise as she could on the approach. The commercial carpet denied her fury, deadening her footfalls.

"Don't be looking at my cards, Lin," said Mini, over her shoulder.

A joke? "It's late, and the power is off, and you'll have to leave today. We don't know where to take you, even if we can get you packed up and..."

Marybeth put her cards down and rubbed her hands together like she was washing them. It was a familiar nervous habit, but this time it felt wrong, put on. Their eyes met. The woman's usual angry scowl replaced with a shark's smile. Lin had the sudden urge to run away.

Violet cleared her throat and laid down her nail file. "You don't have anywhere for us to go?" Violet said, her tone suggesting disappointment, a very personal disappointment in Lin.

Lin shook her head.

Violet smiled sympathetically. "I guess that means we'll go to Tommy's," she said. "What do you girls think?"

"I say, let's go," said Bernice, tapping her cane twice on the floor.

"Well, there won't be any lights out there either," said Ruby, raising an eyebrow.

"Oh, my," said Marybeth, rubbing her hands and casting a rare smile Lin's way.

"What? You've never lived without electricity?" Mini asked Ruby.

"Listen dear," said Doris, winking and touching Lin's arm with her surprisingly soft leathery hand, "We've already packed up. We've had some of the gentlemen put our belongings in the bus. Everything but an overnight bag for each of us. We were just waiting for the right time."

Violet jingled the keys to the van over the table.

"You can't, where did you get...?"

"From little Bobby's office, of course," said Doris.

Ruby shuffled her cards, avoiding eye contact with Lin. "We figured after what that little man did, the van at least was ours."

"And Vi has her license. We're all set," said Bernice, rising in her seat.

"I need to talk to the other staff," said Lin.

"What other staff?" said Marybeth.

"What you should do..." said Doris, "...is go talk to each of the others, and make sure they have someone coming to get them. Then come back to us if you have time. We'll be here."

Feeling a little like she was being hustled, Lin turned to go. It was time. The longer she stayed, the more she felt like the ground beneath her was being washed away. As much as she tried to suppress it, the phrase *the inmates are running the asylum* kept skimming the surface of her mind.

Behind her, she heard Mini Barone say in an overloud whisper, "Does Violet really have a driver's license?"

Lin turned her head just in time to see Violet shake her head and share a grin with her companions. Let them have their fun. What they'd said was true. Of all the residents, they were the ones she worried least about. If anyone could take care of themselves for a few hours, it was the poker ladies.

Lin found herself circling the room taking note of each of the remaining residents. Some had cell phones at hand. Some needed help using them. Sue Bernard had hers out, but her hands shook so badly that her fingers consistently missed the keyboard. "What number?" asked Lin.

"Three. Speed dial three," said Sue.

Lin pressed and held the button until the phone began to connect the call, then placed it in Sue's shaking hand. A crackling voice answered. Sue smiled and nodded thanks to Lin, "Hello, Suzie. This is your momma."

Lin went back to her survey. Ms. Ginny looked positively at peace staring at the flowers on the table. The flowers were from the garden, the last of the season. Ginny didn't have a phone. She would need to call someone for Ms. Ginny.

***

The ladies weren't as well packed as they'd let on. By the time they were on the bus and ready to go, Marybeth was glad that the sun was down so no one could see how disheveled the last minute dash to collect her valuables had left her.

With heavy hearts, they helped Ginny Betts sign into the county home. Ginny hadn't moved on her own in months. Most days, she stared at the wallpaper until someone put food in her mouth. There were times when she seemed at perfect peace, as if the wallpaper held happy memories or some amusing secret. Marybeth had also seen Ginny's face crumble into despair and loneliness so deep that no word of comfort or hope could penetrate. Marybeth had been to that place, too. She knew what it held, and she prayed that she would pass before going there again.

The gook girl, Lin, cried helping them load the bus. Marybeth dismissed the girl's teary admonition to take care of themselves, and laid back on the seat pulling the blanket up tight around her shoulders. It was just the six of them now.

Violet drove the handicap van they called the bus, while the others took turns reading directions from her smart phone. They made one stop at a hardware store to purchase a huge set of bolt cutters. Vi's nephew had passed away, and his land was in probate. She expected the gate to be locked. They could return the tool if it wasn't.

Marybeth looked at her reflection in the glass. It was dark out. Country dark, where the stars were the only light in the sky. The low lights of the bus interior made it seem even darker. The view out the front and the glare of the headlights off the painted lines on the road were impossibly bright in comparison.

They passed what looked like a fairground turned flee market, then turned off the highway onto a blacktop road that may never have had lines painted on it. Violet stayed to the smooth center, avoiding the potholes at the edges. They slowed to what seemed like a crawl, maybe following the road, but just as likely navigating by the light patch of sky between the trees.

If the windows had been open, Marybeth would have been able to hear the crickets and croaking bullfrogs. There were deer in these woods, and raccoons, and all manner of creature. Every once in a while, they would pass a reflector that marked a drive or a mail box. People lived here, but not too close to one another.

They passed the bright fluorescent lights of a gas station standing like some alien port of entry to our planet. Marybeth was caught by surprise. She'd never gotten used to the trees here and how they obscured the landscape. Things would just sneak up on you. She had travelled some. First in the Western US, then in Australia, and then some places that she didn't want to remember. Every place had its own surprises.

Australia had been the one that she loved most. From the porch of her father's house, they could see the lights of their nearest neighbor nine miles away. Marybeth remembered her father's warm laugh when she looked at him with those pleading eyes. He tapped his pipe on the porch rail and smiled so that she could see his teeth in the dark. "Make note of the direction. You can go with Seth and your mother tomorrow," he said.

It took an extra day to get away, but he was as good as his word, and she had the most wonderful adventure riding the open country. Marybeth slept, remembering in her dreams the moonlit outback.

The van jolted to a stop, then reversed. To their left was a white painted gate with a sign above announcing that they were at Blake's Orchard. A rusted padlock hung on the gate. Alongside it, a plastic-covered notice that had long since faded.

Violet wiped the notice and tried to read it. She gave up, and motioned for Doris to join her with the bolt cutters.

"Are you sure?" said Doris.

She nodded in the dark. "I helped buy this place."

The orchard road was not nearly so impressive as the gate. Rain had washed ruts into it, and the tall grass and trees encroached on the narrow path so that it felt like a tunnel. They drove on, the mirrors of the van snagging on the brush.

After a few minutes, the space around the van began to broaden. Below the trees, the land cleared. Suddenly they were free of the brush. Huge tree trunks lined up in perfect rows reaching twelve or more feet up before the first branches arched away, creating a forest cathedral with a ceiling of leaves and stars.

Orchard indeed, a pecan orchard, apples, too. Marybeth slid her window open and took a deep breath. The crunch of gravel beneath the tires announced another change in the road, and before them in the light of the rising moon stood a white clapboard house with a glorious porch that ran all the way around both floors.

Marybeth breathed in deeply. She could find peace here if she could find it anywhere.

CHAPTER 2

Bernice tapped the sofa cushion with her cane, sending up a cloud of dust. She stepped back, her nose twitching like a nervous rabbit. Ruby lifted the wand of the vacuum cleaner to suck up the cloud. The pair had drawn living room cleaning duty, and now that they had liberated a vacuum cleaner from Golden Lawn, they had no excuse to procrastinate.

Bernice had never quite gotten used to the Georgia dust and pollen. The best years of her life had been in the Yucatan where the heat trumped all else. Here, breathing meant sneezing. Even in a house that had been closed up for months, the dust found a way in. Maybe it was always there and only settled. However it got here, they had to clear it out or suffer with it. One step at a time, and eventually they would be settled. They would clean the house, maybe get a few more chairs for the porch, and eventually the power would be turned back on.

The few lights and the refrigerator were currently powered by the emergency generator. In a cooperative effort, Violet figured out that the carburetor and fuel tank needed to be drained, Bernice knew enough to make sure the main breaker was off, Doris found the breaker, Marybeth went for gas, and Mini stood by with a fire extinguisher.

The house was a beauty, but two of the three bedrooms were upstairs. The stairs were a beast on old knees. Violet and Marybeth took one of the upstairs rooms, Doris and Mini the other. Bernice shared a downstairs room with Ruby. She liked Ruby but was just now realizing how little she knew about her. That was bound to change.

The first night was the hardest. Arriving after dark in a house with no power and no running water had been rough. Without the energy to do more, they'd made do with what they could find and gone to sleep. They were short a mattress, so Bernice slept on the couch. The next morning, Violet drove her to the strip of stores along the highway where she found a cheap mattress.

Bernice lowered herself into the chair they'd just vacuumed. It still smelled dusty. They would have to get a wet cleaning machine when they could afford it. Right now finances were as tight as could be.

All of them had lost their life savings to Bob Robbins. Bernice gripped the handle of her cane, her anger rising like lava through a crack in the earth. The joints of her hand screamed at her, but it felt right forcing the pain up where it could be felt, remembered. There had been small victories. Violet and Marybeth had managed to stop transfers from their checking accounts when they became aware that the savings had been raided. That, and the few dollars of cash between them didn't add up to much. Buying things like mattresses would cut into that.

They had enough for gas to make a run to Golden Lawn, and it made perfect sense to raid the supplies at the home while they could still get to them. Doris even suggested that they sell the beds and medical equipment from the home. It was an idea, but after struggling to drag a single mattress from the van into the house, Bernice wondered how they would manage. That there could be laws preventing them from selling the home's property had not occurred to them. They were beyond worrying about what was theirs and what wasn't. Bernice lightened her grip, letting her joints rest and the pain fade into the past.

The breeze from the open windows felt wonderful, the air heavy with the scent of apples and pecans in the orchard. They'd just missed the harvest. No one had picked. Such a shame. She could almost taste a sweet apple right now. She rubbed her dentures with her tongue wishing she had better teeth. That would cost money, too.

The van was back. Marybeth and Doris offloaded groceries. Not much by the look of it. Something touched the top of her head. She swung around in time to see Ruby withdraw the wand of the vacuum cleaner.

"You off in La-La Land?" Ruby asked with a smirk.

"I was thinking."

"Can you think me up some water?"

The kitchen was looking good. Violet's nephew, Tommy, had done a lot of work on the house before the cancer got him. The floors were solid tile, easy to clean but too hard and slick. They needed rugs.

Someone had cleaned out the refrigerator and shut up the house properly after Tommy left. Aside from one block of mold that had once been a loaf of bread, there was no rotten food in the house.

The counters were sparkling clean. Three baskets of apples that someone had culled from the orchard were clustered on the end. Bernice took a deep breath. Apples and pine cleaner. Like a country kitchen. She asked for water, and Doris just about danced across the room to show her the cupboard for water glasses and the pitcher. “The pipes are all clear now,” said Doris. “But Vi will only let us run the pump a few minutes at a time until we get on full power, so the tank isn't filling up.” She spoke the last sentence with her hands on her hips and her eyes boring through Violet’s back.

“The generator doesn’t put out enough power for the pump to run all the time. We’ll burn up one or the other if we run it too much,” responded Violet, without turning from her place at the table. She’d been there most of the last three days. In front of her were piles of papers from Tommy’s files. A box under the table was near overflowing with the pages already discarded.

“What are we going to do with our trash?” asked Marybeth, seeming to read Bernice’s mind.

“Burn it,” said Doris.

“There's a burn ban on,” said Bernice, remembering a poster at the gas station.

Marybeth scowled and mumbled unintelligibly as she left the room.

Lin scowled after her.

It was strange seeing the girl here. She’d texted Doris the day before, volunteering to help at the house in exchange for a signoff on her internship credit hours. It wasn’t a perfect situation. They didn’t have a room for her, so she would have to commute most days. Nothing was perfect.

Bernice touched Lin’s arm, “Don’t you worry, dear. She does that to all the Japanese.”

“I’m Chinese,” said Lin. “Actually, I’m American.”

Bernice shrugged “Well, she thinks you’re Japanese.”

She wiped an apple on her apron and slipped it into her apron pocket before selecting another and bringing it to her nose, Ruby's water long forgotten.

***

Doris took measured strides down the A Wing hall of Golden Lawn. She carried a heavy industrial broom like a bayoneted rifle, aiming it around corners, ready to strike anything that moved. The home was eerily still with creaks and thumps at all the wrong times. Already she had seen the evidence of a break in, some turned over chairs and cigarette butts on the floor in the great room. The window that Lin had closed before leaving was open. She'd closed it.

She was too old to be frightened by an empty and dark building. An occupied, dark building was something else. There it was again, the thump, and the slight change of air pressure like one of the outside doors had just closed. She shuffled down the hall ever so glad for the bright spots where light flowed through the open doors showing the way. Picking up the pace, she jogged into the lobby... and *smack* into something heavy and soft.

A shrill screech shattered the peace. The initial burst trailed off into a terrified wail that rose from the floor where Anita Fulsom-Bright lay cowering with her hands up and eyes closed. The wail bloomed like an old storm siren reaching full power.

"Shut it!" shouted Doris, pointing the end of her staff at the source. The wailing paused, replaced by a series of short, sobbing gasps. The woman looked and sounded like she was having a seizure.

"You-you-you," Doris sputtered. "What are you doing here sneaking around?"

Anita Fulsom-Bright, kept her hands up in surrender. "Nothing, nothing, I swear. I just wanted to know where everyone was." She nodded as if agreeing with herself, and began to push off from the floor.

Doris didn't believe a word of it. This was the daughter of Irene Fulsom. If there was anyone in the home that Doris could call anything but friend, it was Irene Fulsom.

Anita's eyes darted to one of the columns. Doris pointed the broom at her and ordered her to stay put while she stepped cautiously around to look behind the pillar. No monstrous huge dog waiting to pounce, just a box. A box of liquid soap bottles.

“Are you serious? Are you stealing soap from the home?” she said. They had come here for bedding, towels, and soap. She counted twenty-four bottles of liquid soap. At $2 each, it added up. She pulled two and dropped them by Anita. “Take the box to our van and you can have those.”

Anita let out a grateful sigh that turned suddenly to a cunning sneer. “What about you? Are you stealing soap?”

Doris answered by pointing the broom, “I live here. It’s my soap.”

From the B Wing hallway she heard a thump and shuffling. She froze. Violet was the other way, searching the kitchen for food. “Are they with you?” she asked.

Anita, more terrified now than ever, shook her head.

“Let’s go find out who it is,” said Doris, already wishing she were less brave at the right times.

“*You* live here,” said Anita.

Annoyed but just as happy to be away from the sniveling lump, Doris entered the hall at a steady trot, tapping the broom handle loudly on the walls and calling out to whoever was there, “Hey, get out. You hear me, out!” She passed an open door and froze. The window stood open. Papers were strewn across the floor, some shredded and torn.

Something warm brushed her leg.

She yelped and jumped, then chased the fleeing critter down the hall.

Seconds later and out of breath, she slid into the lobby. Across the room, a raccoon slammed headfirst into the glass double doors before spinning, and confused, it turned on her and her broom.

Doris crouched and pointed her staff at the little bear-like animal. It hissed and tore at the wood with its razor sharp claws. On the other side of the doors, Anita loaded the box of soap into the back seat of an S-class Mercedes.

“Oh, you didn’t!”

The raccoon, classifying Doris as a mortal threat, gave its full attention to scratching a hole through the glass door.

Form the other side, Anita raised her middle finger toward Doris.

Doris raised her broom handle to the push bar and opened the door.

The raccoon fled between Anita's feet and into the back seat of the Mercedes. Anita spun reaching for the creature. Not interested in socializing, it swiped a claw at her. Anita slammed the car door with the animal inside.

Bursting into laughter, Doris locked the building door, leaving Anita to deal with the animal. This was justice.

***

"You should have caught it," said Ruby, interrupting the song she was singing under her breath while stirring the stew pot. "We need the soap, too."

"I got some soap."

"Not all of it," said Ruby.

"A raccoon?" repeated Lin.

"It was huge. Those claws tore up the end of the broom," said Doris.

"What if it comes back?" said Lin.

"It will. Maybe we can catch it," said Ruby, wistfully.

Doris looked at her crossways. "Why would we want to catch it?"

"Did you close the window?" asked Ruby, sitting at the table.

"Of course, I did," she said, clearly revising history.

"The critter will come back in and make a mess. We'll need to catch it before it tears the place to pieces," said Ruby. She smacked her dentures. "We need meat!" she said, clearing up what should have been obvious. They had had meatless stew twice this week, and that was the closest they'd come to real food since two days before leaving Golden Lawn. Free bread so stale that it had to be toasted for breakfast, cans of Ensure for lunch, and rice and beans for dinner had become the daily menu. Thank God it was warm enough to leave the windows open. Otherwise, someone would have died from methane poisoning by now.

"You would eat a raccoon?" asked Doris, incredulous.

Ruby chuckled, "Raccoon, snake, mule, or camel. You skin it, I'll cook it."

"What if we don't skin it?" said Doris.

Lin covered her face as if that would hide her shock. "Would you eat cat?" she asked.

Ruby let the girls wonder for a moment while she considered the question. "I don't much like cats. Arrogant little creatures. Probably too tough to eat, but we could try if you can catch a few."

Lin covered her face and fled the room. Ruby burst into laughter, her loose dentures threatening to launch onto the table. Doris' scornful scowl pushed her deeper into the mirthful abyss. Struggling to pull herself together, Ruby spat out a cackle and some word-shaped grunts. Popping out her dentures, she rinsed them and returned them to their station. "You know, we do need meat a few times a week," she said, when she'd caught her breath.

That night, Ruby lay in her bed and turned off the kerosene lamp. She had eaten many a possum, raccoon, snake, and bear growing up in the mountains of Kentucky. She couldn't remember how it tasted except a faint recollection that bear was fatty and cooked well in stew. In or out of season, Pappy had always had meat in the smokehouse. There were plenty of lawmen in coal country that would arrest a man for taking illegal game to feed his children, but they'd always left Pappy alone.

So long ago. There were things that she remembered and things that she only felt the faint shadow of in her mind. She remembered her little sister wanting to go on a date and Pappy getting angry. She pushed that memory away. Those weren't the kinds of things she wanted to think about, the bruises and late night tears. Those were memories best left lie.

She remembered the smell of wood smoke and bacon from the stove, the chill she got walking down to the creek at night, and the flutter of bats as they came out of the cave on the mountain and dove for mosquitos. But the memory topmost in her mind was the one triggered by the smell of kerosene from the lamp. That was a memory that would never fade to complete black. The memory of a night of pain and despair, when her house was burned down around her, and by the grace of a God that was either cruel or loving, she had survived.

Ruby felt the cold track of a tear on her cheek. Burning kerosene was the smell of betrayal, fear, and the kind of evil that she had never come to understand. Her husband, her own husband, had beat her and left her for dead in a burning house. She remembered waiting for the flames to take her and thinking that would be fine. The fire didn't take her, and she wasn't.

Ruby smiled bitterly, tasting the salty tear on her lip. One of the graces of age was the fading of many painful recollections, but some slipped through. Sleep would cure that if she could find it tonight.

CHAPTER 3

Doris celebrated her birthday alone. Her friends would be angry when they found out, something that would happen soon now that Marybeth and Bernice were going through the files from the home. Was it her fault that they couldn't remember her birthday?

She spit a little juice out from the little glob of chaw that she was working on. She'd found the box of still-sealed pouches of Red Man in the apple shed. She pulled the moist ball from her mouth, tore a piece off, and applied it to one of the growing welts on her arm with a piece of duct tape to hold it. Wasps had come at her in the wood shed. She'd won the battle, but at a cost. With the last of the five stinging welts covered, the pain was beginning to subside. Her arm looked odd with the patches of tape, but the chaw would take the poison out in short order and the tape would come off.

The mule skin gloves she wore were too big and rubbed between her fingers. Dori wondered if she could wet and dry them to shrink them a bit. She took one off and shook a piece of bark out of it, wishing she had some water to wash the bitter tobacco from her mouth.

The cart was full up to the top of the sideboards with firewood. It was as much as she could pull up the slight hill to the house. Dori would be the first to deny that she needed to lose weight. She was stout, she told herself. She didn't feel stout pulling the loaded cart. More like winded and tired.

Lester had come to visit the day before. Never saying how he had found them, he'd pulled the wagon and helped her stack wood on the porch for several hours just to be with her. He was a good man. She would never admit it to the girls, but she enjoyed his company as much as his help and would have liked him to come back.

The temperature was dropping, and the leaves were starting to turn. In another week, they would be in full fall colors. So far as she could remember, Doris had never seen apple trees in the fall. She was sure it would be pretty. And maybe now that the lights were on in the house, they could have visitors. Someone had paid the tab to get the power reconnected. She suspected Lester. He was a good man.

She heard the crunch of big tires on gravel and caught a glimpse of white through the trees. Her heart beat faster as she tore the tape patches from her arms. That would be Lester's Escalade. She thought about running in and cleaning up, but that would make the girls talk, wouldn't it? Instead she took her gloves off, taking note of the cracked and worn nails, and sat on the steps. The car would take a while to wind its way through the orchard to the house on the hill.

The big SUV slid to a stop. Like a teenager cruising the strip, Lester jumped out before the dust could settle. Doris glowed. Lester's eyebrows arched up.

Darn it! she had just given him hope again. "Now I'm going to have to hurt his feelings," she muttered.

"What's that?" asked Lester, reaching behind his back and keeping his hand there as if hiding a weapon.

Doris squinted at the man. He was grinning like the cat that ate the Christmas goose. All 140 pounds of him in those tight blue jeans and crisp button down shirt. He raised his eyebrows again.

"Stop it," she said. "You are going to make people laugh and that will make their blood pressure go up, and you know that could cause all kinds of trouble."

Lester grinned and looked around. Finding no audience but his granddaughter who'd insisted on driving him, he handed Doris the pair of gloves that he had concealed behind him. "Happy birthday," he said.

Doris was beside herself. "Oh, Lester, thank you. I didn't tell anybody. How did you…?"

"Don't you worry about that," he said, sitting beside her.

"I don't suppose you had anything to do with the power being turned on?" she tried to sound dry and disapproving. It didn't take.

"I did," croaked Lester, without a hint of defensiveness.

"We'll find a way to pay you back."

"No, you won't," he said with finality.

"This is a pretty place," he said, taking a deep breath of the country air and sliding a little closer to her.

Emily, Lester's nineteen-year-old granddaughter, blushed, suddenly finding something interesting about the apple shed.

"You know," he continued, "I can't blame you for wanting to be here over that big old house in the city. It really is pretty here."

"It's a nice place," agreed Doris, thinking that there was a lot of room here to build another house.

He elbowed her lightly. "Are you thinking what I'm thinking, that there's a lot of room to build out here?"

"Why Lester, you presumptuous old goat, did you just bring me a pair of work gloves and propose?"

Laughter spilled through the screen door behind them, and Lester's ears turned bright red against his white hair. "Maybe I did!" he said, crossing his arms.

Doris laughed. "You are a sweet man, Lester. Thank you for the gloves." It suddenly occurred to her that there may be more to the goings on around here. "Are you paying Lin to stay on?" she asked.

It was Lester's turn to chuckle. "I am, and I'll keep paying her as long as she'll stay."

Doris was already laying her hand on the man's arm to mute him. "Lester, hush up before the girls hear you."

"We already heard him," said Mini, stepping out and passing them on her way down the steps. "I love these things," she continued, turning the volume on her hearing aid back to low on her way to the shed.

Doris passed on telling him that they were so low on food that Lin had grocery shopped for them with the money that he payed her. He was doing more than enough, and she would not burden him with any more. It was something the women needed to settle among themselves.

"I know, I know," said Lester. "I know that you're just getting settled, and it's a lot to think about. But if you don't mind, I'll keep trying."

For a moment Dori was stunned by the outburst. Where had that come from? By the time she realized that she had been shaking her head at her own thoughts and that he thought she was shaking it at him, he was reaching his car door handle. He turned back, his shoulders slumped and one side of his face turned up in a forced smile that didn't quite make it.

"Oh, Lester, I didn't mean…"

"I'll be back," he said. "You can count on that."

The sun set over the orchard, golden light dancing through the leaves turning the house from white to amber. Long shadows from the huge oak between the house and the apple shed lay across the front steps reaching for the pump house at the end of the drive. Beyond the pump house were two rows of young pecan trees, then a clearing with a short pole and power box conspicuously in the center. Tommy had been planning to build a new barn or maybe even a house in the clearing.

Dori thought that was fine. It was a good place to build. Almost more than anything, she wanted to make a go of it here with her friends. They were on the path to doing that, weren't they? Why then was she so heartsick? Dori shivered. The sun no longer warmed her bones, and her shoulder started to ache. Marybeth stepped out of the house and stood beside her. For a moment, Doris thought that she would have to speak. She didn't want to do that right now.

Marybeth lay a blanket around her shoulders and turned back toward the door. "You missed the poker game, but that's okay. I'll take your money tomorrow." The tortured squeak of the spring and slap of wood on wood as the screen door shut announced Marybeth's departure.

Lester was a good man, and she cared deeply for him. Why, oh why, could she not say the right thing to him, ever? "I'm too old to cry like a teenager," she told herself, feeling the sting of salt tears. "Too old."

***

The last rays of sun for the day shot under the trees bathing the steps and the front porch in gold. A light breeze kicked up, and the leaves began to flutter like pixies coming out to play. Leaves broke free and danced in the breeze on the way to the ground. Fall was here.

Mini Barone stood at the porch rail and took it all in. She didn't want to miss a thing. It was all so beautiful. Beauty that lasted a moment then fled like moonlight on rippling water or trees covered with snow.

All so pretty. She'd come out to see if she could get a Wi-Fi connection for her computer. She wanted to let her kids know that she was okay. They cared, but had long since given up trying to control their mother. The notebook sat on the wicker table, alone and powered off. This beautiful evening was to be savored.

Mini grew up on another kind of farm. Hers had been hard and flat and dusty or muddy, depending on the weather, with mosquitoes big enough to carry away young children. Unpainted siding, cracked porch boards, and a rusty tractor seat for a chair were the comforts of her childhood home.

They hadn't even bothered with a shed over the well, but when she was twelve her father had plumbed a line from the windmill to the house. Pappy was allergic to work, and Mini wondered why he had done that until her mother let slip that had he not, she would have left for the city.

The city was Columbia, Mississippi. That town sported a population of near six thousand in 1940, the year that Mini waved goodbye to the dirt farm and southern Mississippi and hello to life on the road.

Despite the plumbing, Ma left first. Not to the city, a nicer place according to the Good Book. That was something they hadn't seen much of on the farm, books and reading. They read in school, which the county made sure they went to, rain or shine. More rain than shine the way Mini remembered it.

She recalled muddy roads with no ditches for the runoff. Walking barefoot and carrying her shoes in a paper bag to keep them dry for school. Lunch of dry cornbread and sometimes figs or pears picked from the trees along the way. Milk from a cow that quit giving when Ma died. Pappy shot the cow for meat and sold most of it to a butcher in town. Instead of buying another, he drank up the proceeds.

It wasn't long after that, he came in one night all liquored up and took Kate to his bed. Mini took down the shotgun and sat ready, waiting for her older sister to cry out for help. Her memory was unclear about the rest of that night, but it hadn't gone well, she was sure.

Come morning, she found herself at the well, washing mud from her hands and feet with Kate doing the same. Her hands red and stinging from hard labor, and Kate pausing every few seconds in washing to stare at her as if she were some especially interesting bug stuck to the windshield of Pappy's old truck.

The red sky of a coming storm hung over them as they walked to school. It was a Friday, and there was a football game that night. They didn't go home. After the kickoff and first few plays, Kate grabbed Mini's arm and dragged her off to the mowed field where the cars were parked. They went car to car until they found one with a full tank of gas. There weren't many that needed a key in those days. They took the car and never looked back.

It was early fall when they left Mississippi. They travelled north to Missouri, then on up to Illinois. Mini had been hungry before, but that was the year she discovered cold and hungry. She and Kate needed work, and the only thing that paid daily without questions was picking. Orchards were now a love-hate thing for Mini. She was convinced that had they not picked apples, they would have starved, but the work was hard and the complications that came with being a young girl on the road harder.

Life was hard. That's just the way things were. Mini never expected easy. Fathers broke children's hearts, children with good fathers ran away, sisters parted ways. It happened in every day, every year, every generation. Nothing of significance ever changed.

The sun had fallen, the very last of it glowing over the horizon. Cold seeped past her thin skin, reaching for her bones. Mini pulled her shawl tight around her. Maybe she could get Lin to help put up some kind of antenna for her Wi-fi so she could use it here. As irregular as they were, she missed the emails from her children. They were busy with their own kids and troubles and didn't need to know about her problems, but it would probably be a good idea to let them know where she was. Eventually, if they didn't hear from her, they would worry. Worry made people do stupid things.

Something *clanged* behind the half open barn door.

***

Mini laughed. She'd come to investigate the light and noise from the barn and found Violet on a milking stool under the tractor, wrench in hand and painted with engine dirt and grease.

Violet raised the crescent wrench like a throwing knife.

Mini began looking for a way out.

Violet lowered the wrench, "I'm not going to hit you. Don't want blood on my tools," she said, almost too low for Mini to hear.

"You'd have missed anyway. I'm small and not too slow," said Mini, her confidence returned. A worn t-shirt, repurposed as a rag, lay across the giant rear tire of the old Massy Harris tractor. She handed it to Violet. "There's grease on your chin. Dinner's on the table."

"Is that what you call it?" scoffed Violet.

"Baked chicken," said Mini, as if announcing filet mignon.

"Baked, dried, degreased, flavor free. We finally get meat, why can't we have it with some of the flavor still in it? I'd like fried chicken for a change."

Mini hesitated. "You really want to eat greasy, artery-clogging, fried chicken at your age?"

"Yes, I do," shot back Violet. "And last I checked, you were older than me. What's the point of being my age if I can't eat something with flavor every once in a while?" She tossed the greasy rag at Mini.

Mini dodged out the door.

Rambling toward the house, she could see the ever changing outline of the sky against the trees. The wind urged her gently to steer right, toward the dark steps. It was cool enough that her hands went to her jacket pockets for comfort. Golden light spilled out of the kitchen and dining room windows, but the front of the house was near dark. Even when there was no shortage of electricity, the women turned off every light not in use.

In the hard times, these ladies, her friends, held it together. But they were like a big spring, wound tighter and tighter. These last weeks had been so full of stress for all of them she wondered how they got by without someone having a stroke or heart attack? Maybe the change was good for them. Maybe getting out and doing new things, or old things, was what people need to feel alive.

She couldn't deny that everyone seemed better off here than at the home. But there was a lot of pressure that came along with the move. Someone was going to pop one of those important blood vessels in the brain. They needed some relief. They needed a party. She grinned in the dark and spun around taking in the starry sky. There was something wonderfully primal about being outside at night in the country. She bent her neck back and kissed the sky.

CHAPTER 4

Anita sat in the Mercedes on the hill overlooking Golden Lawn, engine idling. Her first raid on the home had turned into a nightmare. The blond twit, the brainless old bitch, put a raccoon into her Benz. The shop charged her almost five hundred dollars to get the smell of racoon pee out of the leather seats.

She'd watched and waited for twenty minutes, her personal limit for patience. No one had come or gone. Only three cars had passed. Each time she held her phone to her ear. One of the cars slowed down, presumably to offer help, and she'd waved it on.

It was time. She eased the Benz onto the road and down the long hill to the gates. From there, she couldn't see the sprawling cluster of low buildings. The only indication of anything beyond the gates were the solar powered lights that lined the road through the oak forest to Golden Lawn. It had been a pretty place before the vandals and spray paint artists got to it. Now, in the twilight, it reminded her of a derelict mental hospital. Anita gripped the bolt cutters, prepared to defeat the locked gate.

Moments later, she stood at the mouth of the north wing hall, the other end of the hall an impossibly long way away, glowing faintly in the last minutes of the day. She wondered again why she had chosen to come here at this time of day. Oh! yeah, because mother had demanded her attention every minute of the day, and she could only get away while Irene was busy with her new cooking coach. The woman was 84 years old. *Why did she wait till now to learn to cook?*

Anita turned on the flashlight and started down the hall.

***

Aaron loved to ride his bike. Uphill, downhill, or around the hill, but mostly on warm blacktop. He liked the sound the tires made on the tar, like they were constantly being glued down then pulled up. He liked that sound so much that he sometimes got scared without it. When that happened, like when he had to go up his own concrete driveway, he would mostly get off and walk the bike. He tried sometimes to ride up the drive, especially when Dad was watching, but it was hard, and his front wheel would wobble wildly by the time he got to the garage.

His favorite road, the one he rode every evening that it wasn't raining, was the Golden Lawn road. That wasn't the real name. He didn't know the real name; he liked roads with numbers better than ones with names. He could remember numbers. He liked the long hill, and he loved the gate to Golden Lawn at the bottom. He had never been through the gate. That would have been trespassing, and he could get into trouble for that. Besides, they locked the gate with a chain. He'd seen the lady with the van put the new chain on the week before.

Aaron stepped hard on the coaster brake and slid to a stop. He stared at the open gate and the cut chain for almost a full minute before taking his phone from the handlebar bag and calling the number that he had memorized a month ago.

"Special Agent Jonah," said the voice after only one ring.

"Hi," said Aaron, counting Mississippi one like Mom taught him, then going on. "This is Aaron C… C… Cain. I live near Golden Lawn, and you told me to c... c.. call. If there was anything susp.. susp.. wrong."

"Oh, yeah," Aaron heard from his phone. "You're the autistic kid."

"Asperger's. And I'm not really a kid. I'm twenty-f… f… four."

"Sorry about that, Aaron. I'll try and get it right next time. What's up at Golden Lawn?" asked the FBI man.

Aaron bobbed his head in acceptance of the apology. "Somebody cut the lock off the gate. There's a car in there."

***

Agent Ted Jonah heard everything the kid said. The power was off. The residents all moved out. Someone had chained the gate, and the lock was now cut open. Most interesting to Jonah was the description of the car. A Mercedes S-class, and Aaron, God bless him, had memorized the plate. Robbins drove an S-class Mercedes. It was a crumb tantalizing enough to get Jonah to reverse course from the parking garage to his office to check the plate.

The old man, Special Agent in Charge Stevens, had been on him today about this case. People, meaning politicians, wanted this guy caught. A local news station got the ball rolling with a piece about the retirement home. It didn't look good for the politicians or the Bureau when a guy like Bob Robbins got away.

Unfortunately, it hadn't stopped at the local news. A commentator at Fox was scheduled to run a segment on the investigation tomorrow. The deputy director had been blindsided with the story and asked to comment with the camera shoved in his face. That had taken eleven whole minutes to matriculate down the chain of command where it exploded from the mouth of Agent Jonah's own boss in a string of very un-FBI-like words. "Fix it. Find this sonofabitch and perp walk him in front of a hundred cameras. Do it now," said Stevens.

Six weeks and they had nothing. Nothing.

Now, Jonah was back at his desk, back at the file, and comparing the plate number for the Mercedes to the plate number from Bob Robbins' own S-class. The numbers matched. "That kid gets a reward," said Jonah to the buzzing fluorescent lights.

Seconds later he was on the phone. "Get out of there, Aaron," he said. "Yes, this is Special Agent Jonah, and you need to get out of there now."

"Why?"

Jonah wiped a sudden layer of sweat from his forehead. His own brother was autistic, and while he hated it when he was a kid, he understood the process. "Bad people are there. Do you understand?"

Four minutes later, Jonah was strapping on his tactical vest with one hand and calling for a chopper with the other. He could only get five agents on such short notice. It would have to be enough. The chopper was warming up, and a call had already been made to clear air space for a low-altitude, high-speed run to Golden Lawn.

With the last man aboard, Jonah gave the pilots a thumbs up, and they were airborne before he was settled in his seat. Through the headset, he ordered the pilots to get there as fast as possible. The pilots both grinned as they pushed the Blackhawk beyond the standard maximum speed to almost 200 miles per hour. The sixty mile flight took less than twenty minutes.

***

Anita whimpered, a warm patch growing under her. Three men with helmets and masked faces looked down on her. But she wasn't counting men. She was counting the round black holes in the ends of the automatic weapons. If she had been able to look past the gun barrels, she would have seen the disgust in the eyes looking down at her as the damp spot in her jeans expanded.

"Stand down, gentlemen," a man said.

"Where's Robbins?" the disembodied voice asked. An ID was flashed so quickly that all she saw was the three big letters *FBI*.

An hour later, Anita sat numbly in the Atlanta Field Office interview room. She rubbed her wrists, raw from the handcuffs. Her wet pants had been replaced with orange prison pants. She wondered if she would get her jeans back. They cost sixty bucks.

"Don't worry about your pants," said the one she now knew was Agent Jonah. "You have much bigger problems."

"That makes me feel so much better. Did I say something about my pants?"

"You haven't stopped talking since you got here, but what I haven't heard is where Robbins is."

Anita shook her head. Things were starting to clear up. She felt herself begin to shake, first the shoulders, then the hands, then her whole upper body, and there was nothing she could do to stop it. A shrill animal whine started somewhere nearby. It sounded like it was coming out of the glass in the mirror behind Jonah. She saw herself in the mirror, mouth open and eyes wide. The sound was coming from her. The Whale Guy snapped his fingers in front of her nose, and the animal sound halted, replaced with her own deep panting.

"Ms. Bright, what are you doing with Bob Robbins' car?"

"I took it," she squeaked. "He took everything from us. So, I took the car. Am I in trouble?"

The Whale Guy tossed the file on the metal table and turned for the door. He was going to leave her alone again. Anita felt the familiar surge of panic grip her.

***

"You heard her," Jonah said to Stevens. "She's had the car the whole time."

Stevens shrugged. His eyes were glassy, and when he spoke, Jonah caught a blast of gin. No doubt he'd been unwinding from the hectic day when he got the call about Fulsom-Bright's arrest. He looked Jonah in the eye. "Ten-to-one he's out of the country?"

Jonah nodded. Stevens was an ass sometimes, but he wasn't stupid. In fact, the guy was brilliant, smart enough to keep up with the details of most of the active cases in the office without having to check the files.

"I'd start checking countries that we don't have extradition treaties with," said Stevens. "I'm thinking he planned this whole thing from the start. Maybe before he opened the home. He didn't just stumble into the idea." He tilted his head wistfully and exhaled another blast of gin.

Jonah nodded again, "We found a flat-bed driver that says he was prepaid to deliver the car to Florida, but the car was gone when he went to pick it up."

Stevens raised an eyebrow. "How'd you manage that?"

"The guy's card was still in the console," said Jonah. He tilted his head to the glass behind him. "What about her?"

Stevens shrugged and turned to go.

Jonah examined his prisoner through the glass. Auto theft was not a federal crime. Too bad. He'd love to lock her up just for the pain-in-the-ass factor. But there was more to it than that. At a gut level, he didn't believe her. She knew more than she was telling. Through the glass, he saw her begin to sway in her seat. Before he could even think to reach for the door, her eyes rolled back and her head thumped down on the table.

"Shit! She did it again," he said, watching the dark spot in her pants grow under the table. He lifted the phone and slowly pressed the extension for the US attorney's office in the building. Stevens had wisely requested someone to stay on tonight. Someone that Jonah knew very well.

"Katherine Jones," answered the crisp voice on the other end of the line.

"Is that your special tone just for me?"

"It could be, or maybe I just spoke with another G-Man that broke my heart."

"You know I don't believe that. Your heart is way too tough for a few G-Men to break."

"Wow! Let's not get mean."

For a moment, Jonah thought he had gone too far. He'd dated Katherine, way too rigid to be called Kathy or Kate, for a while, attracted first by her trim figure and long legs. They were nice legs, but they couldn't buy passage around her rock hard heart. Now, here she was sounding wounded.

"You bought that, didn't you? I've been practicing having emotions," she said.

"You're getting good at it," he laughed, relieved that he hadn't really hurt her and disappointed that she still managed to dodge having any endearing personal qualities.

"Look, I've got a hard case down here…"

"I hear that she just melts in the interrogation chair."

Jonah bit his tongue. "I miss you and all the confusion of trying to interpret our conversations, and yes, she does have that super talent. I have a question for your brilliant legal mind. She hasn't asked for a lawyer, and I need to buy some time to figure out how to present her to the ever watchful press or get her past them, whichever. How long can we hold her?"

"You don't care about the press any more than you care about me. You think she has ties to Robbins?"

"Maybe."

"Why don't you let me, the US attorney, interview and put the fear of God in her? Maybe we can flip her."

"You'd do that?" asked Jonah.

"I can scare anyone. You of all people should know that," she said with just the right tinge of bitterness.

"Let me get her cleaned up first."

Katherine laughed. "You do that."

Special Agent Ted Jonah smiled for the second time that day. Catching the woman that stole Robbins' car was not a big break; it was a small break. But if the FBI was good at anything, it was in taking small breaks and turning them into solved cases. He punched in another extension. "Jonah, in interview four. I need a female Marshall. Thanks. Oh! Send an EMT or whoever you've got that manages smelling salts. This woman keeps passing out. And… you'd better bring another change of pants for her."

CHAPTER 5

With a *whoosh*, a ball of flame broke the night sky. Howling laughter echoed off some distant surface. Glass clanked on glass with the dull ring that any travelling man can tell you is thc sound only half-empty booze bottles make. Music, broken strains from a mouth harp whose player seemed short of breath, punctuated the breaks in the laughter. The chirpy squeal of a long neglected cello blended with the crackling of the fire.

Violet, perched on an upended log, took it all in. Ruby, with the harmonica, nodding her head and singing softly when she wasn't pushing some mountain song through the reeds. Doris with the cello half-tuned, striking low raspy notes that seemed to vibrate the very strings of the heart. Mini, Marybeth, and Bernice dancing around the flames of the bonfire, energized anew by the music, spraying mouthfuls of booze into the flames. It was all so rich, so decadent, so perfectly out of control.

Violet tossed a cup of gasoline on the fire and took a shot straight from the bottle of Irish whiskey. Oh! That hit the spot, going down like warm liquid candy with a bit of fire added. She felt the gas cup in her other hand and reminded herself not to confuse the containers. The thought made her giggle and wonder briefly just how much difference there was between the gas and the booze. Both made nice fireballs. "The booze tastes better."

Mini stopped between her and the fire, her short wispy thin frame swaying like a tired belly dancer. "The man spent our money on good booze," she shouted, before swaying off, her bare feet floating over the grass in a way that made Violet wonder if her friend were not truly an aging gypsy princess. *No, too short.* She took another slug from the bottle.

"Here, let me try that," said Bernice, offering Violet her own three-quarter full bottle of tequila in exchange.

Violet took the trade and a sip of the new bottle. The tequila tasted fruity after the whiskey.

Bernice danced a circle around the fire and exchanged bottles again with Violet without breaking stride. "I don't drink. I just like spitting it in the fire," she confessed, before taking another mouthful of cactus juice and spewing it into the flames.

Doris began to sway following the bow as it traveled across the strings singing a song that was vaguely familiar to Violet, the "Kol Nidre." Drawn to the sheer passion of the music, Violet began to sway with it, tossing the bottle of whisky back, taking a long swig, letting the warmth flow through her. The music took her. She lifted her heels, then her toes, and danced around the fire.

Later, they fed small logs to the two foot pile of embers, watching them ignite and vanish into the night sky. Ruby played softly on her harmonica, wetting her lips from a whisky bottle. Violet poked the embers with a piece of steel bar. Mini tested the quality of her breath by blowing into the flames.

They'd needed to blow off some steam, but this was going to hurt tomorrow. Violet chuckled, while she could.

Bernice sat across from her, gazing blankly over the fire. "I don't drink," she said again.

"You know, alcohol soaks in through your membranes," said Marybeth.

"I don't drink," repeated Bernice.

Doris started to laugh first. Then Mini, and Marybeth and finally, unable to resist, Violet joined in.

"She is so drunk," howled Mini.

"Who's drunk?" asked Bernice.

Violet lost her balance and fell off her log.

"Is Violet drunk?" slurred Bernice, mouth agape.

"You are, dear," replied Ruby, kneeling in front of her. "How many fingers am I holding up?" she asked, first holding up three, then reconsidering and holding up four.

Bernice counted the fingers by touch. "Five," she slurred.

Ruby barked a laugh and fell into the trampled grass, her belly rising in explosions of laughter and her feet kicking the ground like a child throwing a tantrum.

"Oh, for goodness' sake," Violet heard her own disembodied voice say. "If we don't quiet down, someone will call the sheriff to see what we're up to."

"And they'll take the booze," added Doris.

"Too late," said Violet.

"They're not taking my booze," declared Mini, hugging the half empty Jack bottle.

"That gook girl would do it," added Marybeth.

"Oh! for goodness sake, why do you call her that?" snapped Doris.

Violet perked up. It wasn't often that Dori jumped on someone, but when she did, it was always good.

"Because that's what she is," snapped Marybeth, primal hatred blazing from her eyes, her fisted hands shaking.

"I just don't understand," said Doris, bewildered.

"She's a Jap!"

"She most certainly is not. That girl is Chinese or Taiwanese, or something!"

Marybeth's clenched fists dropped slowly, shakily, to her lap as if her anger were too tired to go on. "All the same."

"Oh, my. Why do you hate them so much? That war was so very long ago."

Marybeth dropped her chin, then her shoulders sagged. A few minutes later, she began to sob. Her bottle fell to the ground, amber flowing into the grass as tears flowed from her ancient eyes and her body began to convulse out of synch with the moans.

"What's with her?" asked Ruby, waking from a nap.

Violet shook her head, then shifted her gaze to Bernice who was showing some sign of consciousness, staring at Marybeth with her head cocked and mouth open.

Violet wanted to laugh, but Marybeth's sobs were turning to gasps, and with each she slammed her fists down on her own thighs. We're going to need ice, thought Violet, unable to attach herself to the emotional wreckage before her.

Doris sat beside Marybeth and wrapped her own blanket over her friend's shoulders. Together, they watched the flames, prodding them occasionally to grow then fall back to an almost peaceful consumption. They sipped at their bottles and huddled under their blankets and shawls. Violet warmed her arthritic hands as close to the fire as she dared, then cleaned and filed her nails, a habit that came from her years as a mechanic.

Bernice found her cane—almost falling to the ground reaching for it—and began to tap on the rocks around the fire, hitting them about half of the time.

Ruby, sat up and leaned on Bernice's log, warming her hands as well.

Eventually Marybeth unclenched her fists and began rubbing her hands in her normal fashion.

Violet breathed a deep sigh of relief.

"I was fourteen. Tall for my age," began Marybeth, her voice raspy and weary with pain. "When the war started, we were on the way home from Australia. Our ship was taken, and I was taken to the Philippines to a camp called Santo Tomas. It was okay for a while. We were living in a kind of dormitory that I think had been a college. It was exciting. We could get most of what we needed at the fence from the locals."

She paused, her fists clenching and releasing, clenching and releasing. "One day, I was alone going to the fence to get food, and I got stopped by a Jap officer. He had a squad of men with him, and they wanted to inspect me. But it was wrong. There was just something wrong about the way they were looking at me. I fought…"

Her voice tapered into a thin wail as she pulled the blanket tight. "They made me into a comfort girl. I was fourteen, and they made me into a whore. I never, never told…"

Violet sat stunned and watched more than a half century of buried shame and pain pour from her friend.

***

Lin, shivering, listened from her post in the line of trees. She saw them collecting booze and stayed late, suspecting that she would be needed. She wished she hadn't. Somewhere in her heart, was a list of the times that she'd felt alone, an outsider. This night would be added to that list.

It didn't matter that Marybeth was wrong to hate her. It didn't matter that the others supported her. What mattered was that it made her feel like leaving and not coming back. She clenched her jaw, the stinging tears mixed with smoke burning her eyes. Already her mind was elsewhere, wondering what it would be like to go home in the middle of the night. Wondering how to explain her leaving to those that cared. Her phone buzzed in her pocket. The text was from Doris. "Don't leave. It's not you she hates."

CHAPTER 6

Bob Robbins watched the waves roll lazily toward him, the early morning light turning them hues of bright orange and dark blue. The growing ocean breeze negated the need for fans and kept the rumble of passing trucks on the road behind the house at bay for the moment. This home, this castle, was all his, the stone arches and concrete balustrade mirrored in the swimming pool below. Bought and paid for with years of work and planning. A walled fortress by the sea.

The house had been built by a drug kingpin that had run afoul of the local police by not paying them enough to ignore him. Bob was smarter than that. He made discreet inquiries into who he needed to encourage with financial gifts then made sure to keep the gifts regular. That he paid with stolen money didn't seem to matter. He hadn't stolen it in Belize.

Nor did he keep it here. Suspecting that any local authority worthy of a bribe would be able to buy access into his banking information, and aware that the IRS routinely pursued Belize banks looking for tax cheats, Bob kept only a small part of his fortune in the local banks. This country had no extradition treaty with the U.S., but the banking protections were light at best.

He was doing well, he thought, except for the damnable need for help. Even here, servants, cooks, and gardeners cost money. And each seemed to come with another local official who felt that if you could afford to pay one, you could afford to pay another. Yesterday, it had been a cook whose cousin was the city planner for Belize City. A poor planner in Bob's opinion, but one with deep pockets and a cousin in his kitchen. She was a good cook. Breakfast had been German sausage with eggs and toast with marmalade. Wonderful, but at a fifty percent higher rate, the cousin included, than he had expected to pay.

This stuff had gone on forever he was told, but he seriously doubted that the British, when they had been here, had put up with it. If they had, there would certainly have been exceptions for Brian, and Jack, and "dear old Cavanaugh, who had flown in the war you know." The upshot being that all the bribes under the British would probably have added up to annual club memberships for the takers.

Now, Belize was the home of any number of people who carried some sort of authority and well-rehearsed reason to demand a monthly stipend. One had noted Bob's stress at not having the cash on hand and had been kind enough to accept an annual payment via PayPal—three percent added for transaction fees, of course.

Unfortunately, the suspiciously high property tax that he had paid on taking possession of the house had consumed the first six months of his budget. Already he found it necessary to access his safe deposit box in the Caymans to withdraw a bearer bond. Rather than pay an expensive courier—there were a number of them in the Caymans—he had risked using FedEx to send the bond to his lawyer in New York. Jerry cashed it in and transferred the funds to his Belize account for him.

He smiled and sipped his tea. He called Jerry twice a month to stay in touch and check the status of his case. If the FBI had been half interested in finding him, they would have tapped Jerry's phone. Not that it would do them any good. Jerry Goldstein was a damn good lawyer and his most faithful friend, the only one who hadn't raised his rates when Bob skipped the country. Instead, Jerry had set up a special phone that Bob could reach him on that would not be traceable to him. Bob suspected that he was paying $300 a month for a prepaid cell phone, the cheapest of cheap solutions, marked up just for him.

Overpriced or not, it worked. Every other Thursday at 1:00 pm, Bob would call, and Jerry would fill him in on any pertinent changes in the world. Usually there were updates on the home. The power being cut off, the remaining residents leaving, that kind of thing. Not that it mattered to Bob, but technically it was still his property, and it was hard to completely disconnect. There were other issues: the missing car found by the FBI—in Anita's hands no less, the building in disarray, people calling Jerry demanding payment for services. Jerry pretended ignorance and in one case told a food services company to go stuff themselves. A lawyer with a sense of humor. Bob sipped his tea, hiding a smile behind the cup.

Bearer bonds were not the most convenient or cost effective way to keep money, but things had changed in offshore banking. Money transferred could be tracked, that information shared by the bank with other countries with an interest in tracking tax evasion or money laundering. The U.S. was one of those countries. Items in the safe deposit box, however, did not show up in the accounts of the bank they were stored in. Only the hire of the box was recorded. The bank made a show of inspecting the contents that were entered into the box, but that was only on the opening of the account. After that, privacy was assured. Unfortunately, that privacy came at a cost. Bob was forced to either make his box accessible to someone who could retrieve and cash in bonds as funds were needed, or he would have to himself travel to Grand Cayman to access the box when the need arose.

Jerry had been clear that he did not want responsibility for the account in the Caymans. "Bob, if you come up short some bonds, I don't want you thinking I had anything to do with it," he said.

He was either an honest lawyer, or a cautious lawyer. Either way, it suited Bob. "If only the bribes would stop," he grumbled.

"What, sir?" asked Carmine, the cook, setting down his coffee.

He waved her away with the back of his hand. Weren't servants, especially those trained by the British, supposed to have some sort of ability to not hear what wasn't for them? Apparently not here. Bob sipped the coffee and watched the waves crash against the stone seawall below. There were beaches here and there, but few homes had beachfront. Instead, most had deep water docks to park their fishing boats and yachts. He had one of those, too.

It had taken him two weeks to build up the nerve, but with the help of his gardener, he'd taken the forty-five foot yacht, *Desire'*, out for a cruise around the peninsula of Belize City. The brightly colored buildings and roofs astounded him. Until then Belize had been the streets and sidewalks near the banks and stores that he had visited while setting up house. Only from the sea had his eyes been opened to the wild beauty of the city.

Noting his increasing excitement, the gardener shook his head. “It’s not so pretty up close, boss. It stinks.”

It had the sound of good advice and marked a slight turning point in Bob’s attitude toward the staff. Maybe paying them and their third cousins was worth it. The gardener’s brother was a cop. Bob didn't like cops, but if he were ever in real trouble, having one on the payroll could come in handy. Though that had been suggested in their initial meeting, Bob had arrogantly dismissed the idea…and the man.

“George,” he said to the gardener, “tell your brother that I’m sorry for the way I treated him. He could be a useful man to know in this city.”

“My name is Jamie, sir. His name is George. And yes, he can be useful. He drives a taxi when he is not a policeman. If you want to see the city?” he shrugged.

Bob nodded, “Is it worth it?”

“You live here now, sir. You should see the city. And there is very good food,” said Jamie, swinging the boat around to circle the peninsula and return to dock at the house.

Jamie was working down by the south wall now, his red shirt catching a stray ray of sunlight through the palms every few seconds as he pulled or planted. One or the other was a constant here. The staff were turning out to be valuable and informative assets, but it would be careless to forget that they could be sources of information against him, as well. Bob kept a tight watch on his words. There was no need to tell the cook where he was going when he went on an errand. On the other hand, he felt it prudent to let Jamie in on his plans if he were going to town. That he had done only a few times now, but he felt comforted knowing that if he were not to arrive home at a reasonable time, a local cop whose salary he supplemented would come looking for him, if for no other reason than to keep the largesse flowing.

“Jamie?” called Robbins.

“Yes, sir,” said Jamie, jumping up to the side of the pool deck.

“Where can I play golf?”

“Yes sir, not on the mainland, no way. The mainland courses are not so good. But you know, Mister Bob, there’s a good place on the island. Not too far. Ten mile maybe. Real fast by airplane, not so fast by boat."

Bob had a twinge of doubt, but what good was it to live in a place like this if you couldn't play golf? "No plane. Have the boat ready to leave by 10:00. I'll tell Carmine to pack us some lunch and put some beer on ice."

Jamie laughed, a big Caribbean blast. "You a good man, Mr. Bob." The words had a tinge of nervous relief.

Bob squinted into the shadows. "Why did you say it like that?"

Jamie shrunk, "I just mean you're a good man, sir… to let me drive the boat and all."

Bob studied the man in the shadows. There was more to it than that. It was in the eyes. "Tell me, Jamie, what you meant."

"Oh, sir, I don't mean nothin' by it. It's just that people say dis and dat, and then you're so nice to me."

Bob nodded, his whole body rocking in the steel chair. "This and that?"

"Just things, you know, like you some kind of big-time robber guy that come down here to relax. I hope you come to relax?" Another nervous shrug.

Big-time robber guy? That didn't sound so bad. The chair squeaked as he settled back and sipped his coffee. *Not bad at all.*

Somewhere in his dreams, Bob had thought that getting away to the Caribbean would mean really getting away. Too many Jimmy Buffett songs had promised real freedom down here. It never occurred to him that with the changing times everyone here now had a smartphone. Even the people living in those tiny two-story wood houses in the city had iPads and internet. It was insane. The minute he arrived, he felt like everyone had looked him up. Maybe that wasn't such a bad thing. Being thought of as a tough guy could work out to his advantage. If not, there were still the small islands. Some of them had to be available. He could look into that if things got weird. Maybe he should look into it now. "Hey Jamie, tell Carmine to make more coffee. We'll go to the island another day. I have some thinking to do."

CHAPTER 7

Bernice pulled the blanket tight around and brought her feet up under her. A shiver shook her frame. Though she desperately wanted to be out of the house, it was too cold outside.

Lin poked at the contents of the fireplace haplessly with the ash shovel.

"You've got to give it a little room to breathe between the logs."

"I didn't build the stack. Marybeth did," said Lin.

"My, aren't you defensive. So, you *were* watching last night?"

"Does everyone know?" Lin said, using the poker to open a gap between sticks of oak, letting the smoke have enough air to light. Her back remained stubbornly turned to Bernice.

Behind them Marybeth passed through, emitting a grunt on the way.

Bernice tapped her cane on the floor twice hard, her signature move when annoyed. Lin's shoulders lifted in a laugh.

Bernice shook her head. She thought she understood some of what was going on, but the only way to be sure was for Lin to tell her. There was no margin in guessing at people's feelings. "You should tell me about it."

"All my life, I've been different, the outsider," said Lin.

Bernice listened, and Lin told her about leaving China, being adopted, the names kids called her in school, and even her teen awkwardness. Something had pushed Lin's button, and she was in talk mode. Bernice resisted the urge to tap her cane and interject. Finally, Lin let silence take over and hung the poker on the tool rack. The fire was well lit.

"Oh dear," said Bernice, who listened to every word wondering how anyone could get it so wrong. "I'm not much of an advice giver, but it seems to me that you're carrying a lifetime of baggage already. Maybe you need to unload a bit of that."

"I just did."

“I was thinking of something a little more long term.”

“You mean like therapy? God, I don't want to go to therapy. Can't we send Marybeth instead?”

Bernice laughed.

It warmed up enough in the afternoon that Bernice felt comfortable walking outside. Taking her tablet—a wonderful thing for someone like her that loved to read about everything—she walked around the hilltop orchard hoping to find some magic spot where she could make a data connection. She found none.

It felt good to be out. In the daylight, the gravel drive didn’t look so bad. She set a quick pace and soon found herself past the front gate, the smell of warm blacktop reminding her of her childhood, the *tap-tap* of the cane reminding her of her age.

Bernice grew up in west Brooklyn where Germans, like her, weren’t all that common. While her parents struggled with the English language, she was born into it. Still, in a community of mostly Italian and Irish decent, she stood out. She was the girl with the German accent living in a time when Germans weren’t popular. When the war started, Bernice was twelve. It was the first time she remembered her mother yelling at her. Mother yelled a lot that year.

Money was tight, and as tensions grew between Germany and the US, Papa’s prospects for work became slimmer. For as long as she could remember, Papa had worked the docks, getting up far before sunrise and coming home tired and dirty for a late dinner. Only lately, he hadn’t been so tired and dirty. A few times he had even come home bleary-eyed and stinking of beer. Work was plentiful, but not for Papa.

Mother’s normally calm disposition turned more sour with every mention of Hitler and the National Socialists, the Nazis. Papa wasn’t going to work as long as he spoke with a German accent, but the accent was there to stay. She cooked and sewed to put food on the table. She loved to sew, often having fabric left over to make clothes for family. Bernice was never lacking for something to wear, and her clothes were good advertising for Mother's tiny business.

Things were always hard, but for Bernice, the world changed very quickly when the war began. People she called friends still talked to her, but the conversation changed. The games became a little rougher and "hide-and-seek" became "find-the-spy." Bernice was always the spy. She didn't mind most of the time. She was crafty and good at the game, preferring to hide over running. Sometimes she took a bag of sewing or a book so she could have something to do while the others rushed around looking for her.

One blustery fall day, she wandered a few blocks further than normal and found herself surrounded suddenly by older boys. She was thirteen and pretty in a flowered long-sleeved dress that Mutter had sewn from a McCall pattern that had cost a whole dollar.

Five boys, dark-haired and bored, their fathers most likely off to war, spread out around her. Timidly at first, then with more boldness, they moved in, closer and closer until she could feel their breath. They circled like dogs in a pack, until the short one, whose name she had long forgotten, snapped back to her and shouted, "Booo!" making Bernice flinch.

"Who are you? What are you doing here?" asked the boy who was only a few inches taller than her, though fourteen or fifteen by the look of him.

Blonde Bernice, with her crooked lip and handmade clothes, was more curious than intimidated. As the boys stared at her and continued to circle, she was reminded of a picture show she had seen where several men courting the same young woman circled her and danced. Despite her confusion and unease, despite these boys crossing into her space, Bernice was starting to enjoy the game.

"Do you speak English?" demanded the short one.

Bernice, unexpectedly angry, tilted her head and put her hands on her hips the way her mother did when she was about to take charge. "Of course, I speak English. I live here."

"Where do you live?"

"That is none of your business!"

"I think it is. Perhaps the Fraulein is lost."

"Yeah, lost," burst out a boy behind her, his voice cracking.

"I don't think so. I live right down there," replied Bernice, jabbing one finger into the boy as she pointed with another, and taking the moment to check the street sign. For the first time now, she was nervous.

She didn't recognize the street names.

"If she *is* lost… maybe we should help her find her way home," said a calming voice.

"To Germany?" demanded one of the boys.

"I think she lives closer," said the new boy, pushing his way through the circle. "My name is Warren," he said, with a warm smile that instantly made Bernice feel safe. They shook, his hand as warm as his smile. "I'm Bernice," she said, "and I think I may really be lost."

Warren brushed an undisciplined shock of brown hair from his eyes and swung his eyes around the group. Lanky, with joints that seemed to flex where they shouldn't, he stood at least four inches taller than any other boy in the group. Bernice barely came up to his shoulder. She didn't know why, but that comforted her.

"Well, let's find this lady's home." Turning back to Bernice he asked, "Street name?"

"Willow," she said.

"We know that one, don't we boys," bellowed Warren, like a prison guard calling the dogs to chase down a missing man. "Which way do we go?"

"We could go through Pierrepoint! My name is Ronny," said the boy, extending his hand to Bernice.

"That's the long way." said a skinny boy behind her. "We could go down Hicks and stop at Cray's for a soda." Everyone seemed to like that idea and at once began to dig in their pockets for change. "Do you mind?" asked Warren, smiling at her again.

Bernice shook her head. She would love a soda.

Lost in reverie, she had walked at least a mile from the orchard, the sun as warm on her shoulders as the blacktop under her feet. It wasn't quite like home. There were no buildings for the cold wind to whistle between. It was more like her other home. The one Warren and she had made in Guatemala. Flatter and a little dryer here, but, like the jungle, missing the noises of man.

A pickup truck pulled up beside her and slowed to her speed as the window slid down. A middle-aged woman seemed genuinely concerned. "Are you lost?"

Bernice wanted to laugh, but her tablet buzzed in her hand telling her that she had found a mobile connection. She stuttered, probably giving an even stronger impression of confusion. "Not really," she said. "Do you have a mobile hotspot?"

"Yeah," answered the woman.

"Do you mind if I connect for a minute?"

***

The morning talk with Bernice had left Lin a muddled mess. Unable to sort her thoughts or even be sure what she wanted, she isolated herself hoping that in solitude she would find some answers. Her new course hadn't been a stellar success. She scrubbed the upstairs bath top to bottom, refolded and sorted everything in the linen closet, and finally began to clean out the closet under the stairs.

In the closet, she found a wooden box with a heavy leather handle. Dragging it out, she slipped the brass latches and lifted the lid.

"Oh! You've found a nice box of paints," said Ruby, from behind her.

Lin turned to find Ruby's eyes glowing with excitement.

"I always wanted to paint," said Ruby. "And that's no beginner kit. Look at the brushes."

Lin looked. What she saw was a mess. Ruby apparently saw treasure.

***

Ruby held her breath. It was a mess, a beautiful mess. Drips and splatters of paint throughout the box, well-used brushes with clean fibers but spattered handles, scrapers and spatulas with paint in every crease, tools, even some handmade knives, palettes with globs of color stuck to the edges, tubes of paint with as much color outside as in. The palette smeared with hues of gold and warm brown, grape and plum, and reds that seemed impossible. Beautiful, almost magical colors blended and dried on everything, turning the tools themselves into art. A mess. A glorious mess.

Ruby nudged Lin aside. Deeper in the closet, behind where the box had been, stood an easel, a dozen blank stretched canvases, and another box, this one older and almost too heavy for her to lift. She leaned the easel against the closet door and opened the second box, surveying the huge store of artist supplies.

"He was a painter," she muttered.

"I can see that," said Lin.

Ruby spoke over her shoulder. "He painted a lot. He must have left some paintings here somewhere, don't you think? I mean, look at this."

"You really think he left paintings here? I haven't seen anything."

"He must have," said Ruby. "What else would he do with them? Violet says he spent almost all his time here. He was practically a hermit. There has to be something," she said, feeling a twinge of some long absent joy of discovery.

She missed that. After the first few days in the house she'd fallen into a kind of malaise. Not depression. That would be a weakness, a crack in her façade where there was none. Not depression, just tiredness, weariness with a touch of hopelessness tossed in. This was the opposite. This new feeling was the bright light in a room that had been dark so long that the darkness had become normal. Her heart beat fast, her breath quickened, her skin tingled with anticipation.

"We could search the house," said Lin.

Ruby agreed. A search would be good. A search would be essential. A search was going to happen whether Lin wanted it or not.

They'd already cleaned the kitchen and living room thoroughly. That left the bedrooms, closets, and maybe the attic. They started downstairs, checking under beds and in closets. Bernice and Ruby's room was closest. Ruby felt certain they would find nothing there. Still, she pushed aside the boxes in the closet while Lin looked under the bed.

That room finished, they moved upstairs, brushing aside inquiries. The linen closet was cleared. They slowed down long enough to knock on Violet and Marybeth's door before searching that closet and wardrobe as well. Still nothing.

***

In Doris and Mini's room, Mini sat closed-faced and arms crossed on the bed. "It's mine, and I'm keeping it."

Lin scowled and tried to outstare the old woman.

"That face of yours isn't going to change my mind," said Mini.

Lin shook her head and crossed her own arms to match Mini. The old woman smacked her lips and defiantly turned her hearing aid down.

Ruby laughed and began pushing aside the clothes hung in the closet. Behind her, Lin pulled up a stool and stepped up to check the top of the huge wardrobe. "I've got something!" said Lin.

Mini squinted and smacked her lips again before turning up her hearing aid to listen. Her shoulders slumped just a little in confusion and, for a moment, Lin felt the smug satisfaction of vindication. That moment passed. The old woman was hiding something. Mini hiding something couldn't be good.

The painting had a weight to it. The weight of beauty. Through the dusty plastic she could see only a hint of color under the white paper wrapping over the canvas. Lin wiped away the dust but didn't dare open the bag without cleaning the outside thoroughly. Right now there was something else she needed to deal with.

"Mrs. Barone, we're looking for Tommy's paintings, but I want to know what you're hiding."

Mini smacked her lips and glared, her mouth curling in a snarl. "The paintings are in the crawl space under the house."

Lin was at the door before she realized that she had only been given half the truth. She turned back, put on her best schoolmarm face, and looked down calmly at the shriveled old woman who still wore her nightgown this late in the day. In place of the old woman, Lin saw a child, someone who knew that she was an inconvenience and hated it.

She almost bought it, but Mini was never weak, never lacking for pride. This was an act. Either that or worse, Mini Barone was suffering from dementia. Lin raised an inquiring eyebrow.

The trace of a smile flashed in Mini's eyes.

"She's talking about her shotgun," said Doris, from the doorway.

Mini glared at Doris then shot a glance back at Lin.

"Really?" Lin shook her head. "I don't care about your shotgun. Just don't accidentally shoot yourself… or anyone else, please."

"I've never shot anyone by accident," muttered Mini, at Lin's exiting back.

In the hall, Ruby touched Lin's arm. "She's okay you know."

"I know. No crazier than the rest of you," said Lin.

They found forty-eight paintings in the crawl space. Each unique in size and heft. Each wrapped in archival paper, then plastic, with silica bead packs. Carefully, they began to bring Tommy's work up to the living room where they vacuumed the dust from the plastic on all of them before opening the first bag.

The weighty smell of turpentine and chirping chatter of the women filled the air like Christmas morning in a workshop full of little old elves. Lin glanced up when Bernice strolled in only looking up from her tablet for a few seconds to glance over the cleaning operations in the living room.

"Did you see?" said Lin, but Doris turned on the vacuum cleaner at that moment, and the words were lost.

Bernice passed through, barely lifting her eyes from the tablet, then took a seat in the kitchen and began to read, her fingers dancing across the screen.

Lin cut the tape and opened another painting, this one rich in deep plum colors like dark rain-soaked leaves on a forest floor. Tommy had been a master of color, producing visuals that opened emotional gates with dreamscapes of color and texture. This one made her sad. Purple faded to dark, earthy brown, all of the light flowing into the earth at the bottom of the canvas. Ruby took the painting, stood it on a chair, and stood back, transfixed.

She opened another and drew it out. This one instantly brought to mind visions of golden leaves blowing in a cool fall wind. Just seeing it, she felt herself tumbling through life, flying away.

When she next checked on Bernice, she got the impression of tense shoulders and the strained clenched fist of an agitated woman on the brink of an emotional outburst.

Marybeth blocked her view. “I’m sorry,” she said, without preamble. “You never did anything but good for me.”

Lin nodded in acceptance and turned to slip by. Marybeth blocked her. “Can I have the fairy one?”

She meant the painting that was mostly white with shades of gold and one kinetic blurred path traced through it. It made Lin think of fairies, too. “It’s not mine to give,” said Lin.

Marybeth rolled her eyes. “It’s your treasure find, little Lin.”

CHAPTER 8

Violet was an early riser. These days it was a critical matter of moving to get the blood flowing and get warm. Often the first to the kitchen and the first to put on the teapot, this morning she had another reason to be up early. A letter from the county tax office had kept her from sleeping. She stepped into the cool kitchen with the blue light of pre-dawn glowing in the window and lay her hand on the handle of the teapot only to find it was already warm.

“It's been sitting awhile,” said a muffled voice from the table.

She turned her head cautiously around until Bernice came into view, wrapped in a comforter, sitting at the table, the bottom of her chin bathed in blue light that cast soft specter-like shadows on her face. Her tablet, the source of the blue light, was wrapped up in the thick quilt that overlapped the tabletop. She seemed to Violet like a cartoon gypsy sorceress with her crystal ball.

“See anything?” asked Violet.

“Yes.”

The single word sent a shudder through Violet. It had the tone of doom, of bad news.

“I guess you better tell me,” she said, resigned to the worst.

Bernice explained her walk and borrowing the mobile hot spot. It had been a success for her, wonderful to be reconnected to the world and her daily reading. Violet listened, relieved knowing now that whatever Bernice had to say it wouldn’t be that she had cancer or some other incurable disease.

“Bob Robbins is out of the country and so is our money,” said Bernice.

The words hung in the chill air like bricks about to rain down on them. Violet’s hand shook, the spoon rattling in the empty tea cup. She breathed in hard and held it for a long count. It seemed like such an inconsequential thing, something they should have expected. It wasn’t.

It was something they had all hoped against. If there were any hope of getting through this, of regaining some semblance of self-sufficiency, it depended on them getting their money back. There was no other way. By her way of thinking, that hope evaporated when the money left the country. *Damn, damn, damn, and once more around on that.* "What do you mean, he's out of the country?" she asked, knowing it was a stupid question, needing to hear the answer nevertheless.

"I've found seven articles so far. All of them make it sound like it's a done deal. He's free, and chances are he's spent a good bit of our money by now. The big story three weeks ago was that we'd been robbed. Now it's something else. Something more exciting," said Bernice. "There's more."

Violet nodded. *Why not get all the bad news at once?*

Bernice looked down at her tablet, not really reading. "Bobby was interviewed by this underground news blog called 'The Offramp.' It's a kind of Anarchist rag, that caters to the fringe."

Violet watched her friend try to form the words and wondered just how bad it could be.

"You can read it yourself, but basically Little Bobby claims that he earned every penny he stole. I know they're just a rag for misfits and crooks, but they made the guy out to be some kind of celebrity Robin Hood. I can take a lot, but this…"

Violet put her cup down and pressed her hands on the table to steady them. She drew in a deep breath, wishing the action would help calm her but feeling the sinews in her back tighten like twisted steel bands and a kind of coldness wrap around her heart. This was what it felt like to hate, and she despised herself for feeling this way, for wanting more than justice, for wanting revenge. "Where is he?"

Bernice shook her head. "Don't know."

Violet felt her heart lurch in her chest. Bernice was crying. Her friend was crying, and she could do nothing about it. More than anything in the world, Violet wanted the man who made her friend cry to pay. To pay with blood, to pay with his own tears, to feel the pitying eyes on his shabby clothes in the grocery store. To wonder if he would ever be able to afford a new pair of shoes.

She felt the folded letter in her dress pocket. More problems, more reason for her friends to worry. The day after they moved in, Violet had sent a letter to the county declaring her intent to manage the property, assuming there were no legal issues. There were. The orchard was a commercial property. Never mind that it hadn't been operated commercially in over a year. The taxes, late payment fines, and court fees added up to $230,000. Almost half of what the house and land were valued at. The plain and simple truth was they didn't have that kind of money or any prospect of getting it. Not now. Bob Robbins had seen to that.

Oddly, being broke seemed trivial compared to the way that they, the victims, were now seen by the press, even the pseudo press, as somehow not deserving to keep what they'd earned with a lifetime of labor.

***

News of the article spread rapidly through the house. As slight as it was, it threw the entire household into a spiraling depression. The interview was a slap in the face. The idea that someone would track Robbins down just to interview him and celebrate his successful thievery was shocking. Worse, it drained the lot of them of faith and hope.

At lunch, Ruby floated around the room like a ghostly dancer singing songs under her breath. She seemed almost at peace, singing the words to a battle hymn, the forceful clatter of her knife against the cutting board harsh enough to turn heads and rattle already frayed nerves. Marybeth stormed into the room with her hands clasping involuntarily and her footfalls making the floor and everything on it shake. Mini ate boiled peanuts and watched the activity with interest. Finally, she turned up the volume on her hearing aid and asked what was going on.

Ruby swung toward her, huge knife in hand. In her other hand was a printout that she tossed in Mini's general direction. She returned to her task with the *thunk-thunk-thunk* of chopping squash and sweet potatoes keeping time to her song.

Mini read the first page, then left the room without comment. Violet caught just a glimpse of her eyes as she left. Tearless, they burned like hot, angry coals. Looking more closely, Violet saw the wrinkles in the corners that spoke of a deep disappointment. *Maybe we shouldn't have told everyone,* she thought, but it was their story, all of theirs.

So was the letter she held in her pocket.

It would stay there for now. She wanted everyone together and clear-headed when she told them about the tax situation. That wouldn't happen today. They were already overloaded. That was her safety net, her excuse. Driven into their separate corners to deal with the day's news each in their own way, there would not be a single moment when all were together until the poker game, and that time was reserved for small talk. That was fine with Violet. There had been enough bad news for one day. Hers could wait.

The secret was heavy. Too heavy for her to bear alone. On Wednesday, she took it to Marybeth.

"I know," said Marybeth, before she could finish the first sentence. "You think I haven't seen you moping around here, hand in your pocket, thumbing that letter that you grabbed off the pile Monday? Only bad news comes from the government. Which is it this time? Did someone die, or do we owe more taxes?"

Violet was stunned into momentary silence, memories of the telegrams bringing the awful news of her brothers' deaths suddenly taking her back to another country house in another time. She sat, feeling like the weight of her thoughts combined with her own 140 pounds would break the frame of the sofa.

"Lordy," said Marybeth. "I thought I was kidding."

Violet shook her head. "We're going to lose this place. The county is going to take it. We can't pay the taxes," she heard herself say, the words barely audible above the *thump-thump* of her heartbeat in her ears.

Marybeth eased her tall frame into the sitting room chair, gripping the wooden arm so tightly that her knuckles turned pale. She nodded, her mouth a thin line and her head shaking almost imperceptibly. "Oh, my Lord, what are we going to do? I guess we'll have to figure it out."

Violet didn't miss the sarcasm. Certainly her friend was right. They would find a way out, a place to live, a way through. But she had been living with this for several days, and the path looked narrow and dark to her. Three days of worry, and stress, and anger had brought her no great revelation. She had no idea where they would go. It was not in her hands alone, she knew now. It never had been. There were five others that had a say in this.

"You should have told us all sooner," said Marybeth, "Would have been easier on you."

"How long do we have?" asked Ruby, from the kitchen door.

Violet did a quick calculation. "Fifty eight days."

***

They each took the new bad news in their own way. Doris with an uncharacteristic curse. Mini with slumped shoulders went to her room. Marybeth sat at the table watching and thinking. She stared out the window squeezing her hands. Ruby stabbed the knife into the cutting board and washed her hands.

A little after noon they all found their way to the kitchen for lunch where they prepared and ate the meal in silence.

Lin wandered in. Violet watched her open the pantry looking for food then glance around the faces at the table. "Why the gloomy faces?" she asked.

"There's a chill in the air," grumbled Mini.

"Don't you feel it?" asked Ruby.

"Yeah, I guess I do," said Lin, ducking out.

The women ate in silence.

Finally, Ruby threw her hands up and pushed back from the table. "I can't stand this!" she exploded, reverting to her native Kentucky mountain accent. "I can't stand knowing that two-faced, weaselly bastard is getting away with this!"

"Best to keep your voice down," said Marybeth.

"Oh fiddle sticks," replied Ruby. "Keep my voice down? We've been robbed, and that sorry little bottom-feeding turd of a man is going to get by with it. Why do I have to be quiet about that?"

"Who says he'll get by with it?" said Mini.

Violet fixed her eyes on her little friend. An idea was growing, gnawing at the back of her mind.

"The FBI says so, the newspapers say so. Or haven't you heard?" said Doris.

"No, I've heard." Mini leaned back and looked around the doorframe.

Violet thought it was all a bit off. Mini really was losing it, acting as if there was something in the wind other than depression and anger. She let go for the moment, chasing her own thoughts, a whisper of an idea that she couldn't quite latch onto.

Mini dropped her voice and leaned into the table. "Who says we can't get it back ourselves?"

The steady *tick-tock* of the clock echoed through the house. There was that idea again. This time spoken aloud, not just a spider-web-thin concept floating around in her own head. Violet heard the front door close as Lin left the house. A moment passed before Mini took a loud bite of her sandwich, and the whistle of the teapot made everyone jump.

Violet flipped her nail file between her fingers. The idea had been born when Bernice first told her that the money was gone, out of reach of the law. It had seemed like an absurd thought at the time, and she'd brushed it away. Here with her circle of friends, it didn't seem so ludicrous. *Crazy,* maybe, but not out of the question. There were moral issues. Outside the range of the law did not mean outside the range of morals, values, or consequences. But couldn't the same be said for what Robbins had done? Weren't there supposed to be consequences for his actions?

"Let's just say that we could find a way…" she said, "…Let's say that we find the bank, or whatever, where he is keeping our money. What do we know about robbing banks?"

"Good Lord, who said anything about robbing a bank?" said Doris.

"That's a big leap, isn't it?" said Marybeth.

"Why?" said Violet. "We've done everything right, played it safe, and lost every time. Why not take it back?" *…Or at least go out with a bang?*

Mini smiled smugly. All eyes focused on her for a moment while she seemed to struggle forming words. "How to say this?" She smacked her lips and pushed her plate away. "I have some experience in this area."

"Were you robbed?" asked Doris.

Mini shook her head. "No, sweetie, I robbed some banks. I robbed a lot of banks. Stores, too."

***

Mini scanned the shocked faces. Even Violet, so ready a moment before to fix bayonets and charge, stopped twirling the nail file between her fingers. Mini couldn't remember ever saying anything that made Violet stop twirling the file. She was holding the darn thing like a knife. To say her friends were shocked would be a colossal understatement. "Careful, your dentures will fall out," she said to Doris, whose mouth hung open at an odd angle.

"I don't have dentures," replied Doris, her voice trailing off as if she weren't sure.

While everyone else focused on her with deep concern, Ruby sat straight up in her chair with a joy-filled grin on her face. "What?" demanded Mini, suddenly certain beyond any doubt that Ruby was batshit crazy.

"I know a lot about explosives. I know dynamite and plastic, and I even know how to make some of my own stuff," said Ruby, slapping her hands on the table like she was pounding on bongos. "Not caps, but explosives."

Mini felt herself connecting with Ruby's excitement. It should have frightened her. It didn't. It had been a long time since she had thought about robbing a bank or anything else, but there was a certain wild lightning in the air, and the urge to ride the lightning seemed to be catching.

"I'm not much on shooting and all that, but I'm hell on wheels when it comes to planning and logistics," pitched in Marybeth.

"I'm hell on wheels when I drive," said Violet. "I raced cars, boats, airplanes too."

Mini was near breathless at the realization that they had an honest-to-God crew here. A real team. The kind of crew that few could imagine, one that knew and trusted each other.

Doris sputtered, "All my friends are crazy, downright nuts. I guess that qualifies me in some way. But what am I going to do in this band of geriatric, yes I said that, bank robbers? I'm grumpy sometimes, but I really don't think I could shoot anyone. Maybe the little bastard himself but not some guard at a bank. Maybe I could shoot a camera or something, but…"

Marybeth lay her hand on Doris' shoulder, halting the monologue. "Dori, we need you to help with the money, travel, that kind of stuff."

Doris looked at her blankly.

Mini took a deep breath. Brilliant. It was brilliant. Doris may not understand yet, but she did. She scanned the determined faces of her friends clockwise around the table, ending on Marybeth who sat next to her with her hands firmly and confidently clasped together. Barring memory loss and maybe some physical issues, this may be the most balanced, prepared, and capable gang in history.

"Are we going to tell Lin?" she asked.

Universally, heads shook.

Mini felt a laugh coming up from her gut. "Let's hit that bastard where it hurts and take his money. Our money."

***

At 4:00, the poker game started on time, routine took over, and normalcy, whatever that was, returned for a while. The girls laughed at Doris' jokes, Bernice tapped her cane when she wanted a card, Violet filed her nails, Mini turned her hearing aid up and down, Ruby muttered words to an old song, but today, Marybeth smiled a little more and didn't rub her hands together so much.

Lin lit a fire to take the chill off the room and sat back to read and listen to the banter, feeling the change in the air and happy for them and whatever peace they were finding in this new place.

The next morning, she found the six women in the kitchen sitting silently at the table.

"What's up?" she asked casually. The words fell like damp leaves in the forest. She poured herself a cup of tea and leaned on the counter. There was no doubt in her mind what this was. It was a meeting. Something was going on, and she wanted to know what.

Ruby grunted. Marybeth coughed.

"I'm in this with you, you know," said Lin. She sipped her tea and waited.

"What is it we're all in, dear?" asked Doris.

"Making this work," said Lin.

"Yes, dear, we are," confirmed Doris.

"But you have a house to go home to at the end of the day. This is it for us."

Lin felt certainty flutter away and self-doubt invade.

Ruby coughed and covered her mouth. Bernice tapped her cane but wouldn't meet her eyes. She suddenly felt like there were some gigantic joke that she wasn't in on. "Did I miss the punch line?"

"Oh, no. Bless your heart, dear, you didn't miss anything. We're just having a better day than yesterday. You know it feels like that cold front is passing right by."

"Not for me," grumbled Bernice. "I need some pills."

***

Lin left the kitchen, and Ruby turned on Doris. "Did you have to tease her like that?"

Doris nodded, "It wouldn't be right not to."

"You know, we might have to skip the poker when we do this," said Violet, trying to change the subject.

"Nonsense. We'll just plan around it," said Doris.

At lunch, Marybeth passed a note to Violet. Violet nodded and crumbled the note before throwing it away.

As requested, she arrived at the apple shed just before 2:00. The shed was dark when she entered. While her eyes adjusted, she listened to the movement of the wood and the wind blowing through the slats. It was a familiar sound. One she had grown up with.

Gradually her eyes grew accustomed to the dim light—that took longer these days—so she could make out the benches that ran full length against each wall and down the center.

The sorting benches on the far wall were half-filled with apple boxes that had been filled with food donated from pantries for the poor around the county. The reminder was both humiliating and infuriating to Violet. All her life she had worked hard. She had given often to places that collected food for the poor. She had sponsored children of incarcerated parents at Christmas and helped pack shoe boxes of toys and necessities for children around the world. She'd never dreamed that a time would come when she would eat canned food and brush her teeth with a donated brush. One that she herself could have donated.

The anger put some steel in her back. She could do this, whatever *this* was. Even if it was dangerous. What did danger matter at her age anyway? She could do it because it was the right and just thing to do. After all they had been through and all they had accomplished, she and her friends didn't deserve to be left begging for food at a run-down strip mall. She never wanted to look into the sympathetic eyes of a pimply-faced teenage volunteer again. She had not failed in life. She'd been robbed. Robbed people had a right to take back what had been taken from them, even if they had to bend the law a little to do it.

A shaft of orange light from a slightly open door led her to the corner office.

The room was up a short ramp, a few feet higher than the plank floor of the solidly built barn they called the apple shed. Along two walls were narrow windows that would have looked out over the work area in the shed had they not been covered with plywood shutters. A window unit air conditioner was fitted into the wall. The eight by ten room had a small desk, a lockable cabinet, and a flip over white/black board. The floor and walls were bare plywood. The floor speckled with paint of a thousand hues. Tommy had built himself a quiet place to work and paint. Marybeth closed the door and the well-insulated silence engulfed them.

The blackboard sported lines with columns of numbers, presumably from the last day or week of picking. Violet ran her fingers over the lines dragging the colors of chalk with them. She did so miss her nephew. Tommy was a good man that worked hard. Some of the family had suspected that he was homosexual. She knew that not to be true. He was a quiet man that had loved one woman who had not returned that love. So, he had found a quiet place to live and share his feelings with canvas and paint.

Marybeth flipped the board. The whiteboard side included a few notes in Marybeth's indecipherable shorthand. "If you need anything, put it on here, and I will find it."

"I've never been in here," said Violet, nodding appreciatively. "I like what you're doing. Just one favor?"

Marybeth shook her head. "It's not a favor. You're the leader. You weren't exactly elected by anyone, but I think it goes without saying."

Violet nodded. "Let's ask before we assume."

"Whatever you say, boss."

CHAPTER 9

The palms swayed, dropping fronds and fruit around the pool like little bombs. Bob and Jamie retreated to the interior of the house where the cool wind followed, pushing the billowy white curtains.

In the sitting room, the boss chose a comfortable chair while Jamie turned on the lamp and steadied it against a sudden gust of wind. Just this morning, he'd convinced the boss to postpone the boat trip to golf on Caye Chapel. Born and living on the coast his whole life, Jamie had a sense for storms. The weatherman said nothing, but Jamie knew with his first breath of morning air when a blow was coming.

Slipping on the marble tile, he began to close the three sets of enormous French doors. Bob balked until a gust of wind grabbed a newspaper from the table, taking it on a flight around the room.

"Best if I close them all, boss," said Jamie.

The Belize City newspaper, the *Amandala*, was scattered, some of it dry but most wet. Jamie moved quickly to pick it up trying to avoid sliding on the tile, thinking that he hated to scrub news ink from the white floor. He held up the dripping paper. "Sir?"

The boss glanced up from a magazine. "Anything important?"

"Don't quite know, sir. It's all wet."

Bob lowered his eyes to the magazine.

Jamie was pushing the paper into the trash when the page two header caught his attention, AMERICAN FBI LOOKS TO CARIBBEAN FOR CON MAN. In the fold of the paper, he could make out part of Bob Robbins' name. He crumpled the remaining pages of newsprint and covered the headline, then retreated to the kitchen to get the mop.

Later, on the way home, he found a copy of the paper and read about his boss.

***

Lin smeared butter on bread and layered it with ham and cheese. She loved that fresh butter from the local dairy farmers cost less than Mayonnaise. She washed the knife and wiped the counter then took a bite of the sandwich.

Bernice tapped her cane dangerously close to her toes, causing her to dance back against the counter. “Why you do that?” she asked, around a mouthful. “You feeling a little disconnected today? Maybe a little crazy?” she said after choking down the food.

“Don’t forget it,” said Bernice, winking at her.

A loud double boom rattled the window, chickens cackled, and somewhere a dog yelped fearfully.

“Poop! What now?” Lin left the sandwich and jogged out the front door.

“Get an ice pack,” ordered Doris, about the time her feet left the bottom step. By the time she returned, shaking a bag of frozen peas, the situation was becoming a little more clear. Mini stood slightly hunched over, holding her right shoulder in her left hand. Ms. Doris and Bernice stood at her elbows steadying her. Violet cradled a long double barrel shotgun, a wisp of smoke curling from the barrels. Behind them, the barn was spattered in yellow paint. Somewhere between, Lin was sure she would find remains of a paint can that had been blown apart by the blast of buckshot from the old gun.

Mini ground her teeth as the cold peas were applied to her shoulder. “Should have kept my finger off that second trigger. Not the kind of thing I should have forgot.”

***

Lin stood cross-armed in the yard and watched the mob slowly stomp up the steps. Violet hung back still holding the shotgun and eyeing her, the interrogative gaze unnerving. She shook her head. “What do you want me to say?”

“What do you know about guns?” asked Violet.

“Open the breech,” said Lin, for the moment feeling like she was on familiar ground.

Violet examined the mechanism, then chose the lever on top. The gun broke open, and the empty shells popped out far enough for her to remove them by hand.

Beyond that, Lin wasn't sure how to answer the question. She'd fired a half a dozen guns in her life. Her father had insisted that she learn. Beyond the basics of loading and firing, she really wasn't an expert. Taking the the shotgun, she was surprised at how light it was. The barrel was long but thin. She'd never fired a double barrel shotgun. Closing the breech, she pulled the stock into her shoulder and the barrel toward the sky. The gun was definitely made for bird hunting. She lowered it and pulled again. The stock didn't fall easily into her shoulder. It was too long for that, made for a man. A woman or child's gun would have a shorter stock. She remembered that from a day at a skeet range.

She noted the cause of Mini's real problem. The gun sported double hammer and double triggers. She'd let her fingers rest on both triggers, and when she pulled one, the recoil made her pull the other. *That would hurt,* Lin thought, examining one of the empty shells. It had a double zero on the side.

"I fired buckshot once. It hurt really bad. My dad thought it was funny until he saw I was crying, then he wouldn't stop apologizing." She opened the breech and handed the old gun back to Violet.

"What if we were interested in something easier?"

"I don't know much, but my dad has an AR-15. I shot that. It was easy," said Lin.

"Can we still get those?"

"I guess. We *are* in Georgia. I think you can buy anything here at a gun shop or range. They let you try stuff out at the shops with ranges."

A slow smile grew on Violet's face as she turned away.

***

Wet grass clippings clung to Bob's new golf shoes. His partners for the round, a tipsy Brit everyone called Davies and a dark scowling man about thirty whose name had not yet been volunteered, were loading their carts. The dark one growled at his bag, struggling with the straps to attach it to the cart. Davies wordlessly lent a hand. The scowling man didn't thank him.

Bob had never played on an island course; in fact, he'd hardly played anywhere. It had always been his goal to be good, even great at the game, but he never seemed to have the time. Until now. Now, he was learning that wind is a major factor, especially on an island. By the sixth hole, he had lost three balls. The dark mustached man introduced himself as Eduardo at the fourth T, then shrugged and laughed. "You will learn to keep it down," he said, in a way that suggested that he was happy just to be here.

Bob Robbins was a salesman, and whether he liked someone or not, he had a need to understand them and their motivations. To that end, he had, through years of trial and error, developed the capacity to ease into conversation with almost anyone. Observation was first, nodding and smiling when the subject spoke. Eventually the subject—this was science—would wonder if he were really listening. Human nature demanded it.

The subject would ask Bob's opinion on something inconsequential. Bob would consider the answer carefully. It was critical that he answer the first question thoughtfully. For some, the answer needed to be funny, and for some more serious. That, he left to instinct. For all, the answer needed to be relevant enough to draw out another question. His question from Eduardo was coming soon.

He chipped in from six feet on hole seven, and Eduardo spoke. "What makes you play golf, Mr. Bob?"

Bob stepped back to the cart while Davies lined up his shot. There were a lot of answers but probably only one that was relevant to Eduardo, the man who had started the day angry and was now enjoying the fact that he was well ahead in the game. "I find it peaceful," answered Robbins. *True.* "I'm not that good at it, but even when I'm consumed with more frustrating things, golf relaxes me and lets me think." He glanced over to Eduardo who was leaning on the cart nodding.

"The same for me. Everything is about my father's business. Except when I can sneak off for a round of golf. The old man thinks I'm working now, but we just land the plane, and I play a round while my boys you know, do the job. They pick me up on the return, then we go home."

"He doesn't notice that you take your clubs?"

Eduardo stepped up to putt. "He's a busy man, and in our business, people don't talk much about what other people do." He sunk the putt. "What about you, Mister Robbins, what do you do?"

"I'm retired," answered Bob taking a deep breath of the warm island air. It felt so good out here. "And I'm going to learn this game, even if it kills me."

"I can see that," laughed Eduardo.

At lunch, Bob threw back a few beers, the warm breeze and the cool shade doing their part to make him feel truly retired. The squeaky wooden chair felt like the most comfortable place in the world. Even the help was relaxed, Jamie enjoying the company of the bar girl with the blue and pink hair. Bob swung his eyes lazily over to Eduardo who had just asked a question.

"So, I'm looking for a place to keep my money," repeated Eduardo. "Someplace safe, you know?"

Bob nodded. He did know. "I keep mine in the Caymans Bank and Trust." He chuckled at his own cleverness. "In bearer bonds, you know? No tracing what's in a safe deposit box," he said, adopting the timber of Davies' persistent Brit upper class chatter and tapping his beer down on the table just a bit too hard. "They keep a pretty tight rein on what comes into the bank. Trying to please the big guys in the US. I guess it's a reputation thing. Anyway, you can't just go open an account. They run a background check and everything. But if you do what I did and open an account with a small amount of cash, then open a safe deposit box, there's not much that can go wrong."

"You keep bearer bonds in a safe deposit box that is in a big vault?" Ed nodded appreciatively. "It sounds secure."

***

Eduardo Salizar sat in the open air bar and watched the twin Beach aircraft gracefully touch down. He'd lied a little. He didn't bring his clubs on the flight, but left them here where he played almost every week. Davies and Robbins had assumed that he was new to the game, but really he was just frustrated with the stiff straps on the new bag.

So much of his life was about deception that he sometimes felt the lines blur between truth and lie. Stepping from one to the other was as easy and natural as getting out of bed in the morning. He was good at it, something his father found disturbing. Papa was brutal but straight forward, never trusting those that were more devious, even if they were less violent. It was a schism between father and son that seemed impossible to repair. How did you win the trust of a man that would not trust you? Yesterday, there had been no answer. Today, perhaps the answer was to show Papa the value of the very character traits he did not trust.

Today's round had been good. He'd learned something that could benefit the family. He would have to find a way to broach the subject with his father without giving away that he was letting Manuel make the flights alone. He would find a way. This was good stuff, and Papa would want to act on it.

He smiled at the bartender with the colorful hair and ordered water. He wanted to be clear headed for the flight home.

CHAPTER 10

It started with a cup. One of the "unbreakable" tea cups from Golden Lawn. Marybeth stared at the cup she had dropped. It wasn't just a cup. It was a symbol of the place that had been their home such a short time ago. A place that was rotting and falling down now. It was a reminder that she had once been able to sit back and enjoy the life bought with years of hard labor, and now she was scrubbing her own floors until her bones ached from the effort.

She stepped on the cup, trying to put her weight on it without slipping and falling. She could feel it give a little under her shoe. She lifted her foot and brought it down hard. The cup cracked. Another stomp and it shattered. Oh, that was satisfying, but hard on her ankle. She looked to the dish rack for another and found a small plate.

"What are you doing?" asked Doris.

"Breaking things."

"I can see that. Why?"

"This belonged to little Bobby," answered Marybeth as if that explained it.

In a strange way, it did.

Doris assaulted a plate, trying to break it on the edge of the counter. Unable, she dropped it and opened the cabinet where she found stacks of plates and cups.

"Oh, for goodness' sake!" said Violet, "let's take this outside where we can use tools."

***

Lin pulled up the gravel drive, the loose suspension on her eighteen-year-old Accord snapping the wheel back and forth, punishing her wrist. Dad said he could fix it, but she would be without a car for a week while he worked on it. It just hadn't happened yet.

She drove slowly. There was something on her mind that she had to sort it out. Anita Fulsom-Bright's mug shot had been on the news this morning. Frizzy haired and face scrunched up looking like she was about to hurl, but undoubtedly the same woman, and undoubtedly a mug shot. Why? When had she been arrested and why? Lin's father had the volume down on the TV, and she had not wanted to turn it up and alarm him with the story. She loved her father, but she didn't want him to be involved in her work. That was all hers.

Swinging around the last bend where she could see the house, she wondered if Anita was closer to Robbins than they had known. The woman's frequent visits to the home had often included extended meetings with Bob in his office. She'd assumed they were discussing Irene. There was a lot to discuss. But what if they weren't?

"Now what?" she said, steering toward the house. The ladies circled around a giant stump. Suddenly, an axe was raised and flashed down. Were they killing chickens, or cutting firewood? She opened her door, and her ears were greeted with the ringing sound of something hard struck with steel. The axe went up again and came down again. This time she saw chunks of something white fly. Some of the ladies ducked. The axe rose and fell again. The ladies cheered with each drop of the blade.

Lin leaned on the porch post at the top of the steps. "It's getting weird. Kind of barbaric," she said to no one in particular.

"It's fun," said Doris.

"Breaking dishes from the home seems like a kind of transference thing. You know, the object represents a person, kill it?" said Lin.

"Exactly," said Doris.

***

Brett watched the handicap van swing slowly into his empty parking lot. The sign on the side had been sprayed over by an amateur, the original black lettering bleeding through in places. The van was relatively new to be second hand like that. He knew a little about vans and was learning more as budget chairman at the Wellspring Missionary Baptist Church.

It had been a slow day. Every day was a slow day so far at South Dixie Guns. The doors had been opened for thirty-one days now, except on Sundays, and he had made almost enough to cover the rent in this low-rent building. Most sales to date had been ammo. The big plan to sell and build up stock was a bit slow in gaining momentum. He glanced around his store at the half-full racks. Maybe the place would look more full if he moved some of the empty racks to the back. He hit the door release to open it for the twenty something Asian girl who was reaching for the handle. The girl pulled and held the door while six elderly women strolled in and began to examine his guns.

Brett's first inclination was to protest, to tell them that the Whole Foods store was next door or that the Social Security office was downtown. Then, the girl rolled her eyes at him, and he wasn't sure how to take that. "They're safe, sort of," she said. "The sign says you've got an indoor range?"

Brett nodded, feeling control slip away again. He was here alone. How could he manage the range and the store?

"I can help them on the range," said the girl.

"One at a time shooting and we have a twenty-percent senior discount," he said, handing her the release paperwork.

***

Brett took a deep breath and wiped this morning's coffee stain off the counter.

The old women asked a lot of questions. They asked to hold different guns, how to load them, and what it felt like to shoot them. That was a question he couldn't answer. His arms were half as old and twice as large as any of the women. They needed to go out to the range to find out for themselves. There were other ways he could help. "What are you using the gun for?" he asked.

"Why do you care what we use it for? It's a free country still, isn't it?" snarled a woman that could not have topped ninety pounds.

"Now, Mini," said a woman with a nail file in her hand. "The gentleman only wants to know how to help you find the right gun."

The woman with the file introduced herself as Violet as the smaller woman drifted away grumbling.

Brett sighed nervously. "It's all right. Most of our customers value their privacy. Are you looking for something for self-defense?"

Violet nodded.

"Home or out and about?" he asked, feeling like he was getting somewhere.

"Both," answered another woman leaning on the counter over the Glock and Sig pistols.

"More than one gun?" he asked not daring to hope.

"Oh, absolutely," said Violet. "Eventually we'll want one for each of us. Maybe more."

They started with light rifles. A good choice. He kept an eye on the range camera monitor as the Asian girl showed them how to load and ready an AR-15 to fire. The girl seemed to have it in hand. Before long, they had all gotten in a few rounds. Brett enjoyed watching the woman with the cane empty a twenty round magazine into a target while it was still being moved down the range. He began to calculate his profit for the day. It was looking to be a good one, his best in a while.

He went to the used gun rack and retrieved an AR-15.

Two of the ladies reentered the store, coming through the two entry rooms that kept the noise on the range. The tall woman, almost as tall as Brett, introduced herself as Marybeth. "That's a fun rifle," she said. "We'll want two of those and two of the Ruger P-90 pistols. With five extra magazines for each, and we'll figure out how much ammo." Brett froze, stunned for several seconds, then robotically swept a background check form from the shelf behind and handed Marybeth a pen from the can. "If they are all for you, you only have to fill out one form."

The chunky woman with the big white hair, Doris her friend had called her, watched her friends on the range monitor. She turned suddenly and winked at him. The gesture caught him off guard. "Isn't there a .22 version of the AR rifle?" she asked.

"Sure. I have several. But before you try that, I have a modified AR with what we call the Echo trigger. Y'all seem to like to shoot fast. You'll like this. You pull, and it fires once. Release and it fires again. One trigger action for each round fired; so fully ATF approved as a semi-auto. Fast and fun. Just don't forget to release while it's pointed down range."

"Let me try that," said Doris, taking the rifle and three boxes of ammo into the range.

Brett watched the monitor as Doris emptied twenty rounds in about four seconds with the Echo trigger. He could do it faster, but the little bird kept the rifle on target the whole time. Nice.

The ladies spent an hour and a half on the range before they started to tire and occupy the stools behind the lanes. The background check had completed without a hitch, and the two ladies had taken their guns, ammo, and ear protection to the van and returned. Marybeth was entertaining herself with an dummy drill rifle, twirling it slowly when the Asian girl and the others finally came out of the range.

Brett gave Lin a thumbs up.

"What do we owe you?" she asked.

"The ladies already paid," said Brett.

CHAPTER 11

Luis Salizar strolled steadily down the muddy street, throwing up a silent prayer that he could maintain his footing and his dignity. With every step, more of the slick clay mud gathered on his boots, threatening to turn them into skis.

The rain had washed the air clean, leaving behind the smell of damp earth with a tinge of starch that steamed up from his soaked shirt. He carried a poncho that was as wet from condensation on the inside as from the rain on the outside. When he got home, he would change into dry clothes and read for a while before taking a nap. Home was a short hundred meters away, at the center of the village.

He nodded to a woman sitting on her porch, holding a baby. The house was typical for the region. Wooden posts supporting a sheet metal roof with about half of the building covered in siding. Some had screen doors and windows. This one did not. From the street, he could see straight through the house and into the jungle behind.

The woman glared at him in the emboldened way that women did when they had lost their husband in his service. He would take care of them. It was his duty. He didn't like the way they looked at him, but after years of violent living, seeing families destroyed, widows living in shanties and children growing up to work for him just as their fathers had, Luis was willing to accept the looks as reasonable. Who else could they blame? They could blame the Americans like they had for so many years, but that got old. Choices had been made. At some point, you had to let go of the past and accept responsibility for your own life. Once a commander in the revolution, Luis had long since taken that journey.

His men who once followed him for loyalty, then fear, now followed him for money. They didn't question his command. They fought well, but not all of them came home. The woman on the porch, her husband died only two years ago. Not in a battle against the army but against police.

Luis Salizar had long since traded the revolution for the life of farming. No longer would his men risk their lives and their families for a cause that cared nothing for the people. The narcotics his people grew generated enough money to make him rich and to provide for their protection. In the almost thirty years since he had resigned the revolution with a bullet and a sign saying *lamentomos, lo sentimos* (we are sorry), his people had seldom been attacked. Life was good here. The revolutionaries left him alone out of respect, and the government, who knew why they didn't come after him. Perhaps they were tired, perhaps afraid, perhaps they had better things to do.

Luis stood in the middle of the road, rain dripping from the brim of his fedora. Careful of his footing, he turned back and crossed the street to the porch where the woman sat. "Why do you look at me this way old woman?" he asked, standing in the mud, not wanting to dirty her porch.

"My husband worked for you."

"Yes, yes, this I know. Are you not well taken care of?"

"My son works for you now." She waved her hand at the sky. "He flies airplanes."

"Yes, yes, with my son. His name is Manuel?"

The woman gave him a skeptical look and shook her head. "Manuel, yes, but not always with your son."

"What does that mean?" he asked, annoyed with the direction of the conversation.

The woman rocked the baby for a moment. "Your son does not always make the journey. Sometimes he leaves it to my son alone and sometimes with another boy." She said the last word in a way that proved she didn't think the "boy" competent.

Luis groaned. So, it was true. Eduardo was off playing and shirking his responsibilities. He rubbed his chin, wishing he could conceal his irritation and knowing that as always his anger showed in his eyes for all to see. He sat on the floor at the corner of the porch where only the front of his hat and his knees were still in the rain. "Would you keep this quiet, woman, friend, while I deal with it?"

She nodded.

Luis looked through into the house. "Your son flies for me. Why does he not take care of the house?"

"He lives with his young wife in the painted house at the airfield."

Luis used a damp bandana to wipe the rain from his face. This did not surprise him. Nor did it surprise him that the old woman looked to him to rectify the situation. From the first day that he had become leader, he had been judge and arbitrator to everything that went on in the village. They even asked him if they could marry. He shook his head. He had never desired such power and responsibility. He only wanted to live and be left alone.

"I will send a carpenter to fix your walls and install screens. Is the roof good?"

The woman shook her head.

"He will fix that too." He stood, popping the brim of his hat to halt the steady stream of water. The stream returned in seconds. "I will talk to my son, and I will make sure your son has someone trustworthy with him."

The woman nodded and pursed her lips in satisfaction.

***

Doris sat in the parlor drumming her fingers on the arm of the sofa until her nails were in danger of cracking. Lester was on the way, his headlights visible, sweeping across the trees through the window. *Why can't his car break down, or something, anything?* She chewed on a broken nail and tapped her foot on the floor making the Tiffany lamp next to her rattle.

He was here, and there was no use waiting for him to come in. She stood and pulled on her coat, taking a good look at herself in the mirror. *Whatever does he see in me?* She smiled, and the mirror reminded her that she had a good smile. Things were what they were. No matter what she thought of her worth, Lester thought more of her. He had for a very long time. Certainly she had thought at first that it was infatuation. It wasn't. Lester was a rich man. Smart and charming, too. Even the young girls liked him, and, had he been interested, he could have had his pick of any of them to marry. Doris knew that there were many a pretty young girl out there that would trade the chance to have a young husband for the security of an old man with money. She liked the old man for himself, not his money. Yet, here she was.

After an almost silent drive, they took their seats in the dark corner booth of a steak restaurant. She wasn't even sure where they were. Lester's granddaughter had driven, then gone off to shop while they dined. It was a convenient arrangement that gave them plenty of time together.

"You know," began Lester, "this is the first time we have been on a real date."

"Nonsense. I'm sure we had Jello or ice cream together dozens of times." She finished with a laugh that came from a content heart.

"My God, woman, you are beautiful."

"Well, Lester, I was sure you wanted to marry me for my charm, not my beauty."

"I'll take both," he said, spilling his tea and reaching for the napkin to wipe it up. "The only problem with nice restaurants is the napkins," he groused. "They put so much starch in them that they won't soak up a spill." He pushed the tea around the table with the stiff cloth to prove his point.

Doris picked the napkin up and spread it over the spill, trapping the tea.

"Clever girl, aren't you? I need you just to keep me on a straight path. I mean, without you I would have had to ask the waitress to help, that could have taken her away from something important, and before you know it the day would be over and…"

Doris covered his hands with her own and smiled. "Aren't you going to ask me?"

Lester's mouth moved open and shut, his eyes rolled to the side as he examined the patterned metal tiles on the ceiling, and finally he looked back at her, his jaw cranked sideways thoughtfully.

Doris dropped her chin slowly, keeping her eyes focused on him as she did. It was her best come hither look, and it always got her what she wanted.

Lester laughed. "You are irresistible. You are also the biggest pain in the backside that I have ever met. Put those two together, and I guess we have no choice but to marry."

"Well, Lester, now that you put it like that, I feel…"

"Oh no, there's no taking it back. I distinctly recall you asking me if I was going to ask you, and dammit woman, despite the fact that this is the first time I have seen you in three years that I do not have the engagement ring on my person, I am going to ask."

"Oh no, Lester, you need the ring."

Lester cut her off. "I am going to enjoy the rest of my life with the most beautiful woman I know, and I will have the ring here by the time dinner is over."

"Oh dear, Lester, that is going to take some time. Aren't we a ways from home?"

Lester paused in deep thought. "We are about an hour from my house… each way." He bit his upper lip in frustration.

Doris thought it was the most dear thing she had seen in a long time. "Oh, Lester, bring it to me tomorrow.

He stared at her skeptically.

"I won't change my mind. There's just one thing," she finished the last bite of the shared dessert. "I want my friends to go with us for the wedding."

"Go?"

"Oh yes, Lester, didn't I tell you that I have always wanted to get married on a cruise?"

CHAPTER 12

Doris pushed her way from behind the pantry door where she'd been hiding the phone, and Lin's ears, from the *rat-tat-tat* of semi-automatic rifle fire. Lin was at the market, hopefully still unaware of the training going on at the orchard.

It was Doris' job to make sure Lin suspected nothing. It was a bigger job than she'd expected. With her fingers in her ears, she joined her friends in the field where they'd built the bonfire. Violet had mowed it with the tractor and pushed up a pile of logs about thirty yards from where Bernice stood steadily pulling the trigger on a black rifle.

Down range, a tin can rattled and danced as bullets *thwacked* into it. Mini drew a 9mm pistol from her belt, cocked, and fired, whiffing a can on the first shot but sending it flying into the air on the second and third.

"I didn't think she could see that good," yelled Doris to Ruby.

"She says she can see them when they move!" yelled Ruby. "I want to shoot the rifle!"

Bernice turned, grinning, with the rifle pointed safely up and the empty magazine in hand. Ruby took it and checked that the bolt was open, also looking into the chamber to make sure it was clear as she'd been taught on the range. She snapped a full magazine into the rifle, then mashed the button on the side releasing the bolt to slide forward. Adjusting her earmuffs, she looked to both sides of her, then lowered the gun to her hip and began squeezing the trigger rapidly, watching the impact of the bullets walk into the line of tin cans. In seconds, the magazine was empty and the bolt locked back. The cans had been shuffled and several showed sunlight peeking through fresh holes.

A blast of hot air blew back Doris' hair, then another and another. Specks of dirt and unburnt powder impacted her skin like sand in a hurricane, only hot. Streaks of smoke traced the paths of the bullets downfield. Chunks of dirt rose into the air as if in slow motion, and finally a can flew up, then another, and another. One danced further and further into the field until it vanished in the haze of smoke and dirt.

The shooting stopped, and Doris heard the distinct ringing in her left ear. She tried to clear it, but it persisted. Pulling her fingers from her ears, she heard Mini cackle joyfully. "Never mind," said Ruby, handing the rifle Bernice had been firing to Doris. "This is a .22. I want to shoot that."

"Can I?" asked Doris, bouncing on her toes, holding the .22 rifle in one hand and a full magazine in the other. She felt a tug at her left elbow and turned.

Violet examined Doris' hand curiously.

Ruby handed her a pair of foam earplugs. "Step up to the line before you load," she said. Violet turned her head sideways. She wanted to know about Lester.

"He's bringing the ring over today," said Doris, grinning and stepping up to the firing line. Bernice reminded her how to load the magazine. Doris released the bolt, brought the rifle to her shoulder and lined up the sights like she'd learned in Girl Scouts almost seventy years ago. *Tink-tink-tink*, the little rifle spat little bullets down range with almost zero recoil.

They were picking up bullet-riddled tin cans when Doris felt her phone buzz in her pocket. Lin's picture popped up on the screen. She turned to Violet. "Lin's here." She answered the phone while Violet gave the round-em-up signal and pointed everyone to the apple shed. "Hello, Lin, you're back early," she said into the phone, while the others quietly gathered rifles, pistols, ammo, and trash and marched away. "Oh dear. I'm sorry." She winked to Violet. "We were trying the lock to see if it fit and forgot. I'll come open it for you."

***

"We can't use the 'we forgot the lock on the gate' excuse again," Marybeth said to Violet as she scrubbed her hands at the apple shed sink. The others had spread out occupying themselves, trying not to look suspicious. Doris had gone to open the gate that she'd *accidentally* left the lock on.

"Why not? We're old. We forget things. We'll think of something," said Violet, overwhelmed by the logistics of this thing they were doing and simultaneously feeling like they were moving at a pace that would see them all buried and forgotten before they could complete the mission. "We have to find a way for all of us to meet without her knowing what we are doing. Any ideas?"

Marybeth started typing into her phone.

Violet hated cell phones, and it annoyed her to no end when people started texting while they were in a conversation already.

Marybeth responded to Violet's icy stare with a grunt then, "Hush! I'm sharing what you just said with everyone."

"Everyone will have a different idea."

"Good. We can use them all."

At 4:00, the poker game started. The hands were dealt less often, and the game was slower and less contentious than usual. Someone watching closely would have noted two conversations going on at the table: the usual chatter, with an occasional exchange that didn't quite fit that conversation, and another conversation carried on by group text. Sounds were off on the phones, and the text conversation was slow. Marybeth would type a message and send it. A moment later. all of the phones at the table would vibrate at different times. After a few of the phones had received the message, Marybeth might look up and say, "That was for you, Mini." Over the course of a two-hour poker game, with Lin in and out of the room, they held what amounted to a twenty minute conversation that they were all able to share in. Most important, they could see each other's reactions to what was said.

Marybeth kept a notepad at the table. On the front page was a running tally of who had won how many hands. On the second page were her notes from the text conversation. She sent a note to Doris, "You need to clean the pistols."

***

Doris scooted quietly out of the apple shed and up the steps. In the kitchen, she stripped the semi-automatic pistol the way she had been taught, laid the magazine aside, and dropped the rest of the parts into the sink full of hot soapy water. She had just snapped the rubber gloves on when Mini stepped up beside her. Mini watched for a moment then spread a towel out on the counter and began extracting parts from the sink.

“I'm not doing it right?” asked Doris.

Mini shook her head and wrapped the parts up in the towel. “Get the magazine and come with me,” she said over her shoulder.

In the apple shed, Mini spread the parts out on Marybeth's desk and began to dry them. Over the next half hour, she showed Doris how to clean and oil a pistol properly. Doris listened and watched Mini patiently explain each part of the process.

“Were you ever a teacher?” asked Doris.

Mini nodded. “I was. A long, long time ago. That's where I met my husband. Well, the second time. The first time I met him, I was robbing a bank, and he was a teller.”

“Oh goodness,” said Doris, suddenly feeling like she had just opened a door that had been closed and locked tight for a long time.

Mini laughed. “That man looked into my eyes. It was all he could see. The rest of my face was wrapped up in a scarf. But he looked into my eyes like no one ever had. I almost didn't get out the door with Kate.”

“Kate?” asked Doris, fascinated.

“My sister. My partner,” Mini answered, with a touch of sadness. “You know, I tripped on the front steps of the bank, and when I looked back, he was watching me out the window. I never forgot the way he looked at me.” She paused for a moment. “That was in Jackson, Mississippi. I didn't get back there for several years, and when I did, the war was on and he was gone. I wasn't robbing banks anymore. Kate was gone.” She handed Doris the cleaned pistol with the slide locked back. “That's when I got a job as a teacher.”

Mini was reaching for her jacket when Doris stopped her. “You can't leave it there! You have to tell me the rest!”

Later that night, Doris turned off the bedside lamp and pulled the blankets up to her chin. From the other side of the room, she heard Mini chuckle. “He was an Army Air Corps captain. The war was over, and one day I opened the door of my classroom, and there he was.”

"You mean he tracked you down?"

"Oh, heck, no. He tried. He had a whole collection of news clippings about robberies all over the country. Some of them were ours. But he didn't track me down. He was there to talk to the kids about flying in the Army."

Mini went quiet for a while, and for a moment, Doris thought she was asleep. "Did he know who you were?" she asked.

Mini coughed, and Doris could hear her take a drink of water and put the cup down. Outside the wind kicked up, and the screen rattled. Mini went on, "Graham's eyes lit up the moment he saw me. He asked me if I had been right there under his nose the whole time. Of course, he hadn't been there the whole time, but neither had I. I miss him," she said, her voice cracking. "I'm going to miss you, too, when you get married."

"Don't you start that now! Who says I'm going anywhere?" scoffed Doris. The truth was that she wanted to marry Lester, but the thought of leaving her friends was weighing heavy on her as much or more than it was on Mini. She knew all the arguments and had been through them time after time. The big one was money. Lester had it, and she didn't. That would have some impact on where they decided to live. "We pull this job off, and we'll be richer than Lester by ten times," she said.

Mini cackled in the dark, making Doris smile. She really needed to talk with Lester about what would come after the wedding. She didn't want to live far away from her friends. But then, that was what she loved about Lester. She always underestimated him. He was probably already making plans for them to live close.

***

Violet hated lying to Lin and wanted in the worst way to bring her in on the plan, but as much as it seemed right, it would complicate everything. Then again, there was no denying that things were already complicated. Starting with getting time free of watchful eyes to train. Some of it they could do without raising any eyebrows. Some things were more difficult than others. Fitness fell into that category. They needed to be fit. To do this job, they would have to be able to run and jump and carry things like none of them had done in twenty or thirty years.

Cardio was simple. Every time the sun was shining, two or three would stretch and grumble, then go on a power walk. They tried four at a time to have a walking meeting but found Lin walking with them. It seemed that when in doubt, she had a policy of sticking with the group that was going out. The next day, Dori and Bernice asked Lin to walk with them, leaving the others alone to discuss plans.

Other things were a little more difficult. Tire and dexterity drills had to be squeezed in early in the morning before Lin arrived to help with breakfast. The tires were all roped together under a pile of hay in the barn. Before the sun was up, Violet or Ruby would mount the tractor and pull them out into the yard. The rumble of the tractor was the wakeup call for the others to join them to run drills.

Run was a generous word. Doris bobbled, Mini high-step tip-toed with age defying grace, Bernice did a kind of three-legged march leading with her cane, Ruby turned in a respectable and noisy performance, jogging through the tires with her knees high and popping with each step, and Marybeth just walked. Violet inevitably led with her right foot in a strange kind of two step. She tried going slow and stepping into each tire and soon found herself skipping tire to tire. Frustrated at her own clumsiness, she vowed that if anyone commented, she would chase them down and beat them with whatever she could find at hand.

The continuing problem, age and slowness, left them starting late and having to pack up quickly. No one had yet been able to climb the rope in the barn. Violet grasped the rope and let it slide through her hand. It was probably too much to ask, but it seemed like the ultimate proof of readiness.

Plans to make a meeting and training center out of the apple shed were under way. Violet had her part to play in that. She checked the watch, given her almost fifty years ago by Howard. So many years without him, and still she thought of him every day. Once, not so long ago, a man had come along and asked her to marry. She almost laughed at him. Like her nephew, she had one love in her life and no interest in another.

It was time. Violet could smell the turpentine as soon as she opened the front door. "Stop!" she said, not feeling at all like she was acting. The air was heavy with the mixed earthy and solvent smells of paints and thinners. Way too much thinner. The living room floor was covered with a painter's drop cloth but that was just a technicality. The room had been converted to an art studio. Not a good thing in the same house where they would eat and sleep.

"Out!" she demanded. "Get this out of the house!"

Ruby so engaged in painting that she must have forgotten this was a show put on for Lin, looked up from her pallet in genuine shock. Lin stuck her head out of the kitchen wide-eyed. Violet glared back at her, as if this were her fault.

"Hey, I'm with you. This stuff stinks," said Lin.

Violet kept her face straight and turned back to Ruby.

Ruby froze, her eyes confused. Presumably she was now remembering the goal of this confrontation and by the look of it was suffering from stage fright. Her partners in painting, Doris and Bernice watched Ruby for the lead. Ruby moved her lips silently. Her eyes went to the floor in the most desperately injured way. Violet in those few seconds felt so deeply for her friend that she was prepared to relent and just pass through the room in shame. As Ruby's slowly tilting chin rested on her breast bone, Violet caught the slightest smile on her friend's lips.

"Oh, that was rich. You almost had me there."

"I don't know whatever you mean," shot back Ruby, her chin up and the fire lit in her eyes. "And what's wrong with us painting in the house?"

"It stinks up the whole place!" snapped Violet.

"It does," added Lin, from the kitchen door.

Bernice slammed her cane into the floor, the thud dulled by the painter's cloth. Ruby snapped her head around to blast Lin with snarling eyes, and Doris looked at her as if she would participate in her hanging if the opportunity arose. Lin retreated to the kitchen.

"It's cold out. Where are we supposed to paint when it's cold out?" demanded Ruby, clearly back on track. Bernice followed up with a hesitant double tap of the cane.

"Lin," called Violet.

"This is your fight, not mine," said Lin.

Ruby, her back to the kitchen door, let her eyes go wide, delighting in the moment. Violet almost couldn't stand not laughing, but the show must go on. "Lin, I… we need you to hang some plastic in the apple shed so we can put a heater in there. Will that keep it warm enough?" asked Violet of the other women.

"Yeah, it might," responded Lin, daring to re-enter the room.

"Oh, that would be wonderful," said Ruby. "On a good day, we could open the door and see the orchards and get good light. And, when it's cold, we could use some of those big spot lights." She clasped her hands together in excitement that made Violet wonder if she had forgotten everything and really were visualizing this for the very first time. Only her final outlandishly obvious wink convinced Violet that it was at least half act. The wink itself was almost enough to convince her that Ruby was finally over the edge.

"It's the paint fumes," whispered Ruby, moments later. "It was just so strong. And we waited for you for what seemed like forever. I almost finished a painting, but then I couldn't remember what I did with the Sienna. When you opened the door, it was like a breath of fresh air."

While Ruby and the others moved the smellier of the items out to the porch, Violet studied Ruby's painting. It was stunning, breathtakingly beautiful, capturing the view in a way that was both unrecognizable and still a perfect record of the orchard. "It's magnificent," she said to Lin, who was examining the painting over her shoulder. "It's like Tommy's but not. The style is the same but the textures and light are so different, so alive."

"Tommy's paintings always seem sad," said Lin.

Violet nodded. Her nephew's paintings, though bright and cheerful in color and texture, left you feeling like the world wasn't quite right. Ruby's art was almost the polar opposite. The color and texture were likewise brilliant, but when you looked at it, you felt like you were watching angels dance around the canvas. There was a joy, an exuberance, about the image that was electrical.

"She really is good," said Lin, standing back.

Violet smiled. "We need the apple shed ready right away. Ruby needs a place to paint."

Their first planned operation had come off pretty well. Next, they had to build on that success. Violet flinched at a sudden stab of pain in her left knee. She never dreamed that she would be doing military-like training and drills at this age. Between her shoulder, bruised by the rifle, and her hand bruised by the pistol, and the sore muscles all around, probably from working on the tractor, she was beginning to feel old. It felt good to get out and do something, but did it have to hurt so much?

***

"This isn't going to work," said Ruby, staring at the translucent sheeting. "I thought it was going to be clear."

"Oh, I have an idea!" blurted Doris. "Can we take down the thin plastic, frame this side and put a clear window, you know, just big enough for us to see the orchard?"

That's a great idea. They'll want me to do that. Lin had already framed out a room inside of the room, hanging plastic sheeting from the rafters. Worse than the work, she was losing access to a good storage area, the entry of the shed blocked by the studio.

"I'm really sorry," Ruby said to her, the next time she was off the ladder. "You don't have to do the window…"

"I know," she began.

"No, I just mean you don't have to do it today," she said, dancing away.

Ruby moved her easel into the plastic studio while Lin read up on how to frame a screen door into the wall. She would have to make a run to a hardware store and see if she could get plexiglass for the door and window. For now, they would be opaque.

"Thank you," said Ruby dismissively, as she began painting. Doris was setting up behind her. Together, they blocked Lin's path to the curtain door that led to the inside of the shed.

"I need to set up the lights inside," said Lin.

Doris looked at Lin, confused. “I think that someone is already doing that,” she said. Two very bright lights came on some distance behind the plastic.

“Maybe some sheets to diffuse that a bit more,” commented Ruby, not looking up from her work. “Lin, can you buy some cloth? We need bleached muslin from the fabric store. It comes in nine or ten foot widths.”

As Lin turned her car around to head out, she could see the women one by one enter the studio to check it out. It was already 4:30, and by the time she got back, it would be full dark.

***

In the studio, Ruby painted away while the others gathered. Marybeth and Violet came in from the shed where they had been setting up the lights and moving some of the benches. Marybeth had hurt her wrist and held it delicately.

“She’s gone,” said Doris, clearing the way for them to talk.

Ruby was deep in thought. They had just moved a step toward readiness but were still many steps away from being ready. “This is oh so nice. But there are things we don't know,” she said, still painting.

“For example?” asked Marybeth.

“For example, which bank is our money in? You’re over there moving benches around like you were setting up a room. What room are you setting up?”

Mini grunted. Ruby winked at her, and Mini rolled her eyes. “I hate to admit it, but she's right,” said Mini. “We can get in shape, or wear what's left of our joints out trying, but we can't plan a thing without knowing where we’re going.”

The room fell silent.

“And I was feeling so good about this,” said Doris.

“Mini, why don't you tell us what the plan so far is,” said Violet.

“Here we go,” said Marybeth.

Mini took front and center and turned up her hearing aid. “A lot is going to depend on the bank, but there are some basic plans we can make and things we can practice. From the time we arrive until we leave, I am in charge. I will also be in charge of training for the job itself. Everyone has their job. Mine is to get us all in and out alive. My second job is to set it up so that no one in the bank gets hurt." She paused and scanned the faces of her friends and charges.

Ruby nodded in agreement. That was important, and saying it up front would clear up any possible misunderstandings later.

Mini continued, "The best way to do that is to get in and out fast. Push hard, push fast, and keep them scared. Our worst enemy is a guard or employee who isn't afraid. The longer we're there, the more time they have to think. We don't want them to think. We want them hopelessly jangled but not panicked. Once we have them scared, we walk them through the process like lining up school kids to go to the bathroom. Each thing we are going to do, we tell them about, then do."

She focused on Ruby. "When we blow the safe, we'll tell them that we are about to set off a small explosion. We get them all to cover their heads and ears so that no one is hurt. Once we have accessed the vault, we'll tell them that there is another small explosion coming and that they need to keep their heads down and eyes covered. We will take advantage of their need to protect themselves to make a graceful exit. Are there any questions that I can answer without knowing what bank we are liberating?"

CHAPTER 13

Night landings were tough anywhere, but on the tiny mountain runway at Casa Luis, the lights were only turned on when the plane was a few minutes out from landing. That left little time to line up and increased the likelihood of error. Further, there were no landing visual approach slope indicator (VASI) lights to follow to make sure they were on the right glide slope. Manuel and Eduardo had tried several times to install the approach lights properly, but the trees were so close to the end of the runway that the lights were either obscured from the glide slope or too close to the little strip of tarmac for safety. In place of the VASI lights, the pilot, Manuel, sometimes Eduardo, used the trees and runway lights as a glide slope indicator. If they could count twelve lights on each side of the runway, they were high enough, maybe too high. The trick was to line up, then go down until the two lights at the near end of the runway were obscured by trees, then fly level until they were not.

At that point, they would be about a thousand feet above ground and would simply maintain airspeed at 100 knots and vertical speed at 500 feet per minute. All that while staying lined up with the runway lights, keeping the wings level, and conversing with a God that they didn't believe in on non-flying days. If they were lucky, there would be no clouds between them and the runway. The village was very high in the mountains, and they weren't always so lucky. Tonight, they were.

Eduardo gripped his shoulder belts. Tonight, Manuel would land them. He had so many other things on his mind, talking with his father topmost, that he did not trust himself to maintain the concentration needed. Even now he was having a hard time with backing up his friend and confirming that they were seeing all twenty-four lights, twelve per side.

"There are never thirteen," chided Manuel. "If there are thirteen, we are landing at the wrong place. Maybe even Guermo's driveway." It was a running joke. They both had flown enough at night to know that Guermo Rodriquez, a competing drug lord, had a driveway that ran long and straight across an open field that was indeed lit up like a runway at night. Like a medieval castle, the open areas around the compound were for defense. No enemy could approach without crossing four hundred meters of cleared field. The disadvantage, they all knew, was that if the Americans ever decided to bomb the place they would only have to tell the pilots to fly south and look for the big clearing in the jungle, then line up on the lights for the bomb run.

Instead of being killed or arrested, Guermo's defenses seemed to be working. His profits were up, and he was building an army that threatened all of the other producers in the region, including the Salizars. To this point, the uneasy peace between the cartels and producers had held. That could not last forever. Even now, some of Salizar's men were being offered higher salaries by Guermo. Luis was keeping a closer eye on the comings and goings in the village, even posting guards on the road. Eduardo knew his father's ways. The old man was betting that Guermo would attack the smaller, weaker producers first. Maybe he wouldn't even attack. He might just buy them out and take over. Most of the producers would sell, even go to work for him, rather than fight. But not Luis Salizar and his loyal men. Guermo would have to fight them if he wanted their fields and village. Unfortunately for the Salizars, unless they could double their crop, or somehow double their income in another way this year, they would be facing an enemy that they would not be able to defeat.

That was where Eduardo's new idea could help.

"Twelve lights," said Eduardo, counting again. He could feel the slight attitude change of the plane as Manuel raised the nose, bleeding off airspeed, to bring the plane onto the glideslope. He watched the VSI (Vertical Speed Indicator) drop to minus 500 and stay there. For a fraction of a second, he saw the first two lights twinkle as they were blocked from view by trees, then the nose of the plane was too high to see the ground and they were sweeping past the treetops toward the pavement.

He felt a slight waver of the plane and a tug as the wheels dug through the thin upper branches of the trees. A few seconds later and Manuel pulled back on the yoke and flared, allowing the wheels to touch down lightly. Brakes were applied, and the nose wheel touched down on the runway.

The runway lights were turned off before they stopped rolling. Manuel found his way by following the lighter patch of sky, then followed the flashlights of the man on the ground. They parked the plane in a small hangar that was covered with camouflage netting. No one imagined with today's technology that satellites couldn’t find them, but maybe the netting would keep an enthusiastic young military pilot from shooting up the plane for fun.

Eduardo stretched and walked away from the plane to light a cigarette. What he was thinking of was dangerous but maybe not so dangerous as doing nothing. The hangar door screeched as it closed. He would have to get the ground man to oil the rollers. The lights in the hangar were extinguished before the door hit bottom, the only light remaining from his cigarette. A gentle breeze rustled the tree tops. The seasons were changing. It would be Christmas soon, and they would take a few weeks off to celebrate. Sometimes Papa would travel to see friends and family. Not so much anymore. Most of them were dead now from old age or other things.

“Going to talk to your Papa about whatever is on your mind now?” asked Manuel.

Eduardo was startled. He had never gotten used to how quiet his friend could be. Inside or out, Manuel moved silently when he approached, almost always choosing a path that blended with his surroundings. It was a talent that was very useful. Often when Eduardo was meeting someone for business, Manuel would accompany him. Thin and unimposing, he had a face that could only be described as unremarkable. In a room full of dangerous men, Manuel was seldom noticed, until something happened. Then, whoever was creating the problem would find Manuel beside, or worse for the troublemaker, behind him. Manual and his skills were quite useful. But as tempted as he was to let his friend in on his idea, he would not. Manuel was ambitious, and even a trusted friend could be tempted to turn on you for that kind of money. Such was the world he lived in. He nodded his head in the dark. “I'll tell you when you need to know,” he said, starting the Jeep.

Maybe he would wait till morning to talk to Papa.

The choice was not his to make. He entered the house through the side door near the pool and made his way to the kitchen. It had been hours since his last meal and the cook almost always left something that could be quickly reheated.

Papa was in the kitchen waiting. Technically, he was eating, but his lack of surprise at seeing his son, the extra plate, and the half empty bottle of wine suggested more. Eduardo retrieved a tumbler from the shelf and poured himself a glass of wine then sat and put several of the tamales on his plate.

They ate in silence for a while before Eduardo spoke. In his most respectful and humble tone, he addressed his father and boss, “I know you don't like me getting dropped off to go golf, and I admit that now that I think about it I was being irresponsible. You trusted me with a job, and I left it to someone else.”

“You were delegating,” said his father, after a pause. “Delegating is good.” He paused to unwrap a tamale. “However, I would like to know that there are always at least two men on the deal. You know why?”

Ed did know why. For the same reason that he liked to have Manuel at his back, Manuel needed someone to cover his. How did that American song go? “You always carry weapons cause you always deal in cash.” It was true. It was also true that a single armed man had no chance against two or more armed enemies. Also, if anything went wrong and Manuel managed to survive, it would not go well for him to come home without the money and no one to back up his story. It was not good to treat a friend that way.

“I am very sorry Papa. It will not happen again.”

***

Luis leaned back and studied his son. He was not used to this grown-up attitude. Was the boy up to something? Only a few hours ago, he had been so angry he had thought seriously about disowning his only son.

Now, he was more curious than angry and wondered what had changed. He would listen a little more and perhaps give the boy the benefit of the doubt.

Eduardo, perhaps sensing his father's deliberation, paused to sip some wine. Luis watched his son purposely set the tumbler aside and prepare to speak. It was a habit, he realized, that his son had copied from him. One of the many ways he signaled that he was moving from small talk to something serious. What, oh, what could be more serious than what they had just discussed? Or not discussed, as it were, since it was really only Eduardo who spoke.

“Papa, I have, while I was golfing, come across some interesting information.”

Luis found himself pushing his own glass aside and listening intently as his son told him of the millions of dollars' worth of bearer bonds and his plan to get them. It was a good plan, and though he knew that he would eventually give his approval, he felt it would be imprudent to do so without considering all of the implications. There was also a matter of his own pride and need for satisfaction. He had just waited hours for his son to arrive so that he could scold and perhaps discipline him, only to be distracted from his purpose by this *grand* plan.

Despite his violent nature, Luis was quite capable of self-control when called for. It seemed now perhaps to be called for. For his pride, however, he needed to not let Eduardo's indiscretion go so easily.

“I have been quite angry with you concerning the shirking of your responsibilities,” he said with all the calmness he could muster. “It would be wrong for you to leave here thinking that all was forgotten. It is good that you have seen the error of your ways. It does not help that others knew of this before me.” He examined his son and saw nothing but contrition and humility, not always what he wished from his child, but a good thing at this moment. “I will consider this plan of yours, and I will consider your apology. I will also consider replacing you on the delivery flights.”

Eduardo looked up at him, as expected, the shock written on his face. He had not expected Luis to go so far as to cut off his golfing altogether. It pleased Luis that he could do at least one thing tonight that his son had not anticipated. He smiled. Perhaps if the boy did well on this job, he would allow him to play golf on occasion. Perhaps.

Early the next morning, Luis left the casa for a short drive up and over the mountain. From there, he could connect with any number of cell towers that would not track him back to his home village. A precaution that he did not often take, but one that he felt necessary for this kind of call. He also used a phone that was registered under a false name.

Moments later, he was on the way home. The ball was rolling. A call would come to the house within the next day or so. It would be a wrong number. If they asked for Juan, the information was verified; if they asked for Raul, it was not.

***

In Panama, within sight of Costa Rica's southern border is a lone structure of indiscernible use. The building stands on the cleared mountaintop accessible by a single trail that is just wide enough for a small four-wheel drive and is blocked by a steel pipe gate several miles down the trail. Where the trail splits from the main road—itself only a track through the jungle—the split is concealed by what appears to be vegetation but what is in fact plastic and silk fakery that is replaced annually. There are no farm fields or houses near, and the terrain and forest density are such that no one is likely to come to the gates on foot by accident. Should someone find the road and take it, then find their way past the gate and to the mountaintop, they would then find their path blocked by a high razor wire topped fence with a sign in English and Spanish declaring further passage illegal and deadly. No one is allowed past these gates, and why would they want to be? The most tempting thing visible from the gate is a rusted metal building with high grass around it that surely conceals nothing more exciting than snakes and ticks.

On the north and east sides that are not visible from the gate, the building is not rusty. If one were to get past the gate and around the building to see behind the camouflage netting, they would find what looked like a huge golf ball protruding from each of the two walls. If they were to get inside that building, they would find that the twenty-foot golf ball edifice houses alien looking artifacts that in fact are parts of a highly sensitive antenna system.

Only a few people in the world have been inside to see the antennas. The construction itself was classified top secret by the U.S. government. Anyone so interested in the facility to attempt to climb the fence would find no resistance. But anyone that attempted to open the heavy steel door of the building would find it difficult without explosives or a cutting torch. If they were unfortunate enough to get past the door, they would soon find that the structure was booby trapped with explosives that would destroy the antennas and anything or anyone in the building. The fact that the building still stood was testament that no one had been so unlucky. Some young dirt bike enthusiasts had once come as far as the gate. They didn't stick around.

The building and the antennas inside it had been online and in use for more than forty years. Built when America had better relations with Panama, it was unlikely that anyone in the government of that country today knew the site existed. The site is owned, operated, and protected by the National Security Agency (NSA) of the United States. Its primary purpose is to monitor and collect communications in South and Central America.

Signals gathered at the facility are routed to NSA headquarters at Fort Meade, Maryland, where they are listened to by computers and in some cases forwarded to human listeners to parse. Today, only a few hundred messages were kicked up to human ears to listen and interpret. Several were passed to the NSA's own S2F International Crime section, and one message was forwarded from there to the Information Sharing Services Department of the NSA.

Two hours later, FBI Agent Ted Jonah received a classified file containing that message. Luis Salizar, who Jonah had never heard of, was asking about Bob Robbins. More importantly, he had asked for confirmation that Robbins had a safe deposit box at the Cayman National Bank and Trust.

Jonah knew that Cayman Island banks were inaccessible. Still he lifted the phone and dialed Katherine in legal. Moments later, he set the phone in its cradle. Banking protections did indeed include safe deposit boxes. Silently he wished Luis Salizar great success. He should warn the bank if he *knew* it to be in danger of robbery. Did he *know* that? He couldn't be sure, could he? He weighed the file in his hand. Technically, it was classified information, but it struck him as ridiculous to keep the file separate and locked up. Who really cared what Luis Salizar might be up to? He added the document to the Robbins file.

***

Violet woke with a shudder from a dream that faded so quickly it was gone before her feet hit the rug. She wanted to roll back under the blanket and sleep her aching muscles away, but the rules of age were simple, you either woke up to go to the bathroom, or you wore a diaper. She was resolved to avoid the second option until her last breath. Damn the house shoes, she shuffled across the cold hardwood onto the colder tile to do her business.

She stretched before dressing, going over the day's schedule in her head. Losing track rather quickly, she went in search of her little notepad that was filling up quickly now as it was doing double duty. Starting on the front page were her personal notes. Starting from the back were the job notes. The first page of the job notes was noticeably empty. They knew the country, or thought they did, but not the bank or box number.

That would have to change soon.

***

Eduardo loved the village, maybe more than his father did. It was his home and home to all of the people that he trusted and a few that he didn't. He knew them, and, for the most part, where he stood with them. Eduardo was the son of a drug supplier. Not a kingpin, or cartel boss, but something in between, a farmer on a direct marketing track. Maybe *grower* was the best term. The nomenclature didn't matter as much as the facts. *Fact one: the outside world could not be trusted. Fact Two: the people around you could not be trusted.* Even here, in his own village, he could feel cautious eyes watching him. That kid that came around the corner was running straight toward him as if he were the destination.

The child, five or six, with dark brown skin and teeth white as new piano keys skidded to a halt and spun to walk beside him. "Señor Eduardo," the child said, grabbing his pinky finger and pulling him up the street. "Señor Salizar wants to see you at the big house."

Eduardo knelt in front of the child. "How did you know where to find me?" he asked, gently.

The boy laughed and danced like he was running in place. "There are only three streets in the village. I ran until I found you," he explained, shocked that someone like Señor Eduardo would not know this. Eduardo laughed, recalling his own childhood errands, even a few that did not turn out so well for the person he retrieved. It would not be that way for him. It was his own father, after all.

The laughing child pulled on his hand, dragging him up the street. "I get paid more if I bring you quickly," he explained, breathless with the urgency of the mission.

Papa did indeed have a reason for the urgency. He was packing one of the Jeeps for a visit to the fields. There were many fields, and he could be going to one or even all. Attached was a trailer carrying a water tank with mixed insecticide. He was, after all, a farmer first. Otherwise, there was no product to sell. That the products were illegal where they were sold was not the concern of the producer. Personal morality aside, it was dangerous to be a producer. He took three men with him. All carried rifles as well as side arms.

"You have permission," said Luis, without preamble. "Take the men you need. Let me know what supplies you need and discuss this with no one until you are on the boat."

"Boat?" asked Eduardo.

"Boat," replied Luis, handing him a folded, sweat-soaked piece of note paper from the shirt pocket of his fatigues. "Move quickly," he said, clasping his son's hands in his, "and be very careful. I will see you again before you go to the island." With that, he hopped into the open Jeep and waved for the driver to go.

Eduardo took a deep breath. It was a big and dangerous job his father was trusting him with, and he was surprised that someone else had not been given the job. Either Papa had turned a page and was expressing confidence in him, or the old man thought he was useless, and this was a way to get him out of the way permanently. He put the paper in his shirt pocket.

Moments later, he sat at his father's desk and read the note. Papa's plans were clear and simple, covering some operational matters that Eduardo would never have thought of. Despite saying that Eduardo could take the men he wanted, Papa had suggested specific men. The old man's suggestions were to be taken seriously. Thankfully, the list included Manuel. On the third or fourth read of the note, Eduardo began to grasp the reasoning behind the specifics his father had outlined.

He snipped the end from one of his father's Cuban cigars. Papa would be gone all day and maybe overnight. He wouldn't mind what he didn't know about. Eduardo propped his feet up on the desk and lit the cigar. Maria, the young maid, looked in on him. He raised an eyebrow in her direction. Her expression remained solidly neutral. She would tell no one what she saw or heard in this house. Not even Papa. She had a good job, probably one of the better paying ones in the village, and would not put it at risk. After all, someday Eduardo would own this house and this desk, and if she were good, he would pay her salary.

CHAPTER 14

The house was as quiet as Lin had heard in a long time. A breeze, short of winter and long of summer, pushed through the open windows of the dark living room.

Lin gazed out the window toward the apple shed. The ladies were out there painting or talking. For a moment, she thought about looking in on them. Someone swooshed by behind her and out the door. She watched Doris jaunt across the yard and through the modified screen door into the shed studio carrying a pitcher of lemonade. The glass pitcher wouldn't have been allowed at Golden Lawn. On the flip side, the ladies were taking group walks almost daily. That might not have been allowed in the home either, but it sure looked good on Doris, who'd lost at least ten pounds already. Lin was impressed with the ladies' self-determination and drive to be fit. It was so nice that they were looking after one another, too. It gave her a bit of a break.

She sat back in a comfortably worn recliner and opened her book.

***

Bernice tapped her cane hard on the apple shed floor. The second tap landed on Mini's foot. Mini slapped her friend hard enough to leave white finger marks on the parchment like flesh.

Bernice raised her cane to strike. Voices and hands were raised to stop her.

"She's off her meds," groused Mini.

"I don't take those kind of meds," snapped Bernice.

"See," said Mini.

"What's this about?" asked Doris.

"She called me crazy!" growled Bernice.

"You are crazy. You want us to kidnap an FBI agent to find out if they know what bank little Bobby is using. That's crazy."

"I thought it was a good idea," chipped in Marybeth. "Logistically, it's the shortest path to what we need."

Violet's head swung back and forth tracking the conversation like a tennis match. She thought there were merits to the idea. "Aren't there other ideas?" she asked, sure that there must be.

Bernice and Mini continued to stare each other down.

Ruby walked into the middle of the circle swinging her paint brush around like a conductor warming up before a concert, "I don't know what's wrong with crazy. I've been crazy most of my life." Just as she said *life,* she reached out with the brush, tapping Mini then Bernice on the ends of their noses, leaving a glob of paint on each before scooting back to her easel.

In the moment of silence that followed, all eyes focused on Ruby. Doris handed paper towels to the painted ladies but neither raised a hand to remove the paint.

"We'll have to talk about this later, ladies. Lin is coming," said Ruby, returning to her canvas with her back to the silent cluster. "In the meantime, I suggest that we consider all going to the FBI office together and asking that Agent Jonah fellow where the little turd has our money hid away."

Behind her, the ladies scrambled to look occupied. Doris picked up a brush and went to her easel. The rest of the girls shuffled out into the main room of the shed. When Lin entered, they all stared at the lights as if in deep thought. Lin squinted suspiciously at each of them in turn.

"Something wrong?" asked Violet.

Lin shrugged and made for the plastic curtain.

"We were trying to decide how to make these lights better. Also, how to bring up an idea we had that involves you." Violet and Marybeth had indeed been brainstorming on ways to get Lin away from the house a few hours each day, but hadn't gotten further than jotting down ideas.

"Do I want to hear this?" Lin asked.

Violet couldn't think of a single good reason not to test the waters. "We want you to sell Tommy's paintings."

"Mine too," chipped in Ruby from inside the plastic studio.

"Are you serious?" said Doris.

Violet wasn't sure who the question was for. She ignored it for the moment and focused on Lin who had fallen blankly silent.

"Seems like maybe a little too much for her," said Marybeth, leaning in but not really whispering.

"No, I just… I just need a minute… What is on your face?" she asked Mini. "And yours?" she asked Bernice.

"They were face painting," said Doris, winking at Violet.

"How could I take care of you and do that, too?" said Lin.

"Oh, but you do such a good job, and you wouldn't be far away. We could call you anytime we need you," said Doris laying her hand on Lin's arm.

Violet watched Lin shift from confused to skeptical to maybe accepting then back to confused before nodding to them and leaving.

Moments later, Ruby gave the "All Clear," and the room exploded in conversation.

"Too much," said Marybeth.

"She's suspicious. And what's it going to get us?" said Bernice.

"It's not the dumbest idea ever, but…" said Mini.

"It's fine," said Ruby.

Violet scratched her head and sat on one of the tables. She should have asked the others first, but the real issue was that they didn't have enough time alone to deal with this stuff.

"Let's all go to see the FBI," she said. "And I'm sorry, but the cat is out of the bag now on the painting sales thing, and I think we should just see what happens."

***

Lin sat in the sun, feeling her lips and skin dry and disintegrate with the UV and wind. The paintings were well-protected from the solar rays by the pop-up tent she had borrowed from her father, but it was too cold in the shade for her. The paintings didn't care about the cold.

Her spot was either the best or worst that the fairground turned flea market had to offer. Out front, closest to the road, everyone that came in had to pass her. It was also the sunniest spot, which in the coming winter would be nice, but now meant that she had to constantly move the artwork to keep it in the shade. *Why? Why be here at all?*

She crossed her arms and ran her tongue over her lips. They felt like the floor of Death Valley. A number of people had strolled through, checking out the paintings. Most were farmers, themselves selling produce or old farm tools, junk mostly, that they called antiques. One man had offered ten dollars for three paintings. She pointed out that the starting price was three hundred dollars each. The man walked away in solemn disappointment.

Another man, a farmer, knelt in front of one of the paintings studying it. She could tell that he was moved by it and really wanted it. He lifted the price tag and his face fell. "Too rich for my blood," he mumbled. Hands in his pockets, he ambled toward his truck, an eighteen-year-old F-250 with a crumpled tailgate and sagging bumper.

Lin struggled out of her chair and caught up with the farmer as he reached for the door handle on his dusty truck. "Wait," she said, brushing her wind-blown hair from her eyes and bouncing on her toes.

He wore a feed store cap with the brim frayed from too many washings and a corduroy jacket that reminded her of her father's old shop jacket. His beard was roughly trimmed and his face tan, with a scar on his cheek that ran down from his left eye like the track of a tear. Lin guessed it was a leftover from skin cancer surgery.

"Why? Why does the painting make you sad?" she asked.

For a moment, she thought he was going to climb into the truck and leave without answering. Instead, he turned back to her, biting his lip. "Tommy was my friend,. He stood on my front porch for weeks painting that. I still got paint spots on the deck. Guess I could clean it off, but every time I see those spots, I just don't know. Anyhow, I guess you're one of the relatives?"

"No, I'm… Tommy's Aunt Violet is there now. I'm the kind of caretaker/nurse."

He nodded, a gleam of recognition in his eyes. "Tommy talked about her. Had Sunday dinner with us near every week for the last fifteen years till the cancer got him. He told me she put up the money for the land. I don't mean to be indelicate, but I thought she was pretty rich, and I mean…" he glanced over at the paintings, "…she has a caretaker. Why is she selling the paintings?"

Lin briefly explained the nursing home closing and the six ladies at the house.

"Damn," he said, then apologized for the language and introduced himself as Hayden.

"Was it you that cleaned up the house after…?" asked Lin.

Hayden nodded, "I looked for that painting. There was a bunch under the house, but not that one."

"It was inside, on top of the wardrobe upstairs," said Lin, suddenly understanding why it had been set aside. "I think he might have meant you to have it." She shot away before he could respond.

Hayden blinked as she returned with the canvas of bright gold that she called *The Golden Orchard.* She plucked the price tag off and slipped it into her pocket. "I didn't know him, but I think Tommy would have wanted you to have it."

For a moment, Hayden studied the painting, the lump in his throat and watery eyes telling the story. Finally, releasing a deep rattling breath, he dared speak. "Dotty's going to be so happy," he said, his voice thick. "She cried when we couldn't find it. You tell Aunt Violet that if she needs anything, anything at all, you let me know. Anything."

"It wasn't a complete loss," she explained to Violet later, telling her about meeting Hayden. She couldn't bring herself to talk about the disappointments of the day or her tiredness. It all seemed pale in comparison to meeting Tommy's friend and seeing how a little thing like a painting could be so life changing. The house was quiet when she slipped out and behind the wheel of her car. She was tired, so tired.

The next morning, while she cleaned the kitchen, the ladies packed the van to send her out again. This time she brought lip balm.

***

Violet unhooked the tire ropes from the box blade attachment of the tractor and tucked them under the hay, then rang the big dinner bell on the porch to call the girls out. It was time to get busy.

Marybeth had gotten it right. If the flea market would keep Lin away from the house for even a few hours a day, they would need to provide some incentive for her to go back, or she would refuse. Today would be make or break. The phones came out, and the squinting at the little screens began. Marybeth set up on the coffee table with her calendar open. A half hour later, the first return call came.

Mini called out that she had Becka DeMoss on for Friday the 3rd.

That was good, thought Violet, but they needed someone today. Becka couldn't make it today, did she want her on the list or not?

"Put her on the list for Friday," she said.

***

Lin sat alone under the tent wondering again what she was doing here.

A car slid to a stop on the gravel, and a woman as old as any of those that had been in the home bounced out, her shriveled arms clutching a huge handbag. She set the bag on the table.

"Watch this," she ordered. Lin stood, in sales mode. The woman waved her off. It was just as well. Lin wasn't a salesperson.

The old woman walked down the line then back again twice before selecting a painting and bringing it to the table. She paid the full price in cash and left without a word.

"What's going on here?" she said, watching the woman drive away.

No sooner was she gone than another shopper arrived.

The man, Lin guessed to be at least in his mid-seventies, made a show of strolling through the market then took a turn through the rows of paintings. Occasionally kneeling to examine one more closely, he sniffed the paint, ran his finger along the edge of the canvas frame, tested the hardness of the color with a thumbnail to the edge, and examined the signatures with a magnifying loop. Lin stood by watching the process.

The old man picked up a painting and approached, withdrawing a roll of cash from his pocket and counted off four $100 bills. Maybe the flea market wasn't such a bad idea, after all.

A breeze kicked up carrying on it the crack of distant rifle fire.

"Hunting season," said a passerby.

A minute later, she heard twenty or more shots in groups of two that sounded so close together they could have been echoes.

"Stubborn deer," said another passerby.

***

The ladies marched into the apple shed in single file. Cheeks glowing from the cold and exertion, they each handed the unloaded weapons to Marybeth who dutifully checked them in. The last in line was Doris. She dragged the garbage bag full of shot up tin cans and plastic jugs to the far wall. They still had no trash service to the orchard. Marybeth grunted. One more problem to solve.

"Ruby and Dori, you are on weapons cleaning," said Marybeth.

Violet pointed out that one of them needed to be painting, and Marybeth adjusted, sending Doris out to paint.

"She needs the practice," commented Mini.

"I heard that," said Doris, her voice cracking and dry.

"No tire drill today," barked Violet like a drill instructor. "We've just heard from Paul Walters," she said to Marybeth. "He stayed as long as he could but says he was cold and tired so he bought a painting and left."

Marybeth felt like someone had just pulled her drain plug letting all of her energy run out. She had never imagined something so complicated as trying to get time away from one young watcher that was so dad-blamed helpful. She scanned her clipboard. So many things to do and only a little time left. They still didn't know what bank they were planning to rob.

***

Lester sat in his Escalade in a drug store parking lot in Conyers, Georgia. It was nice to have Emily with him. She asked too many questions, but still a sweet kid. Paul Walters had asked to meet him halfway, and that was fine. Paul was doing them a favor. He had no idea why the favor was needed, but…

Paul's town car lurched to a stop beside him, the bumper scraping on the high curb. Seconds later, he knocked on Lester's side window. Lester opened the door and counted out four hundred dollars in tens and twenties. "I had hundreds," said Paul, staring at the stack Lester was offering.

Lester groaned. "Wait here," he said. Surely there was a cash machine in the drug store.

"Just give me the damn money, and don't forget gas," demanded Paul, shoving the painting at Lester.

"Grandpa, what are you doing?" asked Emily as Paul drove off.

"A favor for a friend, and don't ask why, because I have no clue," he said, fastening his seat belt.

***

Ruby followed Marybeth, Violet, and Bernice into the apple shed office. "Is the cruise date solid?" Violet asked Marybeth.

"Solid as it can be."

"What's that mean?" asked Bernice. "Don't ships usually sail when they're supposed to?"

"It's still hurricane season," said Marybeth as Bernice tapped around the room impatiently.

"Marybeth, I need C-4 and blasting caps." said Ruby.

It was like her words had fallen into a vacuum. Marybeth stared past her to Violet, her thoughts somewhere else.

A knock at the door, and Mini joined them, asking for a run to the gun store to get cleaning solvent.

"We have to pay everyone back on the paintings," explained Marybeth. "It ties up a lot of money."

"I need C-4 and blasting caps," said Ruby, again.

"I don't like having Lester pick up our tab," said Violet.

Ruby thought she caught Marybeth's eye and started to speak again, but Marybeth turned away.

"We pre-paid him for four paintings. That's why we have no cash," said Marybeth.

Ruby interjected, "Explosives and caps."

"We need more ammo for practice," said Mini.

Ruby slipped away. Maybe she needed to do her own research then come back. She passed through the shed and into the studio trying to work out where they could find the stuff she needed.

***

Doris loved Ruby, but sometimes she worried about her. Today was one of those days. Ruby had been at the easel for an hour and a half, and her painting had gone from classic Ruby to a Monet-Picasso mish-mash of unnatural colors.

Ruby continued to mutter about plastic and caps. It was starting to get on Doris' nerves. She painted on. Painting was supposed to be therapeutic. If this kept up, she was going to need another kind of therapy. Maybe she already did. Ruby, beyond question, needed help. Doris dipped her brush into the jar and smeared green paint across her reds and golds. “Damn, damn, damn!” *What a mess!* “What in blazes are you rambling on about?” she said to Ruby.

Ruby turned to her, holding her brush up as though she were about to paint the air. She sat that way for a moment, her head cocked sideways and her eyes focused somewhere beyond the opaque plastic walls. “I need plastic explosive. C-4, or Semtex if I can't get the C-4. C-4 is better.”

Doris dabbed at the green paint with a dry brush and made a mess of it. “That sounds like military stuff,” she said.

“It is.”

The green was blending with the red. This was the warmest day in the shed in a while, and Doris didn't want to waste it letting paint dry so she could paint over it. She dipped a towel into some turpentine to try and dab it off. “There are army bases all around here. I read about a government what-ya-call-it where they were selling machine guns that were supposed to be stolen from an army base. Seems like that kind of stuff happens all the time.”

Pieces of paper towel stuck in the gooey paint. She picked them out with the tip of a knife, not noticing Ruby stare at her, deep in thought. Eventually, Ruby returned to working happily on her own creation.

CHAPTER 15

Lin had driven plenty but never the big van in Atlanta traffic. She gripped the wheel until her knuckles turned white and checked the mirror again before turning on her signal. A BMW zoomed around her into the lane she was moving into. She was already committing to the lane change and barely missed removing the beamer's mirror with the extended body width of the van. It would have served him right, but she probably would have gotten the ticket. In the rearview, she could see Violet gripping the *oh-shit* handle. She cringed thinking about how it must feel to be back there and out of control. It was hard enough being out of control in the driver's seat.

It was urgent, they said, that they visit the FBI office in Atlanta. She almost turned them down. She hated driving in the city. The light turned red, and she stomped on the brake, straightening her back to push it all the way to the floor. Her bumper was across the line into the crosswalk. A cop on the sidewalk snapped a hard look at her. She cringed.

She dropped the ladies at the federal building and caught up with them in the lobby security line where Mini slowly emptied the contents of her huge shoulder bag into the plastic trays. Several impatient people waited in line between her and her charges. Mini began to fill another tray.

In the line to the right, the security officer glanced over at the officers waiting on Mini and chuckled. Doris passed through the metal detector. Violet set her hand clutch down in the narrow gap between the x-ray machine and the frame of the metal detector. Doris picked it up from the other side.

What the…? Doris and Violet smuggling a handbag past security!

Violet passed through the metal detector and retrieved Doris' purse from the belt. It was all so smooth that if Lin hadn't seen them get in the van and noticed that Violet was only carrying the clutch, she would never have noticed the switch.

"I make stuff out of them," Mini was explaining a bag of bottle caps that the officer was holding up. "Some people knit; I make bottle cap art."

"Just let her go," groused a man behind her.

They did, then asked the man to step aside for a thorough search.

***

At the desk, six old women asked to see Agent Jonah. The prim receptionist, Pamela Write, an anti-terror specialist with two tours in Afghanistan behind her, stared at the old women for a moment then lifted the phone and called up. Under her navy pinstriped jacket, she wore an elastic waist band that as well as keeping her blouse neatly tucked in, held a Sig P229 within comfortable reach. Every day, she watched hundreds of people march past her desk on the way in and out of this building, and rarely had she seen a group that looked so harmless on first pass but still raised her hackles.

Agent Jonah arrived and escorted the women into the elevator. Pamela watched them until the doors closed, wondering why they made her jumpy. She guessed that the youngest of the women was over seventy-five, but not a one of them walked with a stroller, or even hunched over. They were fit, tan, and fierce. Not like the young marine recruit she had once been, but like the old career guys who shook your hand while they decided how to kill you.

She reached and almost pushed the alarm before shaking her head to clear it. What was she thinking? Six old women and an assistant had just gone up to the Bureau office with an agent escorting, and her imagination was getting away from her. Maybe she needed a vacation. She'd always wanted to go to Israel to see the Mossad museum. Maybe it was time for a break.

***

Lin watched Doris and Violet exchange purses in the elevator in a professionally smooth move.

She tugged at Doris' arm. "What are you up to?" she whispered.

"Oh, dear. Why do you ask that?"

"You, you…" she wagged her finger in Doris' face.

In front of them, Jonah clenched his hands nervously in a way that reminded Lin of Marybeth. Marybeth was not clenching her hands, Bernice not tapping her cane, and Violet not twirling her nail file. Ruby moved her lips to the words of some old song. But even Ruby was different, not looking scared or distracted but focused. They all looked focused. *What the…?*

***

Jonah fidgeted. He didn't mind coming in on a Saturday, but he wasn't sure how he felt about being outnumbered six to one. Seven, if you included the girl. The girl might count for two. She couldn't be more than twenty-five. Fit and pretty with a pleasant glow, she had an energy that seemed to be catching. He could feel her eyes watching his every move. Instinctively, he turned his head to meet the threat.

"I'm Lin," the girl said, extending her hand and smiling in the most disarming way. "I'm the nurse, the assistant. I don't know how they got you to do this, but thank you," she whispered.

Not able to help himself, he leaned down and whispered in a conspiratorial tone, "Any idea why we're here?"

Lin shook her head.

The door opened, and Jonah found himself trying not to watch her too closely.

A sharp pain leapt from his foot to his brain. "She's too young for you," said the old woman lifting the cane from his foot. He wasn't sure he agreed, but he wasn't about to argue the point now. He stuck his foot in the door to stop it from closing and caught up with the ladies in the lobby, wondering if he should have called for backup.

He led them past his desk and to the conference room, where he encouraged them to sit. He took his own seat at the end of the table. They didn't sit. Instead, they lined both sides of the table and waited. *Shit! That's the way this is going to be.* The girl, Lin, stood arms crossed, staring at one then the other.

Jonah found himself wanting to come to her defense. First, he needed to defend himself. "All right," he said, standing and closing the folder. "I have forgotten my manners. I'm used to working with criminals and bank robbers," he continued, moving from chair to chair pulling them out for the ladies to sit.

This time when he sat, he studied the faces around the table. The one closest on his right, who had moments ago speared his foot with the hard tip of her cane, was Bernice Walker, missionary's wife whose husband had been killed by rebels in Guatemala. His foot hurt still, and he instinctively wanted to move away from her. Stubbornness kept him in place. I *have to be in charge, even if every one of them reminds me of my mother or aunt.*

Mrs. Bernice Walker gripped her cane handle threateningly, as if she had read his mind and was preparing to set it right. He moved on, focusing on the thin woman with the disarmingly persistent gaze. He remembered her as Ruby Dunham, no maiden name available. *How did that happen? Lost records?*

He opened the file as he spoke, "Mrs. Dunham, I don't have your maiden name?"

"Well, it's been a long time."

"You remember it?"

"Well, of course, I remember it."

"I just thought we could update the file."

"Go right ahead," she said, looking through him.

Jonah stared at the files and squeezed his forehead. *I'm losing to an old woman.* He shuffled the papers and moved on, glad that he wasn't recording the meeting.

The woman behind Ruby was shorter, the top of her head barely visible above Ruby's shoulder. He checked his memory and couldn't recall seeing her face yet. Her feet, her large shoulder bag, and the shoulder that supported it, he had seen. Not her face. The outdated picture in the file showed what he expected, a small woman with curly white hair. From here, he could see her left hand and rings.

"Mrs. Barone?" The hand moved, and the head bobbed up where he could see her eyes.

At the far end of the table, the woman he assumed to be Violet Wilson cleared her throat. "Mr. Jonah?"

"Agent," he injected.

"Agent Jonah, we are not here to fill in the gaps in your notes."

Jonah kept his face neutral. *Now we're getting somewhere.* "What can the FBI do for you?" he asked, setting aside the pen.

"We know what's in the papers and the news," she said, clasping her hands on the table in front of her. "What we don't know is what's really going on. We don't know if, or when, you're going to get our savings back. We don't know where that man that robbed us is or where he's keeping our money. Mr. Jonah, it's all we've got."

Jonah swallowed. It was always the hardest part of the job, that moment when you had to take the victim aside and tell them that the family member, or life savings, or whatever had been lost was truly not coming back. It was personal for them. It was never personal for the FBI. The day it became personal was the day they started making mistakes.

"They won't get it back, will they?" asked Lin, the disappointment layers deep.

He shook his head, "Not likely."

To his right, someone fell out of her chair.

Doris Kidd was missing.

Jonah launched from his chair.

Lin was around the table at the woman's side in seconds.

"Water," Lin ordered.

The receptionist should have brought a tray with cups. Not on Saturday.

"Water now!" repeated Lin. This was her turf now. Jonah obeyed.

By the time he returned to the conference room, Doris was sitting up and speaking. Lin seemed to have things well in hand, and he couldn't help but feel that her demand for water was about getting him out of the way. Aside from Bernice and Doris, the women were all seated at the table as if nothing had happened.

Is that the way it is when you get old? People just assume that you will die or get better and don't bother to get up and see which? The whole idea bothered him. Wasting the time of these people bothered him. He wished that he could tell them what they wanted to know, but that wasn't his job. His job was to catch the guy and bring him in.

Getting the money back would be a bonus, but it was almost never possible. He had told them that in the kindest way he could.

He helped Doris regain her seat. Lin sat close, watchful.

“Ladies, you can rest assured that we've got every available resource looking for Mr. Robbins. We have a few leads. Nothing confirmed yet, but we will get him. When we do, through due process in the courts, we will recover every penny of your assets that we can.”

They sat motionless, grasping at his every useless, empty, word.

He couldn't remember the last time he had felt so embarrassingly feckless.

Violet Blake broke from staring at him and let her eyes fall to the table with a deep sigh. It was likely the closest he would get to absolution.

***

Ruby was last off the elevator. She checked the floor directory and stepped back on before the doors closed. A smooth four floors later, she exited. The glass panel in front of her announced that she was in the office of the Bureau of Alcohol, Tobacco, and Firearms, the ATF.

“Excuse me,” she said to the girl at the desk who seemed annoyed that her texting had been interrupted. “My girl scout troop wants to meet a genuine ATF field agent. You know, not one of the puffy desk guys. Could you give me the name and number of one of your agents, a real field guy?”

“Ma'am, it's Saturday. You shouldn't be here without a pass or an escort.”

“Oh, I was just down at the FBI office, and they sent me up,” she said. “If you like, you can just give me his name, and we can call the main number. That would be you, wouldn't it?” The girl nodded, clearly not wanting anything to do with this loopy old girl scout.

She jotted a name and number on a sticky note and passed it over. Dalton wouldn't mind, would he? She sort of liked the idea of the dotty old woman annoying her least favorite agent. “Don't tell him I gave you this,” she said.

***

At the van, Violet deliberately opened her clutch in front of Lin and withdrew her nail file. “I didn't want to lose it to those security idiots,” she said.

Lin was just doing her head count when a knock came at the door of the van. Ruby climbed aboard without explanation. *What the heck? First, Doris fakes fainting, and now Ruby goes on tour.* She turned to Doris, “Why?”

Doris winked.

***

Milo Stenopholis loved his mother. He sent her flowers on every birthday, Mother's Day, and Easter. Every Christmas, he sent a personalized card. Something nice that she could pin to the door of her room at the home. Once a year at least, he would visit, usually in the spring, after Easter. He would only stay three days, but that was one day more than his sister, the Bitch, would stay.

This unexpected trip to Atlanta was throwing his gallery schedule off, but it seemed like something he should do. It wasn't every day that your eighty three year old mother had to move out of a retirement home and into a condo. Now that he was here, he could see that it was indeed an essential journey.

His sister, Brenda-the-Freeloader, had decided to help by moving in with mother. *Hadn't he hired a competent live-in service to take care of that? Of course, he had.* He had also signed the lease of a three bedroom townhome and established a bank account with direct deposit to provide for grocery and daily living expenses for his mother and the rotating live-in assistants. He had not, however, counted on the additional expense of feeding, and apparently clothing, his sister.

“Brenda is Brenda,” said mother. “She will always be her own woman.”

“Then, she can pay her own way,” said Milo.

“Nonsense,” said mother, “I like her taking care of me.”

Of course, having Brenda around was not enough. Mother insisted that she needed the live-in nurse, as well. There were things that Brenda could not be expected to do. Milo loved his mother.

As if the cost of supporting his mother, his sister, and the nurse were not enough to push him to the brink, Brenda had introduced a new challenge just today. Having been relieved of the need to care for mother, she was now spending a considerable amount of time rummaging around in the climate controlled storage unit. While retrieving some essentials, Brenda had gotten into some boxes that were not Mother's. Milo knew this because the painting that hung on the wall of his mother's new living room was an original Krasner that had *perished* in the fire that destroyed his first New York gallery.

The fire and the survival of the painting were accidents. Milo loved Lee Krasner's work and wanted to sleep just one night with one of her paintings hanging on the wall above his bed. Against all rules, he took a painting home. Several times in the night he woke. Each time, his eyes would focus on the painting, lit with a single daylight balanced bulb, and he would absorb the nuanced brush work until sleep took him again.

That night, sixteen blocks away, a basement gas leak and a cigarette dropped carelessly into a sidewalk grate destroyed the gallery.

To the art world, it was a catastrophe, and had there been even a sniff of foul play, Milo would never have been able to reopen. Fortunately for Milo, the investigation unearthed a bad gas line. The blame and cost fell squarely on the insurers.

For Milo, the fire created many problems but the largest by far was the potential for criminal charges. One painting survived the explosion and fire, and in the stress of the moment, not able to explain why the painting had not been secured in the Gallery, Milo certified that all had been destroyed. An oversite that he could not easily recover from.

Traumatized by the fiery loss of his business and dozens of irreplaceable works of art, Milo took a vacation. He drove to Atlanta to help his mother close the sale of her house and move most of her belongings into storage while she moved into Golden Lawn Retirement Home. Three years had passed.

Milo sat on the new white leather couch that he'd paid for. The white walls and smooth north light from the window behind him made for a wonderful viewing. He could see why Brenda had placed the painting where she had. *If only she knew.*

“I like it there,” she said from behind him.

Milo nodded. He could not disagree on the presentation. He opened his mouth but chose not to speak. He waited, listening to her tap through the kitchen, and when he heard the garage door go up, announcing yet another shopping trip to spend his money, he stood. From the kitchen he could hear the nurse reading a letter to Mother. He moved on after, “You may have already won.”

Brenda's room was better organized than he had imagined. Not a single box in sight. Her drawers were mostly empty. Almost everything hanging in the closet looked new. He wondered what her story was. What happened to her? Had she had a house fire? Was her latest boyfriend abusive and she had to run? Did it matter? Brenda always landed on her feet. While most with her talent of using people spiraled downward with each failure, Brenda managed to move up.

In the hall, he listened again before opening the door of the room shared by the nurses that stayed overnight. *Ah!* The boxes were found. The closet was full, and the walls were stacked floor to ceiling. To his left was the crate that the painting had been stored in. He would come back for that.

Mother's room was exquisite. Clean and orderly in a way that only paid help can do. It was the antithesis of his mother's known history. Milo grew up in her house and knew that her natural tendency was to collect and never clear out. Without professional help, Mother would eventually show up on reality TV in one of those hoarder shows.

Wow! On the dresser stood a painting that took his breath away. The intense, deep layers of gold and orange screamed New England, but the warm vertical shots of brown and gray brought him home to south Georgia. Breathtaking, complex, intense beauty. He sat on the bed and gazed at the painting for five minutes, ten minutes, an hour? The shadows through the window moved while he was there. Just as he’d needed to see the Krasner hang on his wall, he needed this painting in his gallery. He examined the signature. As suspected, unknown. Moreover, the paint was barely dry, the solvents still perfuming the air.

Milo backed the rented Benz into the garage and loaded up. Last in was the crate with the Krasner and the new painting. Mother was still having her mail read to her. No need to interrupt with goodbyes.

***

Agent Jonah sat stock-still at his desk in the dark office. There wasn't much point in moving without knowing which direction to go. Until now, the ladies had just been names and faces in a file. Names and faces were just facts to be processed. He picked up the phone and dialed his mother from the directory in his cell phone. *I don't remember my own mother's phone number,* he berated himself. As the phone rang, he opened the Golden Lawn file and began to flip pages. He had no idea what he was looking for.

His mother's voice answered. “Hey, mom…”

***

He was almost home. The conversation with his mother, the meeting with the ladies, meeting Lin, and thumbing through the case file all tumbling around in his head as he drove. *That was a pretty girl,* he mused. *Devoted to the people she cared for.* It sounded like a commercial. Pushing thoughts of the girl aside, he couldn't help but feel that he was missing something. Something had happened. Something had changed today. It was more than seeing the victims as human. He did that already. He wouldn't be able to do his job at all if he didn't start out each case keenly aware of his responsibility to help real people. You always started out with the victims and their story, then somewhere in each case it was important to separate from the emotional burden of thinking of the victims and focus on catching the bad guys. It worked better that way. The Bureau knew that. *Hell, they taught that.* This case was harder now that the victims had faces and names that were fresh in his mind. He would have to be careful.

In his garage, he sat in the car, mentally turning the day's pages once more. Ruby Dunham's maiden name, Mini Barone's shyness. *What was all that about?* Then, on the way out, Pam—Gunslinger Pam, arguably the hottest and most dangerous woman in the building—asked about the ladies. The weird part was that it didn't surprise him that Pam thought the ladies were a security risk. On the surface, it seemed absurd, but having spent a few minutes being grilled by them, he understood Pam's concern. There was an edge to those ladies. Under the wrinkles and age spots, there was a sharp edge that deserved some respect and caution.

Page by page, moment by moment, he reviewed the meeting.

He froze, his breath held, mouth open. *Damn! They didn't! The file.* He recalled flipping through it after they left. What had he not seen? The folder from the NSA. Was it missing, or had he just not noticed it? *I notice everything. Maybe not the things that are missing.* "Damn, damn, damn, they got me."

CHAPTER 16

Milo stared in shock at the empty gallery wall. The price card holder hung alone and empty, teasing him with proof that this was the right place, the wrong day. Milo forced himself to breathe. Too many thoughts were contending for the same neurons, and the traffic jam was building to a collision and a very loud scream. Wait for it… wait for it. A burst of air, like a weak cough, escaped. He was hyperventilating. He *had* hung the painting here. He *had* put a price on it, because you didn't hang paintings in a gallery to look at, you hang them to sell. *But the wall is empty! Empty!*

"Juuuddddyyy?"

Judy, *clip-clopped* her way from the office, through the front viewing room to the secure inner gallery. She was crisp, thin, and young, with just enough sway in her walk, and a deep, sugar-sweet, southern accent. The perfectly devastating package for selling art, or anything to New York men.

"Did we sell this painting?" he asked, hoping against hope that she had some explanation that included the words *I moved it*.

"Yes," said Judy. "We sold it for the marked price. Is there something wrong?"

"How much was that again?" asked Milo, resting his shaking hand on his bloodless cheek.

"Eighty-two thousand. I assumed that it was okay to sell it at the marked price?"

She was right to assume that. Especially since she worked on commission and even in New York fifteen percent of $82,000 was a good paycheck for one week of work. He ran the numbers in his head. He had just made seventy thousand selling a painting that he didn't own. Never mind that the cops weren't going to deduct the commission; he was definitely falling headfirst into felony territory. The sale was unintentional.

Right! Who priced a painting and hung it in a gallery unintentionally? And what of the unintentional act of taking the canvas in the first place? Unintentional was a fast fleeing dream, soon to cross paths with a felony conviction.

He would be found out. No doubt about that. New York art buyers liked to show off what they spent money on. Especially that much money. The sale price alone would guarantee a growing public interest in the painter. Whoever that was, it was just a matter of time until the art world found the artist and uncovered the questionable sale. Then what? How long would it take for his other dealings to be examined? How long until Brenda was interviewed and the Krasner discovered?

How far can I get on seventy thousand? Mexico or Canada? Canada was closer. His head reeled with the implications. He would be found out. He needed to get ahead of this, now.

He dialed his phone and closed the office door behind him, shutting it in Judy's shocked face. “Mother?” he asked. “This is Brenda,” came the brittle reply. “Thanks for taking my painting.”

“It was my painting, dear sister.”

“Really?”

“Really,” answered Milo. “Just like the house you are living in and the food you are eating is mine. Now, let me speak to mother.”

“Milo, why are you so mean to your sister? Milo?” said Darla Stenopholis, in a cracking voice. Milo was reminded how seldom he spoke to her on the phone. She sounded so old on the phone. “Mama,” he began, “I need to know about the painting that I took from your room. It was yours, right?”

“You never call me Mama.”

***

He closed the gallery and turned off the lights. Mother had paid for the painting. That was good. But her disturbing ramble about having to return it as part of the deal muddied the water. If she owned the painting, he was safe. Maybe. There could still be a scandal. In his industry, rumor and innuendo were gospel. That he had priced the painting so high that it wouldn't sell was a proven false argument. It had sold. The bottom line was that he had the money and he knew who the artist was.

With a bill of sale, he could make it legal, hopefully before it was too late.

He would have to speak to Ruby Dunham, and explain that he got the painting from his mother who owed him money. Maybe the artist would be more interested in selling paintings than in pursuing any kind of ethics inquiry. Milo shook his head. That wasn't his kind of luck. Until he had a bill of sale in writing, from the artist, he was in trouble. For now he needed to wait. Maybe Ms. Dunham wouldn't notice a missing painting. Maybe. “Shit,” he said, wondering where he could stash the Krasner.

CHAPTER 17

When her friends arrived, Ruby put down her painting knife and joined in moving the benches around to match their best guess of the Cayman Island bank layout. In the two weeks that Bernice and Mini had been looking, they came up with only one partial photo of a lone gunman in the bank lobby. The gunman had been engaged in a failed robbery. The picture was eight years old.

Marybeth handed out guns made of scrap wood and broom sticks, and the drills began. Three runs through a simulated ingress, with changes in each scenario, succeeded in proving only that they weren't prepared for anything.

"Ruby, you're next, with the explosives," said Mini.

"Shouldn't we get this right first?" said Violet.

"We don't have to have it perfect. We just have to learn to adjust," said Mini.

Ruby turned to Mini. "Do you expect me to blow open a vault door while we are in the bank?" There, that was it, now that she could see the relative small size of the bank, there was no way she could detonate generic explosives while they were inside.

Violet injected thoughtfully. "What are you suggesting?"

"I need plastic explosives," said Ruby. "Shape charges to access the vault locks are the only way to do this without using so much stuff that we would blow up the whole building."

"Where do we get that, and why didn't you say something before?" said Marybeth.

"Oh no, I think I know where this is going," said Doris, covering her ears.

"I have a plan," Ruby grinned.

"2:00 pm power walk for Doris, Ruby, and Violet," said Marybeth as they broke.

Ruby detailed her plan to Violet and Doris during the walk. Afterward she wanted to paint, but her sore hip slowed her down. Opening the Ibuprofen bottle and seeing it mostly empty, she realized that she was not the only one that was tired and in pain. They were working themselves hard. Ruby felt like she was in better shape now, far more energetic than she had been in many years, but still there was the pain.

***

Tuesday morning, Doris received an early call. An old friend was at the flea market to buy a painting. Lin was still in the kitchen warming herself by the stove. "I was reading that cold weather inspires people to spend money," said Doris, winking at Violet.

Lin stared at her with disbelieving eyes.

"I read the same thing," said Bernice.

Lin looked to Violet, her eyes begging for grace. With a shake of her head, Violet pushed her out into the cold morning.

Bernice sighed deeply. "I was hoping she would stay so we could take a break."

"Amen to that," said Doris, along with a chorus of grunts from the others.

They listened to the van leave then bundled up for a day outside.

Doris wasn't feeling particularly adventurous, but the only rifle left for her at the target practice spot was a scoped hunting rifle that took cartridges twice the size of the AR-15's.

She fired once and felt like every bone from her jaw down to her toes had been realigned by a particularly evil chiropractor. The big rifle was just too much. "Why did we get a sniper rifle?"

"You have to pull it in tight to your shoulder," Marybeth reminded her, reading the pained expression.

Doris heard the big bell ringing. Marybeth collected rifles and lumbered toward the shed. Doris was thrilled to see the white Escalade, splashes of sunshine making it sparkle as it rolled under the trees.

Lester's eyes scanned the targets and the table with the handguns as he took long strides across the flattened grass to his bride to be. Smiling triumphantly, he whipped out a stack of printed boarding passes.

Doris beamed, throwing her arms around his neck. "You sweet man," she said, pleasing him very much.

Lester built a fire in the fireplace and generally made himself useful, changing light bulbs and even helping clean up targets from the field. If he had any qualms or questions about the ladies' new interest in guns, he didn't let on. If anything, he seemed impressed that Doris could make a tin can dance at thirty feet with a pistol.

***

Lin had enough of the cold. After selling two paintings, both to elderly people—where did these people come from that would drop so much money on a painting, anyway?—she packed it up. She was immensely curious about the gunfire coming from the direction of the orchard. Hayden stopped by and commented on it, as well. That they never heard it from the house made Lin wonder if it wasn't some trick of the ear, sound bouncing off a hill or following a creek.

She wasn't surprised to see the Escalade exit the gate as she neared the drive. Doris' engagement had inserted another level of uncertainty into daily life. She was still concerned that none of the staff would be going on the cruise. She'd checked and been encouraged that cruise lines were accustomed to catering to the elderly and had plenty of doctors and nurses aboard. What else could she do other than make sure the ladies all had updated medical information before they left?

Marybeth, Violet, and Ruby climbed the porch steps. Doris vanished into the apple shed, and Bernice sat in a sunny spot on the corner of the porch.

It annoyed Lin that no one seemed to care about the shooting. What if a stray bullet bounced toward the house? "I heard someone target shooting?" she said, approaching Bernice.

Bernice tapped her cane the usual double tap and answered without looking up, "Could have been anywhere the way sound travels out here."

She waited, but Bernice seemed focused on her reading.

She found Doris in the plastic-walled studio painting and asked straight away about the shooting. "Lester brought some guns for us to shoot. It was fun," said Doris, not looking up from her work. Lin squinted at her but got no more.

The poker game began on time. The fire, tended by Lin, roared. She read a magazine while the ladies dealt cards. Listening to the banter from the table, she was surprised at how little she understood. Someone would answer "yes" or "no" to a question she hadn't heard asked. A time would be given. At one point, she heard Doris say incongruently, "We sail in two weeks." An answer to a question never asked.

Finally, unable to stand it, she rose and went to the kitchen. Returning a moment later, she drifted toward the table. Bernice tapped the screen of her tablet, shutting it off, but not before Lin saw the text message window open. Scanning the table she noted that every one of the women had a phone or tablet out.

CHAPTER 18

The strained rumble of an overrevved car engine, pushed too hard by someone unfamiliar with driving rough country roads, rattled the windows of the house. "Oh goodness," said Bernice, tapping her cane and looking out the window.

"Poop," said Violet, looking out the window. "It's Irene." With less than two weeks and only a few hours each day to prepare, they did not need an interruption like Irene. It was the meanest thought she had had in a long time, but Violet smiled at the idea of Irene not able to get into the house for lack of a ramp. Sure enough, when she opened the door, Irene was in her chair with the wheels touching the bottom step.

Violet put on the smile she reserved for idiots and cops that were about to give her a ticket. Irene's response was a resolute, demanding click of the tongue. She expected access to the house. "Don't you have help?"

"This isn't Golden Lawn," said Violet, allowing herself a smile.

"Well, maybe you two can lift me," declared Irene, as Doris approached from the apple shed.

"Fat chance," cracked Doris, "That chair weighs more than I do."

Irene glanced at Doris and raised a skeptical eyebrow. Doris ignored her and jogged lightly up the steps and into the house. Anita tapped the minivan's horn and pointed toward the apple shed where a small table sat outside the door with pitchers of water and lemonade. Irene backed up and turned her chair, eliciting the second expletive of the day from Violet.

Anita glared at Violet. Violet returned a patient, *you're-an-idiot,* smile. Irene accelerated her chair toward the apple shed, where Ruby and Marybeth were walking through the itinerary and plan for the bank job.

***

From the studio, Ruby saw the minivan approach and swung into action. The day before the guns had been put away dirty. First thing this morning, they had been brought out to be cleaned. There were six rifles, and it took several fast trips to move them all into the back office of the shed.

Irene exited the van in record time and now, bored with Violet, trucked toward the shed, the tires of her chair churning through the gravel, kicking up a cloud of grit.

She must know that she isn't welcome. Ruby remembered a time when every day that the ladies showed up for the four o'clock game, Irene would already be there at the table. The first day, Doris had tried to talk to her, then given up and gone back to her room. It was the first time Ruby had heard Doris curse. And boy did she, loudly enough to be heard through the heavily insulated walls of the home.

After the bout of cursing, Doris returned to the great room and sat at another table. The others joined her while Irene stubbornly anchored herself at their regular table and fumed. Had she asked, she would almost certainly have been allowed to join the game, but each of these women were gifted with a stubborn streak that would not abide someone pushing themselves into their close group. Ruby supposed that it was cliquish and perhaps unkind, but Irene was argumentative, bossy, and everything that they tried to avoid being. Theirs was a clique, but one of true friendship. It was inclusive, made up of people who respected and loved one another. It was also exclusive. For good reason. Had Irene been allowed to join them at the card table, the peaceful nature of the group would have been tested, perhaps broken forever.

Ruby watched the power chair charge past the table, up the ramp toward the plastic covered door, and launched herself to swing it open just ahead of the chair's front wheels. Irene narrowly missed the easels and slowed only a little before pushing through the plastic curtain into the apple shed.

In the shed proper, Mini was stuffing solvent soaked newsprint from the benches into a trash bag. Irene blew past her and seeing the light from the office door, swung toward the ramp. Short of jamming a pipe in the spokes of her chair, there was no stopping her. She sped up the ramp and into the office.

"What in the world are you doing?" Demanded Ruby, following her. Irene didn't answer. Instead, she bellied up to the desk, examining the printed tickets for the cruise, then turning her attention to the computer where a map of Grand Cayman had been left up for the ladies to study.

Ruby's eyes fell to the storage cabinet. Thank goodness Marybeth had locked it before leaving. Irene was a nosy woman, and it wouldn't do to have her finding the cache of weapons.

Irene grunted. "What is this place?" she asked.

"It's our home," responded Ruby, doing her best to contain her annoyance and failing. The servos on the chair whined as Irene swung around examining the room and its contents. Once again, Ruby considered jamming an object into the chair's wheels. Her eyes lit on the stack of wooden practice guns about the same time that Irene noticed them.

Irene shoved the lever forward, swinging right just shy of the corner and reaching for a broom handle gun. She examined the toy for a moment then tossed it back, letting it fall to the floor as she turned toward the door.

At the bottom of the ramp, a landscape timber had been laid on the floor making it impossible for Irene and her chair to go anywhere but out. Mini and Marybeth consulted quietly against the benches. Irene waited several seconds for someone to respond to her grunts then, giving up, powered out through the plastic curtain.

Doris, waiting in the studio, opened the exterior door for Irene to pass. Ruby followed to find Violet and Bernice loading bags of trash in the van, the loud protests of Anita largely ignored.

"You have to take it," said Violet. "We have no trash service out here. It's the least you could do."

"Bullshit!" groused Irene. "The least we could have done is not come at all."

"Maybe next time," said Ruby.

***

Irene grumbled the whole way home, the bags of trash leaning on the back of her seat. She had expected something more out of the trip. An hour drive each way, and the first forty five minutes listening to her daughter complain that she was violating some law or the other by inviting themselves onto private property. *Bull!* No one was going to arrest them for opening a gate. Posted sign or not, she knew the owners and that made it a visit, not a crime. She wasn't sure what her daughter had gotten into that made her so nervous about crossing the law, but nothing would surprise her. The brat had always been impulsive and stubborn. Irene despised those qualities in any person.

As if that weren't enough, the adult child was always getting into other people's business. Another thing she couldn't stand. Demanding to know what her mother wanted with going out to see her friends at the orchard. Mostly friends. Doris had been stuck up as usual, wagging her fat ass around like she was queen of the jungle. How a slut like that attracted a man of Lester's quality was a mystery. Had she overestimated Lester's intellectual and moral fiber?

Those girls and their orchard. They were up to something out there. Lester had as much as said so when she last spoke to him. Not that she was being nosy, it was perfectly reasonable to keep track of one's friends. Asking about them was the way she showed concern. Lester hesitated before answering. Then he came right out and told her that he and Doris were engaged to be married. Lester, poor, blind Lester was going to marry that, that woman of low character. The man was just no good. A good man would have chosen better.

The trash bags were the final insult. Twice, on the way home, she spotted dumpsters that would be likely repositories for the rubbish. Both times she hesitated. Now, she was glad that she had. A new idea had taken hold.

"Back in and take these trash bags into the garage. We're going to see what's in them," she barked at Anita, as they approached the house.

"You must be kidding."

"I'm not."

In the garage, Anita reluctantly did her mother's bidding and set up the folding tables. When the last bag was out of the van, Irene ordered her to close the door and open one of the bags.

"Isn't this illegal?" balked Anita.

"They gave it to us. You might even say they forced it on us," said Irene. "Now open the darn bag."

Anita hefted a black bag to the table and swept it with a box knife. The contents, including the smell of rotten milk, and something unidentifiably sour, spilled out onto the table.

She ran from the room, returning a half minute later with a can of air freshener. Irene snatched it from her hand and began spraying with one hand, her nose covered with the other.

"Get my rubber gloves," commanded the old woman.

Anita fled into the house again. This time she was away for several minutes. Irene grew impatient and began to bleat.

"Hush, mother," honked Anita, her fingers pinching her nose. "You sound like a sick goat."

"You sit here smelling this and see how you sound. Turn on the fan and open the side door." This time, the girl didn't complain. The breeze from the fan brought in a puff of fresh air, but very soon even that was polluted.

"Mother, this is awful."

"I want to know what they're up to! They gave us this stuff; let's see what it tells us." Irene pulled the elbow length gloves up as far as they would go then snapped them to settle her fingers. At her direction, Anita made another cut across the bag, spilling some of the contents onto the floor. Somewhere in this collection of soup cans, milk cartons and bottles there was a clue to what the poker playing bitches were up to, and Irene was going to find it even if Anita had to pick through every piece.

Anita shook her head. "Mother, I am not doing this. You have the gloves, you do it," she said. Irene watched her go, wondering where the child had gone wrong. Enough of that. She raised her chair and positioned herself with the fan at her back.

She hadn't a clue what she was looking for. Cans and bottles she set aside. The bag was surprisingly empty of bills or stubs. She supposed that they burned or shredded stuff like that. In the third bag, she came across a whole layer of crumpled paper. On a whim, she flattened the pages. The first page was nothing, just a sketch of boxes… *perhaps a furniture arrangement?* She set it aside. The next was a similar sketch only less complete. She continued, stacking all of the similar items together.

Eventually she found a bill that had been torn to little pieces and required clear tape to reassemble. Other than Violet's name and address of the Orchard, which she already knew, there was nothing of clear value.

There were Ensure cans. A lot of Ensure cans. "They don't have money to buy real food," she said with a smug smile.

A rough metal edge on a bean can scratched her finger. The can had a hole punched in it from one side to the other, and the poked out metal was sharp. Another can had seven holes in it. Four going in and three coming out. The can rattled. She turned it over and a smashed ball of lead about the size of a pencil eraser fell out. She'd never seen one before, but this looked like a small bullet.

"Let's get lunch," she demanded, her chair whining to life but no one answering.

She was tired from all the goings on and didn't make it back to the garage until late afternoon. This time, with a little help from Anita clearing out the useless stuff like milk cartons, she thought she was beginning to see a pattern. The cans and bottles, there were lots of them, were from target shooting. Lord knows, they were target shooting a lot out there. Hundreds of rounds fired. She had empty cartridges, empty cartridge boxes, and fifty or more tin cans, milk jugs, and small boxes with bullet holes in them.

Then there were the drawings. Most were just block sketches, but several had ovals with smaller ovals drawn on top. Those had dashed lines, like trails, that all started near the same place. The objects were scattered around the page. On some of the drawings, they were numbered.

Irene rubbed her tired eyes. Tomorrow. Tomorrow, she would come back to this and, maybe it would make sense. Today, she had missed her soaps. Thank God for digital recorders.

The last two pages were stuck together. She separated them. What was she seeing? She pushed up her glasses and examined the page through the bifocal. Finally, it struck her. No numbers. The figures had letters, not numbers. M, V, Mb, B, and R. Mini, Violet, Marybeth, Bernice, and Ruby. No D for Dumbass Doris. Maybe she was one of the other shapes. Some were labeled T, others C, and still others with a G. It looked like one of those play diagrams on the Sunday afternoon football games.

Target practice and play sheets. *What was this?*

***

Lester examined the tiny locomotive through a magnifying headset, the single strand of the brush ready to apply a layer of thinned copper enamel to the pipe rail on the side of the engine. His hand shook, and the magnified tip of the brush went rapidly in and out of focus. With a groan, he put the locomotive on its block and dipped the brush into a bottle cap of thinner.

For a while it had worked, coming down here to take his mind off of things. Working with his hands had always been good for that, good for working things out. But not tonight. Tonight, it was all made a little fuzzier by the late hour.

He glanced at the clock. Midnight thirty. Way too late for an old man to be painting a toy train. Doris called around noon, and he'd gotten the distinct impression that he had done something wrong. She didn't outright say he had or hadn't. She simply posed a question in the conversation that he knew the answer to. "I just wonder how Irene found out where we live," she said.

What stuck in Lester's craw and kept him up so late was that he hadn't answered. By omission, he lied to his bride to be, not out of any need to cover up anything but out of his need to be perfect. To not have done something blindly stupid.

He knew that there were issues with Irene. Nobody really liked her. She was pushy and boldly self serving. Even while he pursued Doris, she had outright hit on him a dozen times. Sometimes with a forthrightness that shocked him. Once, she asked him to help her move a box in her room. He was glad enough to assist, but when she closed the door behind him, he got a whiff of Chanel and began to feel like a trapped animal. Lester shook his head. He had gone the long way around, over the bed, to get to the door and freedom.

The woman was a pain in the backside of everyone she knew, but still he had not been able to say "no" to her when she asked where the girls were living. Was it because he felt sorry for her? He couldn't be sure what he felt, except tired.

He picked up a book from the lamp table. Maybe reading would help him clear his mind and sleep.

***

Anita stumbled through the kitchen, her worn pink slippers slapping the floor. She poured herself a bowl of cereal and opened the fridge. No milk.

Her slippers stuck to the sandpaper-like surface of the ramp into the garage making her feel like she would trip and fall forward with each step. She hated the garage when it was cold.

The milk from the garage fridge had ice in it. She shook the jug to break it up. The place reeked of garbage. She glanced over the tables, pausing to thumb through the stack of drawings. They looked like someone had superimposed some kind of play chart on top of the counter layout of a store or bar. *Humph.*

The coffee was getting cold by the time Irene motored into the kitchen. Of course, she complained. Anita made another pot while Irene babbled on about all of the target shooting at the orchard. It took Anita a few minutes to catch on that the cans and jugs with the holes in them were the targets she was going on about. There were a lot of them.

She stared out the window, chomping on soggy cereal. Her mind drifted. Suddenly, she was on her feet, whipping a rolled up sock from her robe pocket and shoving it into Irene's mouth. She finished with double wrap of duct tape binding the old woman's wrists to the chair arms. Satisfied, she sat and ate in peace.

"I said, target practice and play sheets," barked Irene, shattering the beautiful dream.

"What? Do you think they're planning to rob a bank or something?" said Anita.

She froze, her spoon dripping over the table. There it was, that feeling that she had just stepped in something. Only this time, it wasn't her in trouble. She dropped her spoon and trotted to the garage, leaving the slippers under the table.

Irene begged, pled, then demanded that she explain. Anita ignored her.

It was all right in front of her. The old ladies were broke. Bobby had cleaned them out. An envelope from the county was empty, but the Tax Assessors office didn't send birthday cards, did they? Chances were they owed money.

They were broke, but they had money to spend on guns and ammunition. *How much did that cost?* Anita had no idea, but hungry people didn't throw money away on stuff like that. Not these people. They were half-living on cans of protein drink. They were up to no good, and the plans proved it.

The plans… the plans *were* like football plays.

"Mom, they're going to rob a bank or something." *Maybe they already have,* she thought. "Your crazy friends really are crazy."

"They're not my friends," said Irene.

CHAPTER 19

Ruby half-slid, half-ran down the steep red clay bank and into the dried mud of the road construction site, one arm swinging wildly in the air and the other weighed down by the heavy bolt cutters. They tried to make it look innocent in case there were eyes watching. Violet had a jack under the car and a lug wrench in hand, but the moment anyone saw Ruby anywhere near the metal shed labeled DANGER, they would know everything they needed to put them both in jail.

Violet watched as her mountain-born friend reached the shack and without preamble applied the bolt cutters to the lock. She pushed the door open, and for a moment, only her bent over backside in the faded red dress was available for public viewing. Then, she straightened, and Violet could see that she had a box in her hand.

Ruby closed the shed door and hung the broken lock in the hasp. The rumble of construction machinery growing louder, she took three large strides away from the shed, then turned back. She had forgotten the bolt cutters.

Violet half hoped that Ruby would toss them in the bushes before they were noticed. The rumbling road grader was only a quarter mile away and coming.

This was the third site they had visited today. The first had been easy, but full of nothing. The second site had been too busy. Like this site, the explosives shed was away from the digging, but the foreman's trailer had been too close. This looked like it might be a success. Ruby scrambled up the bank, using the bolt cutters as a climbing tool while Violet hefted the jack and spare tire back into the trunk.

Finding the site had not been the hardest part, nor had breaking in been that hard. The hard part had been getting a car. Violet had begged and pleaded with Lin to borrow her car. Sweet little Lin had been suspicious little Lin. “Why can’t I drive you?”

"Because we're going to commit a felony," Violet wanted to, and almost did, say. Being honest would have been so much easier than the half-truths they had been dealing out lately. *We need the money for the paintings, but we really need you out of the way,* would be a good one. Or, *could you take us all to get new glasses so we can see to shoot straight?* Violet tossed the lug wrench into the trunk. Ruby, breathing heavily, dropped the bolt cutters in the trunk but held onto the red painted ammo can with the conspicuous "Explosives" label. The look in her eye made it clear that they needed to be gentle with the can full of blasting caps.

Now to Walmart, so their story for Lin would be at least partly true.

"Where do you plan to get explosives to go with those blasting caps?" asked Violet as they passed the last barrel marking the construction zone.

"From the ATF," said Ruby.

***

Keith Novak transferred from border patrol to ATF one year and three days before. Many times since, he had wondered about the wisdom of his move. On the border, things had been relatively simple. If they were going north, you arrested them. If they shot at you, you took cover then shot back. Decisions were made somewhere else and arrived in the form of orders.

Here, in the ATF, politics seemed to be a daily game. While generally agents supported one another as all cops should, support was buffered with the knowledge that one little screw up could get you moved to the bottom of the promotions list. No promotion meant no pay raise. Keith learned that the hard way. He also learned that you didn't have to screw up to make that leap to the bottom. You only needed a partner to screw up.

He was looking at that partner now with a certain amount of awe. *How could anyone think up such a dumb-ass plan?*

"Look, it works," said Dalton. "We've used this same sting model a hundred times with success ninety-five. You can't do better than that."

Keith couldn't help but wonder if the five percent of failures were all on Dale Dalton's watch. The man had the look of a good undercover man and the vibe of a dumb criminal. Unfortunately, it wasn't exactly an act.

The worst of it was that he was beginning to recognize the cycle but never soon enough to put the brakes on. He could sense the jovial, frat boy, attitude of his partner that signaled the birth of a new bad idea. Dale would laugh and wink and go on talking up whatever idiotic plan he had. If Keith tried to stop him, he would say he was going out to lunch or make up some other excuse, and an hour later, when he had not returned, Keith would know that once again an entry would be made in his file and whatever dreams he dared dream would be on hold for a few more years.

"Is that real?" asked Keith, pointing at the open case full of paper-wrapped blocks labeled C-4.

"Of course, it's real," said Dalton. "You can't fake this stuff. I think it would actually be a crime to fake these labels and duplicate the serial numbers, and you sure as hell can't remove the labels. That's definitely a no-no. It's all numbered batches so it can be tracked."

Keith stared, his skepticism obvious.

"Hey, it's going to work. I promise," said Dale Dalton. "Numbered batches, tracked. We won't have any problem," he said, closing the case with the six blocks of plastic explosive inside. "It's our chance to make a good bust, and you know, maybe not be on the shit list all the time."

Keith wondered if that were even possible at this point. They were on that list because of ops like this. Could they break that cycle, or would this attempt end as all others, in depressed frustration?

"No backup?" asked Keith, sitting in the parking lot of a CVS drug store an hour later.

"You're my backup, buddy," responded Dalton with a chuckle.

"You got to be freaking kidding me. Six pounds of C-4, and we've got no backup?" Keith couldn't believe that he had fallen for it again. What happened to *this is a fuli-on operation?* Or, *we've got a full team on this?* Keith hung his head in shame. *When will I learn?*

"Cheer up, buddy, it doesn't look like anyone is going to show. Probably your standard cop haircut that scared him off. Dalton tossed his own dark curly mane over his shoulder.

Keith scanned the cars for the tenth time just in case someone that could be their contact magically appeared. The '98 Volvo wagon in the corner probably belonged to the pharmacist. The faded red Chevy next to it with the fuzzy dice hanging from the mirror had to be the pride and joy of the cashier. The pickup that just left was loaded with a concrete mixer and enough scrapes and dents to prove that it was the real deal. The Honda two spaces away had just ejected two old ladies. Two more sat in the front waiting for their friends.

An old woman with a wide bandage across her nose stumbled in front of their black government suburban. She caught herself and straightened her healthy figure with uncertainty written across what they could see of her face. She turned back, then back again. Keith knew that feeling. The woman was lost. "Come on. Let's do something right," he said, getting out of the car.

Dalton followed, "What are you going to do, help her across the street?"

"If that's what she needs."

The woman mumbled while she walked. It reminded him of some of the people he had found on the border that had run out of water in the summer. "Ma'am, my name is Keith, how can I help you?"

"Oh for Christ's sake, how original is that?" said Dalton, laughing at some internal joke.

"Robert, Robert," said the woman, grabbing onto Keith's arm. "Your mother told me to watch out for you and make sure you stay out of trouble. Who is this boy with you? Is that the Bradley boy? I think your mother should know who you're hanging out with." She looked up at him in that way that mothers do that makes you want to throw up your hands in surrender.

"Yes, ma'am," said Keith. "That's the Bradley boy. He's always in trouble."

"Yes, he is," agreed the woman, glaring at Dalton.

"Do you need your medication?" asked Dalton with as much smarm as he could load into so few words.

"Yes, yes, I do. Thank you, Mr. Bradley. Shouldn't you be in school?"

“I'm skipping today,” said Dalton, clearly enjoying himself.

“Robert, can you help me find my medicine,” asked the woman wrapping her arm through his. “And tell little Mr. Bradley to come with us. I intend to call his mother.”

Dalton laughed, “Ohhh, we're in trouble.”

The woman, her round face suddenly serious, stared him in the eye, “You are, Mr. Bradley.”

“Well, I'm skipping, so I'll stay here while you go call my mother,” said Dalton, nervously laughing off the threat.

Led by Keith, the woman turned toward the store's main door. Only a few steps along, she slipped and fell to one knee. She was much heavier than she looked, and Keith could barely slow her fall.

“Shit,” said Dalton, rolling his eyes and locking the car with the remote.

Between them, they carried her into the drug store, zigzagging their way to the back where they lowered her into a waiting chair in the pharmacy.

“Stay with me, Robert, just for a few minutes.”

“Ma'am, I'd like to, but my name isn't really Robert.”

“Nonsense. I've known you since before you were born.”

***

From the car, Ruby watched Doris' magical performance. It was so good that she almost forgot to hold the button of her little black box down when Dalton lifted the remote to lock the Suburban.

Almost.

The box that Ruby held cost only a hundred dollars online. It promised to effectively block or scramble the locking codes of most cars built before 2019. Its purpose was to stop a car from being locked by remote.

Ruby watched Doris enter the store, one man supporting each arm. Just inside, Mini passed in front of the door and gave a thumbs up. Bernice would be backing Mini up inside. Only Marybeth had stayed home, everyone feeling that she was too tall and memorable.

Ruby left the Honda and walked as steadily as she could across the lot. She opened the back door of the suburban and breathing a heavy sigh of relief, extracted the aluminum Haliburton case.

She turned in time to see Mini step out of the store pushing a cart and throw a warning hand like a school crossing guard toward her before swinging the cart back into the door blocking it. The agents were coming out sooner than expected, and Mini was buying Ruby a few precious seconds. But for what? She couldn't get to the car without being in view of the doors with the silver case in hand, and it was too late to run.

Violet waved her away. Ruby froze.

Mini's cart slowly withdrew into the store. In seconds, the door would be clear, and the agents would find Ruby with the case of explosives.

Stepping quickly to the curb, she jammed the case behind a concrete trash can and strolled as calmly as possible to the car, passing the frustrated federal agents as they exited the store.

Violet backed the car out, swinging past the door as the other three women exited, turning away from the suburban. She slowed, and the women piled into the car, barely getting the doors closed before she punched the gas. Ruby held on as Violet swung into the street going the wrong way, then dove into the adjacent parking lot and slammed on the brakes behind a hedge.

Ruby jumped out. She had to see the Feds leave. If they didn't leave, or if they came around the building on foot, she would know that the case was found, and they would have to pull a disappearing act.

She leaned on a lamp post and waited, each second more certain that they had discovered the case missing and were searching for the perpetrators. Abruptly, the black Suburban, its dark windows hiding the men inside, swung around the corner toward her. The muscles around her bowels clenched in fear. The suburban came straight at her, then swerved at the last second swinging out into traffic and away.

Ruby felt woozy and suddenly exhausted.

The case! They needed that case! She pushed through the hedge and sprinted across the lot, her slippers slapping her heels.

A minute later, she stared at the empty space behind the trash receptacle with her hands up and open like she was receiving the gift of confusion from God himself. Violet stood on the curb where the extra eight inches allowed her to see over the hedges. "I don't see anyone with a case. If they found it, they would be looking for us, right?"

Ruby scanned the lot and surrounding buildings. "I didn't see another car. Whoever took it could be on foot," she said, thinking aloud and sliding back into the car.

"Which way?" Violet asked, closing the door and slipping the clutch simultaneously.

"Right," answered Ruby, guessing.

Violet eased out onto the boulevard, swinging her head both ways, slowly like some kind of mechanical clown.

"There," hollered Bernice, pointing up the alley behind a hardware store. A man, shabbily dressed, bent with age and alcohol, shambled up the narrow alleyway with a shiny aluminum case in hand. Violet swung the car into an adjoining parking lot, then cut across a patch of grass and sped down the alley, narrowly missing the man before swinging to a hard stop and blocking his way.

***

Freddy watched the women exit the car, dread consuming him. His whole life he had been running from one woman or another and now he counted five, all after him at once. How did they know who he was, and why oh, why could they not just leave him alone?

Freddy Black, king of whatever alley he slept in on a given night, turned and fled.

Behind him, he could hear the angry footfalls of two ex-wives and the one that he had left but never divorced and the daughter that cried and tried to bring him home to a house full of children and nothing to drink. He was terrified.

He was also tired, and weighed down by a fifth of Mad Dog 20/20, half in the gut and the other half banging against his hip, the heavy bottle threatening to jump out of his pocket. Oh, what a dilemma. Slow down and protect the magic juice or run for your life. He chose the third option, the one that hadn't quite gelled in his fuzzy brain. He turned to fight.

The five women crashed into him, grabbing and reaching—just like Ingrid, wife number two—to take his bottle away. If they got it, they would pour it out. They might even be cruel enough to hand him the empty bottle so he could suck the last lazy drop from it. He pushed the bottle deep in the pocket of the ragged sport coat and screamed, "Help! Somebody help me!"

He felt them tugging at his clothes. *Are they really that desperate?* Needing both hands to protect the bottle, he let the shiny case he'd found go. He never heard it hit the ground, but that didn't matter so much, the grabby hands were failing, and he wasn't losing after all. "Heeeeellllp!" he continued to scream. "Hey, that's mine," he said, pointing an unsteady finger at the case being hauled away by a thin woman.

"No, no, this belongs to the federal government," said the woman.

Another one—where did she come from?—slapped him. "Hey," she barked, waving a fiver in his face. "Get another bottle." He smiled and breathed a deep sigh of relief. The woman flinched away from his wine heavy breath, turning toward the open door of the car. In his moment of freedom, Freddy realized that a great opportunity was getting away.

"Will you marry me?" he yelled, as the car sped away.

***

Relieved at the relatively non-career-ruining day, Keith actually enjoyed a fast food lunch with his partner, finishing off his onion rings as they passed through security into the Federal Building parking garage. They'd thought about a sit-down meal but didn't dare leave the vehicle unattended. Even the FBI had been embarrassed recently when weapons had been stolen from their vehicles. How much worse would it be if they lost explosives?

"Where's the case?" he asked, staring blankly at the empty back floor of the Suburban.

"Is this some kind of joke?" demanded Dalton. "I put it right there."

Keith stared at the emptiness, wondering just how far down he could go before they mercifully fired him. Pretty far, he thought, recalling several incidents of incompetence that bordered on malfeasance. *Oh, that was us,* he realized. *So, maybe that doesn't count in our favor.* “I'm going home,” he said to Dalton. “I never saw you today. I didn't come into work. I wasn't feeling well, and you certainly did not pick me up from home to take me to a parking lot where someone stole six pounds of C-4 from you. Got that?”

CHAPTER 20

In the dusty cool of the apple shed, Violet waited her turn then scooted through the mock-up door, rifle in hand and ready. There was a new energy here. The successful acquisition of the C-4 was a milestone for the group. Each of them, with the possible exception of Mini, needed to know in her own way that she was capable of robbing a bank. Stealing explosives from the government seemed to be close enough to put that question to rest. One could argue that they had committed a felony together, but the ladies of the poker club took the more pragmatic view that their tax dollars had paid for the C-4 that they needed. The government owed them that much for letting Bob Robbins get away.

The operation also proved that they could depend on one another when the consequences of failure meant prison time. It was the kind of boost they needed. The ladies were no longer a poker club; they were a gang.

Time and again, they ran through the drills, until finally Doris complained that it was hot and dusty inside. She was right. They needed a change to go along with their new status. It was time to do some real training.

Violet towed the tires out with the tractor and the ladies ran tire drills in the yard, this time with real guns in hand. Mini impressed all by running the tires frontward and backward. From the tires, they zigzagged through the trees to the field where they each fired five rounds before clearing the weapon and rejoining the group.

Next, they advanced in pairs, one firing five rounds, then the other firing while the first loaded another magazine and advanced. The training was completely outside what they planned to do at the bank, but it was fun, and to Violet's mind it was proof that they were becoming a serious force.

***

Lin crept through the dense lowland brush following the voices and gunshots. Whatever the women were up to made a lot of noise. Far more than the squish of wet shoes or the whoosh of briars that finally let go of her jeans. Her white shoes were clay red with a nice smear of mud brown across the top of the left one. *Why didn't I walk up the road?*

A burst of rifle fire was very close. Lin went to the ground, gasping. She'd sat up in a tangle of wild berry vines. Her sweater was snagged in a dozen places, and the thorns had scratched the back of her hand bloody. To extricate herself, she had to let the vine take the sweater.

"It's my best sweater, and I'm not leaving it," said Lin, prying the thorns out of the wool.

Another burst of gunfire. Five shots. It was impossible to tell for sure, but the hollow ringing made her feel like the sound was being blocked by the buildings. If she had any kind of luck, the shooting would be taking place on the other side of the house, maybe in the field where they'd had the bonfire.

She moved on up the hill where the ground was dryer and the leaves and sticks cracked beneath her feet. Lin pulled the last of the thorns from her sweater and hung it over her shoulders. She could see the house now. The next burst of gunfire echoed off the shed. She paused behind a tree like a child playing hide and seek, then snuck a look around.

Doris, in tights and a long blouse, high-stepped through an obstacle course of tires. Lin watched in shock as the old woman ran across the yard, rifle in hand and scarf tied around her head Rambo style. At the tree line, Doris worked her way from one tree to the next until she had a clear view of the field. She withdrew a magazine from her waist band, inserted it into the rifle, fired five shots at a target, then safed the rifle and jogged back to where she had started.

Bernice took the rifle from Doris, cleared it, and began to copy the process.

Lin slid to the ground behind the apple shed, hugging her knees. She'd witnessed something so bizarre and inexplicable that she needed time to process.

***

Lin sat on the living room floor and listened to the impossible story.

"We just want to be able to protect ourselves," said Ruby, repeating the theme of the last twenty minutes. The woman stank of paint thinner. Her fingers danced in the air as she spoke, as if she were painting the words. Maybe she was, in her mind.

"Look," said Lin, "I don't care about the guns or your little trips into the city. I don't care what you do, as long as it's legal, you don't get hurt, and it doesn't get me in trouble."

A sudden hush fell over the room. Marybeth rubbed her hands. Bernice tapped her cane nervously. Rudy stared into space. Mini walked away. Doris read a magazine. Violet would not look at her. The silence was as thick as the paint fumes emanating from Ruby's hands.

"What is this really about?" Lin asked, not sure she wanted to know.

"It's not legal," said Marybeth.

Violet shot Marybeth a laser glare that shut her down.

"Oh for heaven's sake, we owe her the truth," said Marybeth.

"What truth?" said Lin.

"We're going to rob Bob Robbins and get our money back," said Doris.

Lin laughed. Then she didn't.

***

Ruby felt a smile creeping across her face that she couldn't stop. Elton had once told her that she would be a terrific actor, but she couldn't fake sad. He said that no matter what she did, her eyes still twinkled. No one would believe a sad girl with happy eyes. She never told him the truth, that he was the one that put the twinkle there.

Lin was taking it all well. She hadn't shown the slightest sign of fainting. Nor had she run from the room to call the police. Both were likely outcomes that Ruby had imagined. The girl did seem a little angry, though.

"You sit there like you're lined up for a school picture and pretend that this is nothing? Every day I come out here to take care of you, to help you, make sure you don't get hurt. I take you to the doctor when you need it. I watch after you. And you're out running obstacle courses and… Are you going to shoot people? What else are you not telling me?"

Ruby's phone dinged simultaneously with Violet's. She took it from her apron pocket and wiped a smudge of paint from the screen before checking the message. It was from Mini, who stood in the kitchen door just feet away.

"Tell her about the explosives," it read.

Ruby glanced up at Vi. Violet cringed and closed her eyes seeking some internal peace. Ruby knew that path. She also knew that Mini was right. This was the time to come completely clean.

"We should tell her," said Ruby.

Violet nodded, then opened her eyes.

"Tell me what?" said Lin.

Violet shook her head and looked to Ruby.

"We have some explosives, too. Just small stuff. I'm in charge of that because I know about bombs," said Ruby, scratching a spot of paint from the side of her nose.

"You know about bombs? Who are you people? Where did you get explosives?"

"I grew up in a mining town, so I come by my knowing about explosives honest. As for where we got the stuff, we probably shouldn't say. We don't want to get you in trouble," said Ruby.

Doris snorted.

A howl of laughter rolled from the kitchen.

"I should check on Mini before she hurts herself," said Doris.

Lin ignored her and pressed forward. "You didn't answer my question. Are you going to shoot people?" Her eyes traveled face to face looking for someone to see her point.

Ruby could see it but knew already that Lin would be disappointed in her answer. They were serious. They had to be or this wouldn't work. They had all considered the other options and decided in their own way that violence, should it come to that, was a reasonable course of action if it was what had to be done.

It had to be done. The little man had stolen more than money. He had stolen their dignity. It was the one thing that none of them could live without. Each had taken a different path to this place, but all were of one mind regarding the solution. They wanted their comforts, but they *needed* to look in the mirror and see someone they were proud to be. This was the way they chose to restore their souls.

It wasn't profitable to think of what-ifs. Whatever happened, happened. They weren't going to shoot any innocent guards. The idea was to overwhelm them so that shooting wasn't necessary. The training was about having the confidence to project power. They had to look serious so that the guards would take them seriously. A bunch of old ladies stumbling into a bank would be just the kind of unserious show that would get someone shot. She wondered if there was a way to explain that.

Violet spoke up. "We won't have to. Not if we do this right. If we do it right, there won't be any question about who is in charge and no one will get hurt."

Lin shook her head violently, "In charge? How can you be so sure? And how do you think you can get away with this? You don't think someone will recognize you?"

It was Ruby's turn to smile again. "Not where we're going."

***

Hours had passed since the initial confrontation. Lin sat in the corner of the living room watching the comings and goings. There were huge holes in the plan. No arrangements had been made to get to Fort Lauderdale to board the ship. They couldn't carry the guns on a plane without checking them. She hadn't known you could do even that until she looked it up.

Lin would have to help. They needed someone to drop them off in Florida.

In two hours, she had gone from concerned helper to co-conspirator, assisting them in planning a bank robbery. Did the Cayman Islands have an extradition treaty with the US? Would the US send her to the island for trial? Did they have a prison on the island?

"Nothing you do can ever be seen as you helping us do this," Violet said.

She got it. The ladies were old and if caught would probably serve little to no time in jail. She was young and wouldn't enjoy that kind of grace. "I need to know something," said Lin. "I need to know that you are only going to take what belongs to you, and how you know what that is?"

"Oh, that's simple," said Ruby, "We're going to take everything he has. He's keeping it all in bearer bonds in his safe deposit box."

Lin drove home that night wondering just how long it would take for the cops to figure out who robbed only the safe deposit box of Bob Robbins. Maybe the ladies should consider robbing all the boxes to hide their trail.

CHAPTER 21

Eduardo stood on the dock gazing at the *Ellie Maye.* The boat was beautiful. A Bertram sixty-three footer with a custom cabin and twin diesels that would cruise at thirty knots and top out at thirty-four. That would be nice if they needed it, but they weren't planning on needing it. He hadn't been aboard yet, but the best part could be seen from the dock, the putting green on the foredeck. He hoisted his bag and waved to Manuel. Manuel waved back from the bridge and came to meet him.

“It’s a nice boat, Jefe. And we are only borrowing it?”

Technically, they *were* borrowing the boat. For a while, Eduardo would become Roberto Gonzales, son of the boat's owner Javier Gonzales. The real Roberto hated boats, and though the yacht was known in harbors around the Caribbean, the son was not.

“Only borrowing, unless we like it,” said Eduardo.

Manuel laughed.

“You must be careful of my name. I am Roberto for as long as we are on the boat,” said Eduardo.

“Sorry, Roberto. I forgot that you would be coming back a new man. Where have you been while we have been getting this beautiful boat ready, Roberto?” said Manuel, with a smirk.

“I have been with my father. Listening to stories and learning who I am to become for the next few weeks.”

Manuel drew back, and Ed laughed. Manuel, he knew, had been with Luis for two of the last four days. “This father,” he said, waving the new passport and letting Manuel examine it. His friend nodded appreciatively, recognizing the quality.

“This is someone you know well then?”

Ed nodded, “I do, now. He is a business acquaintance of Papa's.”

Manuel and the crew had been busy preparing the borrowed yacht for the trip through the Panama Canal and up the east coast of

Guatemala. The bunkers were full of diesel, the pantries were stocked, and the engines in top shape.

The Coast Guard would inspect them in Panama and ask them where they were bound. Aboard, they would find Roberto Gonzales (Eduardo), his friend Manuel, and a crew of three—captain, chief engineer, and chef and chief steward. All three of the crew, Diego, Mateo, and Jesus, were employees of Luis Salizar.

It worked out well to borrow the yacht. An old fishing boat, like those found along the Guatemalan coast, full of men who were not fishermen would attract the attention of customs officials. A luxury yacht with tanned, well-dressed men aboard would be unremarkable.

They got underway within the hour, then stopped and waited, and waited again. Though Eduardo was prepared for a learning experience aboard the yacht, he was not prepared to wait two days to enter the Panama canal. Nor was he ready to be inspected so many times.

Diego, the captain, had done this many times. He tried to explain the procedures to Eduardo ahead of time in deference to the boss, but eventually gave up and simply did his job.

At Bocas Del Toro, the east coast of Costa Rica, they made port, were inspected by customs, refueled, and took on another man hired by Luis.

Eduardo was glad to be done with the canal. He'd seen the way the pilot looked at him and Manuel during the crossing. It was well-known that Roberto Gonzales was less than masculine. It was his cover, and Eduardo could live with it, but he didn't have to like it.

They cleared port in Bocas Del Toro, then met a fishing boat only a few miles into international waters. In a less than delicate operation, the fishing boat swung a net over and delivered two crates. The crew opened the crates and the contents, six submachine guns, two shotguns, eight pistols, and four M-16 rifles, were stowed below deck.

CHAPTER 22

"Let's take one with the guns and one without," suggested Lin, heading off the argument that was brewing. Lately, they were arguing about everything. Today, it was a group picture.

Violet winked at Lin. They'd come a long way in the two weeks since they'd come clean with her. A long way, but Lin wasn't satisfied. Violet could tell. She wanted to do more, but the rules had been made to protect her as much as anyone else. She was only allowed to help with everyday chores. Nothing she did could ever be connected to them robbing the bank.

The ruse of selling paintings to get her out of the house was over. Having Lin back full time was a blessing. The accelerated training and exercise program had worn them all down, and having the additional housekeeping had pretty much finished them off. The cruise would be a wonderful break, but Vi sometimes wondered if, once on the ship, they would decide not to leave it to do the job.

Packing was done, except for Doris who seemed to change her mind hourly on what to take. No surprise there. It was her wedding, honeymoon, and first bank robbery all rolled into one. They'd voted that someone stay on the ship to cover for them and be an emergency contact. Doris, who would be a newlywed by then, was the natural choice. It fit with Violet's sense of decency that a woman just married would not be involved in a violent enterprise.

That did not go over well with Doris. "Are you sure you want me in the picture?" she asked, bumping Violet's elbow.

Violet would have laughed but for fear of hurting Doris even more. Doris turned and winked. Violet *did* laugh.

Lin looked around, her finger counting heads again. Ruby was missing.

"She's over there," said Lin pointing to the apple shed where Ruby leaned on the warm plank siding, her phone stuck to the side of her head and deep wrinkles of concern creasing her forehead. Violet's mind jumped to all kinds of possibilities, any of which could put the brakes on their plans. But that was just worry, wasn't it? They were just going on a cruise and celebrating a wedding. If anything went wrong, they could dump the guns overboard and move on with life. No, whatever was keeping Ruby would be personal. Maybe something they would have to deal with, but personal.

Speaking of Ruby, Violet couldn't quite reach the shard of rock that was embedded in the pecan tree above her, a remnant of the previous day's activities. Ruby thought it would be a good idea to test the explosives. The blasting caps, she said, were the only thing she was sure about. The detonators were just battery packs and switches that locked to prevent accidents.

Ruby selected a boulder near the fire pit and made a cone shaped charge of plastic explosive to sit on top of the rock. She unspooled wire from the rock to the front porch of the house over two hundred feet away—surely a safe distance—and carefully connected the detonator that Doris called the switchy thingy. It was all very safely in a field on the other side of several rows of trees. They plugged their ears and turned down their hearing aids.

Violet blamed herself. She should have seen the danger when Ruby smiled that calm, I-know-something-that-you-don't, smile. She didn't.

The explosives worked as they should have, the blast flattening skin against brittle cheek bones. Violet felt like a large hand, palm open, slammed into her chest pushing her backward. She heard the tinkle of glass, and looked around in time to see the window panes falling into the living room floor behind her. The boulder disappeared in a puff of gray dust and chips, some of which rained down on the roof above. A few dented the van. Lin got a new dent in her hood.

The cloud of dust began to settle, and Violet looked around to find that everyone had gone to ground behind the porch rockers and tables. Everyone except for Ruby. Why had she not noticed that Ruby wore a hardhat, earmuffs, and safety glasses while the rest of them had been protected only by distance? Ruby stood there grinning and spitting to clear the granite dust that hung over them from her teeth. "It works," Violet read her lips, her ears ringing like church bells.

"Was that really only four ounces?" asked Mini.

Ruby shook her head. "Eight ounces. It was a big rock," she said, before popping her dentures out and spitting again.

Violet's gaze drifted from the rock in the tree to the porch. Lin picked up her phone. "What do I tell the window guy?"

"Tell him it was vandals with rocks," said Doris.

They swept, but they would be finding shards of glass in the house for a while yet.

Ruby put her phone in the pocket of her print dress and ambled over joining the group. Violet pointed out the rock embedded in the tree, and Ruby beamed. "A memento," she said, letting Lin guide her into place for the picture. Before pressing the button, Lin paused, seemingly deep in thought.

"It's not that hard to take a picture, is it?" said Doris.

"That's not it," said Lin. "I just had the thought that, well I thought that we're taking this picture of all of you and you're about to go off and do something really dangerous and…"

"Honey, at our age, getting out of bed is dangerous," said Bernice.

"We should take pictures every day," said Doris.

"Amen to that," joined Marybeth.

"Well, what if something happens to one of you?" said Lin.

"That's why we're taking the picture," responded Mini. "Now, hurry up before one of us keels over. I want you to take one of me with my rifle."

"Me, too," said Doris.

That night, they ate an early dinner then lit the bonfire, this time without the booze. Lin snuck up on them and took some pictures, their wrinkled faces smoothed by the flickering light. Violet's ears caught the mechanical click of the shutter over the crackle of the fire a few times before she saw the pink of Lin's jacket floating ghostlike around the circle.

Ruby entertained them with a demonstration of flammable materials. For reasons that Violet thought she was coming to grasp,

Ruby did not like kerosene or diesel. She had talked of mixing diesel with common materials to make explosives but only as a last resort. Ruby tossed a handful of stale tortilla chips that they had gotten from the food pantry into the flames and they flared like gasoline. The real winner was a can of instant coffee mix that came with sugar and God knows what already in it. The stuff had been left behind by Tommy, and by the looks of the can, it was years old before he passed on. Ruby sprinkled a little into the fire like fairy dust and it sparked bright blue. She tossed the can up, splashing an ounce or so of the granules into the fire, and it *whooshed* up, igniting like black powder. With a content smile, Ruby capped the can and set the remainder aside for later.

Violet heard the click again.

***

Agent Jonah was pissed. On top of his mandate to "solve" the Golden Lawn case and find a way to arrest a man that was in a non-extradition country, he had just been assigned to investigate two ATF agents that were suspected of stealing explosives. As if all that weren't enough, Anita Fulsom-Bright had skipped town. After her rambling session of accusing the Golden Lawn ladies of planning some kind of grocery store heist, Bright had stormed away from their meeting with that light in her eyes—the one that said, "If you don't, I will." Now, she was gone.

Mid-ramble, she had mentioned a cruise, so with the resources of the FBI, namely a phone and an authoritative voice, Jonah spent an hour calling cruise lines. Indeed, Anita and her mother Irene Fulsom were booked for a nine day Caribbean vacation.

It crossed his mind more than once that if he were going to Fort Lauderdale to arrest Bright, arresting the mother with the intent of making the daughter's life more miserable would be justice. It was a worthy plan, but Jonah had always thought that anything worth doing was worth thinking about first. On his desk, was a great example of agents forgetting to think. The gentlemen of the ATF he was investigating seemed so far to be more the victims of spontaneity than malice of forethought. Dumbasses.

Just do it was not a good motto for law enforcement.

***

Flashing the boarding passes, Lin pulled the bus right up into the terminal loading zone with the other shuttles. She pulled to the side and, muttering something about *making sure,* went into the terminal.

Bernice stared in awe. Thousands of people lined up around the warehouse-like building waiting to board.

In 1952, she and Warren had taken a boat to South America, setting out on a journey that Warren would not return from. It had been the most exciting time of her life, marriage then preparing to set sail into the unknown as missionaries. She would never regret going. She only regretted not telling him how much she had loved every minute. Life always had a way of throwing a cruel twist into a perfectly good dream. She had lived the dream, for sure. Starting with boarding a ship in the port of Houston.

Every last detail of the journey was printed on her heart. In the chilly early morning fog, they watched the entirety of their earthly possessions swing in a net above the oily water of the Houston ship channel. Ghostly images of rats that she first mistook for possums scurried around the piles of grain spilled from the huge grain elevators. She wondered if this were how all great adventures started, in dirty places where ladies didn't go? They climbed the plank, almost as steep as a ladder, to the deck of the ship where they met the captain, a small man with a warm smile. The smile was not for them, they learned later, but for his bride, the sea, that he would be with again that very day.

The hawsers were tossed off, and the ship was tugged through the narrow channel of Buffalo Bayou, past the storage tanks and overflow ponds of the expanding petrochemical plants and eventually past Goat Island, then Hog Island, and into the Galveston Bay, where the channel pilot took the ladder down to his tug and the captain became master of his ship once more.

The world had changed so much. When they'd planned this cruise, the image in her mind had been perhaps a nice gentle gangplank that crossed the greasy brown water to a luxury liner. Maybe even a gravel parking lot. This was more like a shopping mall with its high concrete walls and glass doors.

Lin exited the building, her face a concerned mask. “Bad news,” Bernice heard her say, leaning into Marybeth and Violet. “You have to put everything with guns or ammo in it back on the bus. This place is like an airline terminal. They have metal detectors and everything.”

Marybeth gasped. Violet's lips tightened in an angry line. She put her hand on Lin for stability.

“I'm sorry,” said Lin, clearly meaning it.

Is that it? So many hours of planning and training gone to waste just like that?

Mini leaned in. “What is it?” she asked.

“We can't take the guns. They're checking bags,” said Bernice.

Mini shook her head, “No matter. We can get guns anywhere.”

That was true enough, and Bernice knew it to be so from personal experience. Two weeks after Warren's murder, she’d come across a man in a small village who was willing to trade an old Mauser and a few cartridges for her gold wedding ring. She didn't even remember thinking about it. It was the only thing of value she had. She gave up the ring knowing that Warren would approve of her resourcefulness.

Those days were such a blur of anger and confusion. She had tried so hard to forget them, but the memories were all she had of Warren, and she couldn't bear to let them go. The clearest memory of all was of that life-changing walk down a mountain road with her rifle slung over her shoulder, her chin high, belying her weariness. She could still hear the insects and birds and smell the fires as she neared village after village, passing through each without a word to the residents, who watched her through the thick air as though they understood. How could they?

It was a long time ago, but the lesson was learned, and Bernice knew that a resourceful person could find usable weapons almost anywhere. It just depended on what you were willing to pay for them. Mini was right. The setback was bad, but not life shattering.

“Everything, every gun and every bullet out of the bags,” commanded Violet. On the bus, Mini folded down a table and began checking bags. Minutes later, the job complete, Lin pulled the van up to the loading area and began passing luggage to a porter while the ladies gathered their carry-ons.

Age has its benefits, and while others waited in endless lines, seniors were passed to the front. Minutes later, the ladies exchanged boarding passes for cruise ID cards that doubled as room keys. From there, they passed through to security.

Cruise security managed the baggage inspection with TSA oversight. A situation so confusing that Bernice had difficulty telling which was which.

Violet managed to get through with her nail file with little trouble. Dori's bag of knitting supplies sailed through with only a cursory look, but Ruby was made to open her bag for inspection. Two gentlemen in white opened the larger of her bags and gently began removing the contents while Ruby stood by smiling at them, looking every bit like she was enjoying the extra attention. “Will you gentlemen be on the ship?” she asked.

“Yes, ma'am,” answered the older of the two, who was at least fifty years her junior.

Ruby smiled. Bernice felt her breath freeze in her chest. The man was handling a block of C-4. The wrapping had been removed and replaced with clear wax paper, but the brown putty color was unmistakable.

“What is this?” asked the young security man.

“Oh, that's art clay. It's not quite clay, but that's what they call it. Has a little paraffin or something mixed in with it to make it easy to work.” To show them, she took a block and and began to shape it. “Don't let Doris see this,” she whispered to the officer. “She's getting married on the ship, and I'm going to do a sculpture of her and Lester's hands,” she said, turning her body between Doris and the open suitcase.

“Can we let her…?” started the younger of the men.

A short stout woman stepped out from behind the scanner, shaking her head and holding up Ruby's paint box. “Ma'am, the solvents in here are pretty strong.”

“We have a balcony stateroom. It will be well-ventilated,” said Ruby.

“Ma’am, you can take your paints, but if they get complaints about the smell, ship security will confiscate them.”

Lin helped Bernice lift her bag onto the scanner belt. The female attendant diligently paused her conversation with Ruby to watch the bag scan. Bernice turned away, crossing her fingers and closing her eyes to pray. When she opened them, Lin was interrogating her with her eyes.

The belt stopped and reversed. “What is this?” demanded the woman, pointing at the scanner screen.

“My paints?” interrupted Ruby.

“No, ma'am. Not that,” she said.

“Those are knitting needles,” said Bernice, trying to keep up with the search of Ruby's bags as well.

One of the two male security agents, took Ruby's paint box and put it on the cleared table. Holding up the *sculpting clay,* he looked to the older man who shrugged. “We're going to have to run this by the dogs. We don't allow unknown substances on the ship, ma'am.”

“Ma'am, I see the knitting needles. What are the other objects?” said the woman agent. She pointed at the narrow cylindrical objects with the wires sticking out of them, the blasting caps. “Oh, those are our homemade weaving shuttles,” replied Bernice, crossing her fingers in her mind and praying that the ridiculous explanation she’d just come up with would be accepted.

The woman adjusted the scanner. Bernice had a moment to study her and realized that the woman's uniform was TSA, not ship security. *Darn!*

Somewhere in the suffocating crowd, a scuffle broke out and a shrill familiar voice screeched, while a man begged her to stop.

“What in heaven's name?” declared Ruby. The older security man quickly replaced Ruby's art supplies and closed the bag. The younger officer leaned in the direction of the commotion. “Let the TSA guys deal with that,” said the older officer.

Bernice shivered. The screaming voice sounded so familiar. It had to be Irene’s daughter, Anita.

The TSA woman pointed at the scanner, her attention breaking between that, the paint box on the cleared table, and the events unfolding beyond her sight range, "They look like blasting caps."

Bernice squinted and shook her head in bewilderment, an action that reflected her not knowing what to do but could just as well be interpreted as confusion.

"Do you know what blasting caps are?" asked the officer, standing on her tiptoes trying to observe the growing disturbance thirty yards up the terminal.

"Is it some kind of drug?" asked Bernice.

"Don't let her through with that," said the TSA woman to the ship's security men before pushing through the crowd toward the disturbance.

The younger officer waited for the TSA woman to be absorbed by the crowd, then bumped the switch on the scanner belt. "You ladies have a nice day," he said, stacking the bags on the rolling cart and waving for a porter to take them away.

***

Marybeth shouldered a computer bag that got heavier by the minute. Violet carried only a large purse through the short baggage check line. When the art supplies came out, Marybeth began to hold her breath. An elbow from Violet made her release.

When the C-4 came out, she sensed that Violet was now the one holding her breath. She shot an elbow toward Violet's ribs, half hoping that they would be as tender as her own. Violet blocked her with a forearm. "That's going to leave a mark," said Marybeth.

"It will, and you will hear about it later," replied Violet, her focus entirely on the happenings in the line.

A ruckus broke out someplace outside the double doors behind them. Marybeth would have bet good money that even Mini with her hearing aid turned down would recognize the bellowing of Irene's daughter. "What in heaven's name is she doing here?"

Violet strolled casually past the line of older and handicapped passengers. A brief glance around the door and she returned. "The cops are dragging Anita out," she said, chewing on her lower lip. "Irene is there. God help us if they let her through."

CHAPTER 23

They entered the ship from a gangway that seemed like something you would use to board an airplane only steeper. Marybeth looked around in confusion, “Is this the boarding lounge?”

Violet elbowed her gently, “This is the ship. Ain't this something? I've heard about it, but…”

“This is the ship?” said Marybeth, spinning and taking it all in, the rich carpets, dark mahogany, brass, and glass that sparkled in the sunlight that poured in from high above. She drifted to the center of the room and let her bag slide to the floor as she turned, looking up and trying to count the levels that reached up toward the skylights. It was all so hard to accept when you’d spent the last seventy-odd years reliving the ugly memories of life on the sweltering deck of a Japanese warship.

“It's not exactly what I had pictured,” she said.

“Me, either,” said Violet.

They laid back on a deep leather couch, soaking it all in. While the crowd rushed around them in a blur of voices and motion, all in a hurry to go somewhere, Marybeth and Violet were content to be still.

Behind them, they heard Irene complain at having to wait in line for an elevator. They chuckled and kept their heads down.

Long after Irene boarded the elevator, Marybeth lifted her bag, the burden of it somehow less after the short break. She accepted a map of the ship from a young crewman in a red shirt and waved it in front of Violet, raising her eyebrow.

Violet squinted a question at her.

“Can you think of a better time to wander around a cruise ship, and maybe stumble into places you shouldn't be?” explained Marybeth.

An involuntary laugh burst from Violet. “Let's go.”

They had entered on deck three, where the main lobby and theater were separated from the ship's largest restaurant by a galley area that they were not allowed to pass through. From there they took the forward stairs down to deck two and wove their way through the throngs of boarders, most of whom held their passes in one hand while they dragged luggage with the other.

There were whole families and single people of all ages. One girl of nineteen or twenty that looked completely lost, and boys with hairless chests, bare feet, and swim shorts, looking in the wrong place for a pool.

To Marybeth, the ship seemed to throb with anticipation. People were pumped full of the thrill of the journey to come. They could all be going to the bottom of the ocean in a day, but today they were alive, and life was contagious.

Marybeth and Violet made their way down another stairway to what they thought must be the front of the ship or the back. Marybeth wasn't sure anymore. She tried the handle on a door beside the stairs that had a conspicuous sign saying CREW ONLY. It turned easily.

White painted steel stairs led down to a wide common area that was stacked deck to overhead with loaded luggage carts. Sunshine flowed in through a large hatch to the left. A tow motor carried a cart up the ramp toward them. Marybeth backed around the corner and waved her map at Violet. Up the stairs and past a few nodding crew members they went.

The elevators were miraculously empty and fast. They exited on deck nine and zigzagged through the cluster of stewards manipulating carts of luggage. Rounding a corner, they found themselves looking down six floors over glass and mahogany rails into the lobby where they had entered the ship. A band was playing over the echoes of hundreds of voices.

From that vantage point, they could see some of the levels they had skipped on the elevator. Three or four decks below, the marble, glass, and brass of a shopping mall. Below that, the curved stairs down from a restaurant to the lobby.

Children sprinted past them in swimsuits. They followed.

Glass doors slid open and a blast of hot air and racket assaulted them. Hundreds of people gathered on the deck, the cruise director leading them in a line dance. Hundreds more laid back on deck chairs, sipping the first of many mixed drinks. From above and behind, they heard a scream of joy. The waterslide was already in use.

"Wrong way if we're going to our rooms," said Marybeth.

"How can you tell?" asked Violet.

"The slide is forward of the pool deck, and our rooms are at the front of the ship."

Back past the elevators and into the much quieter forward section of the ship, they found the end of the hall and the rooms that matched the numbers on their cards.

Marybeth could not get her card key to work.

Ruby opened the door from inside and waved them in.

***

The ship would be underway in a few hours. In the meantime, there were a whole heap of issues they needed to deal with, and Violet was already exhausted.

It was a nine day cruise with the first stop in Key West. Guns and ammunition were at the top of the shopping list. Mini and Bernice would focus on that. The wedding would be the day after leaving Key West, the first full day at sea. Violet, Marybeth, and Ruby agreed that the wedding was most important for now.

"After that, we can focus on the bank job," said Marybeth.

"Do I have a say in this?" asked Doris.

Violet's ears perked up.

"The wedding will take care of itself. We need to prepare for the bank," said Doris, making it clear that the discussion was over.

"Okay, then…" said Violet.

The girls huddled around the table and the itinerary. They would dock in Cancun the day after the wedding. Violet wondered aloud if they could acquire weapons there. It was Mexico, and while the kind of guns they were looking for were not legal in Mexico, according to the news, they were plentiful.

"Buying from drug dealers?" asked Bernice, shaking her head.

Violet agreed, "I don't much like that idea. And we still have to get them on the ship."

"Maybe we should re-think the plan," said Mini. "We have explosives. If we go in at night, we won't need guns."

"What about night guards? Won't they have at least one guard all night?"

"More than likely," nodded Mini.

"But we won't be there overnight," said Ruby.

"Can we get guns in Belize?" asked Marybeth. "We have a full day there."

Bernice did a quick internet search on her pad.

"Are you sure that's okay?" asked Violet, waving at the pad.

Bernice halted. "No, but I've already done it."

Violet cringed.

Bernice scanned her results then checked the internet connection. "Belize has very strict gun laws and we're getting internet through my 5G, not the ship."

"Can we get internet at sea?" asked Marybeth.

"It's in the brochure," said Ruby. She found the page and read it.

Bernice was shaking her head. "I wouldn't do any searches from the ship. Everything goes through their connection. Risky."

"Start a list. We'll do our searches when we can get a connection off the ship," said Violet.

Marybeth began to write on her legal pad. KEY WEST NEED TO KNOW

"It's 3:28," said Doris.

"Almost time for that safety briefing," added Ruby.

"I've heard those are miserable," groaned Marybeth.

"I've heard you get kicked off the ship if you skip," said Doris.

"Poker when we get back," said Violet.

***

Mini rambled down the corridor alone. It was 5:00 am, and they would make port in Key West in a few hours. The sun would be on the horizon soon, and she wanted to be on the aft deck to see it. She had never seen a sunrise over the ocean.

The previous day's safety briefing, standing in the stifling crowd for thirty minutes, had been a thoroughly miserable experience, but this was a new day, one for discovery, and she wasn't going to miss a single minute of it.

The ship was quiet, incredibly quiet. When she left the stateroom, she thought she saw the white shirt of a steward vanish ghostlike around a corner. It happened so fast that it could have been her imagination. Of course, there would be staff working day and night. She laughed at the idea that perhaps they could put a ship on autopilot and take a nap. Still, the phantom steward and the almost imperceptible rocking of the ship were the only signs of life.

She crossed an open segment of deck in the center of the ship. Circling the pool, she was glad for the non-slip coating. Her size six shoes left clean tracks on the slick, dew covered surface. She was no foot dragger, especially after all of the exercise they had been getting. Mini couldn't recall a time in the last thirty years that she had been in such good physical condition. *If we can't rob the damn bank, I'll be fit to get a job just about anywhere*, she thought, laughing at the irony.

She caught a whiff of cigarette as she climbed the open stairway up two decks, passing a crewman who raised a surprised eyebrow at her on his way down. "Watch those slick steps, ma'am," he said, politely. She would do just that. Drawing her sweater tight, she followed the deck around to the stern of the ship where chrome and glass windbreaks kept it far less windy than she had expected.

She was alone on the deck. Over the gleaming aft rail, she could see the fog roll by below, lights from the side of the ship glowing warmly in the mist above the ship's wake. The thinning fog swirled, obscuring the ocean surface. The eastern sky was light enough that she could see the curve of the earth over the water. She leaned on the rail.

So much had happened in the last few weeks that she was starting to feel that events had taken her. Like a strong river current that won't let you stand on your feet, their world had become complex, layered, and busy. Mini smiled. *You don't see the current when you're in it.* They had been happily floating downstream, gaining momentum, probably toward a fall, and until now there had been no time to step back and look at the big picture.

Mini loved the irony. There was less time now than ever to consider options. They were broke, and they were going to rob a bank. That was the big picture. That they had only explosives and maybe enough money between them to rent a car for a day, that was the small picture, the *in the current* stuff.

The great orange ball of the sun peaked over the horizon. She drew a deep breath. How marvelous. Now, that was big picture. Imagine that, if they hadn't decided to rob a bank, they wouldn't be here, and this moment would have been lost.

Mini allowed herself a moment of wonder before more practical matters crept back in. Even here on this peaceful morning, it couldn't be helped. She found herself sorting thoughts, plans, fantasies into the right categories, pushing out the stuff that could wait and focusing on the one thing that had occupied her for months.

Bob Robbins must pay for his crimes. For that, she was willing to pay a price.

What seemed like such a big thing before seemed so inconsequential now, and for the first time in many years, she was willing to take the chance of her past life being exposed. The statute of limitations had long run out on her crimes. Her family might have a different view of things if they discovered her history. She would chance that for herself, but mostly for her friends. Not a blessed one of them deserved to die poor. They wouldn't, she knew that. One way or the other, they would come back. Their bank accounts may never be fully restored, but they wouldn't be eating dog food, either. She didn't feel like they had quite passed it yet, but there would be a turning point for them somewhere soon. Otherwise, where would they wind up?

These days, the current seemed to be faster and faster toward a disastrous end. First Robbins robbed them, then the county wanted all that money for taxes on a farm that had not brought them a single dollar of revenue. Now, here they were, willing and ready to take back what was rightfully theirs, and maybe a little extra, but with no means to do so.

For some, the idea of robbery was still a problem. Not for Mini. She tried to see herself as an honest woman, but couldn't help but think that once they were there, they might feel like liberating a few other boxes of their contents. It was a difficult thing to consider. They had been robbed, and it had been devastating to them. To consider doing that to someone else, was a hard thing, but a necessary one.

She'd explained her thoughts, and the others were slowly coming around. To rob only the one box would shorten the investigator's list of suspects considerably. Who else would go to the trouble to rob a bank and only take from Bob Robbins? No, the circumstances what they were, they couldn't afford to rob only Robbins' box.

So many things to think about, and up till now, she had been perfectly willing to let the others do the thinking while she offered her narrow expertise. She had given her knowledge. They had taken her instruction and applied it, and now it was her time to give more. There was a way to do that. She would need help, Bernice and her expertise with the internet. It would be risky, in more ways than one. It could cost her dearly, opening old wounds, but perhaps it was time to open that door and see what was behind it. If not now, when would she ever?

The orange ball was half above the horizon. The fog was burning off, and the disk shrinking to what seemed a normal size. *Was it an illusion that the sun was so big, or was it an illusion that it was so small? Was what they were doing so important?* She stepped up so that she could lean over the rail far enough to see below. Disappointed, she could not see the ship's giant screws, only the windows of the restaurants on the lower decks. She stayed there for some time, leaning on the rail, her view below unobstructed.

Something moved in her peripheral vision. Years of living had taught her that unexpected movement added up to danger. There was no unteaching that. The movement was to her right, she dropped from the rail and stepped left, dragging her right foot. The man charging at her missed her entirely and slammed head first into the rail.

"What the…" screeched Mini, noting the steward's uniform worn by the man. *Were they paid so little that they had to rob the passengers?* The man was barely conscious, but his friends were wide awake. They circled her, two male crewmen and a young woman in a white shirt who appeared to be ship's officer, or maybe a waitress. A waitress might be tougher than an officer. She fell into a fighting stance, waiting for them. They circled like a pack of dogs, while she waited for one of them to break rank and charge.

Fifty years ago, her youngest son had asked her to take a martial arts class with him. It was a brave thing for him to do, to show up with his mother. But mom had surprised them. She learned fast and fought like a demon. Always sizing the opponents up and going at their weakest point. Brad hadn't been so fast to learn, and they took the class several times. That kind of training never left you, and today her body acted from memory even after all these years. Three opponents, with the fourth on the ground. Three people too afraid of a little old warrior to come closer. Mini smiled for them and waved them to come on. "Why don't you come on and try something before I die of old age?" she taunted.

The bewildered faces should have told her something else, but at that moment, they were just a sign of weakness. One to be exploited. Mini swiveled to the limit of her aged bones, and lifted her right toe before snapping the lower leg up, sweeping the left knee of the big guy, the one with the smug smile that was now fading to concern, then outright fear, as he fell to the hard deck.

The move was good, but Mini was at her limit, and her shin hurt like hell from the contact with the big guy's bone. She spun left, trying with everything in her not to fall. It may have looked like a sweet dance move to her attackers, but to Mini it was pure desperation and pure luck to be still standing at the end of the move. "Move," was right. She'd slid on the wet deck and now found herself facing the two remaining members of the uniformed gang. This time *they* had their backs to the rail. It was a long fall to the windows below. Mini could help them over the first obstacle, the rail. Until now, there had been a kind of righteous joy in their eyes. Now, there was fear. She danced back and kicked the big guy in the head to stop him from squirming and moaning about his knee. It worked, and his gang friends were horrified. Pain shot up Mini's leg from the new bruise on her heel.

***

Dana Sully was a three year veteran of the sea. She'd worked cruises to Europe, Alaska, and Australia. She'd worked in the galley, as a room steward, and even in the engine room as a cleaning tech. She knew her way around a ship, and she knew just how to deal with this little hellion. As a full security officer, she knew that she should call for backup, but there was no time.

The woman stepped forward and set her foot to kick.

The deck was wet.

Dana went low, sweeping the aggressor's foot forward. The woman fell back, landing hard on the downed crewman. Dana pounced, her cuffs in hand.

There were procedures, but there was no way Dana was going to drag this woman to the security office without more information. First they would take her to her cabin where they would find out why the stubby little Tasmanian devil had gone on the warpath, then they would lock her in the brig.

***

Marybeth stood at the window watching the waves pass beneath the hull. To their right—she could never remember which was port and which was starboard—she could see the shadow of land through the thinning fog. She guessed that to be Florida, maybe even one of the Keys.

She checked her watch. Almost 6:00 am. Violet was out rambling around somewhere, probably looking for Mini. Marybeth wondered, not for the first time, if it would have been easier on them all to have separate lodgings for a change. Maybe even on separate decks. Being all together, even in this huge captain's suite, was like a slumber party. All of them crammed into connected staterooms, with the stress of a wedding and an impending bank heist, maybe that was too much. The stateroom balconies allowed them to see both ends of the ship's and the night sky, she liked that part, but it was still just a few hundred square feet for so many people with so much energy.

Something had to snap.

The door rattled in its frame as someone pounded on it. Marybeth, perturbed at the insistence answered expecting to see the ship's florist.

Instead, she found a ships officer, several bedraggled crewmen, and Mini in handcuffs.

Something *had* snapped.

"For goodness' sake, what is all this?" asked Marybeth as the crew crowded in with Mini in tow.

"I was attacked," said Mini, defiantly pulling away from her escort.

Marybeth could see several bruises on Mini that had not been there last night, one on her cheek, one on her shoulder, and one that was already turning deep purple on her shin. The crew fared no better, one man looking as though he needed immediate medical attention, his eye swollen closed. Each of them suffered some small injury.

Doris wrapped ice in a towel and handed it to the man with the swollen eye.

Perhaps Mini had been attacked, but from the look of it, she had done some fighting back. The problem was that Marybeth knew Mini too well. Whatever had happened, she wasn't innocent, but the defensiveness of the crew, and the fact that they were here instead of the security office had to mean something, too.

Marybeth focused on the young female officer. "Why would the crew of a luxury ship attack a passenger?" she asked.

She heard the quiet slide of soft shoes as Violet entered. She nodded to her friend, then pressed her attack. "Why did you attack my friend? A passenger on this ship?"

"She was going to jump," said the young woman.

Marybeth almost felt sorry for her, but this was not the time for weakness. "Really? What made you think that my friend, this woman that has lived eighty-seven…"

"Eighty-eight," corrected Mini.

"…eighty-eight years. What makes you think that kind of woman would decide to throw her life away?"

The security officer shrank back. "The crew reported a jumper."

Marybeth waited patiently for more.

It didn't come.

"Did she jump? Did she at any point try to jump?" she could feel her voice weaken, tired with age, worry, and a thousand such conversations.

She turned her attention to Mini.

"They attacked me," she said. "I was just trying to see the water."

Security officer Dana Sully, it was on her name tag, closed her eyes. By the time they opened, a new calculation had been made. Marybeth understood that calculation. She had seen it before. As a child, her father had insisted that every time he fired an employee, she be there. Each and every one of them went through this process. First, anger, then, defiance, then regret. Finally, they would see that the options had run out and that there was no other option but mercy. By that time, father had run out of patience.

Marybeth had a better idea. "I think you should remove those handcuffs and dismiss your crew."

***

Dana Sully made her way slowly down the lower deck passageway. Worry, and a little fear, pinching her face into a hard mask. It would have been better if the old lady had jumped, but apparently Yoda's twin sister wasn't interested in dying, she just wanted to watch the sunrise. That wasn't what worried Dana. *She* hadn't screamed that someone was jumping.

The guys that were hurt had slinked off to the infirmary saying they had slipped on the stairs and had a group tumble. That didn't worry her, either. Nobody cared if a few crew got a few bruises, as long as they didn't show. Fights in the crew quarters were far more frequent than issues on the upper decks.

What worried Dana was Marybeth. That woman had made it clear that she was in charge, and in charge meant over Dana, as well. Marybeth wanted Dana at her beck and call for the rest of the cruise. That was her price for not making a stink of this mess. Dana could do as told, or a complaint would be filed, the likely result being her termination.

She rested against the bulkhead trying to find that one magical thought that would solve her problem. No magic, no fairy dust, just the facts, and the facts were grim. She snuck a glance into the infirmary. The white curtain was open, and Parhan, the man who had made the initial call, lay on the bed with an icepack on his knee. Next to him, Fernando grinned happily, apparently the recipient of some decent painkillers. His face, though, looked like the mask from Phantom of the Opera.

The woman was a demon. Who would have dreamed that a hundred pound, eighty-eight year old called Mini could take down someone twice her size.

Parhan flinched back from Dana's piercing stare. “What?”

Back in the passageway, she made time toward the ladder down to the crew quarters and her own compartment. There really wasn't a thing she could do. They had attacked a passenger and gotten their collective ass kicked. If the old ladies said “jump,” they would jump. “I am her bitch,” said Dana punching the metal wall. Eight days. In eight days, this cruise would be over. Maybe it wouldn't be so bad. Maybe Marybeth would ask for a tour of the crew quarters or get her to help sneak some booze on board. Maybe, but that wasn’t the impression she was left with. As light as the woman had tried to make the conversation, she couldn't help but note the vibe in the room.

What was it Marybeth said? “We have a wedding tomorrow and after that another project that we may need your assistance with. Can we count on you?” Of course the answer was “yes.” *What else could it be? “No, I want to be fired and left at the next port of call?”* Dana had chosen that moment to glance around the stateroom. There were four other women there. Mrs. Barone, Mini, had slipped away to tend her bruises. To her right, the woman with the cane watched her with a shark's smile. To the other side, the thin woman with the salt and pepper hair winked at her. In the mirror, she caught the reflection of a serious looking woman in a dress that looked like it belonged in a farm kitchen twirling a metal nail file through her fingers raising an appraising eyebrow. To her right, the one with the huge ball of white hair winked. “I'm getting married,” she said. It was like something from the Twilight Zone.

Ahead, through the stateroom's huge windows, Key West waited for them. Whatever they wanted her to do, she was sure it was going to be more than smuggling a little booze.

It was time to go to work, and her shipboard phone buzzed in her pocket. She answered. It was Marybeth, asking her to bring an icepack for Mini. "Call room service and tell them she tripped. They can get it faster," she responded.

Manageable? Maybe.

CHAPTER 24

They docked in Key West just after 7:00 am.

Violet held her file like a dagger waiting for Doris to stop pacing the stateroom. Doris tossed her head contemptuously, “I'm not stopping just because you're holding that thing.”

Violet snickered.

“It's not funny.”

Violet shook her head. That didn't mean that she couldn't think it was funny. “What's eating you?” she asked.

Dori froze, hands on hips, and glared at Violet. “I'm getting married tomorrow.” She resumed pacing from the stateroom door to the balcony door and back. Violet went back to cleaning her nails and listening to Doris mumble.

“You want to what?” she asked.

Doris changed course, stopping just inside Violet's comfort zone. “I want to tell my future husband what we're doing,” she said, pronouncing every word slowly and clearly.

“You're not talking to Mini. I can hear you fine,” said Violet.

“You're right. Mini might be a bank robber, but she's downright compassionate compared to you, and I don't even want to think about Marybeth. You want me to marry the man, fine. You want me to lie to him?” she shook her head. “I can't do that! I just can't.”

“Amen,” said Mini from the bedroom.

“Anyone else want to chip in? You seemed fine with it before,” said Violet, loud enough to be heard in the next stateroom.

Doris leaned down close to her. “You are annoyed by the fact that I want to be truthful with my husband. Do you see a problem with that?”

Violet could see the point but wasn't ready to concede.

Doris marched out the door.

Mini collected a spiral notebook from the table.

“What about you?” asked Violet. “Are you going to leave, too?”

Mini turned down her hearing aid on the way out.

***

Mini had been on the verge of a much needed solution when interrupted by ship security. Not that the interruption had been such a bad thing. Marybeth seemed to think it was working out nicely. For her part, Mini was proud of herself. Her body was old and ached all over after this morning's fiasco, but her mind was sharp. People seemed to equate hearing problems with brain problems. They were wrong.

In the fight between Doris and Violet, she had sided with Doris, but really came down on both sides, sympathetic to Doris and understanding the needs of the group. Marybeth was clearly on the same side as Violet, albeit for different reasons. Namely that Marybeth was a cold-hearted, single-minded, task manager. That wasn't really fair; she was more than a task manager. *She's a slave driver.*

It was hard, drawing the line between friend and mindless follower if you didn't break ranks every once in a while. She supposed that was what she was doing when she agreed with Doris. She still wasn't sure what she had been thinking other than that what Doris said was more right than the right of the group to be safe. Lord knew that she wasn't going to marry again, but if she did, she wouldn't go into it with a lie like that hanging over her. She might neglect to mention a few things in the past, but that was the past.

It was the past that she was about to dig up. For that, she needed Bernice.

***

"These people are out of their minds," said Bernice, trying not to stare at anyone specific in the Key West street crowd. "A man that age shouldn't wear a Speedo."

"They're out of more than their minds. Women our age shouldn't be wearing bikinis," said Mini. "Or be topless."

Bernice tapped her cane. She needed it less and less these days. Part of her daily workout had been using a machine to do leg lifts. That strengthened her knees and seemed to be good for her bad hip. The walking was good for her, too. She cringed at the thought of trying to navigate the moving decks and stairs of the ship in the condition she had been in a month before.

She carried the cane out of habit. Right now, she was thinking it might be useful to push a few of these overexposed, oily, bodies out of the way. There was some kind of street festival going on, and the noise and booze level was somewhere between that of a middle school lunch room and a pro football game. A man passed them wearing nothing but paint. “Did you see that?” blurted Bernice.

“They painted his thing,” responded Mini, sounding a bit numb.

“Do you think that's bad for it, him?”

“Not ever going to be my problem,” said Mini.

Key West was not a big place, and it seemed that most of the revelry was close to the water. The further they moved inland, the fewer people bumped into them. After a while, Bernice noticed that the roar of the crowd was behind them. Bare skin was all around, but the sobriety level seemed to have gone up, and the noise level down.

They’d come ashore looking for internet access. Based on Mini's request, Bernice suggested that they search from somewhere they would not leave an electronic trail. When it came to snooping, the ship's crew made the NSA look like amateurs.

They had tried to connect to a router in town from the high balcony deck of their stateroom, but everything in range was secured. She imagined that it could be expensive to leave your internet connection open in range of a cruise ship dock.

A block ahead of them, she could see the sign for the coffee house they were looking for.

Inside, they were greeted by a charming man with a long beard and a sunburned bald head. The gentleman introduced himself as Ray, then handed them a laminated rate card and returned to cleaning his espresso machine.

They opted to pay for three hours internet access. At $10 an hour, the rate seemed exorbitant, but it was better to have more time than they needed. Ray promised them that they would have more speed than they could ever need. She hoped that was true. People assumed that old people didn't need fast internet, but at her age, she didn't have time to wait on a slow connection.

They set up under a ceiling fan and went to work. First, Google, Yahoo, Bing, and Facebook. If they had no luck with those searches, they would move on to the criminal record databases and from there to financials. Somewhere they would find her, Mini's sister Kate. Whether she was still alive was in doubt. Mini thought she was, but she would be ninety years old now, and who knew if she still had contacts in the world of spies.

***

Lester trod down the long corridor. In less than a day, he would be married to the woman he had loved and pursued now for almost four years. It seemed impossible that she had actually agreed to marry him. A part of him wondered if she wouldn't jump ship while they were in port. The wild thought that he should have paid security to keep an eye on her crossed his mind. He shook it off. He wouldn't need security. If he did, there wasn't much point in marrying her.

He loved and trusted Doris. Oh, there were some doubts. Call it old fashioned or what you will, in Lester's mind the start of the cruise was like the start of the wedding day. With that in mind, he'd insisted that they stay apart on the cruise until married. Darn if she hadn't just accepted that without a peep.

That set off some alarms. By itself, it probably wouldn't have, but Lester had seen enough fishy behavior lately to justify a bit of suspicion. On the other hand, whatever the girls were up to, he was in favor of it. In the time he had known them, none of them, Dori included, had been in such good physical condition. Lester grinned. He darn sure wasn't too old to be looking forward to his wedding night.

He'd gotten the lay of the ship fairly quickly. The ladies were housed in the forward staterooms of deck nine, the Lido deck. It was a noisy deck, with music videos playing on the big screen over the pool and restaurant crowds chatting it up. The forward cabins, though, were well isolated from the noise. They also had a great view of the ocean. The balcony of the stateroom that they would occupy for the honeymoon had a fantastic, but windy, view of the night sky. Maybe they would drag a mattress out and sleep there one night. Dori might like that.

For now, Lester was staying one deck below, forward of midship. He had a small balcony in a stateroom shared with his daughter and granddaughter, Emily. They were the only family he would have at the wedding. They were enough.

He enjoyed the first night and morning at sea, keeping mostly to himself and taking advantage of room service for meals. He slept part of the night on his secluded stateroom balcony with a blanket wrapped around him and the cool breeze in his face. The ship was not moving fast. It wasn't far from Miami to Key West, and he supposed that though they could go far out to sea then come back, the captain would rather sail just fast enough to smooth the ride and save the fuel. Thirty thousand gallons an hour they burned at full speed, he'd read.

It had been a pleasant evening, but there were a few stiff muscles that needed to be worked out, and walking was the best way he knew to do that. Changes in activity always meant sore muscles. *Better get used to that,* he thought, grinning.

Lester grabbed the chrome rail and jogged down the ladderway to deck six. The air on the lower decks was well airconditioned but noticeably less fresh. He supposed that, when in port, no wind circulating meant that the systems would have to work harder.

He glanced toward the aft of the ship as he turned past the elevators.

Swinging into the passageway toward the front of the ship, he froze. Had he just seen Irene? That made no sense. She wasn't part of the wedding. Why would she be here?

He spun back in time to see the elevator door close. The light above indicated that it was going up.

Lester sprinted up the two flights of stairs, hoping that the elevator would stop on deck eight. It didn't. He half-ran, half-pulled himself up the next flight to the Lido deck.

The elevator door was open.

***

Lester knocked twice and waited.

Doris was surprised to see him.

"I thought you might have gone ashore," he said.

She dropped her chin and squinted.

He cringed. That had not come out right.

"Can I try again?"

Doris stood on her tiptoes and kissed him.

"I'm going to take that as a yes," he said, clearing a strand of white hair from his mouth.

"I need to talk to you all," he said.

"We're not all here, but come on in," said Ruby.

Despite his best efforts, Lester laughed. "Do you know what…?"

"I know what I said," said Ruby. She stuck her head around the corner, "Marybeth?"

"Irene is on the ship. I followed her for a while," said Lester.

The girls weren't surprised.

"I guess that means you knew she was here?" He thought on that for a while. Dori squeezed his hand in way that could have been comforting but in the overly air conditioned room, made his joints hurt.

Doris, looked to her friends. Marybeth and Violet in specific. Something was coming, he could feel it. They'd been hiding something from him. Now he wondered if he really wanted to know what.

Violet shook her head, ever so slightly.

Dori's hand suddenly felt cold. "I can't," she said.

Then she dropped his hand.

"Oh, for goodness' sake," spat Ruby. "Let her… you know…"

Violet looked to Marybeth. Marybeth reciprocated. Neither seemed to be budging. Lester could feel his blood pressure rise.

"That's enough!" he growled. "It was fine when it was all of you in this, whatever this is, together. But this is hurting Dori and that pisses me off."

He stood and jammed his hands in his pockets. They were safer there. He couldn't look at Dori right now. The last he had seen of her face, she wore a look of utter disappointment. Whether in him, or her friends, he didn't know.

"We're going to rob the bank on Grand Cayman where Bob Robbins is stashing our money," said Marybeth.

His eyes went to Doris rather than Marybeth.

She had an odd smirk on her face. He'd seen her smile like that before. The last time was right before she broke into the kitchen at Golden Lawn to steal some ice cream.

She winked.

"Don't worry, Doris isn't going," continued Marybeth. "Someone has to be our eyes and ears on the ship, especially with Irene trolling around."

"You people are insane. Even without Dori."

Doris slapped the back of his hand. It stung.

The door bounced open.

***

Mini read the room in a glance. "Does this mean I can talk?" she asked.

Violet nodded.

"Good. About time. Hi, Lester. Nothing for sure yet, but we have a possible solution to our supply problem," she said, still not sure how much she could say. She looked at Lester, then at Violet, hoping for something. Violet managed to look only a little impatient.

"Hold your water. I'm just catching my breath," said Mini, sitting on the edge of the couch, clutching her arms around her. There were things that she had never told her friends. Things that she would just as soon keep buried. She couldn't say why. They weren't awful, just private, like the last night at her childhood home. None of it was anyone else's damn business, but it had to be said.

"My sister and I parted ways when I was young," she began. "She left me to go places I couldn't go, do things I couldn't do. I talked to her today. For the first time in a long, long time."

She felt a rebel tear track down her face. She couldn't stop it or put it back. It was there for everyone to see. She reached compulsively to turn down her hearing aid. That wouldn't help either. She lowered her hand to her lap.

"I wanted to talk to her for a long time, but I couldn't. Kate was always the stubborn one. Couldn't bring herself to look me up after leaving me. Anyway, I didn't need to tell you all that. I know. But I…

ah, Kate knows people. It was a long shot, but I figured since she spent so many years doing what she does, she would know people that can get us guns. She's going to call me back."

"Where did she go?" asked Doris.

"Germany, with the OSS. After that, I think she was in eastern Europe for a while."

"What was she doing there?" asked Doris, confused.

"She was a spy," said Violet, barely above a whisper. "The OSS was our spy service in the war. After that, it became the CIA."

"We're going to need a lot of money," said Bernice, mercifully changing the subject.

"How much?" asked Marybeth.

"Thirty to fifty thousand, maybe," said Bernice, with a shrug.

Mini took off her glasses and wiped her face on her sleeve. *Damn.*

***

"I don't have that much in cash," said Lester to Doris in the passageway.

"Well, honey, we'll find another way," said Doris.

"Has it occurred to you that by the time you finish paying for this job, you might have been better off keeping the money you…?"

"Why, Lester Bodine, you old… this is about far more than money. That man took everything we had. We left poor Ginny Holt at the county home. That might have been the hardest thing I've ever done. She lost hope, and I have to tell you that if we weren't doing this, I might have done the same."

Lester smiled patiently.

"This is my room. Want to come in?"

He pushed the door open with his heel and leaned back, dragging her with him.

She didn't resist much.

"Oh, Lester, you old devil!" She giggled as the door swung closed.

CHAPTER 25

Anita Fulsom-Bright was back in orange and back in the interview room. Jonah stared through the glass wishing something, anything, would happen that would require his urgent attention somewhere else. He dreaded the moments with her that much. Talking to this woman to get information was like banging your head on a wall to make it feel better. Worse than a waste of time. The interview hadn't started and already his head was throbbing.

The observation room was small, and when the door opened, there was a noticeable drop in temperature. It seemed a little unfair that the interview room was air conditioned and the observation room was sweltering. Pat Tillis, a junior agent but nice guy, stuck his head in. "I need the room when you're done," he said.

Jonah was tempted to tell him to take it now, but that wouldn't go over so well with the director. Tillis stepped in, closing the door and ending the flow of cool air. He stood shoulder to shoulder with Jonah examining the suspect. "She doesn't look that scary."

Jonah cracked a smile. "She's not. It's just that every time I interview her… she has a panic attack."

Tillis cringed. "I heard about that. You had to hose down the chair."

"The cleaning guys did it. But yeah. That's pretty much the way it is with her. And I get nothing. I don't know why we bother. Except that she keeps doing stupid stuff that makes her look guilty. I don't get it."

Tillis rubbed his smooth chin. "I had an instructor at the academy, Waskowski, know him?"

Jonah shook his head.

"Well, he used to say that if you get someone you're sure you won't get anything out of, there's no harm in taking a shot in the dark. Tell her you got her on something and see what she does. What can it hurt?"

Nothing, thought Jonah. *It can't hurt a thing.* Further, it wasn't a new idea. In fact, it was so common that it could be called standard practice. Only he hadn't done it yet, why? Because her antics had made him walk a cautious line and avoid conflict? Damn. It almost didn't matter if she'd done it on purpose or if he'd fallen into a trap of his own making, Fulsom-Bright's behavior had put him off the scent.

Jonah nodded thanks to Tillis.

In the interrogation room, he pulled the chair out slowly, letting the worn plastic feet grate on the floor. He didn't like the squeak the chair made. Anita Bright liked it less. *Good.*

Her lip curled menacingly. For a few seconds, her eyes locked on his. It was the first sign of aggression he'd seen from her. It was change. *Good.* Change was good. He could roll with that.

"How's your boyfriend?" he asked.

No answer.

"Were you planning on seeing him this week?"

A low groan.

The earthy smell of urine filled the room.

***

It was loud on deck nine. Loud and busy. Irene shoved her way through the crowd, jogging the stick on her chair. She nudged the back of a hairy knee. They could move if they didn't like it. This was day two, and she hadn't seen hide nor hair of the wedding party. They were here. She could feel them and would have found them if the cruise line hadn't held her up most of the first evening.

First, they wouldn't let Anita board. That was the police and cruise security. Then, they wouldn't refund her ticket. They said Irene was taking up a whole room and had to pay for it. They gave in. Yes, they did. They gave her a private stateroom, *without a damn window*. "Got to sue," she muttered, gripping her phone and remembering two failed attempts to call her lawyer from the ship. She would have to find a way to get signal from the next port of call. After all they had done, the cruise wanted twenty dollars a day more to give her phone access so she could call a lawyer and sue them. Ridiculous! She wouldn't pay. Not one more penny. But they would.

A large man blocked her way. She bumped him behind the knee.

He smiled over his drink and moved. *Asshole, didn't know he was in the way.*

The woman with him glared dangerously at Irene.

As if the room situation wasn't bad enough, a kid with a badge that called himself a ship security officer, came knocking on her door this morning. The idiot had the temerity to scold her for offering to tip a ship's officer. It was just a tip. She asked for the room numbers of her friends. That was all. And they treated it like it was a crime. How were you supposed to find anyone if you didn't ask?

***

Ruby and Bernice followed, keeping to the shaded areas of the deck. For all of her cunning in finding the cruise and getting on board, Irene was a lousy detective, or whatever she was trying to be. They had followed her over three decks now, and it was just getting easier with practice.

The problem was that they couldn't follow her all the time. Sooner or later, they would have to all be in the same place at the same time. Tomorrow's wedding would be a likely time, and that was when Irene was most likely to stumble into them. Irene was a problem. No one believed that she was here by accident. No one thought for a moment that she would be anything but trouble.

It was too bad she couldn't be part of the team. She was resourceful and clever in her own way. She was also deceitful and frightfully single-minded when it came to revenge. That was the heart of the matter. Irene had a thing for Lester. She despised Doris even before Lester became interested in her. To say her hatred had multiplied would be putting it mildly. Bernice had been in the game room at Golden Lawn when Irene rammed Doris in the back of the knees with the power chair knocking her down, then run over her forearm.

Doris, for her part, had been resilient, regaining her feet saying, "That's why they don't let you drive."

Marybeth and Bernice had helped her ice the bruised arm, but Doris refused to file a complaint. The idea that her love life could be laid out in a police report mortified her. Irene was a problem they needed to fix on their own.

Bernice felt the urge to jam her cane into the power chair spokes, but the results were not guaranteed. The spokes were heavy, and even a non-mechanically minded person like herself could see that the cane could lose that fight. It wouldn't look much like an accident either.

Ruby seemed to think that having something look intentional didn't matter as long as the attention wasn't focused on them. She had begun to count the people that Irene angered in her passage through the ship. So far, there were eleven that she classified as *really flipping mad*, and eight more *possibles*.

The *really flipping mad* group continued to talk about Irene when she was well out of earshot. The *possibles* didn't say much or anything but watched the old bat with varying degrees of disgust, anger, or disdain as she went on to her next victim. Bernice had a few years of life experience and tended to think that the *possibles* were more likely to be the kind that would pursue an opportunity to correct what they perceived as an injustice. They were the kind that would let things simmer then administer justice quietly. She knew that group. She was in it.

Bernice and Ruby watched and waited, for inspiration or opportunity.

Ruby held up her hand. Bernice, moving with the ship, couldn't stop that fast. She ran into Ruby, hitting her in the ankle with the cane. Ruby cringed. It was the third time today.

"Sorry," said Bernice.

Ruby ignored her and the ankle. She pointed. In front of them, Dana Sully, the security officer who'd fought with Mini, watched Irene bulldoze her way across the deck. Dana waved to another officer and pointed toward Irene. Clearly she wanted nothing to do with old ladies. *Too bad.*

Bernice touched Dana on the elbow. The girl flinched like she'd been shot. The progression from surprise, to frustration, to resignation told Bernice all she needed to know. Miss Sully was clearly hoping not to see any of them again on this voyage.

"What's with the lady in the chair?" asked Bernice.

“She's causing all kinds of trouble. She ran over a kid's foot on deck seven, and the mom is complaining.” The girl looked them over, with a kind of standoffishness, like she was talking to the enemy.

Bernice gave her the sweet, *you're-our-friend,* smile.

Dana became even more skeptical. “You already know all that?”

“No,” answered Bernice. And that was the truth. They hadn't found Irene until deck eight. She had bumped into a number of people there but no kids. Bernice caught Ruby opening her notepad in her peripheral vision. They needed to adjust the count of *really flipping mads*.

“Well, your friend there…”

“She's not our friend,” said Ruby.

Dana examined them through squinted eyes. Her lip curled just a bit. Was it disbelief or a lack of trust? Bernice thought a bit of both. *Fair enough.*

“She's trouble,” said Dana.

“That’s why she’s not our friend,” said Ruby.

***

Dana was in the passage to the main engine room. She could feel the tingle of her phone vibrating in her pocket. She tried to answer, but the noise of the engines ruled that out. She stepped into an open machine room and closed the door. Blessed quiet.

The phone rang again and she answered.

“Miss Sully, we need a room key,” said the voice of evil. God forbid I am ever like that when I am old, she thought. Then again, being cunning and tough when you’re old might be a good thing. She tried to toss that thought overboard.

“What room,” she asked, realizing too late that she had just committed to violating ship policy.

“Whatever room Irene Fulsom is in.” said Marybeth.

“What are you going to do?” she asked.

“Disable her chair so she can't be a nuisance.”

Dana swallowed. It might well be the dumbest thing she ever did, but these women had their own brand of crazy that seemed to be catching. She liked it. It would get her fired if caught, but she liked it.

She didn't give them the key. That would have been stupid. Instead, she knocked lightly then opened the door. Allowing a passenger access to another passenger's cabin could be a career-ending offense. A ship's security officer entering a cabin would not be. She entered.

The lights were on, and Irene's chair parked against the bed. Behind the closed bathroom door, the shower was running.

The skinny woman, Ruby, pushed past Dana and kneeled in front of the power chair opening a cooler bag full of tools. Dana recognized the green handle wrap on the tools. They belonged to the ship. *How the hell...?* She let the thought go and stepped back to the bathroom door to listen. The woman was definitely in there.

Ruby removed a cover from the power chair.

To Dana's right, someone made a squeaky throat clearing sound. Dana turned her head, slowly, numbly, to the sound. *This is it,* she thought. *I'm going to be fired and put ashore at the next port.*

The room steward, a Filipino woman barely over four and half feet tall, stood in the dark corner, a towel over her arm. She could have been, had been, mistaken for part of the room, her light green tunic blending into the shadows.

The steward made slow hand motions and moved her lips without speaking.

It took Dana a moment to shift gears from *I'm caught and in deep shit* mode to trying to interpret what the steward was saying. She was no better or worse at lip reading a non-English speaker than anyone else, and squinting didn't seem to help. It looked like the steward was mouthing, “beach.” For a moment, Dana had the incongruous thought she had lucked out and could bribe the housekeeping steward with a little leave time at the next port of call.

Never mind that and rack it up to language differences. The steward wasn't interested in leave, she hated the “beach”... ah, the “bitch.”

The little woman stepped past Dana and leaned on the bathroom door, clenching her fist in front of her in a sign that Dana interpreted as signifying unity or solidarity. *Did the stewards have their own sign language?* This was all so out of her league.

Ruby glanced up at them then went on with her exam of the chair. She stuck a screwdriver under a plastic cover and pried. The plastic popped loudly.

Everyone froze.

The steward put her ear to the bathroom door. A few seconds later, she motioned for Ruby to go ahead.

Ruby muffled the next plastic release with her hand and removed the cover. Beneath was a battery, like a car battery but smaller.

Ruby removed the nut that held the black cable to the top of the battery. She lifted the cable terminal ring and stretched a thin rubber ring over the battery screw. Careful to keep it centered, she replaced the terminal ring, then put another rubber washer on top before replacing the washer and nut.

It was just a thin piece of rubber on each side of the terminal ring, but it was enough to interrupt the electrical connection of the battery to the chair. A test of the battery would show that it was charged, but the chair would not move unless pushed by hand.

Dana breathed a deep sigh of relief. If this is what the the old ladies were going to use her for, she could go right ahead and be used. They were doing God's work. Even the captain, should he ever learn, might give her a pass on this. Except for the bit about letting them into the room. Then, considering the subject, she might get a pass on that too. What choice would he have? Last she'd heard, he was still seeing that pouty lipped Dutch girl that wanted to be cruise director.

In the passageway, Ruby handed her cooler of tools to Dana. Nearing the elevators, the young ship's officer turned to her. "I don't think we should be seen together." She removed the tools from the cooler and handed it to Ruby. "Where did I find these?"

"Lido deck laundry room," said Ruby, nodding appreciatively.

Dana looked away, rejecting the silent compliment.

"Catch you later," said Ruby, heading for the stairs.

Dana waved her middle finger.

CHAPTER 26

The wedding was a small affair on the aft deck above the restaurants. Irene didn't show up until the evening reception.

Violet knew as much as she needed to about the shenanigans of the evening before. Ruby had gone ahead without consulting her or Marybeth. It was probably better that way. Decisions by committee often took too long, and opportunities were missed. It was good that Irene missed the wedding, and Ruby deserved their thanks for that, not a scolding.

Irene stopped her chair just short of running over the captain in the receiving line. "I'm sorry I missed the ceremony," she said to Violet.

Violet grunted. It was as much as she could manage.

"You don't seem surprised to see me," said Irene.

"I saw you get on the ship. You made a big splash," said Violet.

"I had to spend the morning in my cabin while the crew fixed my chair," said Irene.

For once, she didn't seem to be complaining. It was almost as if she appreciated the help they had given her. "They say the salt air got to the electrics." She twiddled the joy stick as if she were moving on, then backed up a few inches. "You don't have to pretend to like me," she said.

Oh, good. I won't. Violet smiled. Her mother would have reached up from the grave to box her on the ear for thinking that, but at least she hadn't said it aloud.

Irene turned her chair, her shoulders slumped, and for a moment Violet felt sorry for her.

The moment lasted only as long as it took Irene to lift her middle finger to her.

***

Italian men always seem to be as charming as they need to be, and the Captain was no exception. He performed the ceremony in full dress uniform. Even his shoes were shined to a patent leather gloss. Though he had met the wedding party before and during the wedding, he chose out of courtesy to wait in the receiving line like everyone else. Doris noted that several junior officers drifted out of line then back in behind him.

It was a wonder she noticed anything at all. Why, with the stress of the planning and the surprises, and trying to find new weapons, she'd barely had time to plan the wedding. Fortunately, her friends had paid more attention than she, and everything had come together nicely.

The crew decorated the aft deck with white rose garland. The flags strung across on ropes the day before had been taken down, and without the popping cloth, Doris had been able to hear almost every word. She had to ask the captain to repeat a few lines during the vows, but for the most part, it went smoothly. Mercifully, the ceremony was over before she could fall down, or best of all, before Irene could find them. The woman had been known to be brutally direct about her interest in Lester, trying to stake out her territory by running over everyone in her way. It hadn't worked one bit. Doris felt Lester squeeze her hand. He had barely let go of it since they'd said those two magic words, but this was a warning squeeze.

Irene was on her way.

They both backed up. It was best to protect your toes, and other parts, around Irene.

The captain stepped up, cutting off Irene's charge. He lurched when the chair clipped his calf but kept his balance and pretended not to notice the source. A split second of raised eyebrow aimed at the newlyweds was his only admission that anything noteworthy had occurred.

He shook their hands and accepted a kiss on the cheek from Doris.

"I didn't see your father here, so as captain of this vessel, I would be honored, when the time comes, to lead you in the first dance."

Doris felt her cheeks redden. She positively adored this man.

Lester cocked his head sideways, examining her, with a smirk.

"Oh, stop it," she said to Lester. "When was the last time a good looking young man asked me to dance?"

"I asked you last night," he said, leading her past the captain and onto the dance floor.

So he had.

***

The reception stretched on for several hours. Marybeth was tired, and the usual dose of Ibuprofen wasn't doing the job with her throbbing hip. Otherwise, things were going well. Irene surprised her by making little trouble. That would have made Marybeth suspicious on a normal day, but not today. Today she was in a forgiving mood.

She wandered over to the hors d'oeuvres table. Ruby had placed a mysterious box in the center, and she was almost to the point of admitting curiosity. She tipped the corner of the box up with a fork. Suddenly, Ruby was there, tapping her on the back of the hand and scolding her, "You'll see soon enough."

Marybeth groused. She was about to move on when the captain, with a jolly laugh, asked Ruby, "Is that it? Is that the sculpture? I love art a so mucha."

"Captain, it is your honor to open the box," said Ruby.

"Oh, no, ma'am, the honor should go to the bride and groom."

Doris and Lester approached, curious and a little fearful. "What is it?" asked Doris.

Ruby waved for her to find out.

Doris held her breath and lifted the box that covered the mystery.

Marybeth gasped, then burst into laughter. In front of them was a near perfect rendition of the bride and groom's hands, modeled in C-4. She could not find the right nerve and muscle combination to close her mouth, but did manage to swivel her head far enough to lock eyes with Ruby who was positively glowing.

"It's my first sculpture. And it's of unconventional materials," she said, winking.

True to his word, the Captain danced with the bride.

Marybeth watched and marveled. Her friends were the most celebrated group on the ship. Everyone, even Irene, seemed to be enjoying the party. True, the woman had some issues, but she was behaving well enough at the moment. Marybeth supposed that even

Irene could be a decent person. She, like the others, had gotten into the habit of thinking that Irene was just trouble. No one was *just* anything. They all had their rough spots and their not so rough spots. "But by God's grace go I."

People changed. For some, it was the circumstances. For some, it was a major life changing event. But people changed. For herself, this cruise was a celebration of freedom. Marybeth hadn't been on a ship since her return to the states in 1945. That had been a passage far worse than the one that had taken her to the Philippines. The war was over, but in her mind's eye, every ship on the horizon was an enemy that would take her back to that island, to that room. That voyage changed her, damaged her, the torture of constant fear and panic draining her so that by the time she arrived stateside she felt like no more than an empty shell of the girl that had once been.

When they said they would go on a cruise, she had held her tongue. She could do it, she told herself again and again. But each day they got closer to shipping out, she felt herself dreading the walk up the gangplank, the smell of salt air and oil, and the constant throbbing of the engines that seemed to match frequency with her nerves, making them jangle so that she often found herself trying to hear above her own heartbeat.

In her mind, the ship was an enemy that she could never defeat. Her fear consumed her. The day they boarded, walking up the plank, she expected to feel the chill of fear and the emptiness of loathsome despair. Like going before a judge. Maybe in the next step, or the next, the fear would latch onto her.

But it hadn't. Instead, she found herself enjoying the voyage. Today, only fifty hours after boarding, this ship was a friend shared with her friends. There was no journey into the unknown. No fear that her dirty secret would soon be exposed. She had cast that away, tossed it into the deep blue ocean water to vanish, perhaps forever.

Oh, the smells were there, of salt water, oil, and decay. The ship still moved under her feet, and the wind blew her hair in her eyes. But the voices were different. The galley food was certainly better. Once you got into the ship, you didn't smell the fragrances of the docks. And the ships she had traveled on had never had a water slide. She tried that on the first day. Glory, what fun, plunging into the pool at the bottom and coming up sputtering like a child just baptized. She'd done that slide until her legs wouldn't take her back up the four flights of stairs. Then, she did it twice more with the elevator taking her the first three levels.

Only two days after boarding, Marybeth felt completely at home here. She could have done with a bit more privacy, but she liked that she lived close to her friends. A week after moving to Golden Lawn, she had more or less felt the same. She recognized now that it wasn't the place, it was the people. These people were her home.

Marybeth climbed the last flight of stairs to deck fourteen. It was the highest point on the ship, other than a few narrow ladders that crew used to access the radar masts. This was the place to be at night. It was still too bright, though, to see the stars. She leaned on the forward rail. Below were several small forward decks that were empty and not lit. She remembered now that the level above their staterooms had such a forward deck.

Making her way down, she danced a little on the stairs, reveling in her new fitness. It was only three flights. She so enjoyed being in good shape.

Deck ten did indeed have a good place to view the stars. Marybeth sat on a wooden bench and marveled at the night sky. It was like the sky over the outback. Like the sky over the California desert. Like the sky over west Texas. Only deeper, darker, and brighter at the same time. It was beautiful, and she blessed to see her beautiful sky once more from this side.

CHAPTER 27

It was dark, and the wind pushed back on the door. Sean leaned into it with his back, bracing it for Grace to step through onto the deck. Darkness swallowed them, a single pool of light from a lantern lighting the center of the deck fifty feet away. The wind roared in her ears and pushed her back. She lunged for the wooden rail and hung on. She felt the weight of Sean's arm around her and for a moment thought, *oh really?* But the weight lifted and all that remained was his jacket that she pulled tight around her, feeling that if she let go, it would blow away.

In the shadows, just out of the pool of light cast by the lantern, she could see a woman sitting on one of the wooden benches, her head tilted back like she was sleeping. She didn't mind the company. She liked Sean, but had only known him a few hours. His jacket smelled like wood smoke and bacon. Like home.

They talked in whispered tones until, eventually, his elbow touched hers on the rail and she realized that he was shivering. She offered to share the jacket. He smiled and looked over his shoulder to the old woman on the bench as if to say, "We're being watched."

The woman hadn't moved. "Should we check on her?" asked Grace.

"Sure."

She had one hand laying in her lap and the other on the back of the bench. She was taller than most women, and her legs were crossed comfortably in front of her. Her eyes were fixed on the starry sky above. Grace sat on the edge of the bench.

"She looks so peaceful." She reached up tentatively and closed the woman's eyes while Sean lifted the emergency phone and called the bridge.

***

The music stopped abruptly, the mics for the band cut without warning. A voice came over the intercom announcing operation "Bright Star."

"What's that?" asked Doris. "Some kind of stargazing?"

Violet shook her head. Not a single officer remained sitting. Most clustered in groups of two or three. The captain left with an officer who had a phone to one ear.

"Some kind of ship emergency, I think," said Ruby.

"What, like the Titanic?" asked Mini.

"You remember that one, do you?" said Doris.

"Most of the officers are still here. Can't be that big of a deal," said Violet. But something *was* wrong. She looked around the room, searching for some clue. Her eyes landed on the young officer she had seen talking to Dana earlier that day. He was a nice kid. "What kind of emergency is Bright Star?" she asked, sidling up to him with her Champagne glass high.

"It's a medical emergency. We have a lot of guests, and sometimes one has a serious medical issue."

As calmly as she could, she handed the glass of Champagne to a waiter and left.

***

Violet sat on the deck, leaning on the painted rail of the ladderway. It wasn't as fancy in this part of the ship as the more travelled area. The deck was painted steel and cold.

The kids that had found Marybeth were leaning on the front rail. The girl teared up and clutched a blanket around herself when Violet was introduced by the medical officer. The young man had his own blanket. He watched everything with deep interest. That was a bright one.

Violet could feel the tears coming up in her own eyes. She wondered why they had taken so long to come. A crewman handed her a blanket and offered to get her a chair.

"No," she said.

She watched as they laid Marybeth on a stretcher, straightened her long legs out, and covered her with a blanket.

The young man, Sean, offered his hand, “Ms. Violet?”

She didn't want to go. It was good enough here for Marybeth, why not for her?

She took his offered hand and when her feet were under her, she saw that her other friends had arrived.

CHAPTER 28

The *Ellie Maye* bumped against the dock's recycled truck tire fenders. The Caribbean coast of Guatemala was nothing like the wealthy west coast. Here the docks were for fishing boats and small rusty-hulled cargo ships. The streets were narrow and mostly made of stone. The jungle came right down to the sea. Shops were concrete and brick and mostly open air. Houses colorful blends of concrete, stone, and rusty sheet metal.

Eduardo loved this place. It was home, and he was far more comfortable here than in the streets of Puerto Quetzal, where every house had a swimming pool and a private dock. The whole time there, learning to be Roberto, he had not been able to find a proper bar, a place open to the street with small tables and wobbly chairs. A place where three-legged dogs begged and stole food, then ran away to return the next day.

Here bars were plentiful, but the old man would not come into Livingston to meet him. Eduardo left the crew in town and took the Range Rover up into the mountains with the man Papa had sent.

The driver focused on the narrow, wet streets, dodging dogs and motorbikes. Papa had sent two men, one to drive and one to shoot. A truck slowed ahead, and the driver checked the rearview to see if anyone was closing off escape behind. Unwilling to take chances, he swung into a narrow lane and accelerated, wet banana leaves slapping the tire on the roof rack. A dozen more turns and the streets became mere trails between the rough shelters that people here called homes.

They turned onto a paved road and slowed to weave between the pedestrian traffic. Eduardo smiled when he saw a three-legged dog. *My country's animal.* Finally, they swung into a narrow, muddy lane. The driver tapped his horn twice, and a sheet metal gate opened in a wall of vegetation. They drove through.

Ed had been here before. He must have been just a child, but he remembered this place. Back then he called it the hidden village. It wasn't a village at all, just a monastery hidden from the world by a wall of sheet metal and jungle. From a deeply buried part of his brain, he retrieved the thought that Papa's brother, his uncle, was a priest. He had an uncle in the church, and he guessed that his uncle lived here. Why else would he remember this place?

Eduardo had never been religious and never had occasion to think much about monasteries. He examined his surroundings. Aside from a monk sweeping the side steps of the church, there was no one in sight. A few goats roamed between the blocky houses at the end of the courtyard.

A monk in a rough brown robe exited one of the buildings and crunched across the brown gravel toward the church. Nearing, he waved to Eduardo to follow.

Inside, they turned into a small stone cell with arched windows that opened into a garden. An older man leaned over the teak desk reading. He finished his paragraph and looked up. The face was familiar. The eyes and nose were right. The chin was longer, and he was much taller, but he was family.

"You do not remember me?"

Ed shook his head, then remembering his manners, tilted his chin down in a half bow to honor the churchman.

"I am not God, and you are not taking communion."

"Forgive me, Uncle, I do not remember the last time I was in church."

"Yes. Neither does your father," replied the priest.

"But this time?" asked Eduardo.

The priest shook his head. "He will meet you in the garden. He will not come into the house of God."

Eduardo had never understood his father's disappointment in God. Not having been introduced himself, he was ambivalent about the deity, but his father had a brother in the priesthood. Surely he had grown up in the church?

Uncle Jose showed him around the monastery, explaining the workings of the place with dry wit and some charm, pointing out that the monks lived a backward life, only emerging into society often enough to realize that the rest of the world was even more backward.

"Only here is it so backward," said Eduardo.

"I think everywhere is backward, from God," said the priest.

Ed counted sixteen monks, most older than his uncle by a generation. Only one was younger than Eduardo. There were no women at all in the compound. That surprised Eduardo. He had always thought that monks and priests only pretended to be celibate.

The young monk jogged up to them, his chin down and feet shuffling peasant-like in the sandals. He whispered in the priest's ear.

"Your father is here," said Jose.

Eduardo met Luis in the garden, a clearing with a small, thatch-roofed shelter.

"You look like a fagot," said Luis.

Ed cringed, "Please don't say that, Papa. I'm working hard to fit the part of Roberto without looking the part too much."

Luis shook his head. "It's not working."

Eduardo shrugged. "Maybe that's okay then, if I am accepted as Roberto."

"That is only the first part of the job."

Ed nodded. He understood and was ready to get on with the rest of his mission. Why they had stopped here was a mystery to him. They could have gone straight to Grand Cayman from Panama.

"No," said Luis. "You should go slow. Take time to prepare properly. Even when you are there, do not rush into the job."

"Papa, the docks at San Felipe are so close. Why did you have us dock in Livingston where we stand out?"

Papa smiled. "I didn't know you were playing the part so well."

The old man had cracked a joke.

He poured some wine. "Don't worry, it's holy wine," he said, making it two in a row.

"You're in a good mood," said Eduardo.

Luis raised his glass in salute. “They are going to feed us dinner. Let's enjoy the evening.”

***

The sun was setting, dinner was consumed, and the jungle began its evening concert. Eduardo stretched and shook his father's hand. It would be a success. He was sure of it.

Walking to the car, Papa gave him a phone number and some last minute instructions,

Eduardo left feeling very good about the job and even about his father.

***

Jose watched the father and son drive away separately.

His brother had always been very untrusting of God, expressing his feeling that every time he got close to God, bad things happened to him. Perhaps he was mistaking God and God's messengers. Jose chuckled, then brought himself into check. Once again, he was betraying his brother and this time his brother's son. It was no laughing matter, except that it was, when you thought about it. Luis, so many times coming here to meet someone in private, only to have his conversations recorded and sent to the Americans.

Jose wondered if he should send this recording in. He was not entirely sure what they were planning. This was not a drug smuggling operation, but Luis had mentioned guns, and the level of operational security suggested more than a family vacation. He copied the encrypted audio to the email and pushed “send.”

CHAPTER 29

Violet numbly sipped her cold coffee.

The sun rose. Six women, the ladies minus Doris, and Lester's daughter Laura and granddaughter Emily, sat quietly in the largest of the forward staterooms. The stewards brought coffee and a condolence note from the captain.

Violet cringed when she read the note. It seemed so selfish to think this way, but the wedding had focused half of the crew's attention on them, and now with the passing of Marybeth, she felt like they were all under a microscope. Angry with herself for even thinking of such trivialities as the success or failure of the mission when her friend had just passed, Violet withdrew into the fog of simple decision making. Arrangements had to be made. Marybeth would not wish to make her last journey through foreign lands in the back of a truck. They put it to the captain that they wanted to keep her on board in the ship's morgue rather than ship her through Mexico where she would be subjected to the undignified border searches. He agreed without hesitation.

The ladies sipped their coffee and tea and kept to themselves. Ruby wandered out on the balcony. Her long hair flew wildly, her chin lifted, singing; her words lost forever to the wind.

Bernice tapped around the room with her cane as if she were blind.

Mini sat at the table and mumbled.

Doris wandered in and asked for coffee. Violet hadn't really thought she would show up. It couldn't have been much of a honeymoon night. Doris looked at her and winked. Violet turned away. What right did anyone have to carry on like that when they had just lost a friend?

Emily and Laura made excuses to go.

The discussion cranked up.

Always the big question, “Why?”

“What can we do without Marybeth?”

“Was it worth her life?”

Ruby shot that one down. "Marybeth didn't die robbing a bank. She died on a cruise. I for one think she was having a wonderful time."

The debate escalated into a sometimes subdued but bitter brawl of words and looks. The ship's horn blew, signaling arrival at port.

Violet felt her feet begin to move. She mumbled that she would be back in a minute, but when she got to the hall, she turned right toward the stairs.

A sign in front of the casino read CLOSED WHILE IN PORT. So much for high stakes gambling. What port were they in anyway? She had forgotten the day's schedule. Where was Marybeth when she needed her? She grabbed a passing crewman by the arm. "Cancun, Ms. Violet," was the reply.

She wandered, eventually finding herself on deck zero with her cruise pass in hand.

She boarded the tender and waited while it filled up.

They shoved off, and she barely felt the boat move on the ride to the mainland.

They docked.

At the street, she stood, staring ahead until she realized that someone was calling to her in broken English. A taxi driver. She got in and told him to drive. After a while, he stopped and pointed at the meter. "No mas, no mas," he said. *No more.* That much Spanish, she knew. She held up her hand, asking him to wait, and after a few minutes of contemplation, she asked him where she could find a race track.

The driver held up a finger begging her patience, then speed dialed his phone and handed it to Violet. After a brief conversation, the woman who answered asked her to hand the phone back to Miguel. Miguel listened and nodded. He set the phone down. Gold teeth gleaming in the mirror, he made engine noises, *vroom-vroom,* as he pulled back into traffic, ignoring the blaring horns.

***

Raymond Gutierrez, driver extraordinaire, had no desire to shepherd unskilled drivers around the coarse at bicycle speeds. He begged the office to send him skilled drivers, skilled amateurs even. Drivers that were willing to push the pedal to the floor, but smart enough not to. Maybe even drivers that could find the line through the turns and put in a decent lap time.

It wasn't to be. Elvira sent him anyone that was willing to pay. She owned the track, and Racing Cancun was here to make money. So be it. He would be bored. He would take who she sent him. He would drive them around the track at a safe speed, show them the corners, try and explain the concepts of power management. When that was done, he would let them drive the six laps they paid for. He would sit comfortably, maybe take a nap, while the next would-be bus driver puttered around at speeds almost fast enough to warm up the tires. When they were done, he would pretend they were naturals. He would even give them the trophy they paid for and stand in the winner's circle with them for a photo. He would then collect his paycheck and go home to his wife and four whiny kids each night. What fun!

It was infuriating. His best years as a driver were being wasted here because of a stupid contract that he signed when he was broke. Racing Cancun had sponsored him when he needed it. Now he would pay them back one peso at a time until his last breath fled him out of pure boredom.

His next driver was an eighty-seven year old woman from America. Carolina, the counter girl, showed him a copy of the woman's license. *Jesus de Christo! Were they kidding?* It would take her thirty minutes to put on the suit. Plenty of time to get coffee.

Raymond flirted with Carolina while she fixed his coffee. It would have too much sugar. She was no barista. More like eye candy for the middle-aged men that came to drive the cars. They never seemed to care that the drive cost twice as much as the listed price when she was around. Raymond could see why.

"You have a wife," said Carolina.

"Si."

"Then, why are you flirting with me?"

"I am a racecar driver. This is not flirting. I am interviewing a potential trophy girl."

"But I am already a trophy girl."

"Those are not real trophies. Those are paid for. You have the potential to be a real trophy girl."

"Do I have to wear the tight shorts and crop top?"

"Oh, no, you could wear a short skirt, or a bikini, or you could go naked if you want."

"Oh!" Carolina turned deep red.

Raymond turned away feigning embarrassment. After a reasonable few seconds, he returned his attention to her to find that her eyes were watery and her nipples were sticking out like traffic cones. *Damn!* He hadn't meant to go so far. "I will see you later," he said, over his shoulder.

She laughed, "Ooookaay."

Shit, he wound his way between the garages. He had a beautiful wife, but here at work he was so bored, and this girl made it so easy to flirt. He would have to avoid the front office for a while. Girls like that were dangerous.

The snarl of a Ferrari teased his ears. Who would be running this early? There were only two Ferraris in the stable. Both were F430s. To his ear, the shifting was slow, too slow to be one of the track instructor drivers. The car shifted down to second, growling through a turn, the sound of a new driver feeling out the car.

Had he been gone long enough for the Brazilian to run a demo lap and put the client in the driver's seat? It didn't seem possible. He didn't remember seeing anyone else on the schedule before ten. Maybe the Brazilian was sneaking a girlfriend on the track. It wouldn't be the first time.

The pit was empty.

Raymond's heart sank into his stomach. *Where is my car?*

As calmly as he could, he climbed the narrow stairs up the pit wall tower. There was no reason to panic. Well, there was, but it wouldn't help. From the halfway point, he could see his yellow Ferrari at the far turn. It was a nice wide turn, and the car wasn't going that fast. A little drift pulling out of the turn proved that the tires were cold. That would change soon enough at the upcoming turns.

The Ferrari swept easily through the first of the series of curves, then shifted down and made a lazy series of sweeping left and right turns before heading into the first hairpin that took it back away from him.

There was one more easy hairpin before the trickiest turn on the track. Coming out of the second hairpin was one gentle curve they called the Woman and a second curve they called the Bitch. The Bitch was small but sharp, easy to underestimate. So many drivers had missed it that the warning paint was worn off in the middle of the curve where they had skidded into the infield. Other drivers had overcompensated, and the warning paint was worn off at the end of the curve where cars had gone into the weeds.

His driver—he assumed it was his driver in the car—took the turn well, obviously looking far enough ahead to make the curve a bit straighter and keep the tires on the track.

The tires, warm and sticking now, drifted only a little on the curve. The Ferrari accelerated out of the series of turns and through the long sweeping right toward the much harder final turn before the pits.

Maybe—he glanced at the clipboard for her name—Maybe Violet would see him and come into the pits. The F430 was in third and winding up, down to second and hard into the turn. She was not coming into the pits.

Instead, the car buzzed like an angry hornet, pushing through third and into fourth gear, flashing past him on the straight. Down to third and a hard push through the dogleg turn before hitting fourth in the second straight and continuing into the turn in high gear.

Coming out of turn one, the Ferrari found a nice line, only dropping into second gear for the tight hairpin away from Raymond.

She pushed it a little hard on the next turn, drifting out, but like a pro, used the steering rather than the brakes to get the car back in trim. Through the Woman and the Bitch, she made a nice, but not perfect line.

Raymond dropped the coffee and reached for his phone. He needed to time this next lap.

Below, in the pit, he heard another car start. The second Ferrari. The Brazilian was warming up. Raymond glanced down. Standing by the car in a helmet, tank top, and short shorts was a leggy blond. The Brazilian waved her away from the car and revved the engine.

"No! No! No! I'm up here," screamed Raymond. It was useless, no one could hear over the scream of the Ferraris.

The yellow F430 Scuderia screamed past the pits. The Brazilian, in the powder blue 430, swung out behind her, accelerating, but with no hope of catching up.

Instead, he ran a lazy lap, only pushing the car as he neared the pits again. The Brazilian was stalking, waiting, warming up his tires. He wanted to race Raymond. Raymond wasn't the other driver.

***

Violet eased through the first lap, getting the feel of the paddle shifters. She tried the left first. Getting no response, she tried the right and almost stalled the car in the pits.

Accelerating out of the pits and onto the track, she shifted easily up through the gears with the right paddle and back down with the left. Nice.

The track was flat, with only a gentle bank on a few of the turns. Cones marked areas that she would want to stay out of. Concrete barriers would be hard on the car if she made a mistake. Best to get to know the track with a lap or two. Maybe she could get that in before the "pro driver" caught on.

By lap two Violet had the turns figured out and was ready to drive. The car was wonderfully responsive but so low to the ground that she could barely see the next turn. Passing the pits, she pushed the engine past the red line and shifted.

She saw the pro on lap three, helmet in one hand and phone in the other, waiting on the flag tower by the pits. Good for him. If he had thought to unfurl the black flag, she would have stopped. He didn't.

Feeling herself come alive, Violet pushed the car through the third and fourth laps. The tires were good and warm, and she only drifted a little on the big turn. There wasn't much to do about that but drive through it.

At the end of the fourth lap, she saw movement in the rearview. Another car was coming onto the track. So, that was how it was going to be. She pushed through the fifth lap, testing her arm strength on the turns. The way she figured, she had two training laps and six laps to drive. That added up to the eight she'd paid for.

Coming out of lap five, she found the blue Ferrari on the straight and slowed to match his speed before they both accelerated toward the dogleg. The second driver—Violet called him Blue—had the advantage after her slowing, but both had to slow for the dogleg.

The second straight away was split by several small islands. Violet took the outside and pushed the car hard. She was a nose ahead passing the midpoint, but going into turn one she was on the outside and fell behind, her nose almost touching the blue F430.

Not knowing how Blue drove, she backed off a few feet coming out of the turn, following into the sweeping series, then the hairpins, feeling like they were going too slow. There, in the awkward first bend of the second hairpin, Blue went wide, overcautious. Then, again, at the second wavy curve, he did the same.

Taking the weight of the steering with her left hand, she stretched her right shoulder and felt it pop. She rotated it to make sure it was good, then laid her hand on the top of the wheel and flew the car through the final turn. Barreling through the straight and into the dogleg inches from Blue's tail lights, she decided that it was time for some strategy. She swung wide around the last island of the straight and aimed for the inside line of the turn.

It was a failing move that left her two lengths behind rather than in the lead, exactly what she wanted. She needed the space, and Blue wouldn't expect her to try again on this lap. Hanging back through the hairpins, she found the line through the next two curves—the ones Raymond called the Woman and the Bitch.

Blue followed the curves. Violet followed an invisible line, accelerating toward Blue just as he swung wide across her path on the second curve. Gripping the wheel so hard her elbows hurt, she blasted past Blue with so much momentum that she almost didn't make the next, more gentle curve. A rookiee mistake, but hey, she hadn't driven like this in years.

This is where it matters, she thought, bringing her nerves under control. No, not control, instinct! Violet let herself breathe. Let herself feel the pulse of the car through her body.

Blue was in the turn behind her. Pulling into the straight, she let the car do what it was made to do. Like a good horse, it knew the way. All she had to do was let it run. Through the second straight, she swung wide of the islands and dove into turn one at almost 140 miles per hour.

Pulling out of the second hairpin, she saw Blue coming through the first. She found the line again through the curves. This time, the little waver of drift was like an old friend.

On lap eight, she saw Blue pull between the cones into the infield. She cackled like an old hen and coasted through the last few turns before entering the pits.

***

Raymond stormed up to the car, but when Violet climbed stiffly out of the Ferrari with that satisfied smile, he could do nothing but throw his arms around her and lift her from the ground. “You, you are amazing! You beat the track record. You handle a fine car like a woman… like a woman, ah, handles… a… a fine car.”

He set her down. She was not so small and not so big. Just right, and very strong for her age. But there was weariness and pain in her eyes, and when she tried to speak, she cried instead.

Raymond thought of how his wife and sisters responded to happy things and extended his hand. “It was a very good race, and you won it fantastically.”

“That's not it,” she said. “I lost my best friend last night.”

“Oh. Then you needed to drive… to see God?”

Violet squinted at him through the tears.

Raymond turned away and raised his hands, waving them around as he explained, “When I am out here, I am a fool, a donkey. I say stupid things, I flirt with women, I argue with my wife. But when I am driving, I am alone with God. When I am alone with God, we talk.”

From the corner of his eye, he saw Pedro, the track handyman and photographer. Carolina would be close behind.

"Madre de Dios," Carolina was here with the top of her tight shorts folded down. "You forgot to button your shorts," he said, refusing to look at the girl.

Pedro snapped several pictures, mostly of Carolina.

"They are sexier this way," she said holding the trophy above her head as she swayed in a circle around him. Raymond ground his teeth. The white shorts were tiny and her breasts, her breasts jiggled beneath a crop top that barely covered them. And still, the traffic cones.

"Madre de Dios," he muttered. "Suddenly, I am hungry. Will you let me take you to lunch?" he asked, focusing on Violet.

She nodded, "Sure, why not?"

"We take the Ferrari," he said, winking.

***

Violet felt the buzz of her cell phone in her pocket as she waited in line to board. Even with the excitement of planning to rob the bank, she had felt like she was trudging through the muck of almost a century of pain and setbacks. Today, she had leapt ahead. She had violated all the rules. Signed a contract, then thrown it away. Stolen a car and returned it to a man that should have been angry but wasn't.

Lunch had been wonderful. A laid-back afternoon in a local bar where the empty beer bottles were swept away and replaced with full ones. As the conversation waned and the sun began to dip below the awning, Raymond staggered to the car, where Violet—more than a little buzzed herself—took the keys and the driver's seat.

About twenty minutes into the drive, she saw the expanse of the Caribbean on her left and realized that she was heading away from the ship. Swinging the car into a U-turn, she'd glanced at her watch. The last tender was boarding in twenty minutes. She stepped on it.

The buzz was a text message, a picture of Raymond with two cops in their blue uniforms and bullet proof vests. They were in front of the yellow Ferrari that they'd chased the last two miles to the dock. The cops had their arms around Raymond's shoulders. He was not cuffed.

The man was a first rate charmer.

Violet chuckled and put the phone away.

She stepped onto the ship. For the first time in ages, she felt solid ground beneath her.

CHAPTER 30

Violet took the stairs up from deck zero to nine. She needed time to think.

No one spoke when she entered.

Bernice offered her a glass of water.

"Where's Lester?" she asked.

"Off with the kids. We saw you on the tender," said Doris.

Violet nodded. "We've got a full day in Belize to either find guns and get them aboard, or get them to the Caymans."

"No, we don't," said Ruby.

Violet hadn't seen that coming. Did she misread the room? Had they resolved not to carry through?

"Little Bobby is in Belize City. It's in the news," said Ruby.

"Page 10 of Atlanta's mostly worthless newspaper," said Bernice.

"All right," said Violet, catching her breath, "we need everything on the table. Everything we know or need to know about Belize, Belize City, getting around, getting arms if needed… All of it by…" she checked her watch "…by 8:00 tonight. That's three hours and twenty minutes. After that, we eat, play, and rest. Tomorrow, we get off the boat by tender or dock. Bernice, do we know which?"

"I'll find out," said Bernice, jotting down a note.

Violet continued, "Tomorrow we get off the ship, gather what we need, and go get the little bastard. Any objections?" She waited a bare half a second. "None heard, let's get to work."

***

They broke early for dinner and ordered room service.

In the meantime, they sorted notes and shared what they had learned.

Ruby and Doris interviewed Dana Sully extensively. The girl was apprehensive but soon caught on that the ladies were looking for information, not assistance. In all, she was perhaps the best source they had. Her view as a security officer gave them a pre-filtered look at the country from a security perspective. Most of all it helped them separate the written law from the law in practice. All of it was useful. The rest was everyday information. All you needed to rent a car was a local permit. To get that you needed a current driver's license. Violet, Ruby, and Doris all had theirs. You could rent a car easily, but according to Sully, the local cops had a reputation for shaking down rental car drivers. There was also the question of whether rentals were GPS tracked. They couldn't be sure one way or the other. To be safe, they would have to depend on cabs.

After dinner, they took in a show, then commandeered a hot tub for the rest of the evening. The next morning, they took the first tender to shore.

***

Mini watched the taillights and tried not to breathe in the heavy exhaust of the cab as it sped away. In front of them was an eight foot tall iron gate set in a stuccoed brick wall that was accented with ivy and in places, perhaps intentionally, missing chunks of the cement plaster. The wall and the property behind it were shaded by huge palms intermixed with eucalyptus trees.

"I know the cops target rentals, but what do they think of Americans hitchhiking?" said Doris, nodding at the vanishing cab.

"Is it locked?" asked Mini, indicating the gate.

Ruby nodded and pointed to the mechanical arms that opened and closed the gate. "You can't force those. On the other hand…" she bent over the post mounted keypad, and after a short consultation with a notepad, started typing.

The gate whined and opened.

"His Social Security number," said Ruby.

They approached the house cautiously clinging to the sides of the stone trimmed gravel drive. The contrasting bright areas of ocean made the shade of the trees seem positively dark. The house was still, the only movement a curtain billowing out onto the second floor balcony.

The garage, a six bay building to the left, connected to the house by breezeway. There were no cars in the gravel circle drive, and the wide front steps looked forlornly unused.

Mini waved toward the breezeway. Ruby agreed.

From there, they could see the ocean and the pool. The dock stood empty but for a dinghy that bobbed into sight every third or fourth wave.

Mini and Bernice scouted the garage. Three cars. The one closest was obviously his. It was cold. Almost certainly Robbins was home.

She drew the massive British Empire era Webley .45 from her purse. It was all they could get on short notice. The ammo seemed as ancient as the gun, but it would have to do.

She turned up her hearing aid and led into the house.

The lights were off. They entered through a wide hallway that passed through a utility room. From the door, they could see shadows dance across the marble floors of a large room ahead. A breeze pushed the door closed. Doris reached for it, but a damper caught it, and it closed with a light thump.

No barking dog, no alarm. Mini could feel Ruby's breath on her elbow. This might be easier than she thought.

She led them into a large dining room. To the left, huge French doors opened to the veranda and pool. The table and eighteen teak chairs were the centerpiece of the room, the marble floor patterned to frame the table. From the high ceiling, a crystal chandelier hung, its prisms chiming.

Above the chandelier were dark arches to the right and well-lit arches to front and left proving that the arched balconies were a feature that continued throughout the palatial house. The dark arches were a danger zone. Anyone could be in those shadows watching.

Something *clanged* to the right.

Mini moved quietly to the door with the warm glow of incandescent light flowing under.

Ruby moved to the far side of the room and glanced through the arched passageway. She gave a thumbs up indicating that the great room on the other side was clear.

Mini backed off and carefully opened a door near the corner from the entry hall. She didn't like passing doors without knowing what was behind. Behind this one was a set of stairs with a carpet tread that led up to the floor and arches above. She closed the door and motioned for Violet to open the door to what she presumed was the kitchen.

Golden light spilled onto the marble and Mini swept into the room, the barrel of the pistol crossing right to left. The room was empty. The kitchen was roughly three times the size of the house Mini had grown up in. It extended the full width of the dining room and to the right behind the stairs. She heard footsteps to the right.

Around the corner, a door was open. Out of it stepped a middle-aged Hispanic woman with a sack of rice in her arms. The rice fell to the floor, and the woman reached to cover her mouth. "No, no, no, no," she repeated, staring at the gun and backing up, her expression vacillating from terror to confusion, then back. "I don't have any money, and Mr. Bob isn't here," said the woman putting her hands above her head. "Please don't hurt me."

"Sit," commanded Mini, the gun barrel indicating the chair with the arms.

Ruby began with the duct tape.

"Not her mouth," said Violet.

"Yes, her mouth," countered Mini. "We'll take it off in a minute."

Ruby carefully placed the tape across the woman's mouth and pressed it on.

"Is anyone else in the house?" asked Mini.

No, the woman indicated with a head shake.

Mini motioned for Ruby to grab a weapon and follow. Ruby chose a heavy rolling pin.

Moments later, they returned. The house did indeed appear to be empty.

Mini yanked the tape off the woman's mouth. "Do you speak English?"

"This is Belize. We all speak English."

"Who are you?"

"The cook…and sometimes housekeeper. I don't know nothing."

"Just answer the questions, and it will be all right," said Mini. Sensing that the cook was close to hyperventilating, she asked for a cup of water. The water seemed to work, and the cook's breathing settled to something manageable.

"Where is Mr. Bob?" asked Mini, barely concealing the sneer in her voice.

"He is gone golfing."

Mini shook her head in disbelief. "His car is in the garage."

The cook shook her head, confused. "They took the boat to the island."

"You just said he went golfing, now you say they went to an island. Which is it?"

"Both. It's both. The golf course is on the island."

"Who is they?"

"Mr. Bob and Jamie. He drives the boat."

"Is Jamie a bodyguard?"

"No," laughed the cook. "He's a gardener and sometimes drives the boat."

"What's your name?" asked Mini, offering another sip of water.

The cook sipped then answered, "Carmine."

"Well, Carmine, tell us everything you know about Mr. Bob."

And she did.

***

Bob would be back sometime around 3:00 pm. That left them several hours to search the house. *For what?* Ruby asked herself. *A safe? Papers, notes, phone numbers? What do any of those things do for us?* Anything could be important. He could even be keeping a significant amount of their money in the house. The question was, were they going to try at all to cover their tracks?

She found the safe. Not just a little box in the floor. This was the real deal, a strong box with a double layer steel door and mil-spec locks. Ruby studied the box. It was almost four feet tall and three wide. The hinge pins were only ¾ inch thick, but the box was sure to have bolts on all sides of the door and removing the pins would be a waste of time. To get into a box like this, you had to either pick the lock or breach the door to access the arms that control the bolts. Mini had taught her that and more.

It would need to be blown.

What she didn't know was still bigger than what she did know. She didn't know what the bolt mechanism looked like inside the door. So, if she were going to blow the safe, where would she place the charge?

"Wow!" said Mini, making her jump. "This is a Whites Strong 334. Haven't seen one of these in years. The lock is a refit. They didn't have locks like this when these were built."

Ruby grinned and asked where the bolts were centered.

There isn't anything special or magical about the drills used to breach a safe. It's steel, so you need a sharp drill bit and oil to keep it cool. They found a heavy duty drill in the garage. Eventually, they found a set of drill bits with some cutting edge left to them.

It took an hour and a half for Ruby to find the tools and drill three holes about four inches apart in the face of the safe. The holes formed the corners of a triangle, and only went through the outside layer of the steel door. She shone a light through one hole and put her eye to another. The hole wasn't directly over the bolt rods but close enough.

***

Violet watched Ruby work on the safe.

Ruby rummaged around in her bag for a moment then came out with a tissue. She carefully unwrapped the paper exposing a severed finger.

Goodness, thought Violet, catching her breath. For a moment, she thought it was real. Now, she realized it was a finger of C-4 from the hand sculpture.

Ruby stuck the finger into a hole and mashed the plastic-like material around the edges.

She brought out another finger, this one larger, and crammed it into the second hole.

The third finger, she help up and laughed. "It's the middle one," she explained, pointing it up at the ceiling of Bobby's house.

Done amusing herself, she pushed a hole in the plastic with a pencil then inserted a blasting cap. She pushed the cap into the plastic and worked the finger into the final hole. “Maybe just a little more,” she said, another ball of the putty in her hand.

“How long till this blows?” asked Vi.

“I’ve got to find a timer. Twenty or thirty minutes,” said Ruby.

“Warn us when you’re ready,” said Violet, from the door.

There were a number of rooms in the house to explore. Some as plain and devoid of personality as a hotel room. Others more interesting. A store room near the breezeway entry was neatly lined with the man's new toys, dive equipment, tennis rackets, water skis, fishing poles, and golf bags.

At first, Violet was surprised to see the golf bags. *Had the cook lied?* Looking again, she saw that they were empty except for a few ancient looking clubs and the rack of shoes had an empty spot.

The library was interesting for a reader but seemed more like a storage room for dusty books than a place Bobby would spend time. There was a pipe on the corner table. She picked it up and sniffed it. It had been a long time since that pipe had been lit.

Rubber shoes squeaked on the marble. Violet peeked out the door. Doris saw her and lurched to a nervous stop. “You scared me,” said Doris, holding her hand to her chest. “Ruby set a kitchen timer to light the safe in fifteen.”

Violet slipped past to the next room. So far there’d been nothing worth seeing here. She took a series of pictures with her phone and looked around the room. This was Bobby's bedroom, the antithesis of the other rooms in the house. Not dirty, just used and mildly personal. The furniture was all matched. Shoes lined the wall by the bed, when there was plenty of room in the closet. The man had strange habits.

Violet sat on the bed and looked through the papers that Bernice had set aside. Out of all this, she did not find a single thread of anything that looked helpful. No money, no account numbers, no passwords, and no Bobby. *What were they doing here?*

“Doris, call everyone to the kitchen in five minutes.”

***

Bob was in a foul mood. He'd played two rounds with Davies and lost both by a single stroke. He would have felt better, but Davies was the course drunk. He never teed off sober. The man swayed in the wind like a palm and still managed to keep the ball on the green.

The boat ride home was smooth, the swells barely topping three feet, but nearing home Jamie informed him that they needed to stop for fuel before the fishing boats got back and the lines got too long. It was nice that Jamie was thinking ahead, but they were running low, and it takes a long time to pump three hundred gallons of diesel into a boat.

Bob, impatient to put the day behind him, called a cab from the marina. At his urging, the cabbie drove as fast as the beat up old car would allow, things shaking and rattling that shouldn't have, but after telling the driver to break all the records to get him home, Bob wasn't willing to renege. They sped down the two lane road, passing in and out of the shadows of trees that probably should have been cleared back ten feet further for safety.

Three minutes after getting into the car, Bob stood on shaky legs staring at his gate. It was open. Only Carmine could have done that, and Carmine knew better.

Thinking that he may need to leave in a hurry, Bob ordered the driver to wait, waving a twenty under his nose, then keeping it.

***

Violet expected her friends to meet in the kitchen.

They were there. As was Bobby, holding a gun on them.

“Shit,” she said, raising her hands.

“Where's the other one?” he demanded.

No one answered.

Robbins read the expressions. “Oh, I see. The longer I wait, the fewer of you there are.” He chuckled and waved the gun around. “What are you doing here? What did you expect to accomplish?” He paced, swinging the small automatic from hand to hand to keep them covered. “What did you think you would do, walk in here and take my money and just leave? Did it ever occur to you that I might put it in a bank? Are you really that dumb?”

“You came into my house and taped up my cook. You ate my food,” he screeched, pointing at the crumb-covered plates on the counter. “Did you enjoy my…" he dipped a finger onto the plate and tasted, "…my goose liver pâté? Did you eat it all?!"

"Carmine, did they eat it all? Did you tell them where it was?"

Carmine grunted from behind the duct tape and shook her head.

Bobby ripped the tape from her mouth.

"Oww! Mr. Bob, that hurt!"

"Did you tell them where to find the pâté?"

"No, I didn't tell them where to find your smushed goose. I had tape over my mouth! Now, will you please untie me?"

"No, I don't think so," said Bobby, his eyes darting around the room. "Not until I figure out what to do with them."

"Call the police," suggested Carmine.

"Can't do that," he mumbled. "Can't do that."

Ruby inched her way around so that Violet could see her lips move and hear her mumblings. "Tick, tock, tick, tock, goes the little kitchen clock."

"Put a cork in it, you old loon!" growled Robbins.

"Tick, tock, tick, tock…"

Great time to lose your mind, thought Violet.

"…something in the oven…"

Please, please stop, thought Violet.

"Tick, tock, tick, tock…" Ruby rolled her eyes up toward the ceiling, and Violet's heart stopped beating. "Another minute, and our cake will be done," said Ruby.

Bob scanned the row of ovens. "You've lost your mind completely, haven't you?"

Ruby smiled and turned, winking at her friends.

Doris choked, "Oh, Lordy."

"Only forty-five seconds till our cake is done," said Ruby.

Mini turned down her hearing aid.

"Why did you do that?" Demanded Bobby, his face red, gun barrel waving all around.

"What?" asked Mini.

"Why did you do that!" he bellowed.

"So I wouldn't have to listen to you," Mini yelled back. Her hand dropped a few inches toward her bag.

Bobby swung his pistol her way. "Got something in the bag?"

"My arms are tired."

"Drop it!"

Mini made a low guttural growl.

"Drop it. Now!" he demanded, leveling the small pistol at her head.

"Okay," she said, letting the bag loop slide down to her hand, and extending her arm. "But you won't like it." She dropped the bag.

The Webley Mark II breech-loading revolver and its cousins were used by British military from the late eighteen hundreds, well into the twentieth century. A well-crafted, large caliber handgun, it was well-suited to its purpose, and many remain in collections around the world today. As a revolver, it has no safety. As an old revolver, it has no transfer bar. The hammer and firing pin are forged from a single piece of steel, leading to the common practice of leaving an empty chamber under the hammer to prevent misfire if the hammer is bumped. Mini did not leave an empty chamber.

Violet closed her eyes and prayed as the bag fell. It cracked against the hard floor, and a muffled but still extremely loud bang followed. Fiber from the purse exploded toward Bobby, leaving a trail in the air that swirled in an odd counterclockwise pattern between his knees.

Violet let herself drop to the floor as she watched a hole appear in the oven behind Bobby. She covered her ears as Bobby began to shoot wildly at the walls and ceiling.

"Cover your ears!" she shouted.

The world cracked open, sucking the air from the room.

The marble floor bounced. The ceiling cracked, a long lazy line forming like lightning across a big sky. Plaster and concrete began to rain down.

Bobby dropped the empty magazine from his pistol and reached for his pocket.

Mini, bleeding from a nick to the ear, reached for her bag.

Bobby fled.

"Let's go, let's go, let's go!" someone screamed.

Bobby ran toward the back of the house. The ladies ducked and ran toward the front. Violet cut Carmine free and pulled her toward the exit.

A shaft of sunlight guided them through the gathering cloud of dust to the front door. Concrete pebbles rained all around. Windows broke, and the tinkle of falling glass sounded like a million fairies spoiling for a fight. The walls of the foyer were pockmarked from shrapnel like the walls of the Alamo.

The chandelier fell then stopped short of the floor by inches, caught by the electrical wiring. The ladies split, going around it like water around a river rock, charging for the door.

Mini slipped. Doris instinctively caught her and swept her forward.

Behind them, they heard cracking and splintering. Vi looked back in time to see Bob's safe fall through the ceiling into the hall.

Ruby spun, clapped her hands joyfully, then spat out a mouthful of dust and scooted for the door.

Pursued by a cloud of dust and the thunderous crash of falling timber, glass, and concrete, they flung open the front doors and fled down the seldom used front steps.

Doris saw it first. Waving, she called for the cabbie to wait.

"You pay for him?" demanded the driver as the dusty women piled in.

"We'll pay. Take us to the port," answered Violet, holding up three twenties.

The cabbie extended his hand. Violet filled it with cash. "Fast!" she said. Looking back, she saw Carmine standing uncertainly by the gate.

"Go!" she said to the driver.

***

Bob surveyed his house from the pool wall. He was outside in the open, and presumably they were inside his home, armed. If he were lucky, the house would fall on them. He reloaded his pistol wondering what had happened in the house. *Had the little bitch's bullet hit a gas line? Or a dive tank in the store room?* He had heard that those would go like rockets. *Shit!* Glass was falling from the windows.

He scooped water from the fountain and washed the sand and dust from his eyes.

Inside the house, something crashed. A fresh puff of dust shot from the broken windows. From the road, he could hear a car with a bad muffler accelerate toward the city. The cab had a bad muffler, he remembered.

"Shit!" He ran toward the garage.

***

In the kitchen, the .45 caliber bullet from the Webley had passed through the oven and severed the gas line that supplied it. Gas hissed from the bullet hole.

In the center of the house, a smoldering piece of paper floated down through the gaping hole left between floors by the falling safe.

The paper fluttered in the draft from the open front door and flared.

***

Bob took almost two steps toward the garage before he felt the thump of an explosion push the air from his chest. This one, much bigger than the first, lifted the roof on his house several inches. What glass that was left in his windows sprayed the grounds. A five inch shard stuck in a tree inches from him. Bob dove sideways into the pool.

Under the water, he watched the glow of an orange fireball cover the sky. Chunks of glass and concrete left trace bubbles in the water as they sank past him.

Bob held to the wall beneath the spring board, coming up for air every few seconds. Dry fronds fell burning from the palms. The roof sagged in the center of the house. Tiles slid off and crashed to the ground. Flames licked out of the broken windows. A door fell out of its frame and crashed to the concrete.

Bob sat on the side of the pool, bleeding from a dozen places, and drained the water from his phone.

CHAPTER 31

The ladies invaded a public restroom to wash their faces and arms and shake out their clothes before joining the line to board the ship.

Bernice found a local router not secured and downloaded email while she could get the connection. Her hands were shaking, and it was slow going. The day's activities had not quite exhausted her, but she didn't think she would be staying up late.

The last time she had been in this part of the world, her husband had been murdered, her house had been burned down, and she had fled the country. *Forty years, had it really been that long?* Some memories faded, but Warren's face was as fresh in her mind as if she had just seen him. It was a young face. Young and handsome. Never to grow old.

They had lived for twenty-two years just a few miles south across the border in Guatemala. They loved in that house, that had begun as a small hut and grown over the years. They raised their children there, then sent them off to school. Mercifully, the kids had both been in the US when the rebels attacked their home and killed Warren.

When they shot him and he fell, she knelt beside him desperate to stop the bleeding, all the while knowing that it was no use. She remembered thinking that she would be next. It wasn't a thought so much as a fact. She pressed rags on his wounds and wondered why the rebels were waiting. *Why hadn't they shot her?*

She heard them laugh as they tore through her house, looking for what? She didn't know. Yes, she did. They were looking for something to break, and when they ran out of things to break, they would come back and break her.

“Run,” whispered Warren. “Run,” he said, closing his eyes and leaving her.

She leapt from a window and ran into the jungle to hide.

Bernice wiped the tears from her cheeks. At least they had cleared the dirt from her eyes.

***

Sully wished they would let them wear wide hats in the tropical ports. Black baseball caps were fine to shade your eyes but left the ears and neck to burn. Standing all day on the white concrete didn't help. She could feel beads of sweat running down behind her ears.

The ladies had just come from the restroom to join the line. She meandered toward them. They looked pale, splotchy. As she drew closer, she realized that the effect was created by a layer of dust. Violet even had a piece of gravel in her shoe laces.

"Looks like you had an interesting day," she said to Violet. *Very interesting?* She glanced down. White dust filled the cracks on Ruby's arms. Same with the others, she noted, checking each. She plucked a shard of glass from Ruby's hair and examined it.

"You can toss that. I don't need it," said Ruby.

Sully wiped the sweat from her neck with a handkerchief. "I think I had better move you ladies to the front of the line," she said with a nod and a wink. "Have your cards ready and move as fast as you can when you get off the tender. Maybe no one will notice."

"Darn," said Mini, tapping her purse, as they approached the security checkpoint.

"You still have it?" said Ruby.

Mini gritted her teeth. "Guess I could drop it off the tender, but that would be sad. It's a good one."

"I don't think the quality of the thing is going to matter much to security," said Ruby.

Sully listened to the back and forth wondering if they had forgotten she was there. "Ahem," she cleared her throat.

"We need you to take Mini's bag and get rid of the rather heavy object in it. Then return the bag when we're on the ship," said Ruby.

"Why am I not surprised," said Sully, looking in the bag. "Would you like me to bring it on board for you?"

Mini perked up, "That would be nice."

"I was kidding," growled Sully.

"You shouldn't kid about things like that with Mini," said Ruby.

Sully sighed deeply. "I'll bring the gun, but no ammo. It is a gun isn't it? Not a fake?"

"Oh, it's real. You like me, don't you?" said Mini, nodding and coaxing Sully to do the same.

Sully laughed. "Did you get out of prison recently?"

"Honey, I've never been caught," Mini shot back, with a smile.

Sully believed it.

***

With only twenty minutes before the start of the poker game, Bernice washed quickly and scampered up to the deck above. From there, she had several unprotected routers within range to finish her download.

She could see a column of smoke several miles up the coast.

In the few hours they'd had on shore, the gang had made a pretty big splash. She hadn't imagined it would go so far as blowing up the house. The others seemed to take it in stride, even enjoy it. That was understandable. They'd made a mess of everything, but Bobby had suffered, and that added up to a job well done in everyone's mind. There was a certain satisfaction in success, even if it was messy. Oddly, she felt more proud of her friends and their performance than her own. It was strange how that worked. Bernice had more confidence in her friends than in herself and was sure the others felt the same.

It was the opposite of arrogance. *Was that humility?* She didn't feel particularly humble, or that she had anything to be humble about. She and her friends had just faced an armed man in his home and gotten away. In the process, they destroyed his home. For all she knew, they may have killed him.

Unlikely. Vermin don't die so easy.

Back in the stateroom, she rapped her cane, and Mini jumped. Someone tipped a glass, and her eyes snapped that way. The table was set, the chips were dealt, the cards were shuffled. There was even an empty chair for Marybeth. She wondered if that were intentional. Violet moved a bouquet of flowers from the corner table to the chair. That answered that.

The game started three minutes late. The shower had washed away the dust and sweat of the day. It felt good to be clean. She glanced around. Despite the exhausting day, there was a new level of energy. Everyone had it. There was also a tension in the room.

Lester removed a glass shard from Doris' leg while she dealt the cards. “Owww!” she said when he pushed it the wrong way.

“You're just going to have to stop blowing up things,” said Lester, putting a dab of ointment and a bandage on the cut.

“That was Ruby, dear,” said Doris.

“Oh, you weren't there?”

“I was there.”

Lester grunted. “You’re an accomplice, then.”

A knock at the door.

Mini jumped noticeably. Bernice felt like jumping but was too tired to react quickly.

“Are we still in port?” asked Violet, getting to the root of it.

“For another thirty or forty minutes,” said Ruby, checking her watch.

Lester peaked through the spyhole. “It's security,” he said.

Mini stiffened. It would be unfortunate if they were arrested while in port.

“Your friend in security,” said Lester. “Oh, come on. Can't you take a joke?” He opened the door.

Mini pushed him aside and drew Dana Sully in.

Sully handed her the purse. It was heavy, just like it had been when she handed it over.

“The ammo?” she asked, hopeful.

Sully rolled her eyes and reached into her pocket. “Don't even load the thing on the ship,” she ordered, handing over the five remaining cartridges. “Put it away,” she said.

“What happens if you get caught bringing something like that on board?” asked Doris.

Dana thought about it and nodded, “I get fired and left at the next port. If I’m lucky, I don’t go to jail in some third world hole.”

“Better not get caught then,” said Doris, with a genuine smile.

"I'll try."

Mini clucked, "We're all wound a little tight right now."

Dana nodded in semi-understanding.

"Upper deck at sunrise?" said Mini.

***

Dana was getting used to the the requests, orders, coming several times a day. "I can be there. It's my watch, so if I'm late, I'm on ship's business. You know, busting old ladies with guns and that kind of sh…stuff."

There was one other thing. She'd wanted to think it over first, but this seemed like the right time after all. "Your ahh, Irene has been… I don't know if you call it spreading rumors or making accusations." She paused, knowing that she must look funny with her face puckered up, deciding what to say next.

"Well, go on," said Ruby, sipping her lemonade, *or was that a margarita?*

Violet twirled her file and looked up from her cards to give Dana a reassuring grunt.

Best to lay it all out there. "She told one of our deck officers, I think she thought he was security, that you robbed someone on shore."

Mini and Violet studied their cards. Doris focused on the ceiling while Lester with his magnifying headset and a needle removed a tiny piece of glass from her leg. Bernice studied her hands on the curve of her cane. Ruby smiled a twinkly smile and slurped on the straw.

"Well, that's just silly isn't it?" said Ruby. "They scanned our bags. Were there large amounts of cash in our bags?"

Violet snorted. Bernice tapped her cane.

Dana squeezed her forehead. "No robbery then?" she asked, looking at Violet.

Violet shook her head. "No robbery." She went back to her cards.

"So," began Dana, wishing that she could stop. "That freshly fired empty cartridge in the thing I helped you bring back on the ship, we're not going to find that someone in Belize has a hole in them that size or anything like that?"

The words hung in the air, the only sound the shuffling of cards.

"No one was shot," Violet answered, over her cards.

"Okay," said Dana, believing them.

She opened the door. Irene blocked the exit.

***

Jamie tossed the line. Mister Bob caught it, barely, and looped it over the capstan for Norbert to pull. It was Mister Bob, only it didn't look like Mister Bob. The man on the dock wore a worn and torn version of what Bob had been wearing forty minutes earlier. This man's face was black with soot. His hair was matted and disheveled like it had never seen a comb. He was bleeding from a dozen cuts and had an animal snarl that displayed a missing tooth.

"Mister Bob, what happen to your tooth?"

Bob whistled when he spoke. "Fuh du toof. We gonna get toos bitches!" He started to step aboard. Jamie held up his hand to stop him.

"Mister Bob, you be hurt mighty bad." He looked up toward the smoldering house. Firefighters were knocking out the last of the glass and pulling hoses into the house. The roof dipped severely in the middle. It was relatively dark in the shade of the palms, the normally white pool deck now covered in debris. Jamie shook his head in dismay, "Nor, run up der an get a medic."

"Mister Bob, let's you sit here in the shade, and we see about fixing you up." He led Bob to a bench on a part of the dock shaded by palms.

Bob spoke, leading with a trail of bloody spittle, "I hit the side of the pool with my toof. Can they put it back in?" He held up the bloody front tooth.

"It's the whole ting?" asked Jamie, examining the tooth with interest.

Bob nodded.

"Looks good, Mister Bob, but I don know. I tink maybe in the US, but not here, mon."

Bob slumped on the bench, drooling blood.

Jamie watched Norbert help the medics lay Bob on the bench and begin to cut away his wet clothes. It was hard to tell where the water stopped and the blood began on the dark pants. Jamie studied the house. The burn marks were mostly on the south end, where the master bedroom and ballroom were. Where the roof was caved in would be near the master bedroom.

The garage seemed untouched. That was good. The boss would be out of his mind if the brand new Mercedes was burnt.

The EMTs examined a three inch shiv of glass angled into Bob's thigh like an arrowhead. One touched it. Bob squealed through the tooth hole.

While he hyperventilated, the EMTs discussed the need to take him to the hospital.

"No hospital," said Bob.

"But sir, if we don't take you to the hospital, we got to take this out here."

Bob growled and looked at Jamie, "Get me tequila."

"Mister Bob, you don drink tequila."

"I do today," spewed Bob.

As Jamie made his way to the house, he studied the damage. It was a shame, but they would have to replace the roof and gut the house. The concrete walls looked solid, though.

Careful to check first that it wasn't hot, he lifted the small boat door into the storage on the side of the house. Cases of booze were stored here. He found the tequila, two full cases, minus only one bottle. The other two cases were just boxes of shattered glass and amber soaked cardboard.

Bob drank half a bottle of tequila, shelling out a fresh, wet, hundred to each of the EMTs for each large piece of shrapnel removed. Each time, they shook their heads and said "No more," and each time they relented under the gaze of the Franklin twins.

Jamie watched Norbert watching the EMTs get rich. Pairs of hundred dollar bills passed through the boy's hands to the EMTs while he got nothing for holding the tequila bottle and sometimes holding the boss himself. Norbert pulled another two hundreds off the money roll before tucking it back in Mister Bob's pocket. Jamie waved him over.

"It ain't fair, is it?" he asked the boy.

Norbert shook his head as Jamie took the hundreds from his hand. "I just got dis job, mon, now I got nuttin."

Jamie knew the feeling. He slipped one of the hundreds off and back to Norbert. "You give me half of everything you get, you hear. When I get somtin, I give you some. You hear?"

The boy nodded.

"Now, put dat in your pocket and go take care of the mon. When dis done, maybe we get a bonus for bein here for the hard stuff. An don take no more that he don give you, you hear?"

With Norbert and the EMTs busy with the boss, Jamie rescued what he could from storage. Dive gear, a spear gun, and cases of booze. He gave a case of rum to the fire chief, and took the rest to the boat where he suspected they would be living for a while.

On the boat and away from all the noise, he paused to call his brother George, the cop. When the boss woke up, he wanted to be ready.

***

George wove his way between the firetrucks, stepping carefully over hoses. The firemen here didn't have much of a budget for replacement gear and treated what they had with great care and respect. Stepping on their hoses would be like one of them stepping on his gun.

At first, the house looked fine, but as he got closer he could see the damaged roof, missing glass and even some burn marks above the windows. The curtains on the south end were charred black where they existed at all. In the north windows, he could see fragments of cloth, once white, singed to yellow.

He circled the house on the garage side, flashing his badge to the firemen. He found Jamie on the dock, his feet cooling in the water. Jamie waved him toward the EMTs who were packing up to go. On the bench beside them lay a man in boxers with a bottle of tequila rising and falling in an unsteady rhythm on his chest. A pile of bloody cloth, presumably the man's pants, lay at the end of the bench. The man's shirt was unbuttoned, exposing a bandage around his belly. George counted four other bandages on his legs and one on the right arm. Some of the grime and soot had been washed from the man's face creating an interesting effect, like he was wearing a hood with a dreadlock hairpiece on top. The clean part of the face sported four small bandages.

"Is that Mister Bob? He bush mon, look bad."

"He's right drunk now, but he…" started Jamie.

"He's only a little drunk," roared Bob, "and he's pissed!"

George squinted, confused.

"Americans, mon, *pissed* mean angry," explained Jamie.

"Oh. Well, I be pissed too if my nice house be burned up."

"Not burn, mon," explained Jamie. "Exploded, then burn."

"Boom, then whoosh," bellowed Bob, his hands thrown wide, knocking the tequila to the deck.

Norbert snagged the bottle before much loss and put it in the boss's hand.

"Who're you?" slurred Bob.

"I your new best friend, mon. You hire me last week. Have another drink. You'll remember."

Bob leaned up on one elbow, gritting his teeth and feeling the hole where the one was missing with his tongue. "Best friend, huh? Well, I'm a little drunk, pissed, inebri… inebriated, but I've been robbed and my house…" he looked over his shoulder to the house, "…awe fuck, my house is a mess." He handed the bottle to Norbert. "I want to catch those beaches and crucify them."

George looked to James for clarification.

Jamie shrugged.

"Beaches, mon," bellowed Mister Bob, his breath threatening to reignite the fires. "You know, that's how you say it in tequila." He fell back to the bench.

***

Bob felt the fish's tail slap him in the face again. Why did he keep doing that? He pulled the spear gun up to shoot the fish.

It was too close. He couldn't bring the gun up far enough. The tail slapped his face again.

"Mister Bob, Mister Bob?" said the fish. "Mister Bob, wake up."

Bob opened his eyes. They were sticky, and when he moved, he could feel something tug at the hair on his eyebrow. It felt like plastic tape.

"Mister Bob," said the man above him, flashing a badge in the hazy space above him.

“Shit,” said Bob.

“Mister Bob, I'm George. I work for you.”

Bob nodded, that’s good. His neck felt stiff. His memory was beginning to return. Maybe. He rolled on his side and puked.

Someone brought him water, and after a few more sessions of projectile vomiting, he was beginning to put things together. The poker bitches had been here. Five of them, he counted in his head. Jamie, George, and Norbert, who he still did not remember hiring, listened to him recount the story of the assault complete with sound effects. He didn't know why, but he couldn't help but make the sound effects.

Oh, it's so beautiful here, he thought. *But why is the dock floating around like this?* He rolled over and threw up again.

When he woke, George was gone.

“We wanted to put you on the boat, but you already thought the dock was moving,” shrugged Jamie.

A phone rang. Bob fished his from his shirt pocket. Water was still seeping from the case.

Jamie answered his phone. “Mister Bob, that was George,” he said a minute later. “He says the women probably came from the cruise ship that's in port.”

“Where is the ship now?” asked Bob, through the haze.

“Leaving soon,” said Jamie.

“Get me on the boat,” Bob commanded.

***

Norbert gripped the rail with everything he had. He had been on plenty of boats with drunk drivers, but never one that insisted on hugging the coast and steering between the boats at anchor at full speed.

The boss stood at the wheel on the upper deck, his body swaying back and forth completely out of synch with the movement of the boat. It was a fine yacht, worth more than Norbert would make in his lifetime. He did not want to see it damaged. He especially did not want to see it crashed while he was on it.

Mister Bob leaned on the wheel as the hull raised and they sped south. The man's filthy hair stood up like short dreads and when he turned, the transition from the clean part of his face to the black of his ears and neck was startling. He laughed, the bloody gap where his tooth had been, the centerpiece of his face.

The cruise ship was leaving. Norbert had seen it at anchor this morning. Since then, the big ship had turned almost ninety degrees and was pointed southeast, out to sea. They headed straight at it.

The boat leaned left. They were on an intercept course with the cruise ship. *Oh, dear God!* thought Norbert. *He's a crazy man!*

Bob laughed and tossed his head back in wind, a trail of red spit trailing behind him.

***

The anchor was lifted, and the first officer had done a nice enough job bringing the ship around with the thrusters. Captain Ricci settled back, coffee in hand, thinking back on the day and how nice it had been to be alone with Lore, the beautiful junior officer with the flowing blond hair, while the ship was at anchor.

Such a nice cruise this had been. Almost no trouble at all. Only one death on board. That had been unfortunate. He liked the old ladies. They were so nice to the crew, but not too nice. Like his nonna, sweet, but no, how did the Americans say, *no bullshit?*

"Captain?" said the first officer.

"Yes."

"Captain, we have a small cruiser on course to cut us off."

"He'll turn," said the captain without looking.

"I don't think so, sir. This looks intentional."

Taking the binoculars from the first mate, Captain Ricci strolled across the bridge doing his best to push out thoughts of terrorism. He had seen the boat on radar from his seat, but radar didn't tell you much about the pilot.

This one instantly made him nervous. He looked like some kind of Rasta Teletubby, with his white face rimmed in black. More telling were the expressions of the men with him. Both were terrified. The boat slowed, the hull dropping, but it didn't slow enough.

As he watched, the man at the starboard rail, dove from the back of the yacht.

“Sound the horn, prepare for collision,” he ordered, watching the boat disappear under them, below his field of view. There was no point in stopping engines. The momentum of the ship would carry it another half mile even at this speed.

He strolled across the bridge to the starboard extension and waited, trying not to hold his breath. A boat that size would barely be felt if it hit them, but it would cause a delay in schedule. If the boat burned, it could do real damage to his ship. If the boat was loaded with explosives, they could be sunk.

The yacht, a forty-five footer he judged, came into view on the starboard side. The pilot turned hard and came to a full stop only twenty meters off his bow. Ricci raised his binoculars. Teletubby man flipped him off.

“Starboard bow and aft thrusters full,” he ordered.

“But sir…” began the first officer. “Yes, sir,” he smiled and repeated the order.

The ship shuddered slightly, and the water to the right of the ship began to churn as the ship's maneuvering thrusters pushed them left. The yacht that had just challenged them began to rock and tilt, the force of the thrusters pushing it away.

“Watch him,” said Captain Ricci to the gathering of younger officers that were now all doing just that. “A smart captain would turn into the wave until it passes. I don’t think this one is so smart.”

The smaller vessel tilted dangerously to the starboard, and Ricci wondered briefly if the captain would do anything to save his boat. He considered ordering the thrusters cut, but before he could, the yacht began to move under its own power…

…and turn away from the ship.

“Shall I cut thrusters, Sir?”

“No, he is a danger to our ship and passengers.” *There, that was on the record.*

The yacht had turned and righted itself, but the pilot foolishly cut power. The wave created by the ship's thrusters had no brake, and no conscience. It rolled over the aft swim deck of the yacht, the force pushing the stern down and lifting the bow.

Both men on the yacht managed to stay aboard as the vessel, bow up and stern under water, was propelled away like a toy slipping from a child's hand in the bathtub. The Captain grunted. It was for them a miracle. Perhaps for him it was better that no one drowned. That also would have caused a delay.

He watched as the yacht, now a hundred meters away, settled, the men still clinging to it desperately. The decks were flooded, the boat adrift. They had either flooded the engine room, or the pilot had shut the engines down out of fear.

"Cut thrusters," he ordered. No use drowning them when the aft thruster passed.

***

Norbert was a good swimmer, but he was grateful for the life jacket that Jamie had tossed over behind him. Thirty minutes is a long time in the water, and it was at least that long before he reached the *Desire'*. The ship's wake had pushed them apart, then the currents seemed to want to take him one way and the yacht another. He wondered, several times, if he should not have just swum to shore. Only one week working for this man, and they were attacking cruise ships at sea. Did that make him a pirate?

CHAPTER 32

"We could have taken his boat," said Ruby.

They'd just watched the escapade from the balcony above the bridge. Unrecognizable Bob Robbins had flipped them off. What happened next was a truly inspiring moment, second only to seeing the safe crash through his house. The ship's propulsion units pushed Bob's boat away, swamping it, leaving him dead in the water.

In the stateroom, with her friends around and Belize behind them, Ruby thought it was a shame that they didn't get the boat. That boat was big and fast, and could carry a lot of guns.

Not that it mattered. Not now. They had what they needed. While in port, they'd received a reply from Mini's sister, Kate. There was indeed an arms dealer on Grand Cayman. All they needed now was money.

Ruby listened to the money talk, trying not to burst. That idea, the one that had been right on the edge of becoming a conscious thought, was back, almost within reach. *What if...?* What if she had a source of money that was on a string? The guy that called her. The one who sold her painting. He had money. Her money.

"I know where we can get the money!" she burst out.

"Ruby, we've got ten or maybe twelve hours," said Mini.

"There's just no time," said Doris.

Ruby shook her head. *Time wasn't an issue with money.*

"We'll need cash," said Bernice.

"Let's hear her out," said Vi, holding up a hand.

"I need a phone that works here," said Ruby.

Bernice pounced. "I can set yours up for that."

"Is this safe?" asked Doris.

"They don't listen to phone calls," said Bernice.

Ruby shrugged. It didn't matter one way or the other. What she had to say wouldn't break any law. They needed cash, and she might be able to get it. She wasn't going say why she needed the money.

"Let me see your phone. I have to go to the ship's app to get satellite access," said Bernice.

Ruby handed it over. Maybe she was too excited. She saw the way people looked at her when she was happy. *Am I too happy, too excited, too everything, and what's wrong with being a little happy? Look what it got me. I just blew up little Bobby's house. Without a doubt that explosion saved our lives. And if little Ruby had been normal and reserved, Bobby would have shot her. Instead, he let her sing her little song that told everyone what was coming, and we all got away. We all got away. We still have glass in our hair, and I found a cut on my shoulder, but...*

"I found one on my leg," said Bernice.

Ruby stared, "Did I just say all that out loud?"

"I guess that depends on what *all that* was," said Doris. "If you mean about blowing up the house and..."

Ruby covered her mouth.

"Ruby dear, you are crazy, but so are we all. We were all in that house, and we all understood you," Vi took Ruby's hand.

Ruby slipped a little. For a few seconds, she couldn't recall what they were here for.

Bernice handed her the phone. "It should be ready."

Ready for what?

***

Mini saw the change. It was so fast. One second, Ruby was full of information and excitement, and the next she was a blank slate. It happened to all of them sometimes, but this was so sudden. "Ruby, you were going to call someone and get money," she said.

Ruby's face contorted into a pained mask. It was like everything she felt inside had come out. But that was Ruby, wasn't it? Always wearing her feelings in the open for all to see. She wasn't *too* happy, she just didn't hide it well when she was.

"I... I can't remember," she cried. "What, what was I doing?"

She pulled her hand away from Violet, wrapping her thin arms around herself and closing her eyes, closing out the world.

Mini wasn't an empathetic person, but this could have been her any day before they left the home. She had been so fragile, so forgetful, and so willing to give up. At the home, she had been able to hide in her room. No one knew how close she had been to completely losing her mind. Ruby hid in her happiness. That was who she was. They had no right to disabuse her of that. There was nowhere else for her to hide. Maybe when she was alone at night, she pulled up the covers and cried a little, letting go. That was her privilege.

Here, they were together day and night. It was like when she and Kate had been on the road, sleeping in the same bed, or in the same car, or under the same tree. They had covered each other's backs when they bathed in rivers and bath houses. Never alone, never private, emotions bottled up, hidden. If you cracked, it wasn't something you could hide. For Ruby, this was just bad timing.

“Come on, Ruby. It's okay. We all have our times,” said Mini.

Ruby gasped for air. “What do you know? You've always been nuts. I'm new at this.”

Lester let out a whoop. “She's fine.”

He cringed under Doris’ glare.

She's been crazy longer than any of us. She just don't remember, thought Mini, laughing to herself.

“What's so funny?” asked Bernice.

“I don’t have to answer that, I'm nuts, remember?” answered Mini.

Ruby wiped her eyes.

“It's not important that you call now,” said Violet.

“It is, too,” said Ruby.

“Do you know who you were going to call?” asked Violet.

Mini thought she was pressing a bit much. “Can't we let her rest?” she asked. It had been a hard, hard day, and they all needed rest.

Ruby flipped through the pages of her contacts. “Milo,” she said. “Milo Stenopolis.”

“Stenopolis, like Darla, from the home.”

Ruby nodded, searching then shaking her head.

"She had one of your paintings," said Doris.

A light went on in Ruby. Not a big one. Not one to jump up and down and celebrate over, but one that gave Mini some hope that this was just an anomaly and Ruby would pull through.

But Ruby's face was falling again. The despair of a moment before was rushing back to take its next victim, a moment, an hour, whatever it could get. *That's the way pain works,* thought Mini, *it steals a little bit of you at a time till you don't remember anything else.*

"Everybody out," said Mini. "Except you," she said to Ruby.

With only a little mumbling, they left. Doris paused at the door. "Are you sure?" she asked. Mini nodded, "Just give us a few minutes. Wait in the hall."

When they had all gone, she took both of Ruby's hands and led her into the bedroom of the stateroom. She helped her lay down and brought her water to drink, then sat with her. After a while, Ruby fell into an uneasy sleep, then a deep slumber.

Mini hoped and prayed that her friend would wake and remember what was so important. Not for them as a group. Not this time. This time, just for Ruby. Just so she could find that place again and her silly smile again. *Maybe it is for me, a little.*

She slipped away, closing the door.

***

You couldn't be mad at someone for having a good idea then forgetting it. *I forget things all the time,* thought Violet. *There's no telling how much I've forgotten.*

She twirled her file. Still, this was bad timing. A lot of things were bad timing.

Except for the occasional double tap of Bernice's cane, *when did she start carrying that again? After the fight with Bobby this morning? Was that just this morning? Good God, no wonder the woman was losing it. We should all be losing it.*

Violet felt herself deflate. She was so tired. So very tired. Maybe what they all needed was a good nap. She studied the faces around her, all quietly attending to something. Except Mini. Mini was doing nothing. She stood on the balcony staring across the sea with the wind blowing in her face and the last rays of the day's sun on her back.

They had turned the corner and were heading east. East, into whatever came their way. Goodness, she needed sleep.

The cabin door opened quietly behind her. She looked over her shoulder, unwilling to expend any more energy. Ruby stood smiling. Not the usual Ruby smile, one a little less excited, but then the twinkle came back, and she knew that Ruby was back, *for now*.

"His name is Milo Stenopolis," said Ruby. "He's an art dealer in New York, and the son of Darla Stenopolis. He took my painting from her house and put it in his gallery in New York with a steep price tag. Said he thought he could just look at it for a while, and no one would pay that much for it." She paused to laugh lightly. "But that's not what happened. He sold it for eighty thousand dollars."

There was a collective gasp in the room.

"W…wait," said Doris, "With that kind of money do we even need to do this thing"

Ruby paused. "Thought of that, and I might agree. I do agree that the money isn't mine altogether. You all had a part in this, and the fact that I put the paint on the canvas matters little. But Milo is bringing the money to me, and this time, I am making the call. We are buying guns with this money, and we are finishing the job we started."

Violet breathed a deep sigh. Moments ago, she had almost been ready to quit. Now they could quit and could still afford to live, but no one wanted to. God bless her, Ruby in her most frail moment had done what she couldn't in her best, bringing the group back on course.

"Are you going to call him now?" asked Mini.

"Already did. He'll meet us at the airport on Grand Cayman in the morning."

"With eighty thousand in cash?" asked Doris, incredulous.

"No. With a hundred thousand," said Ruby, the shadow of one of her silly grins creeping in. "He wants to sell more of my paintings."

***

Milo suffered from reading too much.

If all he read was fiction, he may have been okay, but Milo liked to read hard news and opinion pieces. Just a few weeks ago, he had read an interesting article about people who carried large amounts of cash being stopped, and the cash being confiscated.

The two four-inch stacks of bills on the table before him definitely qualified as a large amount of cash, and, as far as he could tell, there was no way to make that money available to Ruby in the time she needed it without carrying it to her by hand. Cash terrified him. He had lived in New York long enough to develop a healthy sense of paranoia coupled with pessimism. You didn't carry a hundred thousand in cash through customs, like you didn't carry a thousand dollars in your hand and walk through the Port Authority bus station. Either result would be the same.

One hundred thousand dollars in a bag looked suspiciously like drug money. He got that. There should be a way to certify that it wasn't, but that didn't exist. Instead, he had to make do with a formal letter and some gallery insurance papers in the brief case on top of the cash. The insurance papers were a clever last minute idea. What could be more confusing, official looking, or scary than fourteen sheets of legal jargon? If anyone read too closely and saw that it was all about insuring the gallery and art, he could always fall back on the explanation that he needed to show his client that he was properly insured before she signed the contract.

That might be enough to get him through customs.

Now, if he could just stop sweating.

***

The ladies wandered out onto the balcony one at a time, whisper quiet. The sky was dark purple blue, sparkling with the light of a billion stars. The ship plowed through the ocean at twenty knots, twenty-three miles per hour, toward their destiny. The stars were just so beautiful, and the night was perfect, a light breeze keeping them cool. Behind them, the lights were off in the stateroom.

They had a good conversation, Ruby and Violet, before the others joined them. Ruby didn't cry this time. She just nodded, the weariness flowing from her, into the night air.

Eventually, the others joined them. Bernice was last, disturbing the peace with that question that no one else wanted to ask, "Do we have a plan?"

Do we? Was that a question or an accusation? Violet asked herself. What could you plan without knowing the tools you would have?

"Ruby, I don't think they'll have kitchen timers at the bank," she said.

"I already packed my stuff. We'll find something," said Ruby.

"We've only got eight hours on the island," said Doris.

Not much time, thought Violet. *Not much at all considering travel time from and to the ship. Is there a way to buy more time?* "How far is Jamaica from Grand Cayman?"

Bernice brought out her tablet, the light ruining the night vision of the star gazers.

They groaned.

***

Eduardo ordered the guns to be pushed overboard.

The two ships on radar had become three for a few minutes. One had continued on a course past the blip on the left. For a while, he hoped the other vessels would be misled by the third vessel and would leave him alone. That did not happen.

The new vessel was large on the radar, but looking into the sun, they couldn't see it.

It was still possible that the other two blips were just small container ships or big fishing boats. It was also possible that men would live on Mars in his lifetime. Neither were likely. The guns needed to go before a plane, or worse a helicopter from a cruiser, flew over. A helicopter could follow and video them.

Better to get rid of the guns before that happened.

Even without the guns, the men were who they were, and convincing the Coast Guard that they were cruisers would be a neat trick. Eduardo ordered them to shower and put on clean clothes. He chose a light pink shirt for himself. Might as well look the part if they were boarded.

***

The sun rose, and Mini was on the deck alone again. Dana Sully approached silently. Maybe not the wisest thing, but this time she was expected.

“You're sneaky. I like that,” said Mini.

“You're sneaky, and I'm not sure how I feel about it. Might get me in trouble,” shot back Dana.

“Have you been keeping up with Irene?”

Dana took a deep breath before answering. She wasn't keeping up with Irene so much as fending her off, playing defense. “She's a lot to deal with. A lot.”

“We've always found her that way,” agreed Mini.

“I told her that I was investigating her claims.” *I also told her not to bother people that she thought were dangerous. Did I mention that sometimes people fall overboard under suspicious circumstances, or did I just wish I said that?*

“That should slow her down,” said Mini

You have no idea, Sully nodded, feeling a smile creep across her face.

“What's that all about?” said Mini.

Sully shrugged. It wasn't easy to put into words. Since the day they had met, there hadn't been a moment that she wasn't afraid of losing her job, except for those moments when she was too busy working for the ladies to think about it. She still had no idea what they were up to. She was tempted to break into the cabin while they were out and search it. But somehow she didn't think they left notes around describing their agenda for the day. There was that other little thing—if she were caught doing that without the Captain's approval, she would be fired. It wasn't worth the risk. Besides, she had come to like them. The little jobs they gave her were challenges that were, in a way, helping her with her job.

Before, she had divided people into groups; those that were worthy of suspicion and examination and those that were not. She didn't do that anymore. Now, everyone was worthy of suspicion. The mother of five on deck four had tried to bring a pound of pot on at Belize. Dana confiscated all but two ounces and told the woman not to smoke that on the ship. The confiscated weed was donated anonymously to the crew party the night before.

It was all risky. Life was risky. But the alternative was boredom. Sully was tired of being bored. She liked the new, not so bored, Sully.

"Don't go too far, kid," said Mini.

"How do you do that? How do you know what I'm thinking before I do?"

The old lady cackled. "Once you've been down a few roads, you start to know the look of other travelers."

Dana shook her head. She could see that. It was what she saw in the eyes of the mom with the pot and the kids that were trying to reel in a fish to toss in the pool. They were all in some way like her. They all needed to break out of the box they were living in. Dana was well out of the box and liking it out here.

"What about you?" she asked. "Did you go too far?"

Mini looked at her seriously. "I robbed my first bank when I was sixteen."

That took a minute to sink in. *Holy shit!* "Is that what we're doing? Are you people seriously…? Shit!"

She turned away, looking across the water, watching the the waves topped with golden morning sunshine disappear beneath the bow of the ship. So beautiful, so necessary, so dangerous. The same sun that warmed her hands and arms made her tear up when she looked at it. If she looked too long, it would blind her.

"What do you need from me?" asked Dana.

CHAPTER 33

The US Coast Guard boarded them at 8:13 am, twenty-four miles from Grand Cayman, still in international waters. They hadn't given chase. Ed hadn't run. Eduardo had no idea if the boarding was legal. His experience told him that the guys with the bigger guns got to decide what was legal. The Coast Guard had the bigger guns. The only guns.

As per Papa's instructions, all guns had gone overboard. The only thing they had left was a few ounces of pot and the explosives that Bruno had tucked away somewhere. They would find the pot, and they would ignore it. It was a tiny amount, no more than expected on any pleasure craft, and they weren't looking for that.

They searched the boat thoroughly, making Eduardo and Manuel show them around. The search made him nervous. He needed to be above deck where he could keep an eye on things. His men had been separated. *Were they being interrogated?* One young officer entered Eduardo's cabin while another stood watch at the door.

“You should flirt with him,” said Manuel, raising an eyebrow.

“I should shoot you for saying that,” replied Eduardo.

“I'm serious,” said Manuel. “You should play the part of Roberto,” he said, moving toward the guard. “It will make them nervous, and we might get lucky,” he winked over his shoulder.

“You're very young,” said Manuel to the guard, in a suggestive voice.

“Manuel!” called Ed, suddenly unsure of himself. “Manuel!”

Manuel waved him off. “He's just jealous.”

“Sir, I'm going to have to ask you to step back. Seaman Stamp, please remove these men to the main deck,” ordered the petty officer, dropping his hand to his sidearm.

“You see,” said Manuel, on the way up the ladder, “you play the part and get what you want.”

“Madre de dios, we should have brought some women,” said Eduardo.

“And ruin your reputation?”

Topside, they watched the men being frisked and recorded.

It was a fascinating process that Eduardo had been fortunate to never have been a part of before. The officer in charge of the search stood on the deck while a seaman recorded him with a video camera. He made a short speech about boarding without resistance, then let the cameraman record a wide shot, then a close-up of everyone aboard the yacht.

The officer examined each passport and held it before the camera before returning it to the owner. He handed over Eduardo's and ordered his men off the yacht. “Have a nice day,” he said, stepping onto the Zodiac.

***

The leather bench was comfortable, and Norbert struggled to keep his eyes open. All night they had cruised east at twenty plus knots, following the lights of the big cruise liner.

He wanted sleep, needed sleep, must have sleep, but at some point it registered with him that they were following the ship they had tried to ram yesterday. *Was it only yesterday?* It didn't matter. What mattered was that they were following that ship, and Mr. Bob was insane. If he slept, who would watch the boss? Also, they were at sea with half of their fuel burned and no passports. *What did they do with people who landed on foreign shores without passports? They might send me to Cuba,* he thought. *Better than dying.*

The bench was soft. He drifted, dreaming of chasing a great white whale. The captain, wild-eyed, stood at the wheel, his knees bent and feet set wide, crazy hair blowing in the wind. They sailed into the shadow of the whale.

Norbert woke with a jolt. He sat up, hitching up the oversized shorts Jamie had loaned him while his dried on the deck.

The ship was still far ahead. The Captain was just as in the dream, except for the wind in his hair. For now, he was steering from the wheel inside the pilothouse. Still, his hair stood straight up. The back of his neck and arms were filthy with soot and dirt mixed with sweat, and the boxers that had once been white peeked out below the ragged tail of the long button down shirt.

The inside of the pilot house was sparkling clean, except for the area around the Captain and the wheel. There, dirty hands and arms had left black streaks on the console. The leather chair that had been white, was now only white in a few places. Every surface that had been touched was streaked with grey and the black of dried blood.

Jamie walked quietly over from his place near Mister Bob. "We got no gas to git home, mon," he said to Norb, keeping his voice below the rumble of the engines.

"Ya, I thought of dat, mon. Dey gonna arrest us?" asked Norbert.

"Ya, maybe, mon. We goin to Cayman, I tink," said Jamie.

"Get me another beer," belched Bob.

***

The sun was up, and the Captain took his morning briefing, cappuccino in hand. He watched the playback on the security monitor while the junior officer reported, "We retrieved a woman's tank top that hung on the aft port FLIR." He referred to the infrared cameras that surveilled the exterior of the ship. "What size?" asked the Captain. "Two XL. Somebody probably lost it over from one of the upper decks. No sign of monkey business. The yacht is still trailing us. Got him on radar about three miles back."

The captain glanced at the radar. There was a matter of passengers disembarking via tender possibly being harassed by the *pazzo* on the yacht. "Notify Cayman Police. Have their Marine Unit standing by. Also, get me an update on the storm."

"The storm is turning north, sir," said the officer.

"The storm is a storm. It will go where it wants to go. I want an update every half hour so that I know where it is deciding to go at that moment," said Captain Ricci, the caffeine kicking in.

CHAPTER 34

Dana manned the checkpoint for disembarking passengers at the aft hatch. She scanned each cruise card and when the ladies had all passed, she scanned Lester's card and returned it to him as she slipped the five cards that she had palmed from the ladies into her pocket. Her job was done for now. She silently wished them luck and called the next passenger to hold while the gangway was lifted and the tender shoved off.

The guttural rumble of the tender's engines echoed through the narrow entry as the cluster waiting to disembark stirred and began to move aside for someone pushing their way through. Irene emerged, her power chair squeezing past, forcing the other passengers against the bulkheads.

Her lips moved, but the noise of the departing boat drowned her out. For the briefest second, Dana considered letting her roll on past onto the gangway and into the water below. She pictured the 'Tragic Loss' headline.

The noise from the tender diminished, and Irene's angry rantings filled the portal. Sully closed her eyes and hooked the chain blocking the exit. *Maybe I should jump.*

***

Leaving the ship, Ruby sat in the bow of the big boat feeling the spray on her face. It was 8:30 am, and the sun cast long shadows under a cluster of dark clouds.

The water below was crystal clear, and the boat threw a shadow on the sandy bottom. They passed sailing and motor yachts that anchored closer inshore than the big ship. Their gleaming white hulls and chrome fittings bobbed on the increasingly choppy surface.

From her vantage, the island looked flat. A note of disappointment registered. She had expected something like a mountain peak sticking out of the water. It was a warm day for this time of year, but the cloud cover brought an instant chill to her bones. She checked the map on her phone to see how far south they actually were.

The ride was a little nerve racking. Today was a day that really mattered, and Ruby wasn't entirely sure it would work out. Milo had been so quick to agree, so easy to talk to. *Too easy?*

The tender bounced a little on the small waves then slowed and swung into the dock. The ride had taken less time than boarding the boat.

Doris rode with them. Sometime in the night, she and Lester had agreed that she should come. “Oh,” said Doris, as they passed through the terminal shopping tents, “let's get scarves. We might need them.”

“Scarves and hats that we can ditch,” said Bernice.

“Anything to make us look different,” said Mini.

“Do we really have to ditch it? It's so pretty,” Doris held up a bright blue and green scarf.

“Get one to keep and one for… for working in,” suggested Violet.

***

“On behalf of a client, I am making a purchase from an American artist who is on the island,” said Milo, to the Cayman Customs agent in the most precise language he could.

“Sir, our banks have an interest in preserving their reputations and do not accept cash deposits from unknown sources.”

“Thank you for that detailed explanation of your country’s banking rules, or preferences, or whatever they are, but I'm not here to make a deposit. I'm here to buy art.”

“Sir, couldn't you have made a transfer?” asked the customs agent in a polite British accent that was quite disarming.

“I hope that you can see my position, but I don't get to choose what people want or do. The artist isn’t wealthy. She's a breakout artist, and she’s decided that she wants cash.”

The custom man's eyes sharpened, and his finger froze on his page of notes.

“A new artist,” explained Milo. “She's here on vacation with her friends, and she needs a lot of cash. Maybe she has a gambling problem, or maybe she plans to buy art on the ship. I don't know.”

"She's on a cruise, then?

"Yes,"

"They sell art on cruise ships? I've never heard of that."

Milo nodded, back on familiar ground. "Oh, they do. There are several really big galleries that hold auctions on cruise ships. They do it on almost every ship now."

"Really, I had no idea. But you're not on a cruise ship."

"The lady said her ship was in port today."

"And she is going to buy art on the ship?"

Milo had not slept much in the last twenty four-hours. The best he could do was try and draw on the tiny bit of patience he had in reserve. He tried mimicking the Brit's patient demeanor and lowered his voice, "I actually don't know why she needs the money. It's just that, as far as I can tell, a bank transfer can't really be made to the ship. She said she needed the money. I'm just doing the best I can for the artist that I represent."

"So, she's not buying art?"

"I don't know what she's doing. I know what I'm doing. I'm paying an artist for a painting that I sold for her. That's all I know."

"Fascinating. I never get tired of the things I learn here. Enjoy your stay in the Cayman Islands," the agent said, stamping Milo's passport. "Next."

***

The ladies left the terminal via the main gate and entered Georgetown where stone and concrete buildings two and three stories high hosted everything from restaurants to diamond markets. Ruby thought it was like nothing she had ever seen, with industry and pleasure so thoroughly mixed.

The main street in front of the terminal was a wide two lane where bumper to bumper traffic moved steady but slow. Violet flagged a cab and asked the driver where they could rent a car. "All at the airport," he said, reaching to open the sliding door.

He slung them around turns and through streets that looked to Ruby like alleys. Violet held her phone in her lap, checking the GPS against the streets. "We need a map," she said.

Ruby nodded nervously. Milo was due to meet them at 9:30. They hadn't decided where, but they would try and keep it discreet. Everything depended on him. If Milo showed up on time, they would have the money they needed and could go on as planned. If not, they were sunk, or, at the very least, they would have to come up with another plan. She gripped the handle on her small pack. *Could they rob a bank with a single pound of plastic explosive and an ancient pistol?* She checked her watch, then grabbed the seat handle and clenched her teeth as they rocketed around a small traffic circle and turned left.

Leaving the shore, the town changed rapidly from touristy to industrial. Buildings here had small parking lots and solid concrete walls with few or no windows. The streets were busy but not gridlocked, and each intersection hosted a traffic circle. Some were what you expected of a traffic circle, and others were little more than a bump to swerve around.

It took her a few minutes to grasp why the trip felt so odd. They were driving on the wrong side of the road. "Violet?" she said, grabbing her friend's hand and pointing out the oddity.

Violet nodded. "I think I can handle it," she said.

From the seat behind the driver, Mini asked his name.

"Kersan, madam."

"Kersan, is that an Indonesian name?"

"Yes, madam."

"Kersan, we're going to rent a car, and at some point, I want to visit the police station."

"Oh, ma'am, have you been robbed? I can take you there instead of the airport."

"No, no, we haven't been robbed. I just have a fascination with police around the world and want to see the station."

"Oh, oh, that is a very interesting hobby. The station is up across from the Governor's home. Governor's Square, Governor's Beach, all that is together."

"Oh, how nice. We'll avoid that," she said over her shoulder to Violet and Ruby.

"Are the police armed here?" she asked.

Bernice elbowed her a warning.

Ruby watched it all, half amused. She had her own concerns. The phone buzzed, making her jump and almost fumble it.

The ring followed while she tried to slide her thumb across the screen to answer.

"This is Milo," said the voice from the other end. "I cleared customs. Can we meet in the airport?"

"No," said Ruby. "We're going to the car rental. Meet us at…" she looked at Violet. "Violet, what car rental?"

"They are mostly all together," said the driver.

The drive to the airport took less than ten minutes. Most of the car rental agencies on the island were in a cluster of strip mall type buildings on the north side of the airport.

A young man in a black shirt and slacks waved at them from the terminal side of the street. Ruby waved him over, assuming that he was Milo and throwing a huge *thank you* to God for him showing up.

"Everyone gather round," said Violet, as they waited for Milo. "Ruby, we need Milo to rent the car. Otherwise, we'll be returning a rental when we're supposed to be off of the island. How long will he be here?"

"I don't know," answered Ruby.

"Five days," said Milo. "I'm not coming down here and going right home."

"Ruby?" he asked, extending a sweaty hand. "I am Milo, and I am so pleased to finally meet you."

"Mr. Milo, I am so glad you came and so sorry that you had to travel so far just to…"

"You know, it's a terrible imposition to have to come to the Cayman Islands on business and meet a soon to be famous artist. Just horrible. I have no idea what I will do with my time. I might have to breath some clean air, go to the beach, do some sailing, maybe get a tan," he finished loosening his collar around his pale flesh. "I saw some beaches when we were landing that looked fantastic."

"How was the flight? Any trouble with customs?" asked Violet.

"My dad was a cop. A grilling by customs here is a little easier than the screening I got before I could sit down for breakfast."

"Speaking of…" said Ruby, nodding to the bag.

"Oh, yeah. The money is here," said Milo, holding up a messenger bag. "I just need you to sign for it. And if there is anything else I can do for you, please, call on me," he said, bringing out a contract for Ruby to sign.

Violet answered. "Well, Mr. Milo, we are only here a short time. Probably won't have time for the beaches. But we do need one thing."

***

Milo liked the ladies. It was a strange thing knowing that these people that he had known for forty minutes and felt so close to were the same ones he had ignored so diligently when he visited Golden Lawn on holidays.

People were just different when you got to know them.

And these gals were different. Strong, willful, full of something. Joy, tinged with the weight of sadness, perhaps. He hadn't heard so much laughter in years, but even the laughter had a sharp edge to it.

He rented the car for them, then went to another rental agency and rented one for himself with another card. Simple. *Now, what were five strong-willed little old ladies going to do with a hundred thousand dollars and a rental car on a tropical island?* He didn't dare ask.

He dug his toes into the sand of Seven Mile Beach and took a deep breath of sea air. There was a storm coming, they said at the car rental. Even with the clouds, it was a nice day on a beautiful beach.

CHAPTER 35

A storm was brewing ahead. How big or small, they couldn't tell. Jesus and Diego, the only two real sailors on the boat, had zero experience with weather radar. Any storm was to be respected. This one looked especially intimidating on the live radar map. The fishermen stood over the console shaking their heads. "No, Jefe, it's no good," said Diego. "With the wind from the east, we drag anchor right into land," he illustrated with an awkward crashing noise.

He pointed at the map on the screen, then touched the beach on the west end of the island. "Here is good. Protected by the land, and if we drag anchor, we go to sea."

"No land to crash on?" said Eduardo.

"Si, Jefe."

"What about this big bay, North Sound?" asked Eduardo. "Doesn't the land to the east protect us from the wind?"

Diego shook his head. "No, Jefe, the land is flat, the water not so deep."

"I don't like it. It will take us longer," said Eduardo.

"Does it matter?" said Manuel.

"I don't know," said Ed. But it did. It seemed like every day there was another delay, another problem, another hurdle. "How bad is this storm?" he asked Diego.

The fisherman shrugged, "Bigger today than yesterday, Jefe."

"Find us a better place to anchor."

***

Ruby leaned on the handle of the heavy glass and steel door and entered the bank alone.

The lobby was larger than she expected, the marble floors smooth and polished. The layout nothing like the pictures. Everything was fresh. Even the leather couches looked like they'd never been sat on. The bank had been remodeled.

The contrast of the bank's formality to the plain exterior was stunning, as it was meant to be. She felt overwhelmed and underdressed in the grandeur of the high-ceilinged room with the tellers and staff all in black. A young woman in a fitted black skirt and jacket stepped forward and introduced herself as Anne. Her accent was Dutch or South African.

There were three guards, Ruby noted as Anne led her across the lobby, her high heels double clicking on the marble. Ruby paused and touched the thick glass screen that stood above one of the marble-topped tables. Her fingers left a smudge that she hurriedly wiped with her scarf, apologizing to the young banker who pretended not to notice.

A guard wearing body armor and holding a wicked looking machine pistol across his chest nodded as Anne led her into a short hallway and closed the door of her office behind them.

Ruby introduced herself and explained that she was only on the island for a day, but had a sum of $10,000 that she had been paid in cash for her painting that she felt she needed to deposit. Could it be put in a safe deposit box for the day.

"Certainly," said Anne. "But there is no daily rental. It will be for one month, and there is a charge of approximately eighty dollars American for the month." She withdrew a form from her desk and passed it to Ruby.

Fifteen minutes later, Ruby skipped across the street to join her friends.

***

In the shade of a table awning across from Cayman National Bank and Trust, Violet leaned back in the metal chair and relaxed as well as she could under the current challenges. Her friends were around her, the gleaming white concrete of the bank building glowed in the soft light of the overcast sky, and a breeze rattled the awning pole, making the canvas pop. A waiter eyed the clouds warily.

"We don't have guns. We don't have a way to get off the island. What do we have?" said Doris.

"Explosives," said Ruby.

"I don't know what to do with that," said Doris.

"You shape a charge, then make a hole in it and stick a blasting cap in…"

"Bless her heart, she thinks she's answering my question," said Doris.

Ruby looked away and sipped her lemonade.

A sudden gust threatened to blow away an open notepad with a sketch of the inside of the bank. Doris anchored it with her purse. The drawing showed the positions of the guards, counters, tables, offices, and vault.

Violet examined it again. The vault, at the left rear of the bank, was their major concern. To get to it would require them to cross almost sixty feet of open lobby floor. There were counters and heavy tables that the guards could use for cover. The glass plates above the counters and above some of the tables were heavy, layered glass. "Bulletproof shields. Fancy stuff," Mini said, when Ruby described it.

The ladies quietly contemplated their options, while the wind rattled and shook the world around them and a spritz of rain wet Violet's cheek. She liked the wind and rain. It was comforting. The world left you alone when there was a storm.

"I have to get my money back by five," said Ruby. "Regular bank hours are 9:00 to 5:30, but cutoff for getting to the box is thirty minutes before closing."

"That puts us right at the end of the day, but what time does the ship leave?" asked Bernice.

Good point, thought Violet. "We can't be too late, or it will ruin our alibi."

She tore a sheet out of the pad and jotted down a timeline in the left column. The last boat to the ship was at 4:30. The last reasonable time Ruby could enter the boat would be 4:15 pm. She wrote, "RUBY GETS $."

"What time is sunset?" she asked.

Bernice looked it up. "5:45."

Violet made a note in the far right column.

She sat back and stared at the building across the street. While Ruby had been inside, she had walked up and down the street and around the building. There were nine security cameras that she had located. There would be more.

"It doesn't sound good," she said, with a sigh. "I think we should plan on Ruby getting her money back at 4:00, then we go in right before closing. That will be right before dark, and if this cloud cover holds, it will be dark already."

"That gives us the advantage on the approach," said Mini.

"What kind of advantage?" asked Doris.

"It will be dark out and light inside. Just like we can't see them now, they won't see us until we open the doors. But it's not enough," said Mini, her voice fading.

Violet nodded. "I also think that we should have a backup plan. Just in case something goes wrong, or…" she spun her file staring at the bank, "…or we just decide it's not right. Did you ever back down from a job, Mini?"

Mini shook her head, "Not until I quit. But we had the big guns and the guards had sticks and pistols, back then."

"If the vault is against the outside wall, what keeps us from just blowing a hole in the wall?" asked Violet.

Ruby answered, "It will take multiple charges. There'll be steel bar in the wall we'll have to blow or cut. I don't know if I have enough C-4 for all that. We may need other tools, and we just don't know."

Violet could tell by Ruby's expectant posture that she wanted to try.

"Why does that have to be the backup. Can't we just get tools now and make that the plan?" said Doris.

"So, Ruby gets her money, we blow a hole in the vault in the middle of the night as a main plan, or go in the front door and rob it in the morning if that doesn't work?" said Violet.

"You mean while there are people all around looking at the hole that we blew in the wall?" said Ruby.

Bernice looked up from her phone. "This is a full tropical storm. It's coming right at us, and it could turn into a hurricane."

A gust of wind tugged at the awning. "Is that good or bad?" asked Doris.

Ruby studied the buildings around the bank. “This is mostly businesses around here. A good storm could cover the explosions.”

Mini chuckled, “Nobody is going to think that stuff is thunder.”

“Big power transformers blow up in storms all the time,” said Ruby.

Violet checked her note sheet. “So, we have six hours to get the guns and more plastic if we can, find a way to get to Jamaica and meet the ship, and find a place to stay tonight.”

“Not a hotel,” added Bernice.

“Not a hotel,” agreed Violet.

“We'll need to borrow another car, too. We don’t want to be spotted in a rental that can be connected to us, even through a third party,” said Mini.

***

“I don't like this storm. It's huge,” said Eduardo, studying the weather map on the console. Diego stood back, proud of himself for figuring out the new technology to bring up the satellite imagery. A fisherman from birth, he knew little about computers. He did know how to drive a boat in rough seas, a skill they would soon need.

“Manuel, we'll put you ashore here,” said Eduardo. He zoomed into the island and pointed to Seven Mile Beach, that ran north and south on the west end of the island. “Rent a car and meet us up here,” he pointed to a spot on the north shore of the island.

“Diego, we will take the boat around here. Will this give us good shelter?” Eduardo pointed to a small bump on the north shore labeled Anchor Point.

Diego studied the map, comparing it to the weather map. “Si, it will give us a little shelter, I think.”

“We will take the little boat to shore, and Manuel will meet us with the car. We hit the bank before closing, and we're back at sea tonight. Any questions?”

Diego used the new trick he had just learned to zoom the map out where he could see both the island and the weather radar. The winds on the leading edge of the storm would blow south, directly into the north side of the island. He raised his hand halfway.

Eduardo did not notice.

***

Irene watched from the back seat of the cab, feeding a twenty to the driver every fifteen minutes or when he began to fidget, whichever came first. It had been a strange morning. First, to the car rental plaza, *more like a strip mall,* where the poker girls met a young man in black that seemed vaguely familiar. The high hedges had kept her from seeing what they were doing, but they met then drove away in a rental car while she fed another twenty to her driver.

From there, they'd driven around for a while, her driver doing everything he could to make her uncomfortable, jerking the wheel around turns and aiming for every pothole. The metal arm of the folding jump seat beside her jammed into her hip each time they took a left turn, and she had to grab the seat bar for each roundabout.

Ruby went into Cayman National Bank and Trust with a small black bag and came out empty handed. Now, the girls sat in the restaurant across from the bank, drinking and talking while the sky darkened and sprinkles of rain dotted the cab windows. Every once in a while, someone got up and walked around. Violet, the stupid farm girl, walked all the way around the bank building, coming out right beside Irene's own cab, forcing her to duck down in the van. Violet couldn't have seen her through the tinted windows, but why take the chance?

The cabbie followed the rented black SUV through the outskirts of Georgetown and into Bodden Town, where the houses and properties were notably less resort-like. Passing a sign for some kind of animal sanctuary, the driver held his hand up for another bill.

Irene had only ones and fives left. She handed him a five.

He looked at the bill and held it up to her. "This and one more will get you back to the ship."

"I paid you over a hundred dollars. I should get the whole day at that rate!"

"Yes, ma'am, and I make that much in an hour when a ship is in port."

The insolence! She spent all morning and all of her money to follow those women and watch them sip drinks while she sat in the hot car.

“Take me back to the ship,” she ordered, without producing another bill.

The cabbie swung the van in a wide arc across traffic, reversing course.

Twenty minutes later, he unloaded her chair three blocks from the port terminal. Heavy raindrops began to fall. He handed her his own umbrella as if that would make up for leaving her in the rain so far from the ship. She tapped her stick and rammed her chair into the back of his ankle, eliciting a rewarding curse from the man.

***

The island was much smaller than expected, and the roundabouts made it fast to drive. Violet hadn’t seen a stop sign yet. The Land Rover LR4 handled solidly but had all the pep of a steam locomotive. The rain began in earnest when they turned north onto Frank Sound Road.

The man they were going to see, the Dutchman, lived on the north coast of the island. The road swept right, then left ahead. At the apex of the curve, they turned on Old Robin, heading east. Past some townhomes and businesses the road became lonely, with only the increasing rain and swaying trees for company. The wind gusted, and the rain hit them in sheets, making it hard driving.

Violet tapped the brakes and brought them to a hard stop. She had almost missed the narrow drive beneath the trees. It was marked by a post with a security camera housing atop. Tall grass and brush grew on both sides of the drive, leading them toward a forest that appeared impenetrable. A hole appeared as they approached and entered a dark tunnel of swaying trees.

The low, gnarled trunks and limbs reminded Violet of Texas cedars but with thick rubbery leaves. The stubby trees gave way to taller palm and ironwood, and the drive widened as they approached the house.

They parked beside a two bay garage and left the engine running. The house was plastered concrete with a full length porch facing the drive. The windows above were curtained and dark. To the right of the house, they could see between the trees and over the rocks to where the gray of the ocean and the sky merged into one. Light shone from the window to the left of the front door.

She glanced back. Bernice and Ruby were reading from their phones. Violet cleared her throat to get their attention.

"Looks peaceful enough," said Mini, her ridged posture suggesting otherwise.

An arms dealer, thought Violet, *what kind of man would this be?*

***

The *Ellie Maye* yanked at her anchor. Manuel had swum ashore at the west beach of the island. Eduardo and the remaining four men took the yacht north to the anchor point behind a sheltering outcrop of land that turned out to not be that much shelter.

The men grasped the wet side rail ropes of the Zodiac, each in their own way internalizing the terror they were experiencing as the waves tossed them relentlessly up and down. Only Diego had passed on wearing a life jacket. "Madre de Dios," he muttered from the back of the little boat as a swell lifted them. *Why did I not wear a vest?*

Jesus stood, unsteadily flexing his knees to absorb the movement as he pushed the rubber boat off of the wet stern deck of the yacht. With the rising of the yacht, the bow of the Zodiac rose, the motor end staying behind, tipping them back. For one awful second, Diego thought they would capsize, then they slipped off the yacht and back into the void of the swell, free of the big boat.

Diego engaged the throttle and drove them back up onto the yacht.

Up front, Jesus fell forward, his arms splayed wide, grasping the handrail ropes. "Back on the boat! Get back on the big boat," ordered Diego.

Without argument, Eduardo scrambled over the three men in front of him, clawing and grasping for a hold on the Ellie Maye.

Jesus ran the bow line around a capstan, then holding that rope with one hand, lent a hand to Diego. They secured the Zodiac, and soaked and shivering, met Eduardo in the pilot house.

"I am sorry Jefe," said Diego. "I was wrong. The waves are too big. We will try the bay." He pointed to a spot southwest of Rum Point where charts showed deep water close to land. "This may be safer."

Eduardo pointed to a spot deeper in the sound and closer to the town of Savannah, "What about here?" Diego nodded and leaned back on one of the pilot chairs, catching his breath before advancing the throttles. Anything was better than this.

Ed hit speed dial and began to tell Manuel about the change in plans.

***

The ladies sat in the rented SUV, the storm thrashing the world outside.

“I'll get my hair wet,” said Doris.

“We should all go in,” said Violet.

“Use your new scarf,” suggested Ruby.

“Well, at least get us close to the door.”

Violet nodded and eased the car up parallel to the steps.

“Why are we nervous about this?” asked Doris. “He's just a businessman, right?”

“He knows my sister,” said Mini. “Anyone who knows my sister is suspect.”

“You know your sister,” said Doris.

Ruby snorted, and Mini grinned. It had been a long time, but she did know her sister. It made the man even more questionable. “When we're in there, give me a little elbow room,” she said, opening the car door.

“Do you have the lead on this, or should I?” asked Ruby, jogging up the porch steps.

“You talk, I cover,” said Mini, her hand tapping her purse.

***

Coos Flanders, slightly overweight and balding on top, moved quickly to the window when heard the car approach. He was expecting visitors, and as usual, had asked Sean to back him up. Unless Sean was sitting in a rented car by his garage, he was late.

He untucked his shirt so that it covered the Sig pistol on his hip and stood, his left knee wobbling until the cane could take the weight. He was in no shape for a fight, which is why he tipped Sean a few hundred each time he had a meeting. Sean wasn't keen for a fight either, but together they could handle whatever could fit in a single car. Alone, maybe not.

Coos checked the security monitors and stroked his grey streaked goatee. Though always on the edge of a world of violence, he liked to think of himself as more refined and philosophical. The long black hair and beard helped complete the image.

He scanned the clearing. No movement in the trees or grass that couldn't be written off to the wind. It paid to be careful. Monitor three showed the Rover moving up to the door. The car door opened and his mother, or someone who looked very much like her, stepped out into the rain. Others followed, splashing through the puddles to the thin shelter of the porch.

Coos stared at the cluster of women on his porch and shook his head. What to do? They looked so harmless, but Coos had not come to arms dealing by supplying to harmless people. Everyone had at least one dangerous quality, even if it was stupidity. These people didn't look stupid, but they were getting wet from the blowing rain. Coos opened the door. “I'm sorry to make you wait. Please come in.”

His house, humble plastered concrete, was secure and warm, even with the ocean raging only meters away, and he could not deny shelter to such a docile looking group.

“You're not exactly what I expected when I got the call,” he said. “Not from the island garden club, perhaps lost?” Coos had never seen a gang like this and wondered what their whole story was. He wouldn't ask. Better not to know. But still, it must be a good story.

The woman with the cane tapped it on the stone floor as if testing it.

“I'm Ruby, and this is Violet,” said the tall one with the dark hair, waving toward the woman that was perhaps her own height but broader in the shoulders. “I assume you're the Dutchman?”

The small one that had reminded him of his mother stood back from the group. She still reminded him of his mother. She would be the security. He would get to that. “I am sometimes called that. Coos Flanders, at your service.” He bowed slightly and offered them seats around his table. “I'm afraid I don't have enough chairs.

Violet raised an eyebrow and nodded.

Ruby glanced up the stairs into his attic library then around taking in the room and the collections of small things that reminded him of people and places. He had many memories represented in this house.

"I am Coos," he offered, again introducing himself to the tiny woman that had separated herself from the others.

She puckered her lips and eyed him with suspicion. *Definitely the security person.*

"That's a nice bag. What are you carrying?" he asked, commenting on her heavy purse.

"A Webley Mark III in .455."

"Oh my," said Coos, suddenly excited. "I so love the old ones. I collect them, you know. May I see it?"

She hesitated, and Coos realized his error. "I am so sorry, your name is?"

"Mini."

"Mini, it is your defensive, ah weapon. May I trade you mine? I really just want to see this."

Not hearing any objection, he reached slowly back and brought forward his Sig 229, butt first. Mini accepted it and handed him the Webley.

The Webley was a thing of beauty. A cavalryman's gun, it had almost certainly seen action. Sad, really, that so many that carried them had killed with them or themselves died, but the tools were not the killers.

***

Violet watched the exchange with unconcealed interest while moving around the room. The house was filled with book cases and mementos. A woman had lived here once. Someone he cared very much to remember. Her touches were everywhere. Coos was a fascinating man. She had expected someone greasy and corrupt, and instead had found someone more refined but perhaps even more dangerous. She liked what she'd seen of the man, but had to remind herself that he dealt with criminals and could not be as tame as he seemed. Maybe not as honest, either.

Coos swept a curtain back revealing an alcove and workbench. The bench was tidy and the shelves above full of models and parts of models. “A hobby,” he explained, swinging the magnifying light down and turning it on. “I build models. I enjoy it, and it explains the many drawers of small parts if anyone, if the authorities, become curious.”

He unloaded the pistol and examined it carefully under the magnifier. “This is a great thing and very valuable to me. I know that this is not what you came here for, but would you, could you, perhaps trade for it?”

“I like it, but it kicks like a mule,” said Mini, flexing her wrist.

“It was used recently,” said Violet, thinking that the man needed to know that.

He turned to her, his eyes questioning. “Where, and if you don't mind saying, how?”

She took a moment to consider his question while Coos continued to examine the old pistol. Coos had secrets, and kept secrets. No one could run a business like this without being a good keeper of secrets. On the other hand, a man so flexible morally could be a trader of information as well as guns.

“Do I have your word that you will not tell the police?” she asked.

“You do,” he said, facing her.

Violet nodded. “Belize City. A man who is a known criminal.”

“Did you kill him?”

“No,” said Violet. “We didn't shoot him. He tried to shoot us. We dropped the gun and…”

“You dropped this!? The firing pin is part of the hammer, and it fired?” he asked, gleefully waiting to hear the rest of the story.

“It did. And the bullet went into his stove. It must have cut a gas line…”

“Oh, this was the fire in Belize City?”

Ruby snickered.

“That is no problem for me. No one would ever connect an antique like this to an event like that fire. Especially here, so far away. Will you sell or trade it? I would consider it a great favor.”

***

Diego drove the *Ellie Maye* past a host of barely visible sail and power boats toward the south end of the sound. At his request, every man was on deck watching for boats and other obstacles in the unfamiliar waters. They dropped anchor a half mile off shore. Close enough for the zodiac but far enough not be be seen from shore.

Even the act of setting the anchor was laborious in the high winds. When it was set, and the drive in neutral, the *Ellie Maye* swung a wide arch around it until she was nose into the wind. Suddenly they were at the complete mercy of the seas, the anchor pulling the bow down.

Eduardo called them onto the bridge where every man grabbed something to hold onto. Jesus and Mateo were last in, looking green. "We have to go now," said Eduardo.

Looking at the faces, Diego was sure that no one wanted to board the Zodiac in this storm. He was also sure that they would rather chance the small boat than stay aboard the *Ellie Maye* in a hurricane.

***

"You have indulged me long enough," said Coos, handing the Webley back to Mini.

Ruby flipped through a book about the art of Winston Churchill, keeping an eye toward the proceedings.

Mini offered him the P229. He waved it off, "Keep it for now. Let me show you what I have for you. I thought at first that you would need heavy machine guns, but I see now…"

"We need at least one big gun," interrupted Violet.

"But of course. First, we have these," He opened a cupboard exposing a rack of folding stock submachineguns. "This is," he said, withdrawing one and bouncing it in his hand, "heavier than it looks, but with the suppressor it is surprisingly easy to keep on target. Ladies, meet the HK, MP5 in 9 millimeter." He handed the gun over to Violet, then gave another to Mini.

"The version of the MP5 that you have in your hands has a collapsing stock that is adjustable. This will come in very handy for you with shorter arms." He helped Mini adjust the stock length.

"How much?" asked Ruby.

"There is an old saying. If you must ask…"

"…You can't afford it," Violet finished for him.

"It's a matter of how many we can afford," said Ruby, still reading from the book.

Coos nodded in understanding. "The MP5s are twelve thousand American each."

"A few of those, then," Ruby nodded and continued reading.

Violet handed the MP5 back to Coos. "We need something in 5.56. Maybe a machine gun.

Coos hobbled out of the room, his cane tapping an off tempo. Ruby heard a door open then close. A moment later he returned, handing a rifle to Violet and leaning on the counter for support.

Violet shook her head as soon as she felt the weight of the Heckler & Koch HK93 rifle.

"Too heavy?" asked Coos, as if expected.

Violet handed the HK off to Doris, who grunted and handed it back.

"Do you have any AR-15s?" asked Ruby.

"I have at this time semi-automatic only, and only carbines. No M-4s or M-16s. Of the carbines, I have three only," said Coos.

The three carbines, two MP5s, and the HK93 added up to $68,000. Ruby counted out the stacks of cash. "We could do with some flash bangs, maybe a few balaclavas and some C-4 if you have it," she said, holding another stack of hundreds up.

"Ah, the grenades. I have even some smoke, and headwear I have, but I have no C-4."

"What explosives do you have?" asked Ruby, sensing that he was holding something back. "SEMTEX?"

"No, no, nothing like that. I have, ah, I have rocket launchers."

Ruby closed the book, smiling a cat-like grin. As Coos hobbled out of the room, she bounced on her toes, hands clenched and humming.

Doris stared at her, concerned.

"I've always wanted to try one," said Ruby.

"You're certifiable," said Doris.

"Uh-huh, but we need explosives. Rockets have explosives, and I want one!"

Coos tapped his way back into the room and eased himself into a chair, laying the olive green tube of a hand held rocket launcher on the table. “This is an M72 LAWS rocket and launcher. It is single shot, waterproof until opened, very effective, even against light armor and buildings. Very easy to use.”

“I like waterproof. We'll take it,” said Ruby.

“Very good. Now would you ladies care to stay for lunch? I would enjoy the company, and I want to hear the story of the man in Belize,” he said with an amused smile.

Violet nodded, *what a gentleman.*

After a light lunch, Mini pushed her chair back. “Do you still want the pistol?” she asked.

Coos sat back and sipped his coffee. “Yes, very much.”

“Do you have a second rocket launcher?” asked Ruby.

Coos smiled. “Yes, I do.”

“Let's trade,” said Ruby.

“You drive a hard bargain, but I cannot make this trade.”

“But it's such a nice pistol,” teased Ruby.

“The pistol and the HK93 for a second rocket launcher. It is too much gun for you, anyway. You are over-armed. It will slow you.”

Ruby agreed.

***

Manuel watched the Zodiac approach, skidding sideways across the increasingly larger waves of the sound. The gray boat was almost invisible in the storm. Had it not been for the black ponchos fluttering, he may not have seen it at all.

The dock was deserted. A half a dozen boats ranging from twenty-five to sixty feet were on blocks or trailers near the concrete and steel warehouse. One larger party boat bumped against the fenders at the breakwater. The Zodiac straightened as it passed the seawall and entered the slip, partly protected from the wind. Diego drove the boat up the ramp riding the wake and setting the bow down on the concrete.

Manuel, happy that he had not had to make that boat ride, caught the bow line. The six of them carried the boat up the ramp and tied it to a post near the building. Diego insisted on locking the rope. It made no sense, but it didn't matter. They would be back for it soon enough.

It felt good to be in the dry car, but Manuel thought maybe it was an act of futility. He started the rented Isuzu's engine and turned on the defog and wipers to full. They were going to see a man called the Dutchman about guns.

***

Violet drove slowly wondering how bad the storm would get and how it would effect their not yet made plan to get off the island. Loosely they had some idea of hiring a small plane. She had flown for years, but never in anything like this. She'd never known a good reason to fly through a storm. She *had* driven in weather like this a few times. Once, she'd managed to get halfway across Louisiana in a hurricane before finding a high shoulder and waiting it out. It had been a two day wait then. This seemed worse. Maybe it was just her older eyes.

A Jeep crawled along a few hundred yards behind them with no lights. In this weather, lights weren't to see but to be seen. Like on a boat or plane, they became anti-collision lights and only an idiot would drive without them. An idiot, or someone trying not to be seen. She dismissed the idea as paranoia. Who would possibly want to follow them here?

Ahead it was hard to see the lane. A boxy Isuzu SUV came at them, at first moving to their left, then cutting over to their right. For a moment, they played a game of chicken that both would surely loose. At the last second, Violet remembered to drive on the left. She was on the wrong side. Swerving, she felt her tires go off the edge of the pavement into the wet grass before straightening.

The Isuzu passed, a car full of angry men glaring at her.

Violet shrugged it off. *These things happened.*

Ruby cleared her throat and looked up as though nothing had happened. "We need a drill to set our charges and a saw to cut any steel that gets in the way."

"A hardware store," said Bernice.

***

Coos heard the tap on the glass at the rear of the house. The odd pattern stood out to him even with the rain and tree limbs making such a racket. He lifted the jam stick and slid the glass door open. Sean stepped in, flipped back his hood and shed the rain coat. Coos took the wet slicker and hung it on the rack.

"See you brought the patio stuff in. Or did it all blow away?" said Sean.

"It would be in the ocean if I had not," said Coos. Even opening the door for a few seconds had left a blast of water on the stone. "You walked?"

"Of course. Wasn't going to drive in this shite, was I?"

Sean wore his age well. The gray hair of a man in his late fifties framed a lean, tan face. Broad in the shoulders, he showed a bit of expansion at the waist, but most of that was the body armor that he wore on days that Coos called.

"You're late."

"Damn it all. Does that mean I get no whiskey? I came through hell for that."

Coos chuckled. The accent had faded with the years, but Sean was still a hard drinking, hard fighting Irishman. Coos had heard the stories many times over many bottles of Irish whiskey, Scotch whiskey, American whiskey, and Jamaican rum. A northerner but indifferent to the troubles, Sean had chosen to fight for the Crown. After years of service in the SAS, he settled down only to find that his Irish neighbors didn't think well of his choices.

Not inclined to spend the rest of his life looking over his shoulder, Sean took his young bride and shipped out for the islands. It had been a good choice for both he and Coos.

They'd met when Sean was just a corporal in one of the southern African skirmishes, and again several other times over the years. Back then, Coos was an arms dealer with scruples, only selling to the right side. Since then, his morals had become slightly looser. He liked to say that he was selling to collectors, but Sean wasn't there to protect him from collectors.

What's that?" asked Sean, pointing to the movement on the monitors.

"Interesting," said Coos, handing Sean an MP5 and checking the Sig in his own belt. "My client has come and gone." Coos cleaned up quickly and put one of the whiskey tumblers back in the pantry. While he watched the monitors, Sean took up his usual position behind the curtain. Three men exited an Isuzu SUV. Three more stayed in the car.

***

"Madre de Dios," spewed the man who had introduced himself as Eduardo, his face darkening. "Where are my guns?"

Coos answered coolly, "I do apologize, but I was not told who would be coming. The guns you are asking for have been sold. I have alternatives."

"Who was it? Who got my guns?" growled Eduardo, waving off his wiry sidekick's attempted interruption.

"I keep my client's confidence," said Coos, flatly, watching the muscle tick in the man's jaw and wondering how far this would go.

He didn't have to wait long. The angry leader stepped toward him.

Coos pressed the muzzle of the 9mm Sig into the man's gut. It was, he knew from experience, an uncomfortable feeling.

In his peripheral vision. he could see the smaller man circling him.

"Heels on the floor, dancing man," said Sean, slipping out from behind the curtain and into a deep Irish brogue. "I wouldn't want to have to clean this place up. Again."

The little man froze.

"I do not approve of this lot. I really don't," Sean said to Coos. "So, what are ya, drug dealers, terrorists?"

"May I step back?" asked Eduardo.

"Certainly," said Coos, glad for the man's attempt to be reasonable.

Eduardo began to speak, "We have business on the island that requires…"

Coos cut him off, "I don't want to know your business. I want to sell you what you need and send you on your way. Now, gentlemen, would you care for some coffee to get things moving?"

"Keep those heels down," said Sean to the wiry little man.

***

Coos watched the Isuzu's taillights vanish under the trees.

“What was that?” demanded Sean, still at the ready with the MP5. “You let them go with a bloody minigun and two MP5s. Who's responsible for what they do?”

“I am responsible. And don’t forget the pistols,” said Coos, letting the curtain drop. “For the minigun, I gave them only six hundred rounds, and the first one hundred and fifty are blanks.”

Sean laughed, and relaxed a little. “Still, that's nine seconds of lethal fire. You don't think they'll notice the blanks before or after?”

Coos shrugged, “Perhaps we'll ask them after. They could be coming back, but I did not show them how to load the weapon. They will have to figure that out, and frankly, even if they do, they will only shoot for a few seconds.”

Sean tilted his chin down and waited for the explanation.

“Did you see me give them these?” asked Coos, holding up a box of ear plugs.

“Shite,” said Sean, “You're a mean bastard, you are.”

“They are clients, but they are a bad sort. I give them what I must, and I keep the money,” he said counting twenty one hundred dollar bills off the top for Sean.

“How about that drink?” said Sean retrieving the tumbler.

“Does Becka know where you are?” asked Coos.

“I'll send her a text. That sweet girl will wear me out if I stay home with nothing to do.”

***

Manuel tilted his mirror down. Each of the four men in the back were fondling a gun. Two with submachineguns and two with pistols. The pistols were cheap South American knockoffs of the Berretta 9mm. The machine pistols were the real thing, MP5s with short barrels and fixed stocks. Those would do well, but they wouldn't need them.

They had already worked out the plan. The minigun was the key. First, they needed something to bolt the gun mounts to. Without a solid mounting, it would be uncontrollable when fired. A hardware store would have what they needed.

***

Bernice turned on the lights in the low-ceilinged room.

"I'm retired. The beds are clean. No bugs. It's a good roof for this storm," said the woman who owned the shack they were renting for the night.

"We'll take it," said Bernice, letting Ruby pay the woman.

"Are you sure?" asked Doris.

"You can sleep in the car if you want."

Doris huffed, letting the screen door go with a slap.

The rain was relentless. The awning over the door kept only most of it out. A curtain would give them privacy and outside shutters could be closed if the rain blew in. Bernice put a towel on the wet spot in front of the door. Only a few feet outside the door, the street had become a river.

The low concrete house was tucked away on back street away from the beach on one of the higher places on the island. The outside and the inside were painted the same ocean blue. The curtains, with their dolphin and Caribbean motif added green and several bright yellow and orange tones. They'd parked in a narrow drive beside the house. Watching the water flow down the street, Bernice was pleased that they had found a place well above sea level.

Still, the place was rustic. There were only two beds and two cots. Someone would have to double up, or sleep in a chair. Bernice pulled back the curtain to see the promised kitchen. A pull string turned on the lights. The small room with the metal frame table made her think of home.

"Let's play cards," said Violet, dropping a deck on the table.

"It's early," complained Ruby.

"The way I see it we have three hours to plan a job, steal a car, and find a way off the island. Let's play while we can."

And plan while we do, thought Bernice.

"Did anyone notice that little Jeep that followed us?" said Doris.

CHAPTER 36

Lin sat in the jeep with the engine off and the wipers stopped. Visibility was cut to a few yards and less now that the windshield was fogged.

Suddenly, her door swung open.

"Inside," said Doris. "Now!"

***

Lin held the remains of a tiny umbrella dripping on the towel in front of the door. The ladies sat, arms crossed, on the beds, waiting for her to speak. Every few seconds, one of the women would smile like she was some wayward child that needed their encouragement.

Lin could cross her arms, too. Who were the children here?

Doris tilted her chin down in an imitation of a stern parental glare.

Ruby hung a towel over her shoulders and handed her another.

"Can I get one of those?" asked Doris.

Lin relaxed a little. These were her friends. She scanned the faces and saw mirth, amusement maybe, but not malice. She took another deep breath and shivered. She needed dry clothes.

A gust blasted cool water through the screen door.

"Where's Marybeth?" she asked.

***

Captain Ricci paced the bridge, his uniform soaked from walking the upper decks to get the feel of the storm. Thrusters were on to stabilize the ship, but still the decks rolled. Tenders were already bringing passengers from the island, but not as many as had left the ship. Some would choose to wait on the island for the storm to blow over then fly home. He couldn't blame them for playing it safe. This was just a blow so far, but projections showed it worsening.

And that was what kept him pacing. This tropical storm could easily become a hurricane. It was moving slow, and slow moving storms usually gained strength. If he stayed and waited for the last tender, he may have to take his ship and passengers through a massive storm. If he pulled anchor and ran, he would be leaving passengers on land. In either case, the cruise line would lose money.

They could afford that. What they couldn't afford was to be in the path of a hurricane. The danger to the ship and passengers was enormous. So great that Ricci was considering sending the current passengers to the island and taking the ship to sea with only the crew.

"I need to know everything," he said to the first officer.

Davis lifted his clipboard and began to run through his notes. "As of one minute ago, this is still a tropical storm. We have not received any call, fax, or signal from the main office concerning the storm in the last hour. Our last message said that they have the greatest confidence in you."

Ricci grunted. *Of course they do, now. Wait until it costs them a hundred thousand dollars in fuel and even more when we do not make port in time.*

Davis waited for him to stop mumbling in Italian, then continued, "The boat that was following us with the crazy Rasta Tellytubby guy has not been located. RCIP Joint Marine Unit says they are looking. My note, I think they don't want to go out in this weather. In either case, he is not within visual range of the ship."

The captain looked out the full height windows. That wasn't consoling. Even on the lee side, visibility was only maybe five hundred meters. "But he could find us so easy, even if he had no radar?" he said.

"Almost certainly, sir."

Ricci nodded, "Continue please."

"Ah, and Lore says…" Davis' cheeks reddened as he stammered through the message, "Would you like to read this yourself, sir?"

"You read it," said the captain, his mind elsewhere.

"Umm, okay. Lore says come down to the cabin, I assume she means yours, the rocking of the ship is exciting. That's not actually what she said, but…"

The captain rolled his eyes and smiled. It was worth considering. But other captains had left the bridge in crisis, and it never seemed to turn out well. He watched another tender, light on passengers, sprint for the lee side of the ship. Seas were still such that they could board. He checked his watch. 3:05 pm local. Two hours to get them all off or to get them all on. Leaving now really wasn't an option. "Tell her we will get a hammock when this is over."

***

"You can't go with us," said Violet.

"I came down here to help," said Lin.

"You flew down. That means you're here, on the books here," said Bernice.

"Yeah, so are you," said Lin, her eyes deep red and still flowing from the news of Marybeth.

"Not in a few hours," said Ruby.

"Whoa, what does that mean?" said Lin.

"We're not getting back on the ship. We have someone that will make it look like we did," said Violet.

"That's nuts… but actually kind of smart," said Lin. "How are you going to make it look like you were on the ship if you don't get back on the ship. I mean, you'll have to catch up, and that will place you on the island. When are you doing this, anyway?"

"Late tonight," said Ruby.

"It's our best option. The storm will give us cover that we never expected," said Mini.

"We could take a boat out in the morning," suggested Doris.

"A boat? Have you seen the waves out there?" said Lin.

"I still think we can wait for the storm to pass and hire a plane. If we succeed, we'll have the money for it. If we fail, we won't need it," said Violet.

"It's not a bad plan," said Ruby.

"Is there anything you're not for?" asked Doris.

"I'm not for any plan that doesn't let me use my rocket launchers."

"Rocket launchers?" spewed Lin.

"Yes, dear," said Ruby, dealing the cards.

Violet stared toward the street in deep thought. "We need another car. Something fast that can carry all five of us. Think you can get that for us, Lin?"

"You want me to rent a car for you? I already have the Jeep."

"Can't use a rental. We need something off the books," said Violet.

"Sure, I can steal a car for you, but I can't help you rob a bank?" she said, sarcasm dripping.

"It's more like borrowing. We can't take it with us, so we'll only use it for the night. We might need a boat too, so keep an eye out." Violet spun her file.

"I don't know how to steal a car."

"Borrow," said Ruby.

"I guess I had better go with you," said Violet.

***

Norbert cried for the first time since he was six and the old barracks burned with his football in it. It wasn't fair. *Why did he have to get this job right before the boss man go nuts? Don't nobody else need a job?*

"Just one more ting in a long, long string o' bad luck," he sang, drumming a reggae beat on the console.

"De boss he say, follow de ship man,
But de swells be gettin bigger,
By the hour,
And we can't kep up no more,
No more.
We lose the ship in the rain,
And don't know how to use de radar,
So good. So bad."

Norbert was having a good time, and why not? Life was short and looking to get shorter. The boss man was insane following this giant ship through a storm. "Now we follow dis one," he said, pointing at the biggest blip on the screen. The sky was black ahead, "but we got dis radar, ma-n."

He felt a bump under the hull. A scrape, really. Up ahead, floating above the water, something steady and bright white. *Not a ship, a ship be moving. We hit land!*

"Just one more ting in a long, long string o' da bad luck," he sang.

***

"Do you really know how to steal a car?" asked Lin.

"On an older car, you just connect the battery wires and touch the starter wires," said Violet. "But today we're going to try and find one with keys."

They drove slowly, scanning the houses through the fogged glass. "What about there?" Lin pointed at a stone two story house with a Mercedes SUV and a BMW coup sheltered in an open garage. It was only the second open garage they had seen. The other housed a golf cart. Easy to steal, but less than useless.

The door from the house to the garage opened and a young woman in a tight black skirt, white blouse, and black jacket ran out, carrying her heels. She climbed into the left side of the car and the car began to back out. At first Lin was confused, it happened too fast, then, she remembered that the driver's seat was on the right in most cars here. Someone else was driving.

The car backed out and as it passed them the woman bent over in the seat to put on her shoes and the garage door began to slide slowly down.

"Don't these doors have a sensor that…?" Violet began.

Lin flung the jeep door open and ran for the house, wet towel in hand.

She wouldn't, couldn't. Twenty feet and the door had only a foot to go. She threw the towel. Wet and heavy, it cut through the rain, caught the bottom of the door, then flopped across the plane of the door sensor.

The door stopped, then began to open. Lin ducked low and under as it rose, her feet sliding on the polished concrete. She stood, dripping. Violet, high and dry in her rental, clapped. Lin called her with a beckoning finger.

On her way in, Violet grabbed the towel, then went for the button to close the door. As the door rolled down, the old woman shook and shivered, making Lin sorry that she'd made her get out of the Jeep.

The Mercedes was unlocked. Violet began examining the steering column. "Look for keys," she said. She'd just pried the first panel off below the steering wheel when Lin returned jingling a key ring. They were in business.

***

"That was fast," said Ruby.

It was fast. She felt like she'd just gotten here, and already she'd committed a felony.

"I didn't tell you about my rocket launchers," said Ruby. "They're honest to God M72 rockets, and I have two of them!" she said, with just a little too much Christmas morning glee for Lin to swallow.

Lin suppressed the urge to respond to Ruby's crazy-town moment. She'd flown out here to help, to make sure that nothing bad happened to her friends. That's what they were now. Not charges, or clients, but friends. Good people with good hearts that needed her. Only, she was too late for the one that mattered most to her. How did that happen? How did the person that hated her most, that distrusted her most, become the one she felt most responsible for? That was the way of things, she supposed. Now she was here, and the first thing she did was help steal a car. "Borrow" they called it. "Will I have to shoot anyone?"

"No, dear, we're going to be fine. You won't be with us, and the plan is not to shoot them. Now we've got to get moving if we want to make it to the bank in time to get my money," said Ruby.

"Weapons checked out and ready," said Mini.

"Last check," said Violet, breaking away from Lin. "As of right now, this storm is getting worse. Bernice, an update please?"

Bernice waved her tablet in the air but didn't stand. "The weather service says that the storm is stalling over us and is likely to be a hurricane by tomorrow morning, or midday at the latest."

Violet checked her watch. "That settles that. We won't be flying out in the morning. It's 3:30. The ship's app says that the ship will be sailing at 4:30. They want to outrun the storm. The last time that we can reasonably be at the bank and still be expected to be back at the port terminal on time to board the ship is 4:00 o'clock. Does anyone here think we should throw in the towel and go back to the ship?"

She scanned the room. Lin flinched. Mini blinked once. Bernice wiped her glasses.

Violet continued, "They've got three guards, so we'll go let Ruby get her deposit, then we'll come back late at night and blow the vault from the outside of the building. We assume that between the two rockets and the C-4 we can get through. Mini and Bernice will grab any guards that come outside. Once inside, we'll drill and pop the locks off as many boxes as we can in three minutes. If we can't do it with the drill and pull hammer, Ruby will blast the main box. If all goes well, and we get away, we'll ditch the nice car that we borrowed and come back here. The ship will dock in Jamaica tomorrow and will sail from there at 4:30 pm. We have until then to get to Jamaica. The next stop is the US Virgin Islands."

"Security will be much tighter there at the airport," said Bernice.

Lin raised a timid hand. Violet nodded for her to speak.

"You can't use your phones here after the ship leaves. That will kill your alibi," she said, shrugging an apology for the bad news.

That gave Violet pause. With the role modern communications played in their daily lives, she hadn't even considered the effects of losing, or having to set aside, their phones would have. So many things to work out and so little time. The one good thing they had going for them was the storm and even that was causing problems.

"Can we text?" asked Doris.

Lin shook her head, "You have to turn off the phones when the ship leaves. Otherwise, every time the phone connects to a tower it leaves a record."

Too much. Maybe we should just walk away, thought Violet.

"You're tired, Vi. Don't let it get to you," said Doris.

"So right," said Violet. "Maybe after we get Ruby's money we can take a nap."

"Why is this a big deal? We don't need the phones," said Doris.

"If we get separated, we'll need them," said Mini.

"I still have mine," said Lin.

"We did without them for years. You didn't have them when you robbed banks. Why do we need them now?" said Doris.

"Because the other guys will have them. We can't just run down a dirt road across the state line and be free. We're on an island for-Christ-sake," growled Mini.

"You need a nap, too," said Doris.

"It would be nice to have at least one backup option," said Violet.

"I think we need a way to reach Lin if something goes wrong, even if it isn't perfect." said Ruby.

"We can buy a prepaid phone anywhere. They must have them here, too," said Lin.

***

Norbert leaned over the figure laying in the sand. "He look so peaceful, mon,"

"Yah, mon," agreed Jamie, looking at the man that still held his golf club in one hand. *Mister Bob did look peaceful.* "Still breathing, too."

Desire's hull had scraped before coming down hard, crashing into a coral formation, tearing a modest but final hole in the double hull and sinking her in only ten feet of water. They were so close that they would have been on shore in a few more seconds.

It was better this way, thought Jamie, shaking his head. To come ashore, you need a passport. To come ashore from a sunk boat, you don't. "Dat's jus de way it is," he laughed.

"What, mon?" asked Norb.

"We got to leave him, mon. I don think he need us anymore. He be fine here."

Norb hesitated.

"What you want?" asked Jamie.

"Mon, we got to get paid," said Norb.

Jamie reached into the boss's shirt pocket and retrieved the diminished roll of hundreds. He counted eight. He slipped off three for Norb, three for himself, and put the remaining two back in Bob's pocket. "The mon got money on the island. I hear him say it. Let's go get drunk mon. They got good beer here."

"Are there bars still open?" asked Norbert.

"Yah, mon, it not even dark yet!"

"It look dark to me," said Norbert.

Jamie thought he heard the skinny boy's teeth chatter.

***

Bob felt a cool spray on his face. Something tickled the end of his nose. A terrible pressure in his sinuses threatened to explode his head.

He rolled up on his elbows, hanging his head in the sand, then lifting it and letting the salt water drain from his nose.

Sand? “Where the fuck am I?”

He opened his eyes with a struggle. They felt like they were glued shut. He used his fingers to pry them open, then let them shut again, begging the tears to wash out the sand he had just put in his left eye.

Rain fell in streams; he could feel one on his shoulder. He leaned, letting it flow over his head and face. He opened his eye and let the water wash it clean, then closed it again and scrubbed the dirt and whatever else from his face and hair. He chased the stream as the wind blew it here and there and tugged at an adhesive bandage that flopped from his cheek.

He opened both eyes, blinking the water from them. The stream was just one of many formed as the water from a stinging rain fell through the branches of the rubbery leafed tree above him. The tree hung low over a white sandy beach, offering some shelter from the storm.

The sky was dark as night, but in the west, out over the ocean, the gold orb dipped low, sending its rays between ocean and clouds and through the rain to throw dancing shadows from the trees onto the surrounding sand and buildings.

The building wasn't a building at all, but a wall.

Bob stood, his wobbly legs thanking him for being ashore. *How long had they been at sea?* He ducked under a swaying branch and approached the wall. Wiping the stinging rain from his eyes, he read, PLEASE RESPECT THE GOVERNOR'S PRIVACY.

“I've been here before,” he muttered to the rain and wind. “I've been here before. Where’s my boat?”

He looked out to sea. Yachts were bobbing at anchor several hundred yards off shore. None looked like they were doing well in the increasing swells, but none looked worse than the one rocking side-to-side only a hundred yards from the beach. His own *Desire'*, with only the top of the pilot house showing above the foamy green surf. “Crap!”

The rain was cold and began to feel like bullets where it didn't have a tree to slow it down. He remembered this place. There was a road and beyond that, buildings. He began to march, his putter a walking stick, taking cover tree to tree around the pond that formed in the sandy drive. He had parked under these trees once. How strange it looked now with the light of the failing sun streaming through the branches, throwing dancing shadows across the sheets of blowing rain.

***

Ruby felt her feet slip on the marble tile of the bank lobby. *That would suck,* she imagined charging through the door gun in hand and falling on her ass. She thanked God that they'd changed the plan. Explosives were always the best answer. On the other hand, they were now down to two guards, both near the main doors. They could take two guards with ease, if needed. Still, this was the perfect noisy storm for explosives.

Twelve minutes later, her $10,000 in her bag, Ruby walked down the steps, gripping the hood of her mac close around her face. She would have to remember to exchange that for a poncho tonight just in case they were caught on camera. Change her shoes too. So many things to think about. So many choices. Bank robbery was hard work. Choices, choices, choices. If she told the rest about the change in bank staff, would they want to go in now? Easy choice. She wouldn't tell them.

The hood of the mac wasn't worth a darn for keeping blowing rain out. She paused to adjust. Most of the cars in the lot were parked in the shelter of the neighboring building. A flash of lightning illuminated everything. The boxy SUV parked tailgate to the wall was not empty. The wipers swept the glass, showing it full of armed men.

"Blast!" she swore under her breath and forced herself to walk on. Were they guards, extra security? It took every bit of determined, denture grinding, self-control to keep walking when every bone in her wanted to look again. She needed to know who they were, how many they were, why they were there? Information was crucial, and all she had was a brief flash of memory stored in a brain that didn't handle memory well. They had guns, they wore civilian clothing, collared shirts, she recalled, almost tripping on the curb. They definitely had guns, MP5s like the ladies but without the suppressors. The guards had suppressed MP5s and body armor over their uniforms. These men in the car weren't the night guards or backup, then. *What did that leave? Competition?*

Ruby pulled her hood tighter and danced tiptoe through the three inches of water in the street, glad now that they had not parked at the bank where the men in the other car would have seen their faces.

CHAPTER 37

Lester boarded the last of the tenders, dreading the bouncy ride to the ship. The swells were dark and red in the last rays of sun that shot under the blackening sky. He wanted very much to ride out the storm on the island, but he had a job to do. He'd promised his love that he would protect her, and for now, this was how he could do that.

The boat's captain wasted no time, ordering the lines released and pushing the engines to full speed in the same second. The boat strained, and Lester felt the deck twist with the torque of the big engines beneath his feet. The bow rose, and the passengers ducked as they left the shelter of the dock and the hard rain swept under the canopy.

A deck officer scanned the passengers, ordering those few that had not fastened their life vests to do so. The big boat surged across the water, the wind pushing it sideways.

In the shelter of the cruise ship, they swung a hundred and eighty degrees rocking as the stern of their boat slipped momentarily into the stream of the ship's stabilizing thrusters. The starboard side of the tender pushed hard into the fenders, then hung, tilting ten degrees to the side as a swell lifted the tender more than the ship.

"Move quickly, but only on my command," ordered a ship's officer from above. "Send the first four."

The tender's safety officer selected the first four and sent them up the ladder to the boat's upper deck, then selected four more and had them sit on the front bench of the lower deck, ready to go. Lester gripped a stanchion and leaned right to see the bottom of the gangplank extending from the ship. It ended several feet shy of the upper deck of the tender. A passenger leapt from the tender to the gangplank.

Oh darn! Lester moved to the last bench.

Five minutes later, Lester stood on shaky legs on the tender's upper deck gripping the safety line and looking across the gap at Dana Sully.

She wore a strange, confident smile. The girl was either happy to see him, or happy that he was the last.

The officer shouted, and Lester leapt.

His foot slipped on contact with the rubber. Dana caught him, pulling him in.

Behind him, orders were given, lines were cast off, and the engines of the tender roared.

Sully accepted Lester's cruise card and ran it through the turnstile like reader. She withdrew it and wiped it on her pants leg before trying it again. She repeated the process a third time.

Lester watched carefully, wondering how or when she would get to recording the cards of the women left on the island as having come aboard. On her fourth attempt to dry the card, he saw her switch cards. She finished and handed him his card with a smile. “Welcome aboard.” The other cards had gone into her pocket while the rest of the crew secured the hatch and gangplank.

Lester exchanged his life jacket for a towel and let out a deep, relieved sigh, his part of the mission accomplished.

***

Bob washed his face in the sink of the clean tile public bathroom. He examined the cuts on his cheeks and forehead. Several were stitched with one or two stitches. One still had a bandage clinging to it. He would leave that alone for now.

His memory of the last twenty-four hours was returning, but with significant gaps. With some of the things he did recall, he wasn't sure he wanted to remember the rest. He touched one of the stitches and flinched, only vaguely recalling how he got them. From his shirt pocket, he withdrew the two remaining bills. He’d paid cash for the medical treatment, a memory as painful as the wounds themselves.

Bob wrung his boxers out one more time and put them on wet. There were shops in the complex. He saw some that looked closed on the way in, and wondered how big of a storm it was that shops were closing?

***

He watched from the relative shelter of the passage through the building. To his left and across the parking lot were several small clothing stores with promise. The lights were still on in the store in the corner. Bob touched his pocket. It was a miracle that he still had anything left of his money.

A ship's horn echoed dully through the rain. Three blasts. That meant they were leaving. Leaving in the storm? Did cruise ships normally sail in this weather? He vaguely remembered seeing multiple cruise ships at anchor on a previous visit. Would all of them sail? Would the ship with the Poker Club bitches sail? If they stayed, he would get them, he vowed, touching his pocket again. He needed clothes, but if those women were here, he needed a gun. Gun versus clothes? He weighed the needs. "I need a gun because life sucks," he laughed a brittle cackle that echoed in the concrete passage.

The lights of the shop went out, and the door opened. The clerk locked the door and bolted through the rain to a waiting car. The debate was over. Now he had no choice but to steal the clothes. I need a car, too, thought Bob. But clothes first.

He tapped on the store window with his putter. Behind it stood a mannequin, dressed like a millionaire in eighty dollar swim shorts and a tailored print shirt. Bob wanted it all. He tapped the glass again then swung. Thick chunks fell around his bare feet. He swung again. A large sheet fell inward knocking the manikin aside.

Reaching through with the putter, he drove it into the foam leg of the unlucky mannequin. He dragged the dummy out, across the broken glass and into the rain. Lifting it onto his shoulder he retreated to the restroom to claim his prizes.

The ship's horn sounded again.

***

The last blast of the horn aired. The captain checked the radar. It showed no vessels in the way. The ship moved forward, toward the anchor. The chain fell slack, and the two observing officers confirmed the distance. Ricci ordered the chain raised and port thrusters to maintain the slack. The observing officers confirmed that the anchor was out of the water, though not secured. Ricci ordered the forward thruster reversed, and the massive vessel began to swing to port.

They would run west with the storm pushing them, then swing south toward Honduras. There was literally nothing out there for 250 miles. Just the ship and the ocean. With any luck, they would be able to turn back and skirt south of the bulk of the storm and make Jamaica less than a day late. They could skip Jamaica and go on to the Turks but the men were tired and the passengers, as well. It would be best to make port in Jamaica and make up the time somewhere else.

***

The ladies watched the bank through the blowing rain.

With Ruby's news of armed men sitting in another car, they'd felt obliged to move. Violet circled the block, turning her lights off and parking behind a hedge in the lot of the bistro they had been at just that morning. Street and building lights blinked out. The bank lights slowly came back up as the generators stabilized.

The Isuzu SUV containing the armed men crept across the bank's lot. Through the glass wall, the ladies could see the bank's remaining staff preparing to close for the day. It was 4:50 pm. Like any international bank, they would stay open until the established closing hour of 5:30.

The ship was leaving port. Their phones were turned off, and batteries removed to be sure. The new throw away phone was plugged in and almost charged. Mini covered it with her hand. The light wasn't likely enough to expose them to the men across the street, but why take a chance?

A message from Lin. "The storm has just been updated to a hurricane," she read, yelling to overcome the noise of the rain.

"A little early. How does that work for us?" said Doris.

"It doesn't matter now," said Mini, pointing at the bank and changing the subject. "We could let them rob it then come in right after, while the cops are after them, and take the safe deposit boxes."

"Won't they close the vault?" said Bernice, her thumb on the safety of the AR-15.

"We'll find out soon," said Violet. The Isuzu was rolling. She started the borrowed Mercedes.

Across the street, the Isuzu rolled backward up the steps. While two balaclava hooded men swung the bank doors open wide, the tailgate of the SUV swung open. The guards froze, weapons still hanging at their fronts.

***

Devon, formerly Sergeant Devon of the SAS, turned toward the opening doors in time to see the tailgate of the Isuzu swing open and hear the man inside scream for him to freeze. He did. Not because the man screamed, but because he knew that he was looking at the business end of an M134D Gatling gun and that there was no other response than to do what he was told.

Russell, the other guard, had his hand on the grip raising his MP5. Devon shook his head. The M134 electrically powered Gatling gun was spinning up. It could fire fifty rounds of 7.62 x 51mm NATO per second, continuous fire. The mid-weight body armor they wore could stop a bullet from a pistol or even buckshot, but the high velocity round from the minigun would go through the body armor without pause.

Devon raised his hands.

***

Eduardo watched his men disarm the guards.

The alarm had not been tripped. Manuel sprinted across the lobby with Mateo trailing. Mateo split and entered the hallway with the offices. Manuel continued on to the last hallway, where the young bank officer in the tight skirt was exiting the vault. The steel bar door to the cage entrance stood open.

Manuel pointed his MP5 at her head from ten feet. She released the door, raising her hands. The bank was open for business.

Bruno, the safe cracker and explosives man strode past into the vault, battery powered drill and lock puller in hand, wet shoes squeaking on the floor.

Jesus and Diego pulled balaclavas backward over the heads of the prisoners, then duct taped the hands and feet of all four.

In less than two minutes, Bruno exited the vault carrying a black duffle.

Eduardo whistled. The lights flickered, and the generator fell silent as Mateo sprinted from the mechanical room, catching the SUV as it began to roll.

They had done the job in four minutes without a shot fired.

***

Ruby's seatbelt tightened as Violet slid the Mercedes to a stop behind the hedge. "Who's got a good idea?" said Violet.

Ruby spoke up, "Mini's backup plan. Mini and I will check out the bank. You follow those guys, and send Lin to pick us up a few blocks away."

"Stay on the main road so she can find you," said Violet. "And keep your hoods up in case the cameras are still on. Get it done as fast as you can."

The bank was as dark as the rest of the world, and Ruby did not like it. She pulled her hood up against the rain as she and Mini stepped from the Mercedes, marching blind through the water as their friends sped off.

"Should we turn them lose?" asked Ruby.

"No! They'll be fine. They saw a bunch of men attack them. Let's keep it that way," said Mini.

Lightning flashed, illuminating the steps just before she could trip over them. Mini turned on the flashlight mounted on the carbine and swept in front of them. Ruby follow suit.

The young woman, Anne, that had helped her with the box was securely bound, as were the manager, and one of the guards. The second guard had managed to slide across the floor and was actively rubbing his taped wrists against the base of a stone pillar that supported a table. Mini shone her light on the guard's reversed balaclava. He froze. "Who's there?"

Ruby swept the lobby with the light attached to her carbine and continued forward careful of the slick floor.

The jail-bar door to the vault entry room stood open. Behind it on the floor, cash lined the walls, some in bags and some in open stacks. There were two vault doors. The one on the right was secured. On the left, the rectangular door to the safety despite boxes stood open.

Ruby entered and scanned the boxes. Number 1028 was missing. She swept her light across the floor. The large box was on its side.

Empty!

Disappointment and confusion seized her, her light frozen on the empty box, the hinged lid jutting out at an odd angle. “No time for this,” she said, pulling her eyes away, and swinging the light around the vault.

In her hurry, she’d focused on the one box. But a dozen other boxes had been opened, their contents strewn across the floor. A small brown felt bag caught her attention. She hefted it. It weighed maybe four ounces and rattled like broken glass. Just a minute of searching would surely turn up a worthwhile haul of loot, but they didn't have a minute. This would have to do.

Passing a table in the lobby, her shoes still squeaking on the floor, her eyes latched onto the black plastic of a tablet. She grabbed it.

Wordlessly, they left the bank, tucking the rifles under their black ponchos. In the wind, Ruby felt like she was wearing a sail, the wet cloth wrapping around her, sticking to everything from her ankles up and pushing her forward.

They rounded the corner. Under the poncho, Ruby removed the flashlight from the Picatinny rail of the rifle. It was either that or aim a rifle down the street to see.

“What did you find?” asked Mini.

“They went straight for the box,” said Ruby, feeling like she was yelling for all the world to hear above the storm. A fresh blast of water flung from the bouncing fronds of a low palm hit her in the face. It stung but in a way that was refreshing.

“I got this,” she said, holding out the brown cloth bag.

Mini felt the bag. “You think somebody put cut glass in a safe deposit box?” she said.

“I think the more stuff is missing, the less suspicious it looks for us,” said Ruby, a blast of rain lifting her hood. She chuckled and sang an old song as she walked. She’d funded a big part of the job and had as much right to make an executive decision as anyone, didn’t she? “We need to get to the car and catch the others! Can you run?”

"Can't see," said Mini, shaking her hood like a wet dog and starting into a jog.

***

Lin sat in the Jeep, listening to the storm. She'd parked against the side of a building that sheltered her from most of the wind and some of the rain. In front of her, the water was so deep in the street that she could no longer see the painted lines.

Her phone buzzed, and she answered.

"Lin?" Violet yelled.

"Yeah."

An SUV passed in front of her, pushing a wake up into the parking lot.

"There's a car coming your way, SUV, Isuzu I think. Follow it from a distance."

"A long distance," she heard Ruby say in the background.

"On it," she said, dropping the phone in the seat.

***

Manuel plowed through the streets of lower George Town, looking for anything he recognized. For a moment, he thought he was being followed, but the lights turned off into the lot of the hardware store. The same store where they had bought the wood to mount the gun. The gun they had paid so much for and not even fired.

Another car was behind them several hundred meters. That car seemed to be dropping further back. *Good.* Things would have been a lot easier if they hadn't spent ten minutes going the wrong direction. He shrugged. It was hard to tell where you were in this weather. A little misdirection was good to make sure they weren't followed, anyway.

Eduardo checked the mirrors and relaxed, the MP5 muzzle resting on the floor.

***

Mini ran toward the only light she could see, the glow through the thick glass door of a hardware store. The building was mostly concrete, with only a glass door giving a glimpse into the dimly lit interior. Generator power, she thought, realizing that it was only now five o'clock and most of the town was hunkered down for the storm. She tried, but it was impossible to find a dry place for her feet to land. Her shoes, heavy with water sank into the current with each step. A car plowed toward them pushing huge sheets of water to each side. The headlights were blinding.

"Ah! Why can't you be tall enough to block those lights?" complained Ruby, behind her.

Mini's own light was useless. She flashed it up at the car, hoping it would be enough to keep them from being run over. She tensed, checking that her rifle was covered by the poncho. They had seen only one other car out since they left the bank four minutes ago. With so few out in the storm there seemed a good chance that most would be police or emergency.

There were three hundred some odd police on this tiny island. That was a lot. The good news was that most were unarmed. The bad news was that four minutes was a long time to be in the open after robbing a bank.

The car slowed, the rain reflecting light onto the grill.

Mini relaxed. It was the Mercedes with Violet at the wheel.

***

Lin fumbled with the phone, her other hand white on the wheel. She called, and Doris answered.

"I'm on Crewe Street," she shouted at the phone. "Going east, I think. Into the wind."

"Where? What cross street?" she heard Doris ask.

Lin desperately scanned for cross street signs. "Lark... something," she shouted at the phone.

"Break it off," she heard Violet say.

"Good idea," said Lin, turning into a looping drive and shutting off her lights.

***

Mud, from recent construction mixed with the water flowing across the road, making the lines, the shoulders, the road itself, imaginary. Violet felt the tires break traction several times. She ignored it. Cars always did that if you went fast enough.

"Even if they're slow, we won't beat them to the cutoff," said Bernice, her attention fixed on the stolen tablet. "Floor it and take the first left at the roundabout. That may put us in front."

Ahead, the road vanished into a grassy mound. "That's the roundabout," said Bernice. "Stay left."

Violet slowed, plowing through the water that was almost up to the top of the curb. She took the first exit left from the roundabout onto a dark two lane road.

"What happens when we catch them?" asked Doris.

"Getting close. Are you sure they got our money?" Violet asked of Mini and Ruby.

"There were stacks of cash but the box was empty," said Ruby.

"Did you get any of the cash?" asked Doris.

Mini and Ruby shook their heads in the dark.

"This is a good place," said Bernice.

"Ready with the guns," ordered Violet, pulling hard right and blocking the road.

The five ladies exited the Mercedes SUV, dark blotches in the storm.

"I have to pee," said Doris, dancing up and down.

"You better hurry," said Ruby.

Doris ran off into the darkness.

"Use the car for cover," said Mini.

Ruby and Bernice, AR-15 carbines ready, leaned across the hood. Mini and Violet stood beside one another with the MP5s.

"You know…" said Violet, feeling the need to find some peace before the storm, "…this has been good for us, and whatever happens…"

"If you shoot that thing while it's under your poncho, you'll wind up with hot brass all over your feet," said Mini, cutting her off. "And in case you're wondering, I have my hearing aids turned down. These things are suppressed, those aren't," her hood nodded toward the ladies with the AR-15s.

Violet turned down her volume and called for the others to do the same.

Lights appeared on the trees ahead. A car was coming.

***

"Jefe?" said Diego.

"Si," answered Eduardo.

"Jefe, it's dark too early. I don't think we can find the *Ellie Maye* in this."

Eduardo rubbed his face, the day old stubble giving him something tactile to push back on. "Are you saying we can't leave?"

"Yes, Jefe," said Diego, nervously.

"Madre de Dios, why did you not say something before we robbed the bank?"

"I'm sorry, Jefe, I did not expect it to get so dark."

Flashes of light on the road ahead, like blinking emergency lights, interrupted the conversation.

Thunk-thunk-thunk.

Manuel slammed on the brakes. A hole appeared in the windscreen and a bullet tumbled through the car, ripping the head liner and shattering one of the plastic dome lights.

He threw the car in reverse and floored it. He could see nothing behind. He drove by instinct, praying to God that they could stay on the road. Another bullet penetrated the windshield.

He spun the wheel, pushing the car into a J-turn, and within a second they were moving forward, away from the shooters.

"Who are they," demanded Eduardo.

"Police, for sure," said Bruno. "Who else has guns here?"

Manuel was not so sure. He had seen nothing, no bright reflective stripes or logos. *And since when do British trained police shoot first?*

CHAPTER 38

"Who fired?!" screamed Violet, on the edge of being really pissed off.

Ruby raised her hand, barely out of the poncho.

"Get in the car," Violet bellowed. "Now we have to chase them!"

"Sorry," said Ruby, "but I got them at least once."

Violet revved the engine, out of habit glancing over her shoulder to make sure her passengers were ready. "Where's…"

The right rear door opened and Doris climbed in. "Why didn't ya'll wait for me?"

"That's what Violet said," said Ruby.

Violet stomped on the gas.

The tail lights were long gone.

"Call Lin," said Mini.

Doris hit speed dial.

***

Lin snatched up the phone. "Yes," she answered.

The Isuzu sailed by, kicking up a huge wave.

"You want me to follow them?"

"From a distance. Ruby shot them," said Doris.

***

Water steamed through the two bullet holes in the front glass. Worse, the spider web of cracks reflected every stray bit of light in every direction making it near impossible to see.

"Did we really lose them?" asked Manuel.

"Si," said Bruno, from the back where he and Mateo rode with the Gatling gun. "We see nothing."

"We need to find a hotel or something," said Eduardo.

"And ditch this car," said Manuel.

Eduardo looked back. Mateo was ready on the minigun, but so far, no target. The gun was mounted on a sheet of plywood that they had cut to fit. When the job was done, they had intended to dump the gun and leave the car where the rental agency could recover it. Now they would have to dump the car, too.

“You used a fake name on the rental?” asked Eduardo.

“It's real, but it's not me,” grinned Manuel.

Ed checked his speed. They were doing almost 50 kph. He could feel the tires begin to hydroplane.

***

“They just turned right,” Lin yelled at the phone.

Her hands hurt from gripping the wheel. Driving in a storm with no lights was no treat. The road had vanished under water, and without lights she couldn't see the telltale signs that marked the areas that were not road. The Isuzu's headlights ran perpendicular to her, almost 300 yards away.

She turned on her headlights and slowed, looking for the road. Here the water ran off the pavement quickly, leaving it at least visible. Ahead was a major intersection.

***

“Jefe!” said Mateo, from the back. “Jefe, I see lights.”

“Where?” asked Eduardo.

“On the road we just came off of.”

“Get the gun ready.”

“They're gone,” said Mateo.

“Gone?”

“Si, Jefe, gone.”

***

Defying her panic, Lin swung the Jeep in a lazy turn that took her into deeper water then back onto higher ground. She’d made it. She’d found the road. She let herself breathe driving on the higher, wider, road. The car ahead was gone.

Gaining confidence, she accelerated toward a dark hole between several light colored buildings. Ahead lay a large roundabout with trees in the center, but what was pavement and what was turf?

She bumped on the light switch.

Suddenly, a shadow in front of her didn't look right. She swerved uncertainly, "Wrong side of the road." Still on the pavement, she realized that she was in the roundabout, but going the wrong way around. Did it matter?

Illuminated in her headlights, the Isuzu was stopped at the far exit. The open tailgate faced back into the traffic lane that she should have been in. But she'd taken the shortcut, the wrong way around the roundabout that put her broadside to the Trooper rather than behind it.

Between her and the Isuzu Trooper stood two men, cheap ponchos blowing in the wind. Lin swung right, taking the exit, her tires kicking up a rooster tail of water, as she looked back over her shoulder. She was not mistaken. Illuminated by the Isuzu's dome light, two men in the back of the SUV manned a huge mounted gun with a spinning barrel.

"Holy shit!" She pushed the gas to the floor.

***

"Madre de Dios," Eduardo cursed. The plastic poncho stuck to his gun like corn husk to a tamale as he tried to raise it and defend himself. A sheet of water thrown up by the Jeep drenched him, half of it seeming to find the neck hole in the poncho.

He swung, the poncho keeping him from reversing the MP5, and in his own headlights saw the driver and passenger as the jeep crossed to the left side of the road and accelerated into the blinding rain.

"Just a woman," he said, yanking the useless poncho upward over his head and off. The wet plastic hung on the machinegun bolt, dragging behind him. He grabbed a handful and tore it free, letting it fly away.

"Go, go, go!" he shouted, closing the door.

"Do we chase them?" asked Manuel.

"No, it was just a woman out being stupid in the storm," said Eduardo, opening the map on his phone. Madre de Dios, what a fucked up night?

***

Doris put the phone on speaker so Violet could hear. "They have a minigun!" yelled Lin over the phone.

"Okay, but where are they?" asked Doris.

"Behind me. They have a big machine gun, a minigun."

"You've said that twice now. What does that mean?" asked Violet.

"My dad showed me a video once. It was one of those Gatling guns the army uses. A big machine gun."

"I heard you. We've got some pretty big guns ourselves," injected Doris.

"Not like this."

"Then we'll be careful," said Violet turning off the headlights.

"They can't be more than half a mile ahead," she said.

"Next roundabout, if we take the second exit and stay straight, we might be able to cut them off again," said Bernice, tracing the path on the stolen tablet with a finger.

They were in town now, a large parking lot and hedges on the left, buildings blocking the view to the sides, and a stand of trees dancing in the wind in the center of the roundabout.

"Is this it?" asked Violet.

"Go right instead of left," said Bernice. Too late, they were already speeding into the roundabout.

A ball of fire and a ripping sound tore through the night. The heat from the fire vaporized the falling rain, creating a horizontal mushroom cloud of glowing steam that rolled out from the source. Blinding and furiously loud, it reminded Violet of the noise from the racing planes she'd flown.

She aimed to the right of the fiery cloud, trying desperately not to be blinded by the muzzle flash and praying for a miracle. Just that fast, they were through the roundabout and heading north, the noise and the flash behind.

"Are we hit, are we hit?" asked Mini.

"We're all okay," answered Ruby, after a long pause.

"So, that was what Lin meant by big machinegun," said Bernice. "Let's stay in front of them from now on."

"I'm glad I peed," said Doris.

"They're not following," said Ruby.

"If they keep going north, the roads come really close in about two miles," said Bernice.

"Yeah, but how do we fight that big gun?" asked Doris.

"We ambush them from the front," said Ruby.

***

Eduardo could barely hear the screams. The explosion was so loud that at first he thought the minigun had misfired. It wasn't a misfire, but the opposite. The gun was firing fifty rounds a second of high velocity military ammunition, inside the closed space of the vehicle. It had taken him a second to plug his ears.

A second too long.

His head felt like an elephant had sat on it. Ringing pushed from his ears forward to his eyes, making them throb, blurring his vision.

Behind him, Diego and Jesus squirmed in the seat, ears covered, excruciating pain written across their faces. Diego's lips moved, but Eduardo only heard ringing.

"Drive," said Eduardo, to Manuel, who seemed to be the only one not in pain. "Did you cover your ears?" he yelled.

Manuel nodded, his lips shaping words that Eduardo couldn't hear.

***

Mateo knew instantly that he had made a mistake firing without real ear protection. He had stuffed tissue in his ear, but it just wasn't enough. Fortunately, he had not made the same mistake as Bruno. The safe and explosive man had been arrogant and aloof since they had met. Always superior, only speaking to show how much smarter he was than the rest of them. Well, he's not so smart now, thought Mateo.

Hundreds of hot cartridges had poured from the ejection chute of the minigun into Bruno's lap. Bruno desperately shoveled them away, the crotch of his pants smoldering.

Then he did something completely unexpected but perfectly sensible. He lunged for the open rear door and the watery street. It was only a few feet past the gun to the door, and Bruno was a small man. He should have been able to clear it easily. But this was not his lucky day. Several bolts extended upward from the gun mounts. Bruno's shoelace caught one of the bolts, slowing his charge for freedom just enough to allow him to exit the door in a prone position.

Bruno hit the street face first, the rest of his body followed a split second later. He lay still in the four inches of water that flowed down the street.

Mateo watched it all with a kind of sick fascination. Bruno was no friend, but *damn,* nobody deserved to go like that. He touched one of the hot cartridges. It was already cool enough to pick up. He examined the empty brass casing with his fingers. It felt too long. He squinted at it in the poor light. The cartridge extended beyond the normal length, a hollow tube where the bullet would have been before firing. *A blank?*

"What's going on back there?" screamed the boss.

"We need a new loader. Bruno is gone," answered Mateo.

Diego climbed over the seat. "Where did he go?" he asked, opening an ammo can.

"I smell barbeque," said Jesus.

***

Francis Ledet put down the phone. So, someone had finally done it. They had finally robbed a bank here on the island, and of all things, they'd done it with a bloody minigun.

Ledet dressed slowly while he waited for the other men of the Uniform Support Group, the armed branch of the Cayman police, to check in as operators at the Emergency Operations Center (the EOC) called them up. No hurry on this one. Ledet was as British as a Brit could be, and while the image of the British soldier was one of men who would stoically march into battle against overwhelming odds, Ledet was no longer a soldier. He was a policeman now. Marching was right out.

The men of the USG would gather. They would begin an investigation and pray that they did not find the extremely well-armed suspects until said suspects had chosen to sleep. Of course, there was always the chance that when they realized that they would not be getting off the island in this storm they would take hostages. That would be unfortunate, something to be headed off if possible.

Ledet picked up the pace a bit. First, he needed to call Sean and find out how much ammo these guys had for the minigun. Sean always knew. Ledet didn't ask how. It was enough for him that he had access to the information. He checked his watch. Five thirty and black as night out already.

***

Ruby lifted the green tube over the seat. "I've got this," she said, with a sly smile.

"We do have that," said Mini.

"Left here and…" started Bernice.

"…Stopping," finished Violet, extinguishing the lights.

"Tell Lin to turn off the road now," said Violet, following Ruby into the deluge.

"She said, 'okay', then the phone died," said Doris, from inside the car.

"Ruby, can you hit them from here?" asked Violet, the rain streaming down her face.

Ruby scanned the intersection. It wasn't perfect. They were too close to the corner and would only have a second or two to launch an attack. "Somebody follow me with my rifle," she said, running for the steps of the building across the street, her soaked skirt sticking to her legs. Aside from giving some shelter, the raised patio was five feet higher than the flooded road.

At the top of the steps, she leaned on a pillar and wiped the water from her face. It was not so dark as it seemed from inside the car. A few rays of what could have been sunlight shone from her right, then were extinguished. She could hear the ocean mixed with the slap of the blowing rain. The shore must be close. *What a mess. What a glorious mess.*

Doris, winded from the sprint, took a knee beside her, one rifle in each hand.

"Have them ready but leave mine safed," said Ruby.

From her new vantage, she could see perhaps a hundred yards down the road. The distance varied with the wind gusts and sheets of water. It was true dark now, the power off everywhere. The sun was gone to bed, its place taken by the unpredictable wind and rain. How much would the wind affect the rocket?

"Where are you?" shouted Ruby, to her friends across the street.

One, two, then three, flashlights came on pointed at the ground.

"Back off ten yards," she hollered.

The flashlights began to move.

On the street, headlights approached slowly.

Ruby, pulled the safety pin and extended the tube of the single shot rocket launcher the way Coos had shown her. The sights flipped up automatically. Her fingers, cold and stiff, fumbled with the small plunger on top of the tube that had to be drawn to arm the rocket. Time was running out. Her fingers slipped.

She grasped it again, this time pinching until it hurt.

The plunger clicked. The launcher was armed.

Ruby raised the tube to her shoulder. She could barely see the rear sight. Leaning on the post to steady the weapon, she felt the trigger button on top of the tube with the fingers of her right hand. "Recoilless," they had called it. *We'll see.*

She centered the sight between the blinding headlights then aimed right to compensate for the wind. It was just a guess.

She pressed the button.

The flash from the rocket blinded her, and a split second later the explosion rocked her, the wave from the blast deflecting off the glass behind her. Instinctively she ducked behind the pillar, a shield from the shower of splinters. *Splinters?*

***

Mateo looked over the seat from the back. Manuel was driving very fast for the conditions.

A huge flash of lightning split the night, and the pole in front of them exploded.

The pole was in a small roundabout with the yellow painted curb of the center barely visible above the water.

Manuel spun the wheel to the left, tipping the fender into a hedge and throwing the Trooper into a slide.

Diego's face became one with the side glass. Mateo latched onto the minigun, his thumbs planted on the fire button sending seventy-five rounds down the street before he could release.

As the pole teetered, the Isuzu continued in a backward skid toward it until the rear tires made solid contact with the curb of the roundabout. Mateo, minigun, and plywood sailed from the back of the SUV, skimming, then splashing down well past the teetering pole.

Stunned, Mateo stood, checking himself for injuries.

Diego splashed past him, falling to his knees and scrambling for the hedge, splashes like pebbles in the water behind him, too big to be raindrops.

A loud cracking bang and a piercing pain in his backside alerted Mateo to the nature of the splashes.

Bullets!

***

The forty foot pole teetered, suspended by the many sets of wires that it had been built to support.

Ruby dropped the launcher and raised her rifle. The man standing over the Gatling gun needed to leave or die.

Doris fired first, and the skinny man grabbed his backside with both hands, howling above the wind like a wounded rabbit.

"I got him," screamed Doris, with glee. "I shot the little bastard in the ass."

On the other side of the street, muted flashes reached out toward the man running for the hedge. The man suddenly twisted, his leg giving out.

***

Eduardo gripped the dash with both hands. "Could it get any fucking worse!?" A rifle-like crack answered him. He turned in time to see Mateo grab his ass with both hands and scream.

"Madre de fucking Dios," he bellowed, grabbing the MP5 and rolling out into the river-like street.

Holes, bullet holes, appeared in the fender beside him.

Eduardo dove into the water and pushed himself under the Trooper to the other side.

***

Bob let the wind take his new hat. He didn't like the trilby style anyway. It almost gave him less cover from the rain than nothing. At least now the water could run freely across him like it should.

He walked as fast as he could. There were flashes of light and loud noises ahead. It seemed like somewhere he should be.

***

There were many things that Ledet did not want to do. Top of that list today was to go into a gunfight armed only with a handgun when the other side had a heavy machinegun.

One by one, he answered the calls as the men of the USG called in for orders and a sitrep. Answering the third call too quickly, he found himself listening to the insufferable ass, Chief Super Webster. Mercifully, the signal dropped.

Seconds later, he heard the unmistakable roaring confirmation of a minigun. Unfortunately, it was only a few seconds of fire. A sustained blast would have likely depleted the twelve second supply that Sean suggested they had. “Civic duty and all, I should go,” he grumbled. “Why couldn't you bastards go to the East End?”

He chose a camouflage poncho rather than his usual police blaze yellow. Nothing like blaze yellow with blood on it. Stepping onto the balcony of his high-rise apartment block, he overlooked Seven Mile Beach. The wind howled and the rain blasted but mostly over his head and to the side. He was protected here behind the building. He looked around the wall and was rewarded with a blast of cold water in the face. Some lights were coming on in the buildings to the south.

Two rifle shots cracked. Distinct even in the storm. That was close. “Can't have bullets bouncing everywhere, can we?”

***

Bullets bounced everywhere.

Mini and Violet, with over a thousand rounds each for the MP5s, took cover behind a wall, dropping mags and reloading as fast as they could. Rain hit the suppressors and turned to vapor. The Isuzu was shredded, especially in the front where the one man continued to fire from cover.

Bernice covered Violet and Mini with the much slower firing but more accurate AR-15. It would have been more accurate, if she could see. Her glasses were useless in the rain. She wiped them with the back of her hand and in the half second that she could see, took in the scene before her.

The power pole still stood, albeit at an awkwardly strained angle. The wires above were stretched and stretching more as the winds shook the pole. Bernice felt herself being pushed against the back of the Mercedes, her poncho a flapping sail, water lapping at her ankles. She fired, sending a double tap at what looked like a head popping up.

The windshield of the Isuzu shattered. The rear door on the other side of it opened, and she fired.

The door closed.

Sparks flew as bullets hit the hundreds of nails and staples in the base of the damaged pole. Someone had a good idea. She slammed in another magazine and fired, chipping away at what was left of the base of the power pole.

The rear side door of the Isuzu opened again. Another double tap through that and she was back on the pole. She dropped a mag in her catch bag and rammed another home while Mini went to single fire, *tap-tap-tap,* at anything that moved near the Isuzu.

Suddenly, a streak of light and a flash lit up the world.

***

The car was disabled. The engine shot so full of holes that it would never run again.

Eduardo went for the back door. There was nothing to do but run and damned if he would leave the money behind. He opened the door a few inches, and a bullet passed through, spraying him with dull chunks of safety glass.

He slammed the door. Who the fuck were these people?

He stood and emptied a magazine, spraying wildly, before ducking back down.

From the rear fender, Manuel tossed him another mag. He juggled the catch, almost losing it in the water.

He loaded and turned to fire, and in a microsecond of horror, he watched a rocket fly toward the car. The car with the money in the back. Then, in a stroke of tremendous good luck, it missed and hit the pole.

The base of the pole exploded, slamming the body of the Isuzu into them, throwing both he and Manuel like rag dolls.

The doors of the Isuzu exploded outward, pieces of white paper flung into the air. The bonds! Eduardo scrambled, jumping up to catch a floating page that, dancing in the wind, eluded him.

The shooting began again, cutting through the rain around him. He didn't care. Then something heavy and long like a snake struck the water below. The pole was falling, and with it the wires that now carried current. Eduardo dove for cover behind the car, the papers flying away in the hurricane winds.

***

Jesus crawled, face down in the water, an indiscernible lump. He had a plan. A simple plan. Run away!

He lifted his head a few inches, slowly scanning. He was past the traffic circle.

Face half in the water he crawled down the street.

The searing heat of an explosion threatened to ignite his thinning hair. He rolled his head to the side to dowse it, then, not feeling his face burn, dared to open his eyes to the scene behind. The fireball had already receded.

Battered by the rain and kept afloat by the swirling wind, a piece of paper floated to him. It was providence, a gift from God. He was free. Jesus snatched the bond from the air, stood, and ran.

Behind and beside him power lines crashed to the flooded street.

Jesus ran for his life, tears of terror mixing with the rain.

CHAPTER 39

A cage of hot power lines lay across the Isuzu, loose ends dancing in the water, sizzling, sparks flying. The pole lay across the roof of the SUV, crushing it. All was silent but the rain, wind, and the sizzling of electric current on the loose.

Bernice broke the peace with a round into the front tire. No reason that should be standing tall.

From the front of the vehicle, a handgun was tossed out between the wires into the street.

The stocky man with the mustache crouched in the water holding up both hands for mercy. The flashlights from all three carbines focused on him as he lifted the MP5 from the water and tossed it one handed toward them.

It was a heavy gun and a weak throw. The strap snagged on a power line and the gun fell short, bouncing on a tense, hot wire, throwing a shower of sparks with each bounce.

Bernice held her breath. *Could that thing cook off and fire?* Just in case, she stayed low.

Finally, the gun settled, hanging from the hot wire for a last moment then falling into the water.

One of the other flashlights swung up, landing on a man that lay whimpering, caught between the wires and the hedges and bleeding from several bullet wounds in a place that would not allow him to sit for a long time.

Bernice chuckled. *This is the way it should be.*

She turned her light back on the face of the mustached man. So familiar, his face.

The lights, unsteady in the wind, converged on the down men and the cage they were in, circles of swirling rain in the beams.

The face, thought Bernice. *I know that face.*

"Salizar!" she said, the word barely escaping her throat, a sudden terror rising in her.

The man sat up. He wiped the rain from his face, wariness, and surprise in his eyes.

"Who are you?" he asked.

Anger flared, "I am who I am, Luis Salizar."

"Luis is my father. Please, I do not know you."

The son. The son of the man that killed, murdered, my Warren, and tried to murder me. Bernice went cold and numb, the business end of her rifle, rock steady, pointed at the spawn of Luis Salizar.

"Is your father still alive?" she asked.

The man nodded, his chin down and rain dripping from it.

The cold was fleeing, a warm confidence taking its place.

"Bernice?" she heard someone say.

"Not now!"

"Bernice? Are you with us?" asked Violet. "We have to go."

"The money is in the back. Take it," said Eduardo.

"We can't get to it through those wires," said Ruby.

Bernice felt the weight of the trigger on her finger. It wasn't right to kill a man for being someone's son, but this wasn't just anyone's son.

"What do I do?" cried Bernice.

"What do you want to do?" asked Doris.

Bernice thought only a little before answering, "I want to send a message to his father."

"Tell him the message," said Violet.

Bernice nodded, "Tell your father that Bernice Walker lives. Tell him that I did this to you. Bernice Walker did this to you. Got that? What will you lose by failing here?" she asked, inspired by the desperate look on the man's face.

"Everything," admitted Eduardo Salizar. "We will lose everything."

Everything, thought Bernice, watching Violet switch her MP5 to single fire and point it at the man's leg. Two quick tugs on the trigger.

Eduardo screamed, falling to his knees and grabbing his right thigh.

Bernice lowered her aim and squeezed. Two bullets cut a misty path through the rain and into Eduardo's left leg.

She turned to Violet, "Who do you think you are, shooting my prisoner? The message was from me."

"I think I was putting a nice, clean, but painful shot through the thigh away from the artery, so he could live to deliver the message," said Violet, marching toward the Mercedes.

"Well, I was making sure the bastard remembered the message," said Bernice. *And he will.*

"Get what you can and let's go," commanded Violet, her voice muffled by the poncho.

"She said, get your stuff and let's go!" repeated Bernice, pulling her hood open to be heard.

She turned once more to Eduardo, trapped under the wires on his knees. He could bleed out right there, and for that she would be sorry. Bernice reached over the seat for the med bag. Grabbing a handful of compresses, she high-stepped through the deep water and tossed them to Eduardo. He could patch himself up with wet bandages.

In the car, she pushed her hood back, the rain that it hadn't kept out filling the creases in her tired face. She hoped that Eduardo would live. He was, perhaps, a bad man, even a killer like his father, but what chance had he ever had for anything else?

Violet backed down the short street, stopping once with the headlights illuminating the men and the car trapped under the bouncing and sparking web of wires. The rain pounded the Mercedes and swirled around them. "There is no way to get to the money. No way," she said, begging forgiveness.

"Let's get out of here," said Mini.

"Can you get us back to Bodden Town?" Violet asked Bernice.

Bernice nodded, moving her fingers across the screen. "Take the roundabout right," she said, glad to be doing rather than thinking.

Violet swung around the circle then slammed the brakes violently, swerving around a running man.

"I'll get him," said Mini, rolling out and leveling her submachinegun at the man.

Ruby jumped out with a rifle, the tactical rail mounted light blinding the man who stood trembling, hands raised.

Mini snatched the paper from the man's hand. "Who are you?" she demanded.

"Jesus, the cook. Only the cook. Please don't shoot me."

"What is this?" demanded Mini, unable to read the page.

"Is money. B...b…bearer binds," he said, his voice cracking.

Bernice took the bond from Mini. How surreal, interrogating a soaking wet man at gunpoint in the middle of the street in a hurricane.

Mini lifted the suppressor of the MP5 toward Jesus' head. "How were you getting away? How were you going to get off the island."

Jesus mumbled what sounded like a prayer before answering, "The *Ellie Maye*. Big boat."

"Grab him, and let's go," said Violet, waiting only long enough for the Mini and Ruby to shove the man into the car, and stomping on the gas the second the door clicked closed.

Bernice smoothed the cotton bond paper out on the dash. It was what Jesus said it was, a bearer bond. In this case, an ornately engraved piece of currency, with no value printed on it as the bond value changes with the market.

"How much do you think it's worth?" asked Ruby.

They crossed an elevated stretch of highway, the guardrails the only road they saw.

"Stay between them," suggested Mini.

"At least we got something," said Violet.

"I have to pee," said Doris.

***

Bob stumbled toward the roundabout with the fallen pole. A traffic accident, he thought with disgust. I ran down here for a traffic accident?

A broken power line danced in the river that had been a street. The sparks lit the scene, eerie flashes throwing deep, confusing, shadows. A man crawled, under the wires, flat on his belly in the water, bleeding.

That didn't concern Bob. He focused on the ornately printed document that clung to his ankle. He took up the paper. The same green-grey ink, with the same precious inscriptions. His money, his fortune, floating in the street. *How?*

His knee encountered something heavy and hard. He stopped. The world was just. He'd found a gun.

He sat, one leg on each side of the battery driven Gatling gun, feeling the grip for a trigger. Finally, his thumbs encountered a button on each side. He pressed…

Nothing happened.

In the dim light, he could see red and yellow warning stripes on a flip-up cover on top of the double handle grip. He raised the cover and lifted the switch. Now, he pressed the buttons.

The world lit up as a glorious jet of fire from the barrel. Tracers danced in a stream that flowed side to side as the board the gun was mounted on bounced and drifted. Bob corrected for the drift, sending the stream of tracers into the pole, then into the car under it.

Chunks of metal and glass flew from the car. Splinters filled the air. Pieces of a security camera from the pole flew off into the storm. Water hissed and turned to steam as it met the fire and eight spinning barrels of the gun.

Bob pushed his aim lower, tearing through the wrecked car's fuel tank. The car exploded, and for the second time in the last two days, Bob felt and smelled his body hair burn. *Burn baby burn, disco inferno,* he sang. "Burn baby, burn," he cackled, unable to hear anything but the roar of destruction.

The crawling man leaned up on his elbows only a few yards away. "What the hell is wrong with you? The money was in the car!" screamed Eduardo.

Eduardo!?

"You set me up!" screamed Bob, lowering his aim to his former golfing partner. The barrels spun, the battery still powering them, but the gun would not fire. Steam hissed off of the empty barrels. The corner of a bond drifted down, the flames extinguished by the rain as it fell.

The bonds were in the car?

Bob wept.

CHAPTER 40

"Hoy Trip," Ledet said, to the man in the police poncho, feeling like his voice was lost in the wind.

"Jesus, Frank. You don't need to sneak up on me in this, do you?"

"Let's walk slow, Trip. There's some heavy arms up there, and I don't want to stumble into them."

"With you on that, mate. I see you wore a dark slicker tonight," said Trip.

"Turn yours inside out," suggested Ledet.

"It'll be wet on that side, won't it?" said Trip, dripping sarcasm.

"I'd say it's wet on both sides by now, but you can make it easy for the shooters if you like. Just don't stand near me," said Ledet, as they strolled north toward the reports.

Trip ducked out of the poncho and flipped it, almost losing it to the wind.

A roar, like a racing boat on full throttle, broke through the storm.

Ledet pulled Trip into the cover of a wall. "One Piccadilly, two Piccadilly…" he counted.

"What kind of name is Francis, anyway?" asked Trip.

Ledet counted on. "What kind of name is Trip?" he asked in reply.

The night sky lit up several blocks ahead.

"Some people think it's because I'm like the third or something, but really it's just that I used to fall down a lot."

Can't imagine that, thought Ledet. "Trip, that was a good nine seconds of fire wouldn't you say?"

"That was a gun? Sounded like a big motor."

"It was a gun."

"If you say so."

"It was. Now I happen to be of the opinion that that gun is now out of ammunition. But I am not entirely sure of that. Therefore…" he continued, grabbing Trip by the arm and swinging him right, past the

Smoothie King, "…we are going to make a wide circle and examine the source of the gunfire before we approach with our nine millimeter handguns and limited ammunition, lack of heavy armor, lack of communication, and all that. Clear."

"Oh yeah. Clear," said Trip. "Any chance we'll get to sleep tonight?"

"Only if we're dead."

They circled around the far side of the large roundabout from the blazing vehicle. With the storm at their back and lights off, Ledet expected to have the advantage. Still, they were two against an unknown force. Three hundred cops on the island and not one had shown up yet to back them up. The wonders of an unarmed police force.

They picked up another USG man, Danny Hannah, on the median wedge at the north end of the circle. Danny had a bag of guns in his truck. Lots of guns, and teargas grenades. "You're a godsend, old man," said Ledet, giving him a wet kiss on the cheek.

"Don't know how to take that from a man named Francis," said Danny, wiping his cheek as more rain fell.

"Just hold this grenade while I pull this little pin," joked Ledet, relieved to have real weaponry in hand.

They continued to circle wide around the burning car, entering the passage between the financial center and the shopping mall. In the mall lot, parked against the building on the lee side from the storm, they found the missing unarmed police. Five cars, parked neatly in the marked spaces, the men gathered all in one car.

"Danny, take a look around the corner. Careful now, I think they have a minigun," said Ledet.

"Is that what that ungodly noise was?" said Danny.

"Fifty rounds a second of pure joy. I think they're empty, but be a dear and find out," said Ledet, tapping on the window of the first police car.

"What you want, mon?" asked the driver, a police sergeant.

"USG," answered Ledet, realizing that he had no markings that could be seen. He held up his MP5 as proof.

The man in the car leaned back as if that would protect him.

"That building behind me? That's the financial center, right?"

The sergeant nodded.

"Was the bank robbed?"

"No, mon. Don't know, mon."

"That's good police work. Thank you," said Ledet. "We're going to check it out. Want to come with us? Could be fun."

"No, mon. No gun," said the sergeant, eyeing the MP5.

"All right, have it your way. But I'd turn this car around so you can get away fast. You know, just in case," he winked.

"What you got, Danny?" he asked, squatting behind the former SAS man.

"I got a minigun alright. Looks empty. Still spinning, though. One man sitting on the gun base, thumbs down on the triggers. Nutter that one. I think he likes the pretty fire from the carbeque. Americans call it that. A down power pole with hot wires here and there, and bodies asunder. Mostly alive," reported Danny.

"Good then. Trip, go get them."

The big man stood, ready to go.

"No, damnit, just kidding," said Ledet, grabbing Trip's poncho and pulling him back.

For good measure, he took his own survey.

"Alright, keep a spread, as wide as we can. Danny on point. I'm left. Trip, stay away from the wires. Let's take the big gun first."

They moved quickly.

Seconds later, Danny rested the suppressor of his machine pistol against the back of the laughing man's neck. "Easy does it now. We're going to get you some help. Maybe some nice little pills to make you forget. Just put your hand behind your head slow like."

***

The wind howled, the trees shook, and the ocean rose above the rocks in swells that only failed to overflow the land because they were being rebuffed on this side of the island by the wind. Ruby stood at the brink where ocean and sky were one angry mass and swung the strap of the rocket launcher, letting it fly over the rocks and into the water. It cleared. She did the same with the second empty tube, then ran back toward the headlights of the car.

She felt her feet slide, the wind pushing her. A bit of palm frond slapped her shoulder as it flew past. It had been a stroke of luck or genius finding this place. Bernice's doing, finding that the satellite images for the island had been downloaded to the tablet stolen from the bank.

From the satellite maps, they were able to find an empty lot with ocean frontage only a quarter mile from their rental house. Judging by the concrete steps and walkways, a large house had stood here once. The property adjoined several acres of forest, with a clearing that connected by trail.

Ruby felt a strange sense of vertigo passing though the swaying trees that lined the trail. In the clearing, Jesus, still taped hand and foot, lay in the back of the Mercedes with Mini and Violet leaning in interrogating him.

"Where?" Mini pushed the muzzle closer to the trembling man.

"In the water. Southeast in the North Sound." His face collapsed as though he had just given away the secret that would end him.

"In the marina?" asked Violet.

"No, no, by little boat," answered Jesus, helpfully.

"Where?" asked Mini, Violet, and Ruby, simultaneously.

"Hirst Road," said Jesus. "I think, Hirst Road. At the end. Big building."

Violet broke for the car.

"Don't go back to the boat. I will shoot you if you go back to the boat," said Mini.

Jesus nodded, accepting the warning.

"You didn't see us. You didn't hear us. You might not remember your own name. You got that, Jesus?" said Ruby.

"Yes, ma'am."

"Yes, what?"

"Yes, person I never see or hear, or remember because I not see or hear."

Ruby smiled.

"You've had enough fun," yelled Violet, over the storm "Let's go."

Ruby closed the hatch.

Violet tossed the keys into the darkness as they climbed dripping into the Land Rover.

"Where's the tablet?" asked Ruby.

"Under the seat in the Mercedes. I wiped it for prints. The battery is dead anyway," said Violet.

Lin was at the house when they arrived. Ruby checked her watch, 6:50 pm.

***

Dry and fed, with the storm rattling the roof above, Violet settled in and dealt a fresh deck. They were late, but as Doris put it, "It's four o'clock somewhere."

Ruby hummed as she sorted her cards. It sounded familiar. Everything seemed so normal.

"What about the guy you brought back? Did you get rid of him?" asked Lin.

"Of course, we did. We left him with the car," said Violet. "Seven card stud, straight."

"You killed him?"

Violet put down her cards and looked Lin in the eyes. "We did not kill him."

"I shot someone," popped Doris, "Got him in the backside twice."

"We left him in the car on high ground," Mini said to Lin, leaving the table and returned with a bottle of Irish whiskey and plastic coffee cups.

"Will this melt the cups?" asked Bernice.

"Not if you drink it fast," said Doris.

***

Around 9:00, with a warm belly and a fuzzy mind, Violet spread the damp bearer bond on the table. It did look like a giant piece of currency, which she supposed was exactly what it was.

She sipped her whiskey in the light of the storm candles and examined the bond. All that for these little pieces of paper. But they didn't do it for the paper, did they? They would leave this island, if they could, with this one little piece of paper, knowing they had won the real prize in destroying Bob Robbins.

There had been another explosion and fire at the scene of the fight with Eduardo Salizar and his men. Lin confirmed that. The bonds were gone. Their savings burned up. Gone.

Violet scanned the room, sipping her whiskey. Bernice puttered around the kitchen, her cane beside the bed, far from her. Ruby leaned back on a cot, chatting with Lin. Mini sat on her bed reading the Gideon's Bible found on the nightstand, an icepack on her ankle. Doris, at the table, sorted the poker chips and put them away.

The day was done, and they were all here. All but Marybeth.

Violet raised her cup in salute, "Here, here, to Marybeth."

"To Marybeth," they all answered, gathering round.

"To Marybeth," they drank.

There was one more thing to do, but for now they could rest and remember their friend.

***

While the world slept, the category three hurricane washed the remains of the *Desire'* to sea. Other boats had weighed anchor and run before the storm, their captains praying that they could somehow outrun nature's most fearsome beast.

Thirty foot swells slowing them, the cruise ship ran as fast as she could until the waves relented allowing her to sail at full speed. Pounded by moderate seas, the ship aimed southwest for the northern coast of South America, turning to the southeast about fifty miles from land. She would circle the Serranilla Bank and approach Jamaica from the south. The full speed run around the large circle would put her in Ocho Rios, Jamaica, a day late and cost hundreds of thousands in fuel, but the passengers and crew were safe with only a few complaints and light injuries.

Captain Ricci ordered the engines brought to half speed. There was no use going so fast just to sail back into the storm, and the engines needed the rest. "Message to head office that we are securing from the run, we are in safe waters, and will conserve fuel until we reach

Jamaica. Ask them which stop we should skip," he said to the attending deck officer.

***

Lester rode out the storm in the upper deck staterooms, wishing he could be below where the motion would be less upsetting. Upsetting also were the two attempts by Irene to barge in. Each time, he'd been forced to meet her at the door and lie, telling her that the ladies were asleep.

"I thought you would be with your… with Doris," said Irene.

"I am," he said, closing the door.

Later, the persistent knock came again. With rain slamming against the glass of the forward stateroom, he could have ignored it, but the thought that Irene may go to some extreme and call security, prompted him to respond.

He opened the door, his feet spread wide to keep his balance. Again, Irene pushed her foot in the door. This time, the rocking of the ship altered her course, turning her chair away from the door in mid-charge.

Lester snickered.

Irene looked so hurt that he almost felt sorry for her. Then, he remembered her insults and manipulations over the years. He was not a mean man, but she was not his friend or anyone that would ever be his friend.

"I'm sorry, Irene, we're trying to sleep."

"I'm alone down there," she said.

"I'm sorry. That's not my fault."

"Yes, it is," she replied, driving her chair away.

CHAPTER 41

A little after 3:00 am, the storm quieted.

In the darkness and silence of the shuttered house, Mini could imagine men outside readying themselves for a gun battle. She took the MP5 with her to the window. It was heavier now. Somewhere in the night, she had become weaker or the gun had become heavier, a dead weight in her hands.

Peeping through the crack between the shutters, she could see little. The sky was lighter, the moon shining through the clouds now giving enough glow to see different shades of darkness. The trees that were standing were mostly still. A light breeze shook the rain from the leaves that were left, but on the ground, nothing moved. Somewhere on this island, men were looking for them. Not here. Not yet.

Mini touched on the phone on the table. The light was enough to illuminate the whole room. In the corner, Lin sat up. Their eyes met in silent understanding. *It was too quiet.*

The phone screen timed out, and blackness fell like a curtain of wet velvet.

Mini went back to the window, looking, searching, for anything wrong or out of the ordinary. *What was ordinary about any of this?* After a while, the trees began to shake and bend, then the rain began to fly. The eye of the storm had passed, and the real storm was back.

Mini slept uneasily.

***

Ledet stepped across the crime tape into the bank. He was not an investigator, but it didn't take one to see what had happened here.

Remnants of duct tape and balaclavas lay on the floor, a large area of which, near the door, was wet from the storm. Puddles on the floor showed where the perpetrators had trod back and forth to the vaults.

Strange that they hadn't taken the piles of cash in the cage outside the main vault. They had come and gone, passing right by it, twice.

The detective, a former Scotland Yard man if ever there was one, touched on that again, “You're sure?”

“Certain,” said Devon, the guard. “They came, they left, they came back on foot. It was like they forgot something. In and out, it was.”

The Yard man scribbled a note.

“What about you?” asked the detective.

“Ah, just hanging over here trying not to drip on your evidence,” replied Ledet.

“I can see that. I can also see that you've got a keen eye for the evidence. Been out in it, have you?” he asked, pointing at the blood dripping down Ledet's arm.

“It's not mine. Belongs to one of the fellows who did this, I would think.”

“I'm Banks. Detective. New here and all that. It sounds like you've done my work for me.” Banks extended his hand.

“Ledet. Uniform Support Group.” They shook.

Ledet rubbed his chin, thoughtfully.

“You've got more?” asked Banks.

“We got your Gatling gun,” offered Ledet.

“Really! I'd like to hear that story.”

“Not such a big deal. They were out of ammo by the time we got there.”

“I won't tell anyone if you don't,” said Banks. He paused, examining Ledet's face. “There's more. Isn't there?”

A lot more. Ledet was a former soldier, not an investigator, but anyone could see that the bullet holes in the wounded men he had rounded up didn't match the number of actors known to be involved. Who had shot up the crew that he policed up? Not the cackling man with the minigun. That would tear a man to pieces, not puncture him neatly in both thighs.

“Coffee or tea?” asked Banks leading to the leather sofas away from the crowd.

“I was hoping to sleep tonight,” said Ledet, feeling that dream slip away. He slipped back into the couch as he spoke, “You've got three parties I think. The nutter on the minigun may or may not have been part of the second group. For all I know, the man just wandered in. We have a few guys living in the shadows around here, but I don't know them by sight." Ledet felt like he was rambling.

"Why do you think there were more?" asked Banks, his interest piqued.

Ledet took a minute to sort his thoughts. The couch was comfortable, and the stress of the last few hours had worn him down a bit more than it would have say ten years ago. But he had a job to do. In all the rush to deal with the armed men before him, he had pushed out thoughts that there were more out there. Now, with some distance from the incident, he studied the situation and could only come to one conclusion.

"All right, then. On approach, I heard rifle fire. 5.56 mm, if I had to say. NATO round for M-16, HK93, FN, M-4, and a lot of other light battle rifles as well as some sporting guns like the AR-15. We had three fellas with bullet holes in them. Once we took down the minigun—that was the nutter with no ID—we put down one fella that wanted to fight, then rounded them all up. That would actually be the fourth man shot. Anyhow, one was shot in the legs with low velocity. Didn't pass through," he explained.

Banks waved, and the bank assistant in the tight black skirt strode over.

"You asked me if we needed anything."

She nodded.

"Can you get some water for my friend here?" asked Banks.

"Certainly," she said, with a South African lilt and a friendly smile for Ledet.

Looking down, Ledet saw that her feet were bare. He scanned upward, catching her doing the same to him.

"Big gun," she said, her eyes on the MP5 laying across his lap.

She spun, still smiling, and with long bouncy strides, marched away. Ledet couldn't help but watch her graceful legs as she skipped over the footprints and drips that constituted evaporating evidence.

"I wouldn't play down the taking the minigun story too much. She's fragile, you know. Might feel the need for a man that can protect her," said Banks, dryly.

Ledet didn't answer.

"Back to ah… back to the.. where was I?"

"The bullet didn't pass through," prompted Banks.

"Yeah. The second guy was shot twice in the bum. Both rounds went through, one side to the other. Large exit wound. That was probably 5.56. A pistol, even a big one, won't do that. Third guy was both pistol and rifle. I suspect, from what I could see in the fire, that when things cool down we'll find that the car was shot to hell with low velocity, then with the minigun."

Voices were raised at the other end of the bank lobby. Ledet's tired mind tried to focus on the job at hand, but some of it came through. "You were flirting!" someone said. He couldn't see from the couch, but supposed the voice to come from the fellow in the black suit, a manager he reckoned. Just the kind of guy to whine like a baby when a woman looked at another man. Ledet smiled and leaned back on the couch his hand resting on the MP5.

"Your water," said a male voice.

Ledet opened his eyes and accepted the bottle from the tanned, thirty something man in the black suit. There was just something too perfect about him.

"Did you come to flirt with me, too?" said Ledet with a wink.

The tan face flushed red.

Ledet closed his eyes and laughed as the victim of his wit stormed away.

"You get the point," he said to Banks. "Lots of bullet holes, not a single 5.56 rifle on the scene that could have put them there. Yeah, the rifles could be under water, but I don't think so."

Banks did get the point. "There'll be a manhunt then. Damn if this storm didn't make a mess. I don't think anyone in the world could have planned this. Did *you* know there was a hurricane coming? Never mind that. Either these people are criminal geniuses, or they have the luck of the devil."

Ledet laughed, "Now *you're* rambling."

"I am rambling, but I've got a bloody right to ramble, haven't I? Any evidence is gone in the storm. The streets are empty. There are no witnesses. Who could plan something like this?"

Ledet shrugged. The man was right. Any evidence was gone or at the very least fouled. They could call the TV station and ask citizens to report anything amiss, but that was a two-edged sword. With most of the phones out of order, a nosy citizen could spot something and not be able to call it in. That could put the citizen in danger, even inspire a hostage taking. Unfortunately, this night was just beginning.

"You'll want to rest while you can. I think that young woman has a couch in her office," said Banks.

"Not so sure that would be a good idea," said Ledet, thinking the reverse.

"You might need to get out of those wet clothes," suggested the detective.

"And what if we were to come across those shooters while I was lolling around in my nothing suit?" said Ledet, because that was his kind of luck.

Banks laughed.

"Seriously, I've got me, and I've got Danny over there. We've got no comms, no rifles, and only the armor we can wear. We're not taking on any armed squad anytime soon." Ledet studied the inside of his tired eyelids. Only eight o'clock, and already worn down. "What's that girl's name?"

"Samantha Goodall," answered Banks, drawing out the last name.

Ledet laughed. That fit. "I wonder if Miss Good-all has a towel in her office?"

At 3:45 am, Ledet found himself awake and dressed, his clothes almost dry. There wasn't a towel in Goodall's office, but there was a fan that he employed to air dry the clothing he could spare.

Staring out the thick glass walls of the bank, he wondered how they withstood the pounding of the wind and rain. The eye of the storm had passed while he slept. He reckoned that's what the break had been. He had never been through a hurricane before. It was an awesome force of nature, that frankly would have scared the hell out of him had there not been more dangerous things around to steal his attention.

CHAPTER 42

The sun didn't rise on Grand Cayman. Violet slept late. She made her way past the empty beds and cots into the kitchen to find coffee percolating on the gas stove

Outside, the wind whistled and howled, and anything that was not tied firmly to something very heavy took wing. The street was a river, carrying anything too waterlogged to be airborne. Power lines and TV antennas crisscrossed sky to ground in every direction. A few houses up, a car rested nose down in a ditch with the rear wheels in the air. The ladies were subdued, sipping coffee and chatting at low levels. It was 9:00 am, and the storm carried on like it would never end.

Violet poured Mini a cup of coffee and watched her friend fidget impatiently. Clearly, she had something to say. Likely something that would stir things up.

"I think we need to move before the storm ends," said Mini.

"Right," sneered Doris.

Violet agreed with Doris but wanted to hear Mini's thoughts. "Go on."

Mini spoke, "This island isn't so big that we can hide from three hundred cops for even a day. When the storm breaks, they'll set up road blocks and maybe even have the port police out. A boat full of old women isn't going to look normal."

"So, you think we should take a boat?" said Violet.

"I think we should take *the* boat."

"You think Salizar's boat will survive the storm?" said Violet.

Mini didn't answer.

Ruby moved the coffee cups aside and spread the plasticized travel map they'd gotten from Lin out on the table. "Where'd they anchor?"

Mini pointed to the supposed location, about a half mile off the pier at the southeast corner of the big bay they called North Sound. "There's a big warehouse or boat storage, or something here by the pier. Can we go there and be ready for the storm to break?"

"What if the boat's gone?" asked Lin.

"Then we stay off the roads and take a small boat to the airport," Mini suggested.

The storm raged and rattled the roof, but the room was silent but for the occasional loud sip from a coffee cup. It had been a long journey, and now it was coming to an end. Violet wasn't sure what end, but it seemed likely that they would be caught here on the island by the very storm that had been mostly responsible for their success. Violet let her thoughts ramble on for a while before reeling them in and focusing on the map. There were three islands shown in separate boxes on the plastic paper. "Do you have cell service?" she asked Lin.

"Wi-fi only."

"How many people on Little Cayman Island?" she asked.

Lin typed it into her phone. "About a hundred and seventy," she said.

"Oh, we could take a boat to the little island and…" started Ruby.

"Then we'll be stuck on the little island," argued Doris.

"Who didn't get her cornflakes this morning?" snipped Ruby.

"I didn't get anything," said Bernice.

"You'd be off the main island, though," said Lin. "Isn't that good?"

Violet sat back and flipped her nail file while the others argued. They seemed to be well and truly stuck on this island, and as raw as nerves were, it might be for the best if when they were caught they got separate cells.

"What about the airport?" asked Lin, her voice barely heard in the uproar.

"What about the airport on the little island?" she asked again, this time much louder.

"What about it?" asked Doris, dismissively.

"That's not even an airport," said Bernice, checking the maps on Lin's phone. "It's just a runway. No buildings even that I can see."

"Exactly," said Lin. "Just a runway. No buildings, and nobody there."

"So, how do we get there?" asked Doris, doubt dripping from every word.

"We take a boat. The boat from Salizar if we can, or another, if we have to. Once the storm is past, we could probably make that distance in a fishing boat," said Mini.

"I'm not going to sea in a little fishing boat," said Doris.

"A big fishing boat, then," said Mini.

"One step at a time, then?" asked Violet, searching for middle ground.

"What do you mean by that?" asked Bernice.

"I think I know what she means," said Ruby. "We go to the dock and wait. When the storm clears, we find the boat, or another one… One step at a time, until we're home."

Violet nodded. There was more to be done. "Lin, you need to go back to your hotel. It would be good for you to be as far away from us as you can be. Call Lester and tell him to charter a plane and meet us on Little Cayman. Can you do that?"

***

The road to the dock was easy to find once they got past the fallen trees, fallen power lines, and roads that had flat out vanished under the mud flows.

The building was a boat repair house or hangar. Violet wasn't sure what to call it, but she *was* sure that Eduardo Salizar's men were idiots. They had locked the Zodiac boat to a post with a rope. When the time came, they would only need a knife to steal the boat. Between them they had several. The building wasn't so simple. The huge airplane hangar type doors were padlocked with massive locks.

Wet and half crazy with hunger, the ladies hunkered down in the car to wait.

"I have to pee," said Doris.

Ruby let out a shrill laugh.

"Behind the warehouse," said Mini.

"You can't be serious? In this rain?" argued Doris.

"You are not doing it in here. It's way too crowded," said Bernice.

Doris *hmphed* and exited the car, leaving the door open just a few seconds longer than anyone else felt necessary. Even against the building as they were for shelter, the spray came in, getting everyone wet.

They sat quietly for a while.

Ruby checked her watch again. “It's been ten minutes. Should we go find her?”

The words were barely out of her mouth when the door opened.

“There's a back door that's open,” said Doris. “They have nice bathroom with towels and everything.”

Violet backed the Rover around the building.

***

Eduardo opened his eyes, but try as he might, he couldn’t focus them. He closed them again.

A voice from the darkness asked him how he felt.

“Like shit,” he said, in English, the language the question was asked in.

“How are your men?” asked the voice.

“I don't know,” he answered.

“How many are there?”

The voice was annoying, with all these questions, but it felt easier, somehow comforting, to answer. “Five, and me,” he said, drifting back to sleep.

***

Banks gave way to the Irish nurse, angrily pushing him toward the door. He had as much as he was going to get for now. Maybe as much as he would get period. Including this one, five men had been found. One was almost certainly not with this crew. That left two on the loose, who could be the riflemen he was looking for.

His boss, the Chief Super, was already counting heads and saying the job was done. Banks thought that a bit premature. For one thing, under the layer of grime, the nutter that wouldn't stop cackling was Caucasian. The others were all of Hispanic descent. Not to say that whites and browns can't mix, but on this crew, it seemed unlikely. Second, the white nutter had been the one manning the minigun that destroyed the robbery vehicle. That was a hell of a schism to form in a gang in such a short time. Again, not likely. More likely that the crazy man was an outsider, competition, or just a homeless man out for a spin in the storm.

Banks still wasn't convinced that it was the Gatling gun that stopped the Isuzu. The minigun had been in an Isuzu for the robbery, probably this same vehicle, suggesting that gun had been ejected from the car when they hit the pole. Did they hit the pole? Did the pole by some stroke of luck break in the storm? Parts of it had been found stuck in the plaster sign across the street. *Explosives?* More likely than a hard gust of wind. He congratulated himself for that bit of brilliant deduction, then gave himself an at-a-boy for being able to think at all with so little sleep.

Ledet and a team of six met him in the hospital lobby where the staff eyed them inhospitably, probably as much for the water they were dripping on the floor as for the weapons they carried. “You just can't hide a squad machine gun under a poncho,” said Banks.

Sheets of rain pelted the glass doors.

Banks almost regretted having brought the USG armed response men with him. They deserved a rest after the long night they had just spent on alert, but it had been expedient to bring them along. The hospital was roughly in the epicenter of the action of the previous evening, and there was still no effective communication between police units. Cars that were close could talk to each other directly, but the distance was limited.

Amateur radio operators were set up at the hospital and fire stations. Calls were being relayed by hard line to the hospital from the EOC, then forwarded to emergency responders by the radiomen. The amateurs were doing a bang up job of it, but there were precious few on the island, certainly not enough to put one in each police car.

“Hoy inspector!” called one of the USG men. “There's a call for you on the hard line. Chief Super, I think.”

That would be it. The Chief Superintendent of Detectives would be calling to congratulate them on the successes of the night and perhaps even offer some assistance. *Right.* He barely knew his new boss but didn't think it likely that the man would be helpful. Still, here's wishing. He lifted the handset to his head.

"Blake, is that you, Blake?"

"Banks here, sir."

"Quite right, Banks. We've got your bank robbery all wrapped up nice and neat now, haven't we?"

"Not entirely, sir…"

"What I'm trying to say, Banks, is that now that we've got this robbery mess in hand, we need the USG team back here at the EOC," said the Chief Super.

"Well, sir, I don't think we've got this entirely wrapped up, as you say. We've got at least one, maybe two shooters still on the loose."

"Nonsense, man. We have a jail full of them, and we need our USG men to deal with this hurricane."

Banks could see that he was getting nowhere with the Chief and be damned if he was going to let the armed squad go shuffle papers when he needed them rested and ready to corral a team of armed criminals. "Well, sir, I can try. What I mean to say is that they've already left and we have little or really no radio communications." He waved at the men to get their attention and held his finger to his lips.

"Blast it, man, wasn't that one of our men that answered the phone?"

"Yes, sir, it was. But he's gone, sir," lied Banks.

"Bugger, we need those men. Blake, when you see them, send them to the EOC. In the meantime, you can help here, as well."

"Yes, sir. But if I'm up there, I won't be able to pass your message on to the USG team."

"Blake, do as I say," barked the Chief.

"Will do," said Banks, closing the circuit with his finger then replacing the handset.

"Bloody fool wants us to play secretary and get him coffee," mumbled Banks, leaning on the counter. "You get some rest. You are not here," he said, pointing to the cluster of wet and tired armed police. "And you don't see them," he said to the nurse at the station. Banks considered himself a decent judge of character, and the Chief, he judged, would not be leaving the comfort of the EOC to come look for him.

"How's it look out there?" he asked a hospital staffer who had just come in.

"Bad out there. Stuff down everywhere."

Good, thought Banks. *It could take me hours to get to the EOC in these conditions.* "I'm not here, either. Take a message for me if anyone calls," he said to the nurse.

***

She walked through a grey world, where the wind pushed and tossed frighteningly large objects around and the rain pelted every exposed inch of flesh painfully. It was a scouting mission. Violet got as close as she dared to the top of the breakwater. Still, she could see nothing but frothy waves that came from depths beyond her vision to crash alarmingly close to her own feet.

Leaning into the wind and fighting her way back to the shelter of the boatworks, she wondered for a moment if she could spread her poncho covered arms and fly. Just lean into the wind and let her feet rise out of the soggy, cold sandals and fly. A fresh gust pushed her hard against the steel building. "No. No flying today. No visibility," she said, laughing into the wind.

She welcomed the dark safety of the building. Even with the water running under the door and wind straining the roof, it was better than being in the car that appeared to have moved a bit on its own while they were inside.

Little pools of light seeped in under the doors and eves and where rivets were missing from the sheet metal walls. Blasts of rain occasionally spritzed them from the eves where chunks of foam insulation had been blown out. Outside the office, someone had creatively connected a marine battery to an LED flood light, lighting most of that corner of the building and giving it a safe, homey feel.

In the center of the giant space, two white hulled sailing vessels road out the storm. Somewhere in the dark, Ruby wandered around searching for God knows what. Maybe she was just checking out the boats.

Lacking electricity or a fan, they dried their clothes on lines over the gas stove overnight. It worked, and almost everyone had at least one dry item of clothing.

For Violet, it was socks. She had one pair of deliciously dry socks that were now going on her feet.

“Call it what you will…” she said to Mini, savoring the warmth of the socks, “…I don't favor going out in that in a small boat without being able to see our destination. It might not even be there.”

Mini nodded. “I'll clean your gun for that pair of dry socks.”

“It's my last pair,” said Violet.

“I found a box of cereal!” hollered Ruby, from direction of the machine shop.

“I would have kept that to myself,” said Mini.

***

Banks hadn't given up. There were two more men out there. Chances are that the ones that got away were not so badly wounded.

“Sir,” said a regular officer, a Jamaican. “Are you the inspector?”

“That's me,” said Banks.

“We just brung in a man without ID. He's banged up bad. They got him down in the ICU.”

Banks thought it worth a try. Halfway to the destination, Nurse Joy blocked his way. She looked down at the cuffs in his hand. “The man is already handcuffed to the bed,” she said.

“Who said these were for him?”

“Off with you now,” she said, blushing bright red.

“You're Irish, aren't you?” he asked the curvaceous redhead.

“Wouldn't you like to find out?”

I would, actually, Banks admitted, *but first, I have to find the sixth man on the crew.*

“Banks?” said someone behind.

It was Ledet.

“The hospital dispatch passed on a message from the EOC. The bank manager, Trevor Miller…”

“Your sweetie-pie, from last night?”

Ledet, the armed man, looked at Banks blankly. “Yes, that would be the one.”

“Go on.”

“He's reporting his car stolen,” said Ledet.

“You don't think he had anything to do with this… do you?” said Banks.

“It is a bit much to accept as coincidence on the face of it. On the other hand, for all we know the storm could have got it.”

“Well, on the face of it, we don't have much to go on right now,” said Banks, thinking, “…and if you had a mind to interrogate Mr. Miller, it might generate our first real lead. Might even give you a leg up with Miss Goodall.”

Ledet smiled. “It might. Might look a bit suspicious, though.”

“Can’t let that stop us.”

“I reckon not. I'll get the regulars to bring him in. Maybe let him sit for a while until we can get up there to question him,” said Ledet.

“Now, you're thinking. Then, of course, you should question the woman separately,” added Banks with a wink.

“Wisest course of action. I agree. Maybe over dinner. You don't happen to know where to find her, do you?”

“She's got her own place but has been staying with Miller, comforting him, I suppose.”

“After the robbery?” asked Ledet.

“Before, apparently, seeing as they drove in together in her car.”

***

Ledet met Miller at the main station in West Bay. It took almost an hour to get there in the storm, and, at several points, he wondered if it were worth the risk. Arriving at the EOC, he noted that the sky was lighter. The rain was not.

Miller turned out to be a dead end, a waste of time, a dud.

Ledet gave brief thought to interviewing Miss Goodall. That could wait. He wanted to see her next when he had time to explore a little… he clamped down on that line of thought. He had work to do, a man to find, and a missing car that may have been used in the crime.

A cluster of unarmed regular cops stood around the coffee maker in the EOC call center. He grabbed one by the elbow. “You guys know we're still looking for a man?”

“No mon, we don't know that.”

“We put it back over the hard line,” said Ledet.

“Yeah, we know, but the Chief Super, he say no. You got them all last night. Good job that.”

Ledet turned away. Nothing quite like having your own guys squash your investigation. Not really mine, he thought. But why not? he swung back to the cluster. “We're looking for a black Mercedes SUV… Stolen last night. Might be part of the robbery, so keep an eye out for anyone near it. If you come across it. You know, while you're out there,” he said, waving them toward the doors.

***

Toby, a three-year-old Scotty escaped his owner and made a run for the woods.

Dierdre McLaney couldn't bear the thought of losing her friend. She raced after the dog, finding it hiding under a Mercedes in the vacant lot next to hers. Toby firmly in hand, she dared a look through the glass. A man was laying still in the back, bound with tape.

Dierdre went door to door looking for a home with a working phone. There weren't any, but there was a kind man who let her stay in his home while he sent his grandson to carry the message to the police.

At 10:27 am, the rain was feeling ever so slightly less like bullets. Ledet's men surrounded the Mercedes and breeched it. The body was still breathing. He was, in fact, snoring.

“No habla English,” he said, waking.

Danny slapped the side of his MP5 hard, pushing it toward the man. It was a useless move, did nothing, but always seemed to deliver the proper amount of intimidation. Jesus, as it turned out his name was, babbled unintelligibly, but at least it was in English.

***

The crash of rain on the metal roof tapered to a dull roar.

Violet took her socks off and scouted barefoot. The rain had indeed slowed. She couldn't see the boat, but had at least a quarter mile of visibility. The time was near.

"Load up," she said, entering the boatworks.

***

At 10:42, a new blast of wind threatened to push the police Range Rover off the road. Banks, his hands a bit shaky from the constant correction of the wheel, now wished he'd let Ledet drive.

A power pole, pushed from the saturated ground by the wind, lay across the road. With no way around, they left the Rover and continued on foot, Danny grumbling about having to clean his rifle again.

At the ramp, they found nothing. A party boat tied to the quay rose and fell eerily in the gloom, banging against the fenders on each drop.

Banks followed his instincts to the edge of the seawall. Somewhere, he heard a motor. *There,* out about two hundred yards, *movement on the water.* "Do you see that?"

"I see it," said Ledet. "Rifle!" he ordered.

Danny stepped up with a scoped HK93. In a futile attempt to keep the optics dry, he brought the rifle up before popping the scope covers up. "Got em. Looks like four or five in dark rain gear in a Zodiac," said Danny, his finger near the trigger. "My glass is going to get wet real fast in this."

"Hold your fire," said Ledet. "We don't know who they are for sure."

"In this?" said Danny, lowering the rifle as he snapped the covers over his scope. "You think an honest, sane person is going to be out there in this?"

"Can't say for sure," said Ledet. "I wouldn't do it, and I'm neither completely honest or sane."

"There's that," said Danny.

"Call the Marine Squad," said Banks.

"Call with what?" said Ledet.

"Right, you are. No radios," muttered Banks.

CHAPTER 43

The illusion of visibility had come and gone. The Zodiac, as large as it looked on the ramp, was a floating speck on the massive swells. Violet knew that these weren't really "massive" in terms of waves, but they were big enough when you were at the bottom of one and couldn't see out of the hole. *Scary. Maybe the dumbest thing we've done yet.* "Can we turn around?"

"Why are you asking us?" screamed Doris. "You're driving."

Violet looked back. The quay was hidden, but she thought she could find land by heading straight into the wind and rain. *Just keep the raindrops coming straight into the eyes and that will do it.*

She waited until they were near the crest of a swell then turned the boat, letting it slide back down the mountain of water. "Lay down in front," she ordered the poncho covered lumps.

"Land ho," said Doris, choking on the rain ten minutes later.

It took them another five to make their way into the shelter of a channel. Dozens of boats jammed the passage, some sunk, some overturned, and some even stacked on top of one another. Violet threaded the small boat between them, careful of debris that could snag the Zodiac's prop.

Water flowed past the businesses and the houses that lined the waterway forming rivers that cascaded from the channel walls around them. The channel water was low, the storm sucking it out faster than it could fill.

The houses on one side were lit. On the other side, they were dark. "Let's find a house," said Mini.

"You're off your meds again," said Doris, with a smile in her voice.

"Why not?" said Violet.

"How do we know which one is empty?" asked Doris.

Violet nosed the boat into a slip behind a house that had no lights seen from the channel.

Ruby timed a short jump to the concrete dock, with the bow line in hand. The poncho threatened to trip her in the jump, but she managed to keep her footing and make her way up the stairs. A few seconds later, she scampered back down. “Someone's in the kitchen,” she said, not bothering to hide her voice in the whistling wind and rain.

“The house on the other side looks empty,” she said, teeth chattering and hair hanging in her face.

Minutes later, they tapped on the glass back door of the house. A huge dog, a boxer, jumped, slapping his paws on the glass and barking at them repeatedly. Violet balked. She wasn’t afraid of dogs necessarily, but this one had an impressive set of teeth.

“For goodness’ sake, he’s scared,” said Doris, pushing to the front and opening the unlocked door. “He just wants some company.”

***

One more suspect was now in custody. That left one on the loose. By the Chief Super's orders, suspects that were not wounded were to be taken directly to HQ for questioning. A long drive that neither Ledet or his men had time for.

“Does he look ill to you?” Ledet asked Banks.

“I'm not sure,” said Banks, his confusion showing.

“No, I mean, doesn't this man look a bit peaked? Maybe even dehydrated by his ordeal?”

“Are you going soft?” said Banks.

“I'm not going soft. If the man is ill, we have to take him to the hospital.”

“Well, that would save us some time and trouble, wouldn't it?” said Banks.

At the hospital, Banks took the man to the exam room himself, the Irish nurse following his every move.

Ledet found a dry spot in the corner and slept.

***

“Storm’s letting up,” said Bernice, looking out the window of the commandeered house.

Violet had observed the same. The raindrops that had sounded like sheets of bullets hitting the house now sounded like individual bullets.

Even so, it was hard to imagine going back out there. "We have to go, don't we?" she said. It would be so easy to just stay here in the comfort of this house, with that big dog laying on Doris' lap, and just not worry about the future. Wouldn't that be nice?

Only a few hours ago, they had been fast asleep. No one had snuck up on them in the night. But the math was simple, the longer they were on the island, the greater the chance that they would be caught. It didn't help that they were now breaking into houses for shelter.

"We should go in an hour," she said, sounding as weary as she felt.

"We need to call Lin and have her pick up the car," said Mini, collapsing on the couch.

Violet would have nodded, but that required energy.

***

"Ledet?"

Ledet's eyes popped open.

"You startled me, Danny."

"We got a call. A house alarm set off about a half mile up the sound from the ramp. It might be worth checking out," said Danny, raising his eyebrows expectantly.

It might be, and it might not be. "At this rate, I'll be your age before I get around to calling that woman."

"Is that what you were dreaming of?" asked Danny, with a smirk.

Ledet watched the rain run down the doors. "So, you really think this could be something?" he asked Banks.

"I'm not letting anyone go in there without an armed squad until we know for sure," said Banks.

Ledet buckled and straightened his vest. "Once more into the breach, dear friends…"

***

Stray rays of sunshine lit the dock. A river flowed into the channel from the neighboring yard, the base of the wall between the houses washed away. The channel water rose and fell regularly.

Violet pulled the starter, her elbow aching with the effort. On the third try, the motor grumbled to life. Ruby shoved off with a paddle, and they were under way.

***

Banks heard a motor as they approached the house. A small, whiny, boat motor.

"Back, back to the car," he yelled to the squad.

Whipping out of the circle drive, he floored the Rover and felt the dreadfully slow acceleration. They could see nothing of the channel but the tops of the taller boats bobbing up and down. Somewhere below them on the water, a small boat sped along.

The houses ended. On the right, between them and the channel, was a boat yard, many of the boats laid over and even a few that had been flipped. Through the carnage, he caught a glimpse of movement. *Faster, we need to go faster!* Again, movement. This time, he could see it down a ramp. A rubber Zodiac with five poncho covered figures aboard, the one in front holding a rifle.

"They're armed," he shouted, flooring the Range Rover then slamming on the brakes. The road was blocked by boats and debris. Bailing from the car, he ran for the channel. The rain, the damnable rain, stinging him in the eyes, blinded him as he zigzagged through the maze of boats, ropes, and rubble.

He heard the outboard motor more clearly now, winding up to full speed and achieving a *zip-pop, zip-pop*, sound as it skipped over waves.

In front of him, Ledet pulled up. Banks bent beside him, catching his breath and watching the little boat skip away into North Sound. The first rays of a reborn sun bounced off the water, diffused light making a rainbow of the mist.

"Can't shoot through a rainbow, can you?" said Ledet.

"I think there must be a law against it," confirmed Banks.

***

"Oh!" gasped Doris, "Look at that!"

Though the rain still fell in blinding sheets, light spilled through the clouds striking the foam tops of the waves and sparkling like diamonds. Suddenly, the sky opened to the north, and rays of sun diffracted in the rain creating a rainbow across the water.

"Follow that rainbow!" shouted Ruby, releasing a primal howl of joy.

Violet cranked the hand throttle, finding that sweet spot where the boat rides the waves rather than being pummeled by them. She said nothing about the armed police she'd seen ashore. If they were fired on, they would know soon enough. She set a course into the sound, keeping the buildings ashore visible to her right. When they spied the concrete seawall of the boatworks, they turned north to search the mists for the *Ellie Maye*.

CHAPTER 44

Violet's heart sank. The boat was anchored alone and in the right place, but it hardly qualified as a yacht. More like a thirty-five foot fishing boat. They circled, rifles ready in case someone aboard disagreed with the inspection.

"What was the name?" Violet yelled to Mini.

"The *Ellie Maye*," replied Mini.

Violet breathed a sigh of relief. This boat was called *Divorce*. She swung the Zodiac north, wondering how long it would take to get a police boat on the water after them. She pushed the throttle to full, ignoring the ache in her arm from steering it.

"I see something," yelled Ruby, from the bow. "It's big."

Violet eased off the throttle letting the little Zodiac drift past the yacht with the wind. It was a beauty. Sixty or more feet of deep hull, ocean worthy yacht. "Get ready up there," she said to Mini.

***

The stern swim deck of the yacht was high and bouncing as the bow was held low into the waves by the anchor. Mini rolled sideways onto the swim deck, tucking into the corner, flipping the safety off on the MP5. She ached all over and hoped to God she would find Tylenol on the yacht. She pulled her knees up as Ruby followed, taking the other side of the wide deck.

The rain fell at a nice steady rate. Still cold, still heavy, but no longer blowing at sixty plus miles per hour. Forty, maybe. Soaked through and cold, Ruby tied off. Above them, they could hear nothing.

Mini turned and took a few seconds to pray. It was only a few steps up, but she had no idea what waited for her on the main deck. Knees high, she sprinted up the steps feeling every snap, crackle, and pop of her tired joints and hoping that whoever was on the boat couldn't hear her coming. At the top, she stepped left behind a seat and went to a knee, sweeping the muzzle of the machine pistol right to left.

In the shadow of the wheel house, something moved. Mini felt Ruby take up the position to her right. Finger lightly caressing the trigger, she stood in a half crouch, her poncho waving behind her like a flag, and scooted forward, toward the movement. A tarp, the tie-down broken, flapped in the wind.

Mini triggered the attached light and scanned the cabin. Empty and dark. She waved the others aboard and sat on the leather bench to rest.

Violet fell immediately into removing panels to hotwire the boat.

Doris went below, returning on wobbly knees with food, real food.

Ruby came up from the engine room, smelling of diesel. “The bilges are running. She’ll be dry in twenty minutes or so.” She tossed a set of keys on the console for Violet.

The yacht swung around the anchor point with the slow change in wind direction. “Does anyone know how to lift the anchor?” said Violet.

“Is there a manual?” said Bernice.

***

The bow rose as the slack increased on the chain. Violet engaged the anchor windlass, pulling in the slack, only to have the wind push them back and have to begin the process again. Like that, they took in the anchor, ten and fifteen feet at a time.

Finally, she felt it break free, and the big boat began to turn in the wind, the out-of-control speed of the turn like flying a plane on a gusty day. The wind and water pushed, and the only way to maintain control was to let go and fly with it.

Violet pushed the throttle forward and turned the wheel. The big boat heeled to the right as they came around, then settled with the wind behind and began to move forward. “Bernice, I need help navigating.”

CHAPTER 45

"Look, until the Royal Navy and the Americans get here, we're on our own," said Captain Maynard of the Joint Marine Unit (JMU), the island's version of Coast Guard. "From what you tell me, the people you are after stopped some criminals then ran away. If they are no longer a threat to life or property on this island, then they are not my business. Not today."

"There were a lot of men shot last night on our watch. We very much need to capture these men," said Banks. It was as close as he would come to begging.

Maynard lifted his hat and ran a hand across his bald head. He, of all people, understood the personal importance of law and order. At his core, he was a cop, but his job today was one of rescue and recovery. "If they're in the sound, we'll get them. If they're on the open sea, we don't follow. We don't have the time, and frankly I'm not taking this boat out in this mess."

"Thank you," said Banks, waving for Ledet and the USG boys to board the patrol boat.

***

From her place at the radar console, Bernice saw the flashing lights first. "Police boat," she blurted out.

"I see them," said Violet. "Can he catch us?"

Bernice had no experience with radar, but the legend explained most of the symbols. She traced a line with her finger from the icon at center screen to the approaching blip. Two lines appeared showing the current path of each vessel and the time they would meet.

"Two minutes," she said, feeling a little like the woman from the old Star Trek that always repeated what the computer said.

"How fast will this thing go?" asked Violet pushing the throttles full forward.

Bernice grabbed the console to steady herself. On the left, she could see the wake as the police boat turned to meet them on the new course. The boat was much smaller, the men on it holding on to the rails, their weapons useless on the rough seas. “You have to turn left, west,” she said to Violet.

“That will put us closer to them,” argued Violet.

“I know, but it's either that or take this thing across land.”

“I don't see any land,” said Violet.

“I don't either, but it's there on the chart,” said Bernice, pointing to the screen.

Violet swung left, closing the gap with the police boat to three hundred yards.

“It's not enough,” said Bernice. “Not enough.”

“They're going to come alongside,” said Violet. “They don't know who we are. Everyone put on your ponchos or stay down were they can’t see you.”

“Take the wheel,” said Violet, handing control to Bernice.

Seconds later she was back, her poncho on, and her hood up. She pushed the throttle forward again as though she could wish more speed from it.

The police boat was a hundred yards to port and closing. Through the rain, she could see buildings ahead, just to the right of their path. She couldn’t turn away from the smaller boat. Her only hope was to outrun it.

She turned a few degrees port, feeling the wind push her from that side as she closed with the police boat.

“Are you nuts?” said Doris from the floor.

Violet head checked the position of the patrol boat. Fifty feet and closing. Could they board?

“Prepare to be boarded,” said the man with the bullhorn, whatever else he said drowned out by the rain and engines.

Twenty feet, and only the top of the smaller boat could be seen from here. NOW! She swerved the yacht toward, then away, from the police boat, using her wake to push the smaller vessel away.

It worked for a few seconds then the boat closed with them again.

“They've got some kind of hook on a harpoon thing,” said Ruby.

Violet swerved again, buying them a few more seconds. “Do you still have the flash bangs?” she asked.

***

Ruby pulled the pin on the can-like grenade that was designed to stun with a bright flash and disorienting sharp sound. Peering over the rail, she tossed overhanded, slipping and feeling the rope around her waist catch her as she did. The grenade flashed, …then sank harmlessly in the water.

Doris wrapped her end of the rope around a cleat and met Ruby at the door with a second grenade.

Violet eased the boat closer to the police boat. Ruby pulled the pin and tossed. They swerved away as she released. The grenade again flashed underwater.

Doris brought another. “Last one.” Ruby pulled the pin and held the spoon until she was at the rail. She let the fuse lever go and counted to two before throwing a smooth overhand. “Got it,” she said, so sure. But nothing. No flash, no bang. The police boat inched closer.

Smoke poured out of the bow cockpit. Thick, dark yellow smoke.

“Tear gas,” Ruby hooted with joy. The police boat turned hard to port and cut power. Ruby watched the men gasping for air in the acrid smoke and tear gas mix as the *Ellie Maye* rounded Rum Point to freedom.

***

Lin called for the tenth time. On the third ring, Lester answered.

“Who is this?” Lester asked.

“It's Lin.”

“Lin, what are you doing calling me here, and why don't I have you in my phone? I got, I don't know, ten calls from telemarketers, and it was you the whole time…”

“Lester, Lester, Mr. Bodine?”

“Yeah, what?”

“I'm on Grand Cayman, using the hotel phone. The ladies need a plane to Little Cayman to pick them up today.”

“Oh, that explains it. What the hell are you doing on the island?”

“We need a plane to Little Cayman,” repeated Lin.

“I can't do that,” said Lester. What he said after, Lin couldn't understand.

“Can you repeat that?” said Lin.

“We’re still at sea. We went wide around the storm. We’ll dock in Jamaica this afternoon or tomorrow morning. The captain hasn’t said which,” said Lester.

“Then you can't rent the plane?”

“I can't,” said Lester.

Lin ended the call. It was on her now to find a plane.

***

Out of the sound, Violet set a course northwest.

“Why?” demanded Bernice, when Violet refused to turn east toward the smaller Cayman Islands.

“Let's assume that the little dome thingy on the police boat was radar, then what's the best thing to do?”

“The best thing to do is get where we need to go,” said Mini.

“I happen to think that the best course is one that misleads them. I thought we would go twenty or twenty-five miles northeast, then turn due east to Little Cayman,” said Violet.

“Then what?” said Mini.

Violet’s shoulders sagged as she let her hands drop from the wheel.

“Yeah, then what?” asked Ruby.

“We wait for Lester. Unless you have a better idea?” said Violet.

Ruby grabbed the console with both hands to keep her feet under her. “Do you need help with that wheel?”

Violet nodded, “Yeah, but I think I better do it.”

“When we get to the little island, we should scuttle this thing,” said Mini.

“Really?” said Ruby, clapping.

As advertised, Violet made the turn at roughly twenty miles, the rain becoming more intense with each mile, again pounding on the deck and windscreen in blinding sheets. She had never been to sea in anything like this, and it scared her. Especially the lack of visibility.

The fear brought out something in her. Call it bravery, or stubbornness, either way it was her better self. She managed the wheel like she was testing each swell and finding a way through or over it. The gusting wind pushed from starboard, driving them north in a wide arch that would eventually take them to Little Cayman. Fatigued and mumbling to herself, she braced against the captain's chair to leverage the wheel. Still, she grew more confident as the day passed, steering with the sea, predicting the next gust of wind or wave that would push them. She was developing a connection with the ocean. She was good at this, even if she were new at it.

"So what was your deal with Salizar?" she said to Bernice.

"I didn't hate him. Oh, I hated his father at one time. Maybe still do. Even when it's the right thing, forgiveness isn't easy," she turned away, staring out the starboard portals into the storm. Shoulder to shoulder with Violet, she read the everchanging weather radar downloaded from some satellite and compared it to their path. The rain was just a drizzle now, but visibility was still less than a mile.

"Luis Salizar killed Warren," said Bernice. "For thirty-three years, I've not forgiven that man. I've dreamed of revenge but… I couldn't kill his son just to hurt him."

Behind her, Ruby snickered, "You shot the little guy, didn't you?"

Bernice ground her teeth. "But I didn't kill him. After all that, I didn't want to. I just wanted to send a message."

"What is this, Oprah?" said Mini. "You are what you do. How far to the island?"

Bernice traced the line. "Two hours twenty minutes."

Violet pushed the throttles to full, and the computer began to recalculate.

"One hour and fifty minutes," she updated.

"Plus the time it takes to scuttle this thing. Can I set the charges early?" said Ruby.

"NO!" came a unanimous chorus.

***

Ledet slouched in the hospital waiting room chair, done for the day. Banks was a nice enough fellow, but he for one was glad that Captain Maynard refused to follow on the open sea.

Banks wanted the shooters badly and was willing to chase them into the storm. The storm was a place that Ledet was tired of being. He had been wet, mostly dry, partly dry, or only a little dry, for eighteen hours now, and that was enough.

Banks, though, was not done. He was on the landline to a charter service at the airport. Fly? In this weather? Was the man bonkers?

"The man says he won't fly anywhere near the storm, now or later," said Banks, hanging up the phone with obvious disappointment.

"Well, imagine that," cracked Ledet. "He doesn't want to die."

"Says he's flying a tourist out to Little Cayman though," mumbled Banks, falling into a plastic chair. The man across from him woke, adjusted his grip on the blood soaked rag on his arm, and drifted back to sleep.

"The storm went west. Little Cayman is east," Ledet reminded him.

"It just seems that he has the wrong priorities."

Not for him. Ledet, adjusted the rolled up vest he was trying to use as a pillow.

"What if they go to Little Cayman?" asked Banks.

"Didn't you say that was the destination?"

"No, no, our suspects. What if they go to the little island?" said Banks.

"I'm no detective, but weren't they heading northeast, roughly toward Cuba, when we last saw them?" asked Ledet, annoyed with this new direction of query.

"Yes, but that could have been misdirection."

Wishful thinking, thought Ledet. "Did the storm steal your prize?" He sat up, dropping his makeshift pillow. "You felt the seas, us bouncing up and down on the sound like a bloody cork. On the sound! In protected water! Of course we had our eyes full of teargas and smoke, slipping around in vomit. I doubt they were puking so maybe they had a different mindset. I puked twice. Did you notice that? I don't remember you tossing up. So, why is it so damnably personal? Is there some reason that we can't leave these guys to someone else and have a bloody rest?"

"Well, in point of fact, they did attack us. With the teargas, you know," said Banks. "And they were only four miles out when we lost them off the radar."

"And that means what exactly?"

"Curve of the earth, rain, wind, rough seas, apparently all of that affects radar. And as you so colorfully pointed out, the seas were far rougher out of the sound than in. It's all rather complicated, according to the captain, but anyone who knows the least thing about radar would know that they would be clear out of our range in a short time. Out of radar range, they could turn any direction and we wouldn't know. I do see your point though. I would have liked to have caught them personally rather than let them just drown."

Ledet felt the weight of his eyelids pulling them down. His working relationship with Banks had survived the first fight. That was a new one. Most fights he got into wound up with someone shot or at the least badly bruised. "I don't like teargas. The smoke was nasty. And bobbing up and down. You know we lost a rifle? Trip dropped it right overboard along with his breakfast. I recon the Chief Super will have my ass over that."

CHAPTER 46

The western shore of Little Cayman was just visible through the light, on and off showers. The seas were down, almost gentle in the way they caressed the hull of the *Ellie Maye*.

The Zodiac was ready, loaded with everything they would take. Having no idea what awaited them on Little Cayman, they were taking everything, including the guns. Ruby, last off the yacht, rolled her legs over the side of the rubber boat and let the others pull her in.

Bernice shoved off with a paddle. The Zodiac rode low in the water. Violet got the nod from Ruby and goosed the throttle sending the little boat skittering toward the thin line of white sand and green trees in the distance.

The light rain and ocean spray chilled them below the fast moving clouds. Violet loved rain, the way it cleared the air and made everything fresh, but she had just about decided she didn't care to be out in it anymore. As they neared land, the traditionally clear green ocean water of the Caribbean became muddy with the runoff from the island. Branches of driftwood and palm fronds, even a lawn chair, littered the approach.

"It's all rocky to the right," reported Ruby from the bow. "There's a beach to the left."

That worked, since the wind was already pushing them that way.

The motor choked and sputtered. Violet let off then goosed it to give it more air. It sputtered again, then died. She pulled the handle. It sputtered but didn't catch. She opened the gas cap. Empty. "I'm too old for this stuff."

"Seems to me, the older we get, the more this kind of stuff happens," said Mini.

"Paddles," ordered Violet.

A half mile never seemed so far. As the wind and the current pushed the overfull boat toward hundreds of miles of open ocean, they fought back with sweat and weary muscles. Twenty three minutes of hard paddling and praying brought them to the beach. They collapsed on the sand.

After a while, Mini took a knife to the boat. She walked it ten yards out to sea then pushed a hole in it before shoving it off.

She'd just waded ashore when a flash reached them across the water. A second flash, then a huge orange ball of flame reached up into the sky. Ten seconds later, the rumble of the explosion reached them.

Violet watched the ball of fire rise into the sky and shook her head. To her left, Ruby grinned, the glow of the flames lighting her face.

They kept the ponchos on, even when the rain stopped and the cool wind made them pop like flags. Above, the clouds were rolling on to the north. Ahead, the narrow path led past a deserted house. Deserted or not, Violet felt safer within the anonymity of the poncho.

The trail led them to a washed out road that took them to the north end of the airfield. Some debris remained at the sides of the paved runway, but the center had been cleared. A tractor, red painted engine and dozer blade standing out against the grey primered body, sat at the end of the runway, wet but unfazed by the storm.

Each in their own way, they eased to the ground, sitting on the edge of the tarmac. Ruby checked her watch and opened the deck of cards. In the sunshine, Violet's bones were warming. She took off the poncho.

A lone figure approached on foot as they played. A man in a grey sport coat and navy trousers, a wisp of white hair flopping in the wind. They paid him little attention, but covered the guns with ponchos.

"Should we have tossed them?" asked Violet.

Mini shook her head and raised the bet.

The man carried a folded umbrella and a Bible.

"Oh, dear," said Ruby. "I think God sent someone to preach to us."

"I'm here for the guns," he said, in an unplaceable accent. "Coos thought you might want to sell them back," he said, scanning the sky.

"You're not a preacher?" said Doris.

"Heavens, no. I just like to read."

They could hear a plane, like a mosquito in the distance, growing closer.

"I'm Bartholomew," said the man, offering his hand to Violet. "Coos usually offers twenty-five percent for returns. He can't resell those here. Ballistics, you know," he said. They took the deal with the promise that Coos would send them payment.

"Well, don't that beat all?" said Ruby.

***

"Are you telling me we could have flown out?" Violet asked Lin as she stepped off the plane.

Lin pulled her out of earshot of the man with the Bible. "There were cops everywhere. One of them was trying to commandeer our plane, and you would have had to go through security and passport control."

"It's good that we came this way, anyway," Violet said, thinking of the journey and the finality of destroying the yacht.

Minutes later, the twin Beechcraft King Air lifted off with five passengers for Jamaica. The ladies were asleep before they reached altitude. All except Violet, who insisted on taking the stick of the powerful plane. In the clear night sky, she could see the lights of Jamaica from fifty miles.

"You have an agreement with Lin?" Violet asked the pilot.

"I'll take some time in Jamaica and return for her in two days," he said.

With the help of the pilot, they dodged customs in Jamaica, staying in a hotel that catered to tourists that couldn't afford resort prices.

In the morning, they hired a driver to take them to Ocho Rios, where Lester met them for lunch and some leisurely shopping before giving them their cruise cards. In the shade of the tent market, Bernice held her tablet up for Violet to see. She had pulled up the online version of the Cayman Compass newspaper. At the top, a photo of Eduardo's Isuzu ablaze confirmed Lin's story of the fire and Violet's opinion that the bonds were gone.

The ship sailed at 4:30 pm, a half hour after the first cards were dealt. A quiet, almost solemn, cloud had settled over them all. Violet spun her nail file. Ruby sang so softly that only Doris, sitting next to her, could hear the words of the old church hymn. The ship moved so imperceptibly that had they not had the large windows, they wouldn't have noticed.

Lester stood from his place on the couch behind Doris, to check the door. He checked the hall both ways before closing it.

Ruby retrieved a bottle of tequila and some shot glasses. Doris helped her open it. Ruby began to pour. She looked questioningly at Bernice, who nodded to go ahead.

"To Marybeth," said Violet raising her glass.

"To Marybeth," they chorused.

"To a job well done, even if we came up empty," toasted Doris.

"Here, here," said Bernice throwing down the second shot.

"Easy girl," said Ruby, who was drinking half with each toast.

"I like this stuff. Warms me up right good," said Bernice.

"I'm with her. Fill it up," said Mini.

"Wow," laughed Lester.

"What's that man doing in my room?" said Bernice.

"That man is my husband," said Doris.

That dark wet blanket that had hung over them was lifting. Violet could feel it melting away. "To the one piece of paper we did get. I feel like framing it more than cashing it."

"To paper that looks kind of like money," added Bernice.

"To watching it burn," said Doris.

The bottle was a third down, already. "Order another bottle, Lester," said Doris. "You asked what you could do. Get more tequila."

"And a new deck of cards. Ruby has marked all of these with her artsy fingers," said Violet.

Mini cackled. Violet felt the warmth of love and fellowship take hold of her. These were her people, all here, all well, except for Marybeth who was still here in spirit.

"Here's to diamonds," toasted Ruby.

"Here, here," they cheered.

Ruby poured another round, stumbling a little and catching herself on Violet's chair.

"What about diamonds? Is that some kind of metaphor," Violet had a hard time with that last word.

“No, silly, the diamonds.”

Violet shook her head. *Was she missing something?* “I don't get it.”

“You didn't tell her,” said Mini, holding up the shot glass for a refill.

Ruby set the bottle on the table, took a long swaying, squinting look at Violet. “I don't remember. Oh, God, I've lost my memory again!”

“You remember losing your memory before?” asked Doris.

“Of course, I do,” smiled Ruby.

“Then, you can't have lost your memory.”

“But I don't remember telling you guys about the diamonds.”

“I don't remember that, either,” said Violet.

“Me, either,” said the others.

“Oh!” said Ruby, stumbling out of the room.

A short moment later, a brown felt bag sailed through the air and bounced off the table into Violet's lap. She opened the bag carefully feeling the weight and crunchy feel of the contents. Sparkling reflections lit the ceiling and walls as she poured the bag of precious stones into her hand. Beautifully cut stones, each at least a carat, some much larger.

“Oh, darn,” said Bernice looking over her shoulder. “How are we going to get that through customs?”

“That's easy,” said Ruby.

“You sure about that?” asked Violet.

Lester started laughing. “I’ll be damned.”

Ruby poured another round. “To diamonds,” she said, raising her glass.

“To diamonds,” toasted Violet.

CHAPTER 47

Jamie and Norbert slept in a hotel lobby. In the afternoon, they found a bar that served good cheap drinks and didn't expect large tips. They started drinking just before 4:00 pm.

Sometime around 6:00, a thirty-something man, British by accent and hard like a soldier introduced himself as Francis Ledet. “I heard part of your story. Love to hear the rest,” said Ledet.

“You should have seen de mon,” laughed Jamie, sloshing his beer. “Standing der on de bridge with de golf club like a sword in his hand. Follow dat ship he say.” Norbert laughed and spilled beer.

Ledet asked for the bar phone. “Hey,” he said into it after dialing a local number, “you need to come to the Blue Rhino. We'll be here a while. Trust me on this.”

A while later, an older man with a traditional British mustache joined them at the table. The gentleman wanted to hear all the stories and paid for the drinks all night long. It was a good night, full of laughter. At the end, Jamie had a few hundred dollars left, and Norb fell asleep on the table.

The British men stumbled out of the bar a few minutes after midnight.

***

Ledet had found his limit after thirteen beers and uncounted shots of whiskey. “Damn this storm, the walls are still moving.”

“Storm’s over. That's not the walls moving, old boy,” said Banks. “Where's a policeman when you need one?” he asked, leaning on the wall. “Some tough old birds, wouldn't you say?”

“Yeah. Kind of glad I didn't shoot them.”

“I'd say,” agreed Banks.

Ledet chuckled. “I reckon I'd like to buy them a drink or two for what they done. Kept us out of the line of fire. Kind of emascu… emasculating, though.”

“Quite. A regular public service,” said Banks. “I'm very tired, you know. If I were to go home now, planning to report all this tomorrow, with all the ah… well, you know with all the events of the day and the drinking, I might forget what we heard tonight. Might even think I dreamed it all up.”

“What did we hear tonight?” asked Ledet. “I think I've already forgotten.”

“Are you going to throw up, or are you really able to keep all that in?” asked Banks.

“No, I think I can keep it. I would be… a little more sure of that if the stuff around me would stop moving.”

The cab arrived. After a brief argument with the cabbie, they convinced him that Ledet would not puke in his cab. A block later, the USG man leaned over the seat, excused himself, and threw up.

Banks walked with him the rest of the way to the beach apartment, then called another cab for himself.

***

Irene knocked at the stateroom door. This time she was going to get in and see the girls. If she wasn't allowed in, she would go to the head of security herself. That Sully girl had been running interference long enough.

Ruby opened the door. “Oh, hi Irene, you're just in time for tea.”

“Tea? Since when do you drink tea?”

Ruby closed the door in her face.

***

The ship passed the normal stop at Grand Turk to make up for the lost day. They made port in Nassau in the Bahamas where they all tried snorkeling. At lunch, they toasted their missing friend and all the others that had passed since they had known each other.

It was a somber group that boarded the ship that afternoon. One more day at sea.

“Ruby, do you want to go to an art auction,” asked Violet.

“Where?”

“On the ship. They have them right down by the big restaurant.”

“On the ship?” said Ruby. “Don't that beat all.”

***

It was sunny and warm when they docked in Fort Lauderdale.

Ruby was nervous. They'd distributed the diamonds in each carry off bag, running them around the edges, under the seam tape in the side pockets. There were a lot of diamonds. In her own bag, the stones rested around the binding of her sketch pad, under her clothes, and in among her paints and brushes. A really good eye might see them on a monitor, but what were the chances that anyone was looking that close?

Captain Ricci saw them in the main lounge and broke away from the pretty young woman he was charming at the moment. "Aww, so sad to see you go," he said, hugging each in turn and ending with Ruby. "I want so much to see the sculpture again. It was sei magnifico! Ha."

"Oh, that is so sweet, but it's in a million pieces now. It just didn't hold together under the stresses, you know," said Ruby, hearing Doris snicker behind her.

"Oh, so bad. So sorry for the rough seas," said the Captain, hugging her again.

"Oh, my. You sure you don't want to come home with us?" asked Ruby.

"I could, but I got, a," he pointed his thumb to the young brunette.

"I see. Yes, she's very young and pretty," said Ruby.

The Captain shrugged an Italian apology.

The ladies marched down the ramp and into the warm terminal building with its stairs and escalators and guide ropes to customs.

"They did it. They did it. They robbed that bank," cried Irene to the customs and TSA officers, waving the newspaper in their faces.

"Do you know this woman?" asked one of the customs officers, cutting across the ropes.

"Yes. She's a little touched," said Ruby.

The officer nodded. "I understand, but we will have to hand search your bags," he said.

"Ohhh, I see," said Ruby. *Dammit all!*

"Get them all! Search them all! Strip search them!" screamed Irene, almost climbing out of her chair.

"Oh, shut up, Irene!" barked Ruby, unable to stand it anymore.

For their part, her friends seemed to be taking it well. Mini was the worst, rubbing the handle of her bag nervously. Violet had her nail file out. It wasn't like they would take it from her now.

The officer laid her bag on the steel table and unzipped it.

“I got this,” said a familiar voice.

Agent Jonah flashed his badge, holding it long enough for everyone to get a good look. “Got it?” he asked the officers. “Is there anything in particular you are looking for? Drugs from Jamaica, illegal perfume, millions in cash?” he shook his head, offering them the correct response.

“Ah, no?” said the customs man.

“Good answer,” said Jonah. “Zip the bags and show us to a room where we can talk.”

A few minutes later, Agent Jonah closed the door of a well air-conditioned room with white walls lined with tables. Judging by the posters offering helpful hints on searching, this was a training room, or one used for the unhappy few that got dragged away for cavity searches. Sure enough, a box of rubber gloves sat in the center of one of the tables. Ruby shivered.

Jonah began, “Ah, I just wanted to tell you that Bob Robbins has been caught. He was on Grand Cayman. You ladies were right there where he was. In fact you, Ruby, were at the same bank less than an hour before it was robbed. His box specifically was robbed.

“Relax,” he held up his hands. “I know this sounds like I'm doing a Columbo moment, but we already checked ship records and know that you were off the island before the robbery. On top of that, the Cayman police have the suspects. Apparently, Robbins, we don't know how, caught up with the guys that robbed him. We're working on the idea that he may have known them and been working with them at first.”

Someone knocked at the door.

“Enter,” said Jonah, annoyed.

A customs agent stuck his head in. “We searched the dead woman. Nothing there,” he reported.

"Did you have a warrant for that?" asked Jonah, shooting the man a look that would have scared anyone. "Do you ladies want to pursue this?" asked Jonah.

"I do," answered Violet, her whole frame shaking in anger.

Ruby watched the action unfold, not able to do a thing about it. Violet stepped toward the balding customs man, her anger flaring. "That's my friend, and you had no right to touch her." She lifter her fist, ready to slug the little bureaucrat. Jonah's strong but gentle hand stopped her.

"I'm very sorry. We'll take care of this. I'll take care of it. You don't have to worry. You don't need to go to jail to fix this."

Violet held, letting the little man escape.

Ruby let herself breathe.

"Are we okay?" asked Jonah a moment later.

"So, what about our money?" asked Mini.

"Good to finally see you, Mrs. Barone. The money is, unfortunately, gone. Robbins had it in bearer bonds. They were destroyed in the fire after the robbery."

"Fire?" asked Mini, feigning surprise.

"It's a long story. Do you want to hear it?"

"Maybe someday," said Violet, slumping.

Ruby watched her deflate. It had been a long few weeks for all of them.

"Oh," said Jonah, "Anita Fulsom-Bright is back in jail. Turns out, she was with Robbins. His girlfriend, in fact."

Doris snorted, "That explains the long meetings in his office."

Jonah coughed, covering his mouth. "Yeah, that might."

"What about Robbins? Has he been charged yet?" asked Ruby.

"No. We're waiting for a mental competency hearing." He tried to leave it at that. The ladies, to a woman, crossed their arms and waited for the rest.

"The man has cracked," said Jonah. "I don't think it's an act. There's not a thing that comes out of his mouth that makes sense. Explosions, fires, chasing ships, radar, and golf. The guy talks all the time and says nothing. He accused you of attacking and burning down his home. We checked. The local fire guys say that it was a gas explosion, probably an accident." He threw up his hands then rested, his speech done.

"You flew down here to tell us that?" asked Doris.

"Not entirely. Irene Fulsom has been making calls, lots of calls. Filing reports and all kinds of nonsense. We saw trouble coming, and… anyway, I thought it was the least I could do to try and head her off. Right now, I'm not sure I helped much. I guess I'm trying to buy back a little good will."

"Is that how you spend the taxpayer's money?" jabbed Mini, a slight smile creeping into her voice.

"You are being very helpful," said Ruby.

"Are you going to arrest Irene?" asked Doris.

Jonah cringed and shook his head, "I hope not."

CHAPTER 48

November turned to December, and December turned to Christmas. The day after, Agent Jonah drove the blacktop road through middle Georgia. He didn't get down here much. An Oklahoman by birth, the east always seemed like one big city to him.

Stopping for gas, he heard rapid rifle fire. Someone got a new toy for Christmas.

A few miles down the road, he found the sign for Blake's Orchard. The sign looked fresh, recently painted. They hadn't changed the name. He would have to ask about that.

It was a shock to get out to open the gate and find that it was quiet. No rumble of traffic, no airplanes, just good country quiet. He hadn't heard that in a long time.

He hadn't warned them that he was coming, and he hoped that it was all right. He didn't forget the shooting he had heard from the gas station, but he wasn't worried about being mistaken for a poacher in the black FBI sedan.

The gravel drive was smooth and well maintained, his tires kicking up a little white dust.

***

It was a good Christmas. Quieter than usual. Less stressful. No one worried about who would have to be comforted when a relative didn't show up.

The banter around the house was as bright and snappy as always.

Lin stayed full-time with them at the house now. Just a day after Christmas the windows were open letting in a nice cool breeze. Of course, the fireplace was burning too. Lin heard the growl of a car coming up the drive. There was that little steep part where even the quiet cars strained enough to be heard.

Through the trees, she could see a black car on the white road.

The ladies were in the apple shed cleaning their new toys after a morning of fun. Lin was getting more comfortable with guns but wanted a little time to herself.

The man that stepped out of the car was tall, blond, and handsome by most standards. Lin remembered him but had never seen him not wearing a black suit. He managed to look uncomfortable in the sport shirt and jeans.

She dialed Violet's number from memory. "Agent Jonah is here." Agent Jonah? Didn't the man have a first name?

***

Jonah stood in the living room, admiring the art and trying to ignore the pretty Asian girl that watched him. The first time he'd met her he'd been stunned by her beauty. More so now. The paintings were beautiful, as well. Clearly, Tom had been a great artist, but the stuff signed by Ruby was extraordinary. Way beyond his pay grade, according to his research. There were other paintings, well-framed and signed with names he didn't recognize. The ladies were doing well.

He worked his way around, admiring the depth of color. On the big wall, the one he would have expected to see a large painting on, hung a small frame. No matting, just a nice frame with glass. It wasn't even lit well.

He stepped closer.

Behind him, Lin grunted.

"What is this?" he asked.

"Oh, that's been there a long time."

The vibrato in her voice informed him that she was lying.

He touched the top of the frame. No dust, even in the carved edges.

Beneath the glass was an intricately printed, multicolor document about two thirds the size of a notebook page. It looked like money, but much larger and with no value printed on it. The paper was cotton bond, not even paper really, more like stiff cloth, and the right and lower edges appeared to singed. It was wrinkled, like it had been wet, then dried.

It was a bearer bond. Jonah had seen one like it before. "Do you mind?" he asked. Not waiting for an answer, he lifted his phone to take a picture, centered, focused, then changed his mind and lowered the phone.

Chuckling, he turned to find Lin wearing an approving smile.

“It's been there a long time,” he agreed.

She is so beautiful. He forgot himself and the purpose of his visit for a moment. “Ah, ah, I guess I better go.”

Meeting the ladies on the steps, he handed Violet the folder he carried. “As promised, that's the whole story. As far as we know.”

Halfway to his car, he turned. “I'm hoping that someday you will tell me the rest of it.” He winked and left.

“Son-of-a-gun!” said Bernice.

EPILOGUE

In early spring with the apples beginning to blossom, the ladies sat in the afternoon shade. Somewhere, not too far away they heard the *whop-whop-whop* of a helicopter. It was pleasant out, the evenings long and the afternoons warm.

The house, its English stone work still new, had an expansive porch that reminded Ruby of some of the open air places in Jamaica. It also reminded her of pictures of houses in Australia, and that reminded her of Marybeth. It was beautiful out, and today she was painting apple blossoms in spring.

Ruby painted profusely these days. Milo was building a following of her work in his gallery. Though she couldn't see how it would profit him, he had even suggested that she make a deal to sell her paintings through the galleries that auction work on cruise ships. It seemed appropriate.

Nothing she had done had sold for the massive price of the first painting. That wasn't likely to happen again in her lifetime. But ten and twelve thousand a piece was good money that kept them well fed. She even painted some smaller pieces for the gallery to sell for less. She refused to paint duplicates. Everything was an original.

With just a little smell of paint thinner on her hands, Ruby joined the others at the table, and leaned back in the splotchy shade of a rustling pecan. In the fall, those pecans would pelt everyone and everything on the open part of the patio. She would have to put up a canopy then.

Doris laid the deck of cards on the table. In a few minutes, it would be 4:00 and the game would begin.

Lin was out with her FBI man. Tommy's house, a hundred yards up the hill, belonged to Doris and Lester now. Lester was somewhere in the orchard tending the trees, a new hobby for him.

Violet slid her nail file through an official looking envelope, opening it. “It says it’s from the state department,” she said.

“Don’t open it now. It’s probably bad news,” said Doris.

“Another tax bill,” said Ruby.

Mini grunted in agreement.

“Not a tax bill, but it could be bad news if you want to call it that,” said Violet, reading. “They want us to go to work for the government. Says here that we have a unique set of skills that have come to their attention.”

“Wonder where they got that idea?” said Bernice.

“Sounds more like CIA than State Department,” said Mini.

Ruby hummed.

Doris dealt the cards.

The End

LOVED THIS BOOK?

Help other readers find it by sharing a review on Amazon, Barnes & Noble, or Goodreads.

For exclusive discounts and giveaways on your next favorite read, visit Bill's site and subscribe to the newsletter.

–

www.billhawkinswriter.com

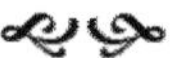

ALSO BY BILL HAWKINS

KATE AND MINI

With the nation on the brink of the second world war, sisters Kate and Mini flee their troubled Mississippi home in search of a better life. But life on the road soon spins out of control. How long before the explosive baggage of the past catches up and the real trouble begins?

Mini is fifteen and awkward even for a Mississippi farm girl. Kate, seventeen, projects sophistication and the kind of beauty that attracts trouble. Together, they hit the road for the big city. But fate and hunger drag the girls back to farm work where Kate's looks and Mini's temper attract trouble and the attention of a sensationalist media hungry for any story to calm the fears of the coming war. Where will the girls' whirlwind romance with violence and fame take them?

ABOUT THE AUTHOR

Born and raised in Houston, Texas during the oil boom years of the sixties and seventies, Bill began working at age 12. Through the high school years he worked as a machinist, painter, roofer, hardware store clerk, carpenter, sheet metal worker, and mechanic at a motorcycle salvage yard. He met interesting people, including drug dealers, bikers, a world class physicist, a CIA field operative, a guy with a machete scar across his face, and an English teacher named Dell Gunter.

When he wasn't working, Bill was playing ball, working on cars, building things in his father's shop, writing in the journal that Dell Gunter insisted he keep, or reading Bradbury, Forsyth, Tolkien, Tolstoy, or Solzhenitsyn. Gunter nudged Bill to pursue his dream of writing, but his life took a different course when he accepted a scholarship to Texas A&M to study electrical engineering.

After graduating with degrees in Broadcast Management and Anthropology, Bill picked up a camera to make a living as a freelance photographer. One thing led to another and with his natural drive to write and entertain Bill began to sell DIY articles with a humorous twist to photography and firearms magazines.

Bill's long and twisted path took him into the tech industry, and eventually back to his love of the written word where he insists that he will succeed or die trying. Bill has written five screenplays, six novels, and two novellas.

Made in the USA
Coppell, TX
05 June 2024